C000101793

'What isn't against the laws of physics is just a matter of engineering.'
Twenty-first century scientist

The first time I saw her, I thought she was from the past. A ghost I mean. Her face was partly in shadow and her clothes rustled like the sound of whispered secrets. It was always just a question of time, for someone like me. The house lent itself to the feeling of not quite seeing someone. The sensation of a room just vacated. The musty ripple of a disturbance in the dust that connected to nothing and the smell of pipe smoke late at night caught in dark corners, like quiet unanswered questions. When I sat by the fire and listened to the room and watched my cat watching someone, I hadn't minded the growing realisation that I didn't live alone after all. A house that was noisy with history, waiting for recognition real or imaginary. People spoke about the need for peace and quiet, but the true silence of an empty life was overrated.

Other people's thoughts were like lift music, the annoying background to a destination, not something I listened to or even noticed much any more, until the day someone 'thought' me a direct question and I answered and how strange that was for me. The madness in my head usually stayed there and didn't involve other people.

The old house, really half of a Devon long house, was unexpected in its ordinary appearance, low and comforting with the echo of past occupants. It was built on the edge of a valley close to Exmoor. In my mind I could see the long-ago someone who had looked at the sheltered slope and savoured the light that would warm the house, summer and winter. The past was a gently shrouded sunken outline, shaped by the wind and weather of the moor. The planted trees and cottage garden waited and the oversized landscape was stretched into undulating folds.

At some point in Victorian times the wealthy farming family had decided the house was too small and had built a gothic monstrosity half a mile down the road. The little building was demoted, divided into two workman's cottages and left to watch the changing seasons.

The local council had added a few square careless dwellings in the 1930s but the valley was generous with its view and this was the way villages were made.

There were huge swathes of Virginia creeper climbing its pale stone walls and the cottage garden was overgrown, full of blousy roses and rotten apples. The fields were dusty with crops and the sky was a deep, peaceful blue.

I wandered through a late summer, picking up the pieces of smashed pottery thrown out by impatient owners with careless hands. In my mind I furnished the house and its garden with the familiarity of several lifetimes. Hundreds of years passed before my eyes like the flutter of birds' wings and the past felt generous with its memories.

I had abandoned the possibility of caring for the garden by winter. The leaves lay thick on the ground and you couldn't see the gate at the end of the path.

Ted appeared one morning saying, "The postman says you need help." He didn't say much more than that for the first three visits, but began making the paths places you could walk again. I found him peaceful company and he made me laugh.

"Have you ever done stand-up comedy?" I asked.

"I was a teacher for twenty years," he shrugged, "So yes." It was through him that I finally met my reclusive neighbour who owned the other half of the house, Edie.

Edie was part of a mystery that hovered at the edge of my awareness and not just in my head. No matter how hard I listened I couldn't hear anything. A stranger to me, but not I thought to my cat, who came in sometimes smelling of whispered secrets.

Edie had lived in the house for as long as anyone in the village could remember and yet no one had any stories to tell about her growing up, no little tales of childhood, or her lovers, or any family. She had never involved herself in any of the village life and despite the prying and curious old eyes and the general view of country people they did 'leave err be.'

Not the local vicar though, who I had seen on several occasions and in all weathers, standing on the doorstep, abandoned and bewildered by the lack of response.

Memories of course were like sunshine and shadows, it could be impossible to make out the true shape of things and I knew that I was on a spiral staircase of craziness which was not a difficult place to get to.

Ted, with a combination of cunning and oily charm, had managed to get his hands on both sides of the fence, as it were and my garden began to look like the one next door, full of flowers and green and not lost in old leaves.

I was standing in a puddle of weak sunshine one early spring morning. The big old trees had buds on them and at the base of each were late snowdrops and early primroses, like little pieces of possibility sitting at the feet of giants. The house sheltered in the curve of the hill and the frost hardly lingered past sunrise. The morning was full of promise and clear air. I heard the click of the gate opening, hidden by bushes, the murmur of conversation echoed in my head. I felt strange, restless, as if impatient for what happened next. The buzzards were wheeling and keening above the hills as if they knew something and were trying to warn me.

Ted appeared through the arch of clematis, he wore jeans and a sweatshirt and those clunky orange coloured boots that looked rather uncomfortable, but were part of the uniform of country life. He walked up the path with a tall, rather beautiful, older woman by his side. She was wearing what my mother would have described as 'floaty' clothes. Her eyes were tired blue shadows and she walked as if she'd just recovered from a long illness. I squinted at the shape of her, it was as if she was blurry around the edges and I was looking at her without a pair of much needed glasses.

Their conversation seemed to be all about the plants along the winding path, which they examined with the quiet, careful hands of real gardeners.

Lavender and rosemary had caught at the clothes of visitors to the house for five hundred years, wafting the scent into the kitchen and protecting all from witches and evil. I could see the flutter of shadows closing in from the past and tried not to look and I wondered what the past would have thought of me, I would have been burned at the nearest stake probably.

A moment in time to gather my thoughts, though I knew who she was, I placed her in my mind as part of now and shook off the dark clouds, a gentle drift of something that was not quite a sound, Edie. Barely a whisper in a window before, here she was.

They both looked up from examining the small, just-opened, pale flower of an early daffodil and as if I had spoken their names out loud they came towards me. I gave up trying to focus on either of them, though I knew there was nothing wrong with my eyes.

We sat in the garden drinking tea from the china cups my mother had left me and I smoothed my fingers around the familiar gold crinkled edging. We talked about the early spring flowers and tipped our faces up to catch the faint warmth from the pale sun, as all creatures did after a long winter.

She asked me if I lived alone, and made no comment when I said I didn't know. The illness was like waiting in a station for a train that would never come. The tiredness just didn't end and there was no relief in sleep. I think people thought I was mad, I thought I was and I was careless.

Ollie sidled over and with cat curiosity he stalked us, his prey really the ginger biscuits the same colour as his fur and the whorl of his beautiful eyes. His overacting a total dislike of strangers broke the barrier of the bubble between us and there was that something with a sharp edge that crept along my spine, like reality, only fixed by warm whiskers.

Actually he didn't care who had turned up, as long as the biscuits came out of the tin, the only container in the kitchen that had resisted his breaking-and-entering skills. Unlike the cowardly fridge which had given up without a fight.

He had been sunning himself on the garage roof and his fur was hot and crackled from stored electricity. He leaped into Edie's lap with a total disregard for the full cup. The hot tea scattered over her clothes the seat and the cat. Edie juggled with the cup, saucer and her dignity with the skills of a circus performer to admirable effect.

I stood in the kitchen until the giggles had stopped, recognising that I hadn't done much in the way of laughing lately, enjoying the sensation that felt like mental champagne and wondering why these people had made me feel nervous.

By the time I got back, my puma sized ginger cat had returned to Edie's lap. I made as if to remove him again, but she waved my exasperation away and scooped her arms around acres of orange fur. "Don't worry," she laughed, "I know when I'm being honoured." It felt as if the 'neighbours' were normal after all.

I didn't remember them leaving, which meant nothing, I had lost whole days to the illness. Somehow, I had mislaid my life in a careless moment. And now I couldn't find it. It was not so much a death sentence, more one of life without parole.

Ted had one of those faces that was neither young nor old and was hard to visualise the moment you turned away. Even the colour of his eyes was debatable and I always remembered eyes and what they could give away.

It had happened one day in the garden. I thought he'd asked me a question and he'd just thought it and because I had felt so ill, I'd answered before checking. I looked at his face. It was impassive and expressionless. Quiet. Maybe he hadn't noticed, that I'd read his mind though I knew it took an ability to speak a thought in the same way as it did to hear one.

There was no sudden realisation of telepathy. It was the tiny step between the end of intuition and the careful measure that was the beginning of something more.

Without the clever or cool and the possibility that there was some geek there lurking in the corners of my mind, school was a silent nightmare. Maybe no one felt as if they really belonged, but there was a big difference between not belonging and trying hard not to shape the hidden lie into something other people could see. I was not one of those children who sat and waited around for adolescence while listening to loud music. I wasn't bullied, not much anyway, just left alone. A small group of misfits formed an alliance and we were butter-flies among the bees. We became witnesses, who lived on the periphery and eventually wanting to belong became a piece of the pattern of my life and not a goal.

The illness had a name, chronic fatigue syndrome. There was nowhere to go with a syndrome; I would have liked to ask the doctor who told me to go away and find myself a good book, what he thought I should do about the memories I was collecting that weren't mine, but he looked as if he had 'One Flew Over The Cuckoo's Nest' in his professional collection. It should have been called something else too because the Victorians cornered the market in fatigue. The bone-crunching tiredness left you half-awake and half-asleep night and day. There was no cure and as time went by your life was just a shadow of what it once was, but then maybe we all lived in the shadows.

I wrote my diary late at night when it was possible to measure emptiness and time passing in spaces of endless. It seemed to me my life was now full of things I hadn't done. I couldn't sleep and the whispering I seemed to hear more and more, was quieter at night. I'd spent my whole life fighting the black cloud.

Maybe it was only ever one story told a million different ways and it was hard to see where the line between pain ended and the loneliness began. My mother had been the type of un-anxious psychologist that parents queued to bring their 'little problems' to. After I had told her about the old man who had appeared from the shape of the evening shadows and read me stories, instead of bundling me off to see a specialist, she told me that he was one of the people who came before and not to be afraid. I remembered that I had rolled the thought around in my mind. Not about the 'came before' but the 'afraid' part, as he sat in the corner watching me and smoking his pipe, smiling, at peace with his world. It had never occurred to me to be afraid of him. I was four and particularly admired the shiny buttons on his red jacket.

She must have watched with the puzzled eyes of all careful parents who realised something was not 'quite right,' but she seemed to deal with the fact that this was not going to be a passing phase in my life with equanimity. She showed me pictures of old military uniforms when I was six and I picked out my friend with delight. We moved house, which, I had thought at the time, was only fair as he had been there first.

My brother Sam said that having a parent as a therapist and a little sister who was quite clearly mad, was enough to send anyone into therapy. He took up rock climbing instead. My mother said that he'd done it deliberately, though this was not, I thought, a professional diagnosis.

The '206' was part of a daydream made real through a nightmare. Flying in England, I was told before I started, was a neat trick, only done by people with more money than sense. It was really a conversation with clouds. But you had to be one of those children who threw themselves off high objects expecting wings, to understand that. I was able to pay off my mortgage and take flying lessons using the money my mother had left me. My instructor explained that not everyone who flew had a natural talent and I was sure I had proved that, like everything in life it was just slog. We had an interesting time. After what felt like a million bumpy landings and an allergic reaction to an endless parade of weather reports, I passed eventually and I was a fully fledged 'puddle jumper.'

Sam bought himself a piece of a mountain in Scotland with a one room bothy on it. He lived there in almost total isolation, a place with no thought or tired horizon. My pain and loss could recede high in the air, in the sun and the clouds. His was healed by earth and endless mountains. Our lack of roots became our collective wound. He thought all his troubles could be solved by staying in one place. I thought all mine could be solved by moving every year. Either way we barely spoke again.

Lives that began fragmented rarely turned into the pink fluffy kind. It was amazing that my mother was able to get pregnant twice, considering the short amount of time she and my father had spent together. She assured me neither of us had been an immaculate conception. He died, in a landslide in Guatemala, never having seen me. Some people didn't plant trees and never really loved anything and they didn't need people, except on the periphery. I can't say I minded. He had built roads and bridges in faraway places, most of which were still standing. I had never seen them.

It wasn't as if my dreams came unravelled. I just stopped dreaming and a life without dreams was a life without hope. The illness measured forever better than any clock could.

After several loud hints from my slightly damp cat I lit the fire against the spirits of the dark night. The rain spattered against the windows. I hadn't bothered to replace the curtains removed by the previous owners; anyone nosy enough could help themselves to the sight of Ollie and me. The evening had been full of dark clouds and the wind battered the old walls and made the trees sigh. I hadn't been out all day and I felt closed in, wishing for the unexpected to save me from myself and as in the saying, 'when the gods want to punish us they answer our prayers.'

I turned from lighting the fire, it spluttered, the wood slightly damp. The face caught in the window gave me a nasty scare, the dark rippled for a moment and I gasped and took a step back at wild hair and blank eyes. Someone lost in the dark. Me.

I transferred my gaze to the mirror near the front door. The single lamp in the corner cast a kinder light. My eyes were still brown and not quite so hopeless. You couldn't see the lifetime of incomplete thought that kept me a prisoner. I released the held breath. "I'm still here, somewhere." My voice sounded hollow with relief. Ollie purred his contentment and washed, close enough to the fire to have made combustion a real possibility. I pulled my fuzzy hair back into a pony-tail, trying for a more controlled look.

As I turned, my heart stopped. It didn't actually, but it really felt as if it had. She was looking at me. Which, I remembered thinking, was something that ghosts weren't supposed to do, stuck fast in their own story. Not entirely unexpected, but still a surprise. She was not what my unconscious mind had imagined. Smooth dark hair, pale skin and lots of silver rings and a long dress, part of the shadows, but real. Rather solid in fact. Ollie put his face up to be tickled under the chin. He sniffed her outstretched fingers and she smiled. I was not the world's leading authority on ghosts, but the space between not seeing someone and them being there, couldn't possibly be so clearly defined. She didn't shimmer or float, she was just there and then not. I looked back at the mirror in the hall. "Nothing," I said, "Can come from talking to ghosts but trouble."

The valley, close to Exmoor, must have been part of the great ice age conspiracy to reinvent the landscape and for the last five hundred years the old house had sheltered in its carefully sculpted hollow.

By pure chance the national grid had been designated to deform the view for a neighbouring village, which I was assured by the locals was fine, because they married their cousins there anyway. Apart from a few telegraph poles and lines, the aspect of the hills couldn't have changed much and life hadn't changed much either. People still rode their horses through the lanes and rush hour consisted of a long wheelbase Land-Rover with hay on the back. There was a lot of amazing geography in the south-west of England.

No one could understand why I wanted to buy the house. Not even the estate agent who, momentarily suffering from a conscience, tried to steer me towards something closer to civilisation. I couldn't have offered a reasonable explanation. Except perhaps, that I was always entertaining ghosts in the silence and where better than here?

The house was four windows and a door, much like a child would draw it. Downstairs was really one big room, but the Victorians, who'd built the monstrosity down the road, had added a wall and called the other side the kitchen. There was a large landing upstairs with two bedrooms and a small bathroom. It had been considerately decorated by the couple who'd sold it to me; with white walls, wood floors and amazingly no flowery stuff anywhere. I hadn't made much of an impression on the shadows.

I must have had some idea of what I could do. My mother certainly must have known, but in her own way, tried to protect me from being *different*. I wondered how much of her own innate intuition, bordered on the telepathic. Once the door was opened it was impossible to close and at least here I had had some anonymity. I became a watcher again, like my childhood, a non-participant and this was a quiet corner of England a place where life unfolded, with very little noise. Old friendships drifted unkempt and people found me, rather than the other way around. I tried to keep very still, hoping that fate wouldn't see me.

I found comfort in strange places.

The local vicar, Father Trethowan, was a keen and relentless amateur historian. He wrote articles in the local paper about the history of the houses and families in the village. His knowledge and information was never clouded with the circumspection usually required by sensitive situations and he had upset several families by revealing long-since hidden skeletons of the past. He was oblivious of the effect he had, expecting everyone to be as delighted as he was. I thought he was wonderful, whiskered and portly, with dirty glasses and the air of a frustrated genius. The first three pews of the church were always empty. You would have needed an umbrella during the sermon. He was also a kindly and much loved friend during dark times, an angel without wings. Or even much of a sense of personal hygiene.

———

In my twenties I had trained as a nurse. My mother was against it for all the right reasons. It was on the official list of jobs that people like me shouldn't have done. I felt like an emotional husk by the time I'd stayed long enough to make a point. My mother hadn't been keeping score.

I travelled for a while, phoning home from the Canadian Rockies and the Great Barrier Reef. Anywhere that it was easy to be no one. I washed dishes in some seriously awful places and was able to use my nursing skills to diagnose early onset food poisoning. At least their plates were clean for a while.

Eventually you had to put down roots, or try to. My mother was living in Salisbury, Wiltshire at the time, near the cathedral, in a small yellow town house on three floors. I could stand on the dark, curved stairway and feel the long skirts of the women who lived there once brush past me. You stepped straight out of the front door onto the street. I walked over Salisbury Plain with next door's dog, a lurcher named Strider and followed the old paths used by Romans and Saxons and tried not to get run over by tanks whilst my mind was elsewhere. If you half closed your eyes and listened to the wind, you could nearly see the lost Legion of the Ninth marching into the past.

I drifted into office work, anything that didn't require too much close contact. And eventually I began writing for local papers, usually historical articles and short stories. Gradually I was able to make a meagre living. I worked from home, which was a succession of bed-sits, graduating to the smallest flat anyone had ever seen.

It was possible to do any business with prospective editors over the phone and by post and eventually by email. Most of them were pleased not to have to pretend to be nice.

'The smallest flat' was in a town called Marlborough in Wiltshire. It was one large room with a little bathroom and a cupboard of a kitchen. I had a futon and a coffee table and two hundred books. The front windows looked out over the street and there was a patch of garden at the back which belonged to the ground floor flat. I was living there when I first met Oliver. I had just started a parachuting course.

I returned from Netheravon, black and blue from throwing myself out of an aeroplane mock-up, starving hungry and filthy dirty. An immaculate cushion of orange fur, he was asleep on the futon when I arrived back. Of indeterminate age and, initially, sex because it would have been rude to look, we shared a tuna sandwich and my pillows. There was that dream, where you reached out your hands and pushed off with your feet and pretty soon you were flying over the rooftops. I gave up flying in my sleep when I took up parachuting.

With skydiving I had found a place where I could let myself be, it was sixty seconds of empty sky, a snapshot of colour inside your head, all sensation and no shadows. I just had to try it, because it was not dying that was frightening, it was never having lived.

The illness had crept up on me like winter. It happened in my head as well as my bones. Constant flu, acres of antibiotics, the world closed in. Life began and ended at the front door.

The World Service muttered into the background of a dark night, telling me the meteor shower was going to be the biggest in twenty years. I sat by an open window in the stillness of the house, with a hot water bottle and a feather downie wrapped around me. Two layers of thermals and a woolly hat completed what must have been an overwhelming picture of sartorial elegance. The frost on the grass reflected into the moonlit sky. Mysterious paths appeared clearly marked in the fields. I wondered if I followed them, what I would see and resisted the temptation. Some places once they'd pulled you in were difficult to break away from. It was easy to get lost in the things from the old times, long before real history, they were the most beguiling.

I thought about my ghost. I wondered if she'd lived here once and couldn't quite leave and I wondered if that would be me one day, lost in an old house watching time going by in someone else's life.

It was odd that the ability only linked me to the past. If the future and the past were connected in a continuous tightrope walk of relativity then you would have thought that the future would be easy to see. Maybe it was all around me and I just wasn't looking hard enough.

Ollie had wormed his way into the space between the folds of the quilt and was rumbling his satisfaction. I had read somewhere that the resonance of a cat's purr could heal broken bones, his purr could heal spirits and I hugged him through the downie. He grumbled a bit and resettled himself. Ollie didn't do open displays of affection unless it included food.

It was strange that people thought the stars were cold, when they were full of fire and warmth and promise, the universe's message in a bottle that you could read through the curve of the glass.

The show began quietly and was difficult to see even with powerful binoculars. I shut my eyes, sometimes I could see better when they were closed. Not so much of a shower, more a child's sparkler fizzling out. It was odd that they seemed to stay in my head, even when I'd given up and curled on the bed with Ollie, me still in my layers, feeling cold as old bones.

The stars continued on their way without me, my mind still seeing the echoes of them. But like other people's dreams, they didn't belong there.

Real sleep, of course, had eluded me. I could do that exercise when you lay there practising breathing techniques and rearranging the kitchen cupboards and your past emotional decisions. It must be done with your eyes closed, otherwise it didn't actually count.

I pounded the pillows and downie for the millionth time, moving Ollie around with my foot, until he retired grumbling to the furthest corner of the bed, out of the reach of restless limbs. Occasionally I *thought* I slept, but it was that sensation of self-induced coma which after four hours drove me to reach for my diary. Sometimes there was nothing else to be done.

The diary contained observations, people, things I didn't want to forget, the odd quote. Sometimes dreams, not as in ambitions, but the ones that happen when your eyes wandered away from reality, awake or asleep. Mr Payne, the local farmer had stopped me in the lane earlier in the day. Ollie had been seen stalking his racing pigeons. I apologised and tried to look contrite. I drew a little sketch, not very flattering, in the margin, of a grumpy farmer complete with tractor. He then went on to tell me of how he was going to have to hire a pyrotechnic to move his mother-in-law into the flat at the back of the farm. I think he was aiming for pantechnicon, but who knew. This was the man who had had a condescension problem in his downstairs bathroom.

Something moved as though a connection had been made, in the shadowed half light of the lamp in the corner. The door was open into the dark well of the landing and a sound filtered through the sensation. It was a high pitched noise like the thin quiet whine of a distant saw starting up. I realised it was coming from my cat. His fur stuck out and his eyes were black pools sunken deeply into shadows. Something hovered just out of sight and I listened desperately for anything that would be a recognisable relief. The thick walls of the house were quiet, without answers. Where everyone had demons, mine were just more interesting.

Another small sound began to compete with the continuous ululation of the cat's high pitched fearful growl. I turned and looked at the window where an unhelpful moon had gone behind a cloud. I saw the rocking chair in the corner of the bedroom moving quietly as it settled in matched time with a ripple of disturbed air. Ollie hissed gently, his teeth fully exposed and the ridge of hair along his back spiked out.

I tried to focus on the shape appearing in the chair. It trembled, a dark, growing blank space with no shadow. I could hear something that felt like footsteps inside my head and I thought for a moment that I could see an old man. My throat was scratched with a lack of oxygen and the metallic taste of terror.

A rumble began, as close as an earthquake. Ollie hissed again and the shadow seemed to claw the air reaching towards me with the upturned talons of a dead crow. A memory tried to push past the fear but I couldn't see it in the smothering darkness. Close to the edge of it I could hear voices. The light bulb exploded and I screamed into the echoing silence. There was a loud banging on the door.

Ollie and I did our impression of an Olympic trampoline team and cleared the bed in one and as I lurched towards the doorway I heard a low angry shriek follow me. It sounded like loss and sadness and something else I didn't want to think about; I just wanted to get away.

I didn't actually breathe until I wrenched open the front door. I threw myself onto the path and screamed again as I found myself tangled in someone's arms. Ted. I barely noticed the pathetic excuse he gave for his providential appearance and gratefully accepted his warm coat which smelled of comfort and wood smoke. He watched me carefully as I explained; his face lost the benign hippie look and took on one that reminded me of the people who fight in small, nasty little internecine wars for money.

"Interesting," he said, after I stumbled over the mixed belief of the not quite figure I thought I had seen. It was odd how someone could make the word 'interesting' sound like a three dimensional anxiety attack.

I stood on the front porch waiting, while Ted disappeared into the dark house. My feelings had returned to the slightly embarrassed thoughts of night-time childish fears and a low level buzz of still needing to look over my shoulder. I could see the shooting stars from the previous night inside my head again, together with other things I couldn't quantify.

Ted came back; he had turned on some lights as he came down the stairs. He looked at me, standing in the shadows of the clouds on the moonlit path, seeing stars and said, "Um." I handed him back his coat shivering in my pyjamas but still reluctant to go back into the house.

A bedroom window opened next door and a calm voice said, "Is everything okay?"

"I'll be over in a minute," Ted whispered. The window closed.

"Um," said Ted again.

"What was that?" I asked him carefully, seeing more of the unknown than I really wanted to take in and not sure if any answer would be the right one. It was like the old paths in the grass, that walking them would take you to places you didn't need to be.

"Tomorrow."

"Tomorrow will do," I said tiredly, and followed the complaining Ollie back into the house. Ted looked at me for a moment, back to the enigmatic hippie as usual and then turned to go. "Ted," I said, puzzled and forgetting for a moment the rules of telepathy, "Who's Rani?" He didn't turn around.

My ghost came to see me later that night, in a barely there kind of way. I was making a drink, standing in a pool of light in my kitchen, surrounded by quiet and she appeared on the edge of the darkness, a peaceful apparition. The house had taken on the sense of a thunderstorm on the horizon. Something in the walls watched with careful eyes and there was no possibility I could have gone back into the bedroom and slept. I knew with complete certainty that whatever I had seen was something that haunted me, not the gentle ghosts of the past that belonged to the house.

"Are you checking up on me?" I asked my night-time friend. She looked at me. I felt calm and peaceful as if talking to her was just a telephone conversation with the past.

"Don't worry I'm fine, just a bit of a strange day. I think my gardener is trying to frighten me to death," I added, "Not that he's really a gardener."

She listened, head on one side, there and not there and then she was gone. There was a good chance, I thought, that I had completely lost it.

I slept on the sofa downstairs with the dreams of thoughts that I knew didn't belong to me and I saw places I knew I'd never been. It felt as if I was on borrowed time.

The rationalisation of the early morning light followed the restless night. I drank coffee sitting on my quiet doorstep and reached some conclusions which made as much sense of the dark corners as the complete absence of answers could. My cat continued to prowl the walls looking for something and we agreed to disagree on what that was.

The little edges of confusion and disquiet rippled with the sound of voices. There was a hurried fear of low conversation. The cup in my hand shook and coffee spilled. My ghost walked through the arch of clematis, with Ted and Edie.

Ted said, rather inappropriately, considering the circumstances, "We're running out of time. You'll need this." He stuck a small silver disc to my T-shirt.

The house and my cat waited for me to catch up. I pulled myself to standing and walked back in through the doorway and the questions heaped up like old snow. Some of the fear had come into the room with them and it was mine now.

"I'll leave you to it," said Edie. She wafted out of the door looking more ghost-like than my ghost and I thought, without thinking, that she was getting more fragile every time I saw her.

"Thank you," I said. "Would anyone like tea?"

"Shall I make it?" Ted asked, walking towards the kitchen door. "Rani, do you still take sugar?" I wondered, and not for the first time, if Ted was trying to give me a heart attack. Rani smiled. Oh no, I thought, another mind reader. Her smile grew and I resisted the temptation to pinch her to see if she was real.

"Rani O'Leary." She pointed at herself, long dark hair green eyes and was taller than my five feet seven inches. I hadn't noticed before, when she was still my ghost. She looked about thirty, except for something about the eyes, which were older than Edie's and full of the layers of tired that came with impossible decisions and endless compromise. There was something about her mind too, which was as closed to me as my front door, but still whispered the warnings of those paths not taken.

The fact that I had gone from the only person I had ever known who could do it, to one of a quartet in the blink of an eye was part of the panic, we had become more obvious, a blip on the cosmic radar. The steel shutters of my childhood came crashing down and I reached back to my eleven-year-old self for the coping strategy of hiding inside my head. It wasn't as successful as it had used to be.

Ted had performed the introduction with a cup and saucer in one hand and my china pig sugar bowl in the other. A scattering of white appeared on the carpet because the lid didn't fit properly.

"We've met," I said and then I realised, because they let me, where they really came from. I wasn't surprised. When you had felt as if someone has cancelled your future without consulting you, other people's futures didn't hold so many complications.

"Do we speak the same language?" I asked Rani, touching the disc Ted had attached to my shirt.

"No," said Rani. "My home language is mostly Punjabi. I'm actually speaking Basic English at the moment, because some of my own language doesn't go through the translator very well. Basic is a mixture of your sort of English, a type of Spanish and something that's a lot like Chinese."

"*Okay*," I said, doing my best to quantify what 'a type of Spanish' could possibly be, "Why are you here?"

Rani and Ted sat side by side on my tiny sofa, elbow to elbow, in not uncomfortable proximity. Ted was back to looking every inch the ageing hippie. My inner self drifted an unguarded thought about impossible relationships, something about which I was an expert. Rani looked at me over a non-existent pair of disapproving bifocals, managing to look remarkably like my mother or someone's mother anyway and Ted shuffled a bit.

Rani answered the spoken question with a question, "Do you know what you are?"

"I can read people's minds sometimes, and sometimes I can send and there are other things. But no," I thought about it carefully, "I don't *know* what I am."

"You're a telepath."

There it was the T word, out in the open like a shadow of wings on my heart. She carried on. "It has not been possible to duplicate telepathy and we *have* tried. There are no natural telepaths in any other species we have come across, with the notable exception of Gurber's race and they're not telling. You are as unusual as," she hunted for an appropriate example.

"A rocking horse in the Grand National," I added helpfully.

"Quite so," she said after a pause, in which I think I could actually hear the translator she wore behind her ear, buzzing in the hope of a suitable conversion.

"How many do you know of then?"

"In recorded history?"

"Yes," I said, shrugging, I had no idea what I was fishing for.

"Mine or yours?"

"Rani!"

"Well," she said reluctantly, "Twenty-seven."

I gasped in surprise. Somewhere out there I had thought there were people like me, that I would find a place where I wasn't alone. I thought for a moment, their reluctance to discuss it was like a magnet for stupid questions. "So what happened to them?" They didn't exactly glance at each other, but they might as well have done.

"Well," said Rani, choosing her words carefully and not succeeding, "Three of them went mad."

"Is that what would have happened to me?" Again there was a pause, where they both walked a fine mental line, then chose the truth.

"Probably," Rani answered.

"So, basically, what you're saying is, if I *don't* go with you the chances are I'll end up as mad as a frog." The translator did some cartwheels.

There was a power in a really long silence along with stillness. In the space in-between, the clock struck the half hour before anyone spoke. I knew they were not telling me much, that the fear of the something was still there and that more than anything they both needed to get me out of the house. I just wasn't sure if I wanted to go.

On the subject of Edie I could sense that they were closed minded and closed mouthed. But I asked anyway, "What about Edie; is she part of this?"

"Edie has her own story, she's not part of yours," Ted said, his face serious and oddly worried.

"Ted," I said, laughing in spite of myself, "Sometimes you're a real idiot!"

"I was trying for enigmatic." He sounded hurt.

"She's slipping away," I said quietly and to neither of them. Like my mother did, I thought.

"Who are you, Ted?"

He looked at Rani. "I'm a time-walker I go up and down the timeline."

"Ted found you," said Rani, which was odd, because I hadn't realised I was lost.

"When you were my ghost, how could I see you?" Rani looked panic-stricken for a moment and I could sense a lecture in quantum mechanics looming. "Just a simple explanation will do."

"A hologram telephone call," she answered.

We sat for a moment drinking tea and it felt like the 'neighbours' were calling for all the right reasons. I went into the kitchen to get some cake, trying to add to the sense of barely-there reality. I reached for a knife from the open cutlery drawer. A slight tapping sound made me look up. I expected to see the robin at the window in a suicide mission for crumbs. Something edged at my vision as if the pane of glass was rippling. I dropped the knife and backed up towards the archway. A small spiral of smoke began to take shape and the tapping continued like the frantic claws of the previous night, insistent and creeping, holding on to me with its fear. The cake fell off the table and the crash of the plate snapped a nerve in the room. Ted flung himself at the shadow, fighting nothing and Rani pushed me behind her. A small gold line appeared up from the floor and across all three of us, like a clear shield. Rani's grip on my arm was a vice of terror. The kitchen slid into silence except for the out of breath sound people made when they have run a long way.

"Is that what you meant by madness, am I going crazy?" I whispered. They tried to lie; it would have made it easier for them to persuade me to go.

"No," she said eventually. "That was something else."

We picked up the shattered food, and Ted walked around with a small device checking the walls with Ollie, who was trying hard not to say I told you so.

"Is there anyone you need to tell if you went away for say, a year?" Rani's face said a million words more than her mouth had spoken, because there was no one.

There was nothing as sad as an empty marriage. All promise gone. You spoke but never really said anything and if you brushed past each other too closely, the death of familiarity, you performed a stranger's apology. The fact that I knew he loved me didn't make up for the growing realisation that he didn't like me and I grew tired of being wafted about on the hurricane of someone's arrival and departure.

The last phone call had been barely discernible; the lines from the Antarctic were not notoriously good. He told me how the sea voyage had been and I could hear the pleasure he had from being cold and tired and wet in the slight raised tone in his voice. It was most people's idea of hell but Max's idea of heaven. We didn't stand a chance. I could have blamed his mean and destructive family; he could have blamed my ever-increasing distance.

Either way it didn't matter any more.

Ollie sat in one of the boxes Ted had brought around. He was purring loudly. "Of course I'm not going to leave you behind," I said. His purr changed tone slightly and he curled up with one paw over his eyes in furry orange contentment. We were on the landing, where I was trying to organise my life. The boxes were grey and felt cool to the touch. Ted had said they were made from something like a type of Teflon. They were self-sealing and I played with them like a new toy. We were all children in the future.

I looked around me. The house waited, much as it always had in times past, listening. I packed. Apart from my books I had never owned much. I had always liked space and light in a home and 'things' weighed heavily on a troubled mind. You couldn't run and hide with a load of baggage.

The old rooms had changed shape and use over the years; if I looked hard enough I could see them. It was not a habit to get into because you started bumping into the walls that were actually here now. In one of the bedrooms was a chair and mirror and in the other a blanket box, an old wicker basket and my bed. I had moved the rocking chair onto the landing because it kept making me feel watched.

Ted had said, in answer to that vitally important question, 'what should I wear,' "Anything you feel comfortable in." The cupboard in the main bedroom wasn't exactly packed with possibilities.

I did, however, belong to the club which believed you could never own too many shoes.

"You need to talk to the vicar." Ted's hippie hairstyle seemed to have taken on a new lease of life. Mainly due to a few twigs and leaves, which I hoped, were there by mistake rather than for effect.

He stood under the trees and looked as much a part of this time and place as his hair would allow. But I knew that he wasn't from here, or now. That he didn't belong, any more than I did really. He began removing the leaves.

"Why?" I said after a suitable pause, in which I'd tried to read his mind and failed.

He smiled. "I don't seem to be able to reassure him about your impending journey."

"Is the vicar telepathic?" I laughed.

"No, he's just a crusty old fart with a heart of gold and not very receptive to suggestion."

I now seemed to be able to focus on Ted; somehow I could remember what he looked like when I looked away. Not Edie though. I was ill not stupid and I hated the feeling that someone was messing with my head and I couldn't do anything about it. It was strange that I hadn't asked too much about what was going on. I thought about asking Ted what he thought. In the absence of an unbiased opinion a biased one would have to do.

It was one of those real spring days that made the possibilities of a special life an inevitable experience.

Ted had cleared the muddle of nature left to its own devices, without stripping the garden of its charm. He was leaning on a large fork. "Are you sure you're not running away from yourself?"

"No, of course not," I protested. He looked at me, head on one side, serious as secrets. "Okay, maybe I am. It's a perfectly good strategy and if I go maybe I will be able to get this," I pointed at my head, "Under control."

"We take our ghosts with us wherever we go Bea, and no one can be sure that it will be any easier to deal with there."

"In my case, you got the ghost part right." He laughed and then I did; the easy laughter of old friends just beginning and I buried the disquiet in a place for later. "I'm going to miss this, aren't I?"

"Yes," he nodded. "But you'll find other things to feed the spirit. Are you scared?"

"No, I've never been afraid of 'out there.' Out there is where we belong."

He laughed, "There are people who live in worlds that you can't even imagine and they're the ones on this planet." He thought a bit and then said, as if giving me a clue, "Keep an open mind." Which was strange, for a telepath, keeping an open mind was not usually an option.

I turned to go back into the house. "Tea," I said. A vision of a plate of chocolate biscuits dancing little jigs swam into my mind. It looked funny and creepy at the same time, which went for just about everything else that was happening in equal measure. It was the way it felt digging up old bones, history in each handful of earth, but archaeology was as much about destruction as it was about discovery. I went to look for the biscuit tin.

The church steps made me dizzy, like a film being fast forwarded. I tried not to touch the old door. It was odd, some churches gave away nothing. This one was packed like a school library with barely smothered whispers.

The vicar was sitting in the first pew. Still as sleep, his breath was a pale cloud on the cold air. I walked down the small central isle, my feet creating havoc with sun beams and dust. I sat down next to him and we contemplated the light through the fifteenth century windows and a thousand other ghosts.

"I've done it again," he said mournfully.

"What?"

"Upset Mrs Pendleton Smythe, I don't understand why she doesn't want to know about her husband's family." He looked at me pleadingly for a moment. "It's fascinating," he said, warming to the subject, "I've just discovered a very strong connection to Charles I."

I interrupted him. "Mrs Pendleton Smythe's husband comes from a long line of lying thieving bastards and they have more skeletons in their ancestral wardrobes than you've got in your graveyard."

"He looked sadly at me for a moment, seeing the historical riches slip through his fingers and sighed, "I suppose you're right."

"She's probably afraid of being sent to the Tower of London. Enough of her ancestors ended up there."

He looked at me over the top of his speechlessly dirty glasses. I took them off the end of his nose and cleaned them on the sleeve of his voluminous cassock. He put them back on again, dragged himself back from the seventeenth century and regarded me owl-like through the two bottle ends. "When are you leaving?"

"In a couple of days," I answered. He nodded and turned towards the altar.

We sat again in silence for a while and as I got up to go, patting his shoulder, he said quietly, "Travel safely and remember you don't just see with your eyes."

I had finished packing. There were six boxes of books and four boxes of clothes and shoes, as well as Ollie's travelling basket. In amongst the clothes, I had wrapped a few pictures and some china. The house looked empty. It felt as if I'd already left and the walls were waiting for their next people.

Why would I *not* go? There was nothing to stay for except more silence and what came after the silence and those things without a voice.

I went to see Edie. It went against everything that had been forced into my brain, but I wanted to believe that my mind had strength.

She opened the door, ghost-like to my eyes. They were really good I could hardly remember why I was there. She smiled. "You're as bad as the vicar. Ted can't put him off either."

We walked through her sitting room, a mirror image of my house, but with more colour and clutter and lots of floaty things to go with the clothes. The kitchen was bigger than mine and it looked as if actual cooking took place there. The day was crisp and clear with the promise of warmth, but my bones felt cold and I was glad to sit by the Aga and drink tea.

"Are you scared, Edie?" I asked, for no reason that I could understand. I knew she was ill and it felt like the 'something else' that lived in the dark places without a name.

"You're going. Good." There was no apology for reading my mind. "More tea, I can't answer any of your questions."

"I know," I said. I couldn't remember any of them anyway. I was no match for Ted.

Rani came to the door in the late afternoon; she stood on the doorstep looking at the fields, all ploughed and ready for crop sowing. "I was born in a place like this," she said, half to herself. I didn't know what to say, she looked strained and tired and a little lost, a shipwrecked soul in the past. The last few days had been difficult for all of us, but Rani seemed to be suffering over something, or someone.

"It's Edie, isn't it?" I asked.

She shook herself out of the shadows and looked at me. "I can't tell you anything, but I promise it will be all right eventually, can you live with that?"

Her jeans, pale blue jumper and ponytail made her look like a busy mum who'd just done the school run and was on her way to get the supper. I wondered if she had family somewhere out there, maybe in the place where she was born that was like here, but not here. I made her a cup of tea and we sat at my tiny kitchen table talking about nothing as the evening grew darker. Then for no reason it was time to go.

All the boxes had been picked up by Ted earlier; he gave me a tight hug as he left, pressing his face against mine and that more than anything that had happened frightened me. I could feel the collective doubts swarming around us like disturbed bees and the fear of unspoken shadows.

I picked up Ollie in his basket and my backpack and shut the front door feeling as if I was betraying a friend. The house didn't judge me, the way it hadn't judged partings for half a millennium. It just added my being there into its spirit and settled quietly into the fields behind us until all I could see were chimneys and the light that Ted had left on.

We walked in the starlight up the hill, following old paths which made me dizzy with the past. A small copse of trees, looking like a group of giants at a cocktail party, were near the crest and we stopped. Rani looked around hopefully. Pulling a small device about the size of a credit card from her pocket, she pressed a sequence of lighted keys then with a sigh of exasperation tried another sequence.

Technology clearly wasn't any more reliable in the future I speculated to myself. I felt like offering her the method I used on the television remote which involved banging it on the floor and some shouting. Out of the gloom on the edge of the trees a form emerged, the outline shimmered and then settled into a dark, smooth, square-shaped craft. A doorway slid quietly open on one side.

Rani looked at me and I looked up to the half moon in the water of the dark sky. My thoughts echoed out into space, like a seal on the waves of the morning. I knew they weren't telling me everything, I knew they weren't telling me anything. I just knew where I was going and when. I thought the threshold of a different time was always going to be a lonely place and it didn't really matter because I had been lonely and I was good at it.

"Are you ready?" She asked. My uncertain feet kept on walking and I thought about a saying my mother had taught me. 'Give me the strength to find my way, give me the courage to live my dreams.' I felt like sailors forever turning from safe harbours and walked in through the doorway of the craft.

The inside was darker than a bat cave; I put out a hand to stop from bumping into anything and found nothing to steady myself with. Rani walked past me and pushed me towards a seat. My eyes gradually became adjusted. There was a large figure in a curved high-backed seat in front of a bank of dimly lit controls. He barely looked around, but I could see strong hands tapping the console in controlled order, like a silent piano. A quiet deep voice said, "We need to leave immediately."

I put Ollie's travel box on the seat beside me and looked for a lap strap. Rani took the seat next to the pilot. "This is Commander Stirzeker," she said. He didn't look up, but carried on with his procedures. "If you push back into the seat," she said, "It will strap you in." I did as I was told.

"Ah!" They both looked around. "Sorry," I said, "It brings new meaning to the words, 'make yourself comfortable.'" They looked at each other then carried on with what they were doing. The seat hadn't finished with me. It settled itself into my shape and two straps snaked out from the edge of the cushioning and snapped together.

I looked around. Four seats, two at the front, two in the middle, closer to the sides of the craft and facing slightly inwards. The inside was smooth curved walls with sloped consoles and large windows at the front and down the sides. There looked to be an internal door into the back of the craft. Lights flashed temptingly. "Don't even think about it," Rani smiled. The overall shape was pointy at the front and flattish at the back.

The craft lifted quietly and smoothly, slightly front end first, but with no forward movement. I felt obliged to say something positive. In the now discernible gloom I could see he'd swung around in the chair, the glitter of light from the console reflected in thoughtful eyes.

It wasn't a ship and it wasn't a flying saucer. The layers of atmosphere gave way reluctantly to the endless stars of real space. First there was only up and then, or so it seemed to my over-stimulated eyes, there was only down. The semi-circular canals in my inner ear did an out of step cha-cha and I covered my face with my hands for a moment.

"Are you okay?" Rani asked nervously, "You're not going to be sick are you?"

I moved my fingers an inch and looked at her. "The thought hadn't actually occurred to me until you mentioned it."

She looked really worried and I looked at the disapproving back. "Don't panic, Commander Stirzeker," I said, "I promise not to throw up."

"You were right Rani," the disapproving back interjected into the quiet. "Even with the translator on I don't understand a single thing she's saying."

"How does this work?" I asked Rani, who was also tapping the key consoles in front of her. "It isn't exactly a classic flying saucer," I muttered to myself, "It must have some sort of anti-gravity ability." The commander looked at me for a moment, a speculating expression in the shadows and plains on his face, though I still couldn't see him properly, and then he looked away. Rani didn't turn around. But I knew she was smiling.

We travelled for twenty minutes or so without anyone saying a word. Ollie had settled in for a snooze. A shape went passed the window on my side and I found myself whispering loudly, "The moon!" The square shoulders in front of me froze in stunned disapproval. Rani just laughed. If you were going to hide a spaceship, a geosynchronous orbit on the other side of the moon would be the place.

We were closing fast on a wall of silver-grey. As there didn't seem to be any nervous little movements betraying panic, I decided that to express my 'concern' would earn me more disapproval. The wall became a vast dark opening and we 'slid' gracefully across the floor, coming to a halt in front of about a dozen people, half a dozen other flying craft and various other unidentifiable objects.

"Welcome to the Starfire," said Commander Stirzeker. I could now see him in the sharp light of the docking bay. He was tall, with dark blonde hair and the sort of grey eyes that made you think of cold water; he wore a close fitting brown uniform with blue lines on the sleeves and shoulders, to go with his close fitting mouth.

The door slid open and a few eager faces crowded the entrance. A combination of smell and thought appeared like a brick wall inviting me to walk right into it. The team of people were waiting patiently for me to do something. Not all of them were from around here either. They all, rather oddly, seemed to be wearing small clear face masks which gave them a rather interesting lupine look.

Someone in a brown-green uniform took Ollie from me as we left the spacecraft. "We'll bring him to your quarters this evening, after quarantine." He disappeared with my unusually quiet cat through a doorway.

"This way," Commander Stirzeker indicated. He and Rani were heading towards a steep flight of steps.

"I'm not too good with steps; this might take me some time."

"Why?" His brow creased in a frown.

"I'll let Rani explain the finer points of chronic fatigue syndrome. I'm going to need to concentrate on breathing." Rani gave me her arm and I staggered upwards like an old lady who had bought all the bargains in the shop.

"Doctor Pui Quan Chan," Rani said, as the doors to the docking bay hissed quietly closed behind us. The doctor took a step forward to greet me, or so I thought. I held out my hand, which she completely ignored and I winced as something cold was sprayed in my face.

"It's nice to meet you too," I spluttered, laughing.

"Its nothing personal," said Commander Stirzeker, as he presented himself for a face spray. Rani was next.

"Right, that's the decontamination over. Sorry," she added as she removed her face mask, "We find it easier than trying to inoculate the whole crew against your twenty-first century bugs." She held out a fine-boned hand and shook mine briskly. Small, with intelligent warm eyes that had just the right amount of crinkle in the corners to make her beautiful and a mass of black hair. Her uniform was like Commander Stirzeker's except with green flashes and she had a snake in gold on one shoulder. We moved off down the curved corridor. "Captain Witherspoon is waiting for you in the briefing room," she said looking behind her.

Rani and the commander glanced at each other for a second. No more than a flicker of an eye movement each. But it spoke volumes. Okay, I thought, this looks as if it's going to be interesting.

She wasn't what I expected, but then no one ever is.

Captain Witherspoon greeted me with a firm handshake and offered fresh coffee and a welcome chair. The briefing room was large, with several unoccupied seats scattered around in untidy groups. We sat at one end of the table in the middle of the room. One wall was all holographic screens of space. It looked as if someone had taken a child's coloured crayon set and drawn great sweeping lines in the sand which was some sort of course plotting programme. There was no Earth suspended there, just a few pale stars I didn't recognise.

My wandering eyes came back to the small group in front of me, looking like the interview board for a job I wasn't sure I wanted. They all shuffled a bit, except the captain, who I didn't imagine had ever shuffled in her life. She had smooth, black skin, impenetrable black eyes and her uniform, which was the same brown with dark blue as Commander Stirzeker's, fitted like a second skin on a muscular body: there was a small gold star on the collar. The silence was loud, if not actually deafening. I waited, because that was what people like me did.

"I don't support the Star League or the Global Government's plan for telepaths." She paused, not I think for effect. She seemed really angry about it and there was some other emotion that I couldn't quite get.

"I think we should manage with what we've got." She paused again. I said nothing. It would have been rude to interrupt. "It's nothing personal."

No, I thought, it never is. It looked as if prejudice was alive and well and living in the twenty-fifth century.

We walked across the corridor to a set of double doors; a small sign said 0103 with no clue as to what was behind. I was still reeling from the welcome speech. Rani touched the sign and it lit up. The doors slid open. "Wow!" I said. In fact the wow factor was off the scale. It was like being at the top of the rain forest canopy, massive trees grew up through the centre of what looked like a huge arboretum and I could hear birdsong.

"Hydroponics," said Rani.

"Really," I answered. Thick, dark vines hung down from the balcony. I looked down to the next level and the next, a sea of green. The walkway on all four sides was covered with plants. The sights and smells literally knocked you over. I looked up; you could see the stars through a clear dome.

"I must go," announced Commander Stirzeker.

Which was a bit embarrassing as I hadn't realised he was still with us. My thank you landed on a closing door. I looked at Rani. "In four hundred years we've come a long way."

"We had help," said Rani, "Gurber's race has given us lots of technology."

"You mentioned Gurber once before." She looked at me, adding nothing to the non-committal smile. I took the hint. "What now?" I asked.

"Let's go and have a look at where you'll be living." We walked down two levels, past the curious and the contemplative, out into another endless, curved corridor. To a door which said 0309.

The rooms were large, sparsely furnished and full of plants. "We thought it might make you feel more at home," Rani explained. My 'quarters' surprised me. I was not sure why. After the welcome talk by the captain, I thought I might be travelling in the cargo hold. The door had hissed open onto a large living room with a comfortable seating area on one side and somewhere to eat. Shelving, empty for now and opposite the still-open door, floor to ceiling windows. Slightly curved, they showed the Earth.

"Can I come in?" I turned at the sound of the voice.

"Ko-Yo-Na," said Rani, "This is Bea." A bird of paradise in a tight grey uniform walked into the room and we shook hands.

"Welcome," said Ko-Yo-Na. "I brought you a new Com/T, a communicator/translator. It will mould itself to the shape of your ear." She hooked the small device over my ear. A small bubble fitted into the ear canal, attached to a clear wire that looped over the top of the ear and a tiny silver disc rested on the parotid bone. She removed the temporary one Ted had given me. "Better?" She inquired.

"Yes," I managed to say. It wasn't that she didn't look human; it's just that she was so exotic. "Thank you," I added. She looked a little disappointed. "I understand from Rani that you're going to be teaching me about the ship. I'm really looking forward to it." She smiled, or I think she did and ducked her head as she left through the doorway. She was very tall.

"See you tomorrow," she said.

Rani walked me down the corridor explaining that I needed a medical. "It is mostly accommodation on this deck." The corridor curved around towards the centre of the ship, empty except for us.

"Where is everyone?"

"It's a big ship." She laughed. We stood in front of a door. "This is the tricky bit," she said.

"I don't do tricky bits," I muttered nervously, as the door slid open onto nothing down or up.

"It's the only way to get up or down, apart from the maintenance shafts and hydroponics."

"Point them out," I said, peering downwards.

"Watch," she walked past me into the lift shaft. Interestingly, it was just like skydiving, resting on a cushion of air but without a parachute.

I had loved parachuting and seen people who really made it look easy. For me it was difficult. It was one of those sports that needed your undivided attention. But it was fun. I enjoyed the challenge of the training and the sense of power when I reached terminal at about twelve seconds. Since I'd discovered flying, I hadn't done more than a few jumps a year which was just enough to scare myself witless. The illness had put paid to both.

"Hello again," said Doctor Chan. The room was half office, half health club and not much medical centre. Her desk was cluttered, which somehow surprised me because her mind was like a filing cabinet. The beds were spaced up against the walls and the office area was in one corner with a small lab in the opposite corner. Each bed space seemed to have a holographic wall around it, but you could see they were empty except for one. A man sat on one of the further beds. Another man in the same brown-green uniform as the doctor was examining his patient's arm.

A loud expletive made us all look over at them. "Sorry," he said looking around.

"Well," said Rani, preparing to leave, "do you think you can find your way back to your quarters?"

"Are you *joking?*" I replied.

Doctor Chan smiled. "I will take you back."

The medical was intrusive and thorough. It took place in one of the alcoves surrounded by a now opaque holographic 'curtain.' I could see out but no one could see in. She told me it worked both ways or not at all, as required. The clutter on the desk translated itself into a series of tests, inoculations and a great deal of grunting and tutting from the doctor. She looked at the readings the computer was spitting out.

"Am I dead yet?"

"No, but I don't know why," she replied, still looking at the readings. "You must feel *dreadful.*"

"I could have just told you that," I muttered.

"I'm going to try and rebalance your system and you should start to feel a little better in a few days. What caused this?"

"I have no idea. There's a lot of speculation, in my time, but no real answers and no solution," I added bitterly.

"We don't have anything like it now. But I will add it to the database, you never know." She pushed a small clear syringe into my arm. It hissed its liquid into the skin.

"What's that for?"

"You don't need to have a monthly cycle unless you wish to reproduce."

"Ah." I nodded gratefully, if she hadn't brought it up, I would have.

"What have you got for stretch marks and sagging?" She looked at me, sniffed and picked out a small cylindrical device.

"This is for the stretch marks. For the 'sagging' meet me in the upper exercise room at six am ship's time tomorrow."

"Thank you." I said, taking the cylinder.

It took me a few minutes to work out there was someone at the door. I was sleeping on the couch and had drifted off looking at the stars. The steady hum of the ship's engine was better than a vacuum cleaner or a washing machine on spin. My watch said I'd been asleep for an hour. My body said it was the middle of the night.

The door chimed again and a wave of impatience wafted into my sleepy thoughts. "Don't be so impatient," I muttered under my breath. The door opened. Commander Stirzeker staggered in with Ollie's box under one arm, balancing two of my personal containers in the other. I leapt up to help.

"I thought I would see how you're getting on." He went out into the corridor and brought in another three boxes. He looked stunned as several pairs of shoes fell out onto the floor and opened his mouth to comment. A muffled siren noise sounded.

"Sorry," he said and caught hold of my arm.

"What sort of sorry?" I asked.

"We're about to time-jump." We jumped. It was as if someone had taken apart my brain and put the pieces back in the wrong place and it hurt. Ollie howled, still in his travel box. I felt like joining in. I opened my eyes carefully, trying to find auto focus.

"Are you okay?" His grey eyes were close and crinkled with concern. He seemed to be holding me upright, which was odd because I usually did that on my own.

"Rani says it plays havoc with her too."

"Oh bugger," I said, finding my voice and not much else.

"Call me Zeke," he said laughing. He let go of my arms and I fell over. "Sorry again," he said as he helped me up off the floor.

"What was all that about?" I asked through a cold wet flannel, lying down having been the only possible option. Commander Stirzeker's voice came from a long way away and sounded as if he had a bucket over his head. Or maybe it was me wearing the bucket. I peered out from under the flannel that was now dripping down my neck. He was sitting on the other end of the sofa, looking almost worried.

"Well, travelling into the future is the easy bit; travelling back in time is much more complicated. You are aware that there's a difference between instantaneous time travel backwards in time travel and faster than light travel?" I raised the corner of the cloth again and looked at him with one eye.

"Okay what about the difference between a black hole and a worm hole?"

"I'm sure I did once," I said, covering my eyes up with the flannel again. He continued, warming to the subject and not taking the hint.

"Basically a worm hole is a black hole with an exit." He was quiet for a moment. I risked another look. At least the room was slowing down.

"What?" I asked, sitting up.

"Just checking you're still with me." He smiled and it was nice to know he was able to. "The time-jump requires space/time foam and inflating a worm hole and a stack of particle physics calculations. It's not something we do without guidance."

"I'm amazed the human race has developed the capacity."

"We had a lot of help." He didn't elaborate and I didn't ask. But Gurber's race came to mind.

I thought I might give walking a miss for a while. At least the stars were back in the windows instead of in my head. "Most people are haunted by their own past," I said and now I'm one of them, I thought.

"You have the power to change all that." He smiled again. "But remember 'even a god can't change the past.'"

Great, I thought, I had to come across the only spaceman that could quote Socrates.

Six am is early whenever you are. The upper exercise room was on the second floor according to a smiling Rani. I felt dreadful. My head ached from not enough sleep and I couldn't shake off the feeling that I was dreaming. On the whole the reality factor was a little low.

Doctor Chan had come to see me late the previous night and given me a needle-less injection into the crook of my arm. It stung a bit, but left no mark. "This should get you started; we may need to do this for a few days. I'll do some more tests next week." She smiled when she said, "See you tomorrow."

Ollie and I had curled up on the bed listening to the ship. I was not usually okay in small enclosed places, but the windows were huge. It felt as if the room was in among the stars and I spent most of the night getting my diary up to date because it pushed the unanswered questions into a place where worrying on a spectacular scale about going off with strangers was less likely.

The early morning corridors were full of much too cheerful soldiers, they all said 'good day' in ones and twos. I began to feel like a nodding dog after about fifteen minutes. There were other people wearing a variety of uniforms and clothes wandering about.

The door to the lift shaft swept quietly open and I looked down. I stood there for a full minute then closed the door with me still on the outside. "Okay," I said to myself, "Where's hydroponics?"

By the time I had run down the corridor and up the stairs in hydroponics and taken far too long to find the exercise room, it was six-thirty and Doctor Chan was tapping her foot and I had done about as much as I could possibly do for the day. We started with what felt like Tai Chi and went onto what felt like torture. I did my impression of a limp lettuce and then found myself agreeing to another session. But she had asked me to call her Pui.

My introduction to the twenty-fifth century began in the engineering section. This might have been a ploy on the captain's part to keep me as far away from the ship's bridge as possible. You couldn't get further away. The bridge was at the front of the ship and the engine room was at the back. Still, Ko-Yo-Na seemed friendly enough, for a six and a half foot Amazon with black teeth and a punk haircut.

"Right, the space-drive is based on the original zero-point engine." Her voice crackled with enthusiasm and I found myself focusing on the tattoos that seemed to begin around her neck and disappeared into various bits of grey uniform. "What level of particle physics do you understand?"

"Well."

"This may take longer than I thought," she muttered, struggling with the various methods of teaching she had probably used in the past, some of which I was sure had involved physical violence.

"Ko-Yo-Na," I interjected into the silence, "Why don't you just go for it and I'll try not to ask too many stupid questions."

The engine room was enormous. Curved walls which glowed with light travelled upwards to three floors. It was noisy with busy people working at various consoles, some sitting, some walking about, all talking and all making a great deal of effort not to notice me. The central structure was spherical and covered in textured metal plating. It reached almost to the third level, which considering what it was able to do was amazing. It should have been the size of a small star; clearly it was the size of a small star on the inside.

"The crucial aspect at the core of a zero-point engine is that it runs without liquids or solid fuel. It requires a small amount of solar power and the rest is based on tapping the quantum fluctuations of empty space."

"That would mean that a vacuum has an energy field?"

Ko-Yo-Na looked seriously impressed, which was again very difficult with no eyebrows. The whole engine room was not listening in so obviously at this point it was making me feel hysterical, like waiting for a punch line you already knew.

"A vacuum is full of ripples of energy called zero-points in the space/time fabric. We basically tap that energy by interfering with the fluctuations."

"Is it possible to meet your team?" Ko-Yo-Na stopped with what would have been I was sure a really interesting introduction to the subatomic layer of the power system.

"Yes," she said uncertainly, "Yes of course."

As if by magic the turbulence in the entire room desisted to the necessary level for pin dropping and everyone seemed to have something to do on the main concourse.

Meeting people in large numbers when you hadn't seen more than one person a week for a few years was a bit like waltzing through a mine field. We did a bit of mutual curiosity, a lot of hand shaking and then my head started to ache. After about the thirtieth introduction, starting with a name, in some cases unpronounceable, a rank, then a job title, Rani appeared.

"Thank you," I said, as we walked into the corridor. "I was beginning to suffer from sensory overload." My head was really painful and I rubbed my eyes.

"Come on," she said, "You've done enough for today."

The corridor lighting and floor cover seemed to be subtly different from a few hours ago. It was a little disorientating. "You'll get used to it," Rani explained. "It's to alleviate boredom. The fiber-optic strands change colour."

A group of crew wearing a variety of uniforms walked by and they greeted Rani by name and smiled their recognition of me. They were taking and laughing and their minds were busy. They made me smile. "I don't understand the different uniforms Rani, what's that about?"

"The ship is tri-service, with army, space navy, marines and civilian technicians. We also have crew from other members of the Star League. It can be confusing. Ah, someone I want you to meet."

Torriff was not very tall. In fact we looked each other in the eye which on him was a most remarkable feature, rather like a crocodile's. His uniform was leather-like and decorated on the wrists and collar. He had sharp ridges over the brow bone and above his ears. His face looked thin, almost gaunt. Hairless, with a lizard-like skin, he could have been a frightening sight. But he had the air of an ageing academic and a combination of humanity and serious intelligence, which was both attractive and endearing. His arms were long and his fingers were beautifully marked, like an Indian prince at a wedding. I held my hand out and he took it. He felt of warmth and sadness. We chatted for a moment and then walked on. It was like being the new girl at school, so much to work out, to understand.

"Tomorrow," said Rani gently.

She told me, as we walked back to my rooms, that the war with Vaneria had lasted ten years and had been over for nearly as long. Bloody aggression had drifted into peaceful mistrust. Torriff's had not been a popular posting. I knew how he felt.

I still had the impression that I was dreaming, but the milky coffee seemed real enough. Rani tapped a few keys on the wall console in my quarters. I had been too afraid to touch it, the thought of a lecture from the captain on hitting the self-destruct button, whilst floating in space, had kept my over-exercised curiosity in check. A large hologram shape appeared. "The Starfire," I said. Rani nodded.

The ship was roughly arrow shaped with huge bulging cylinders on the underside and a knobbly bit at the front that was the bridge. A vast bubble on the top of the ship behind the bridge was the clear roof of hydroponics. It looked untidy and not particularly aerodynamic. The hologram changed shape and metamorphosed into the corridors and different levels.

"Two docking bays," said Rani, "level one and level nine, it's mostly cargo into the lower bay and larger SSVs."

"SSVs?"

"Space to surface vehicle," she explained. "You arrived in one. Accommodation is on the third to seventh levels. Two restaurants, one coffee bar." The hologram changed as she spoke, showing the different areas in a thin, three-dimensional light show that took up half the room.

"What's this?" An odd shaped room defied definition.

"Engineering, as seen from above," she laughed. "Level seven to nine." I couldn't say I recognised it from my brief visit but I'd been looking up, not down. "The working areas are spread all over the ship."

"Laboratories are mainly on level one and so is astro-cartography. Team sports are usually played in the cargo bays and there are various recreation rooms. That's about it," she added. "Oh and there's a laundry for nanotech clothing," she pointed to her own attire, "On level nine and a recycling centre."

"How do I know what time it is really?" I pointed to the holographic clock, which was showing a five hour difference to my now useless watch.

"We run in Standard Time on the ship." She looked at my puzzled face. "It's like GMT? We do hours and days and weeks," she screwed up her face, "well, it's similar." I adjusted my watch to the holo/clock with a sigh.

"What about hydroponics Rani it looked amazing. Are there really birds in there?"

"We spend a long time in space, its home, so it fulfils a practical function, as well as an aesthetic one. And yes, there are birds. Watch out for the parrot on level three, it's a bad-tempered little zudloc!"

***

Star-drive wasn't what I'd expected. You could still see the stars but they didn't stay in the same place for long. There was no sensation of speed. No whooshing. Not much in the way of wavy blue lines, a real disappointment in fact.

A star-jump on the other hand, was all blue lines and whooshing. It took a lot of important rushing around, some tension and a fair amount of maths. This last factor was probably the most important, as getting it wrong could mean we ended up inside something, like a planet for example. The longer the distance, the better the mathematics needed to be.

The countdown came as a bit of a surprise, but as no one else seemed to be too bothered, I carried on walking up the stairs in hydroponics. A voice behind me said, "You'd better hang on to something." I turned. "Na-Es-Yan," said the spitting image of Ko-Yo-Na, pointing at herself by way of introduction. She held out her hand and I went to shake it as the disembodied voice counted down.

"In three, in two, in one." I looked up to the clear dome. Something like the northern lights flickered and danced. Na-Es-Yan held onto me with one hand and the balcony with the other and we whooshed.

"So," I said, after my head had stopped performing the hangover effect, "Two birds of paradise?"

"Err?"

"You and Ko-Yo-Na must come from the same place?" She was wearing a similar uniform to Ko-Yo-Na's, not quite so many bits of brass on the sleeve, but the grey outfit, tattoos and black teeth were the same.

"Tyranox. Its part of the Star League," she added helpfully.

"Are you in engineering too?"

"I'm a xenobiologist. There's a team of three of us." We were walking down the corridor on the first level. "This is my lab, come and have a look?"

There were lots of things in twenty-fifth century jars, not glass, you could push your finger against it and it gave like a firm jelly. The laboratory occupied two rooms on the port side of the ship which were interconnected. The walls on the 'outside' were clear from within, like the mirror in an interrogation room in one of those police procedural films. You could see the windows on the other side of the corridor which were curved and full of interesting faraway stars.

Na-Es-Yan walked over to a large, complicated-looking console. "You might find this interesting, it's my current project." She tapped lighted keys similar to the set up on the wall in my living room. A vast hologram of a shape appeared.

"What is that?" I shouted.

She laughed, "It's a space whale."

The creature did look a little like a whale. In as much as they were probably the same huge size. The streamlined shape began at one end with no eyes and mouth and ended with a tail fin like a ship's sail that

seemed to be able to expand and contract in shape. It was bioluminescent and a beautiful green glow trailed around it like smoke.

"Amazing, it's just amazing!"

"We are studying these creatures, but we know very little about
them so far. They travel in deep space and live to a great age. We think
they migrate using some sort of magnetic field."

"What do they live on?" I asked, as a young man in a light green
uniform appeared from the interconnecting room.

"We don't really know," he answered, his pale blue face shining
with enthusiasm. "We think it has the ability to convert photon particles into digestible energy." He held out a pale blue hand. "Neff.P., it's
nice to meet you Bea."

The three of us gazed up at the creature, a combined and mutual
fascination tying us together with the invisible lace of understanding.

"What else have you got?" I asked enthusiastically to their laughing
faces.

Rani's quarters were full of contradictions. A huge antique book
collection sat side by side with holographic computer games, vibrant
colour and clutter, but with a hidden order.

Lots of throws, the kind my mother would have loved, paintings
on the walls and a tapestry in some sort of silk above the bed.

I thought, much too loudly, **"I bet her clothes cupboard is worth
a rummage."** She laughed as she put a massive chocolate cake on the
table with the aromatic tea.

"Will my kitchen do that?" My voice was full of hope.

"Not without help from you," she laughed.

"Rani, the captain's not the only one who doesn't think I should be
here."

"People are always wary of what's different."

"Commander Stirzeker doesn't think I should be here."

"I hope you didn't come to that conclusion by reading his
thoughts?" Her brow furrowed in concern.

"*Actually* he's rather hard to read, but you don't have to be a telepath to know." She nodded. The cake was a serious challenge.

It was hard to believe that four hundred years into my future I would still be worried about being different. We sat in companionable silence eating cake and sharing thoughts about nothing much.

She said, into the quiet, "It's nice for me to have you here." I nodded, but I wasn't sure to what.

The lessons with Rani began at once. I felt as if I was being trained up for something imminent. "Rani, am I being trained up for something?"

"Not exactly," was the exasperating reply and then there was more of the same relentless pressure. It was something just out of reach, like a childhood memory or a dream in the morning.

I felt my way around the practice box which was made of smooth wood with a metal catch. I just couldn't see inside. After about the millionth time, I think I reached frustration overload. "What am I supposed to be doing?"

"You're still trying to open the box the old-fashioned way. You need to look through the wood to see inside."

"But how do I do that," my voice squeaked in irritation, "There seems to be so much noise. I can hear a bunch of people on the outside of the ship swearing about a communications coupling. Someone in engineering is upset about a letter from home and Captain Witherspoon has a headache!" I threw myself on her sofa. Rani reached over and rescued her cushion from its probable death.

She smiled. "Just think of it as another muscle to exercise."

"My head is like a waste paper bin at this moment, full of other people's rubbish. I just can't seem to block anything out."

"Well you're going to have to learn," she said firmly.

I looked at her. "This is about stopping me going crazy isn't it?" She didn't reply and pointed at the box.

I tried again. My thoughts felt like a wisp of smoke moving against a draught from the opening door. Somewhere I could feel the silence gathering like a storm on the edge of the moor. It frightened me a little and I gasped and opened my eyes.

The door chimed. "I wonder who that is."

"You mean you don't know?" I said, with disbelief and slightly out of breath as I tried to cover my disquiet.

"Sometimes I like it to be a surprise." Commander Stirzeker came in.

"Oh good, rescue," I said.

"That wasn't my first thought," he laughed.

"No, your first thought was chocolate cake."

They both answered at the same time, "You're not supposed to do that."

"Ah!" I put the cushion over my face in the hope of a quiet death.

We ate most of the cake. "Tell me about Gurber," I asked. They looked at each other.

Commander Stirzeker shrugged and waved chocolate-covered fingers. "Gurber's race are very old, they call themselves the explorers. They certainly seem to know a great deal about the galaxy, their maps are highly prized. We think they come from the Rim, but no one's really sure."

Rani said, "We owe a lot of our technical development to them and we can't time-jump without them, but I'm sure what they give us is infinitesimal to the scope of their collective knowledge."

"They say they are here just to observe. Rani thinks they're observing us," he added with a smile. "And their attitude to time is unconventional."

"What does *that* mean?" They both shrugged content with cake and secrets.

"I am going to get so fat if I keep eating like this."

"Its calorie free cake," said Rani.

I looked at her. "I've died and gone to heaven!"

Ollie had settled in well, once he realised the cat box didn't mean 'the vet.' However, he voiced his disapproval long and loud about the house arrest. And somehow I wasn't surprised when I came back to my quarters to find him missing. "Rani."

"Yes, Bea?"

"Do you have any idea where my cat is?" Silence.

"We'd better put out a ship announcement."

A few minutes later my Com/T buzzed. I had just got out of the shower and wrapped a towel around me. I picked up the device and held it to the back of my ear, wet skin and hair dripping all over the floor. "Yes?"

"It's Captain Witherspoon. Your cat is in my quarters."

"What!" How did he get *there*?"

"I'm not sure." She sounded relaxed about it anyway. "He was here when I got back."

"So he got out of my quarters and into yours without anyone seeing him. How is that possible?" She laughed which was not a sound I'd heard before.

I walked down the corridor, in slightly damp fashion, to the captain's quarters and pressed the door buzzer.

"Come in." Captain Witherspoon's living room was huge with massive windows on the far wall and beautifully furnished, with what would have been serious antiques in my time. I was conscious of my wet hair and hastily thrown on jeans.

"Would you like some tea?" She waved a cup at me.

"Tea," I found myself repeating it like the demented parrot in hydroponics. "Yes, please."

Ollie was lying on his back, with all four paws in the air. I think he had been sleeping on her lap and I think she had also been asleep, she looked really tired.

"Have a seat." I sat. The tea was in a china cup. "We had cats when I was growing up."

"Ah," I said as if this explained everything, which it didn't. The door chimed.

"Yes." A man in a smart brown and green uniform with an air of quiet ruthlessness and a large grin added up to what could only be a Gurkha. "Commander Limbu, this is Bea Markam."

I walked back to my quarters, without my cat. He would be back when he felt like it. As the captain had said, where could he go we were in space?

She was a puzzle, younger than I had first thought and not quite so angry; more sad if anything. I wondered what she knew that I didn't, apart from everything and then I thought I was glad I didn't know. Sometimes when you were flying into darkness it was nice to know someone else was navigating. Ollie obviously liked her and cats were a great judge of character. She'd talked about her own childhood on Mars, which was a good indication that she hadn't been put together by a team without a sense of humour. I wondered if I would ever understand her without reading her mind. A heinous crime, which would get me put off the ship on the nearest airless lump of rock, so Rani had told me about a thousand times. My life was divided into trying to prevent some people's thoughts from sending me crazy and trying not to read the minds of people whose minds I couldn't read anyway.

———

I contemplated my room, overall colour green with peaceful walls and flooring, the size of my whole house in surface area. Rani had said that all the quarters were about the same. I think most of the marines and some of the techs bunked together, but generally the rooms were large and individual.

Apparently some psychologist had discovered that people crammed into small spaces for long periods of time tended to kill each other.

The 'kitchen' could do practically anything if Rani were to be believed. However I was under the impression that cooking would still have to be involved. I had spread my treasures around in amongst the copious plants, pictures, cushions and books, all the things that looked and felt like home. The room was half-empty still, not untidy, no cluttered corners, unlike my head.

Ollie had a small space for ablutions which looked as if it was filled with a fine, pale sand and had a built in waste disposal unit. There were other pets on board, though I hadn't seen any except the parrot. Ollie's escape and evasion skills must have been unusual.

The bedroom was the same colour as the living room with one large window. I had filled the shelves with my books and the cupboard with my clothes and shoes, but it still looked empty. I was planning to ask Rani where she got her floaty things. The bathroom was window-less and contained what you'd expect to find, plus a few things I hadn't worked out.

And the view; I knelt on the well-cushioned seating and touched the window which was as cold as ice. Not made of any kind of glass of course, more like the rigid jelly the specimen jars were made of in the lab, but thicker, I hoped it was thicker. You could fill your head with stars if you looked long enough and I never could resist stars.

I began to feel like a human being again with a pulse, instead of a ghost among shadows. After a few days of Pui's treatment, one morning I woke up feeling different. I couldn't figure out at first what it was and then I knew. I'd been asleep all night. I cried for the first time in a long time because when you felt as if you were dying, you couldn't afford the luxury of self-pity. I was going to have to start writing my diary at other times. I hopped out of bed and only groaned the normal amount.

There were short, round people on board, but the cook wasn't one of them. He looked like a cadaver which was no reflection on his cooking. Tariq Azel had been born on the Earth's moon. Initially, during the early days of settlement, the gravity system had been rudimentary, which caused the birth of some very tall thin people indeed. Gradually it became their normal and part of the culture.

The ship had two restaurants and a coffee bar. The little cooking area in my room once I'd worked out the 'kettle' provided any start to the day I could tolerate. However by midday I was usually so hungry I could chew furniture, any later and I could start throwing it. I was lost and starving. Rani had introduced me to Tariq and the upper level restaurant, and I had checked the ship's hologram map before I left my room. I could see quite clearly that it was on the first level somewhere near the back. I just couldn't find it. A smartly dressed young man walked by.

"Hey," I said grumpily. He stopped and smiled at me. "Where's the upper restaurant?"

"Two doors down on the right, I'm going there myself, Mac Ibarra." He held out a hand. I shook it. He was good looking with dark skin and his hair was long and tied back. "I'm going to be teaching you how to use a space suit soon."

"It's nice to meet you," I said hurriedly. "But if I don't eat soon I'm going to be starting on the carpet." He actually looked as if that might be an interesting possibility, but led the way to the restaurant anyway.

The doors slid open onto a large room. Tables were scattered around in relaxed order and the view from the windows was stupendous. A bar ran all the way along one wall in what was obviously self-service food.

"Tariq!" I practically threw myself at him. "I am really hungry." He laughed; he had dark skin, pale blue eyes, and a nice smile.

"This way; only take meals from this end. We have a lot of different dietary requirements on board, some of which could make you feel terrible."

I greedily filled up a plate with a variety of food and found a near-empty table. I noticed that someone was looking at me with great interest, Torriff.

"Hello again," I said with a full mouth. He nodded. I began to realise that we were in a corner by ourselves and we seemed to be the subject of some interest. Torriff's plate contained what looked like something from the forbidden end of the buffet. It was a shade of green that would never have been seen on Earth in any time. I was glad he seemed to have finished. He looked down at his plate and smiled a face full of fearsome teeth.

"It was vegetarian, if that's any help."

What a waste of teeth, I thought. It took me a moment to realise that it wasn't me that was engendering the wave of disquiet from the rest of the room. It was Torriff. War was never over in some people's hearts. I smiled back at him. The room was warm with people and tables busy with talk, the smell was like a school canteen but somehow comforting. I caught at Mac Ibarra's arm as he walked past to collect his coffee, "So tell me about the space suit lesson?" He paused for less than a heartbeat nodding politely to Torriff who returned the nod with a smile.

"Sure, let me get a cup of coffee." He sat down, took a few loud slurps of his drink and said, "You're going to hate it."

I decided to sleep in the information headset for a few nights; it was linked to the computer in my rooms and was a little disconcerting. But Mac Ibarra had said that he did it all the time, particularly when he needed to cram for something important. I fell over more than once the first morning, with a bad case of spatial disorientation. But Rani was pushing the telepathic training hard and I needed to know what I didn't know. My dreams had become disturbed and disturbing and I began to wake with sweat pouring off me sometimes crying for no reason I could remember. I did however begin to understand a bit more about how the ship worked and who the members of the Star League were. I could even match the different uniforms to the appropriate planetary systems.

I was working out on the treadmill and talking grumpily to myself about nothing which was a really bad early-morning habit. I had programmed the holographic screens to give me a river in the dawn light, it didn't look like anything on Earth and the water was a pale pink with the occasional splash of something that was clearly not a 'fish.' The running machine had all the usual stuff, the bit that moved under your feet and a timer; it also had a personality and was sulking because I had turned the advice off. I had always hated it when inanimate objects tried to tell you what to do. Pui was late. Something about a broken arm and a concussion on level six which made me wish I'd thought of it.

A voice said, "How's it going?" I slowed to a walk and looked behind me. I lost track of direction slightly, caught my foot on the non-moving edge of the machine and went flying. He helped me up with a look of concern, confused with amusement. Amusement won. "Are you okay?"

"Oh great, Commander Stirzeker, that thing hates me and now it's laughing at me."

"Did you hit your head?" He looked worried.

"Just add a few more bruises to the ones Doctor Chan is inflicting every morning." I grumbled through gritted teeth and turned off the running machine, rubbing my stinging back and covering my mental discomfort with the physical ones.

He leaned forward. "What are those marks are on your fore-head?" One rough finger tip touched my face. He really made me feel uncomfortable, as if he was someone I knew but couldn't remember.

"Actually they're from the info-headset," I answered sheepishly, backing off from the finger, "I've been sleeping with it on." Our faces were still too close. My proximity warning light was going off and I found myself pulling further away, which was unfortunate as I came into contact with the wall and then tried to look as if that's where I was planning to be.

"You'll make yourself ill, who suggested that stupid idea?" He had moved forward making us look like we were engaged in some sort of mismatched dance.

"Ma... actually I thought it would help me get to know what's been going on," I fumbled.

"It might be safer to just ask." He had a point. He smiled and I found myself smiling back, the eyes that had seemed like cold grey water were now doing 'hidden depths.' He somehow still seemed to be too close and I disengaged myself with as much dignity as I could muster which wasn't very much, just as Pui Quan Chan arrived. She looked suspiciously at both of us.

"Unless you're planning to join us, Zeke?"

"Not a chance Pui, I've done one of your workouts." He smiled and went through the open doorway. It closed quietly behind him. Pui looked at me her face a picture of oriental inscrutability. For some reason I felt as if I had been up to something.

I didn't go looking for Gurber, he found me. I was lost as usual. "I'm lost," I said to a puzzled engineer who was hurrying in the opposite direction. "I can't find the bridge, I know it's at the pointy end, but I keep ending up at the flat end." He laughed and indicated a lift shaft.

"You need to go up another level, turn right," this was said kindly and slowly, "then all the way along to the end." He watched me step towards the lift shaft, a smile still on his face, and then hurried on his way. I moved away from the lift and walked towards hydroponics, trying to translate his instructions from there. The up one level went okay; everything after that went wrong. Which was odd because most of the time I usually knew my left from my right. I could hear bubbling, the corridor was quiet and empty but there was a gentle vibration that seemed to be inside my head as well as under my feet and in lieu of anyone else in the vicinity to ask for help I went through a large doorway hoping not to end up having to make embarrassing excuses for being there. I stepped into space and it was all around me. I held my breath which would have been pointless in reality. In a second I was standing in a large empty room.

"**Soorrry,**" a voice bubbled in my head all telepathic no sound. I turned around.

Gurber was everything an alien should be. I hadn't realised that I had actually been a little disappointed up to then with the rather humanoid species I'd encountered on the ship. But Gurber could only be described as an amorphous blob of jelly. I began to feel a little faint.

"**Breeeathee,**" a voice in my head said. I scooped in a great gulp of air and laughed.

"**Beeeaaa.**"

"Yes, how did you know?"

"**We are interested in you. You arrre,**" there was a long pause, "**Necessary.**"

I probed gently and inexpertly for further clarification and got in return, nothing but a sense of kindly amusement. Much as an adult would feel for a very small child. I tried to ask some simple questions. It was difficult, I'd never attempted to communicate a conversation telepathically before. Rani and I hadn't reached that section of the telepathic training manual. "**Zeke says you come from the Rim?**"

"**Nearly there.**"

"**Do you travel alone when you explore?**"

Gurber was very amused by this. "**We are always with each other.**" Now I could see why they were a mystery they did enigmatic better than my cat.

"**We will expect to see you tomorrow. We are astro-cartography.**"

I'll just bet you are, I thought. "Okay," I said out loud. I found myself outside the door and looking for the bridge again. His voice had sounded male in my head and deep but he had referred to himself as we. I tried not to tie myself in knots over this and then gave it up as a lost cause; much the same as finding the bridge without an escort.

"Basically, the pilot controls can be accessed on both sides of the console." Commander Stirzeker had begun teaching me how to fly a space to surface vehicle. This was nothing special in that everyone on board had to be able to demonstrate basic flying skills. In my case, I thought, it would have to be a very basic demonstration.

The SSV was similar to the one we had travelled in from home to the Starfire. There were not so many flashing lights though and therefore suitable for teaching the average idiot. It was parked in the upper docking bay and much interest had been expressed in my impending first lesson. The crews working on the vehicles and equipment seemed very amused that Zeke would be teaching me.

He had an odd way of talking. Something to do with his punctuation seemed to be in a different place. And he breathed halfway through a sentence which changed its shape and nuance. Also he was right up there with the average windmill. I resisted the temptation to bite the finger that was waving close to my nose.

"The controls are all touch activated, but can be voice activated in an emergency. The computer will only respond to specific commands. You can't ask it what its opinion is."

"Why doesn't 'it' have a voice?" I asked.

"They tried that for a few years but some people began to develop strong feelings for it." He looked really embarrassed.

I gasped with laughter, "You're joking?"

"Right, this is the SSV's main systems," he said, indicating to his left, "Life support, for example. Over here," he pointed to his right, "Are scanners and surveying systems and this is weapons control above the flight controls in front. I sighed, a big dramatic sigh. "You can fly a 'plane can't you, I mean in your time?"

"Yes but can I fly a computer in this time that's the question and one other thing?"

"Yes?"

"Where's the brake?"

He looked slightly stunned and his hand mimed a moment of exasperation. "This is going to take a little longer than I thought."

"You do that a lot, you know."

"What?"

I mimicked his movements in an exaggerated manner. He looked puzzled and then laughed, shaking his head then looked away suddenly as if worried about something.

"Life's a bit of a pain isn't it?" I said.

The space to surface vehicle was awful to fly and we hadn't even left the docking bay. The holographic images that the main computer had thrown up around the small craft were realistically disconcerting. I had crashed twice in half an hour. Once into an asteroid which had been minding its own business, the second time into another vehicle which had no business cutting across in front of me.

Commander Stirzeker, Zeke had been reduced to one word and a whole lot of expressive hand movements. "Again." He waved towards the start up controls. Grinding my teeth but only a little bit and very quietly, I tapped the green keys in sequence.

The upper docking bay was on the first level at the back of the ship. The cargo docking bay was vast and another eight floors down. The smaller vehicles usually landed on level one and it was busy with crew and technicians. Every now and then a body would appear on the edge of the hologram space images, disconcerting me and infuriating Zeke who would rap on the forward windows and indicate with an expressive thumb, as if hitching a ride for the person to move. "Again," he said, throwing himself back into the seat.

At this point I would have welcomed a meteor storm. Rani, however, interrupted on the main com in the SSV. It sounded unnaturally loud and made me jump. "Bea, can you come to my quarters for a lesson?" Even to my buzzing ears it sounded pathetic. I wiped my sweat-soaked palms and tried to look surprised.

"Telepaths," he said and pointed at me and then at the door; much as he had at the people in the docking bay who had annoyed him. His eyes had gone back to the colour of cold water and I was out of there like a bunny out of a hutch.

I had been on the Starfire for nearly two weeks though it had felt longer somehow. I had abandoned the info headset for the more comfortable method of asking questions and I had foolishly asked about Ko-Yo-Na's home world.

We were walking down the corridor to the briefing room. We had regular briefings, where different groups got together and discussed things. As I was supposed to be learning how to be Rani, this involved attending all or nearly all of the ship's meetings that she attended; I had a suspicion that there was a meeting where they discussed me. I did my best which mostly fell far short of adequate and tried not to fall asleep in the boring parts which was more often than you would think. Ko-Yo-Na was explaining the finer points of sharing a biological mother with Na-Es-Yan, something that seemed to have nothing to do with parenting. Children were brought up in what sounded like a collective commune and began their education at an extraordinarily young age. While we were chewing soft toys they were being bombarded with technical information. She was easy company, calm and quiet, with the watchful attitude of a bossy older sister and incredibly proud of her current posting on the Starfire in charge of engineering. Lieutenant Commander Sofred from Katinad, another Star League planet was, she told me, her assistant and in the 'male phase' of his life cycle, something I was going to need a conversation with Pui about.

The Katinads were few in number and quiet, with grey skin and hair and seemingly of both genders. Information overload at this point was alleviated by the view. We were on the outer edge of the ship on level one and the huge curved windows showed a nearby star system in all its glory. I stopped and touched the 'glass' tracing the shape of the stars on the smooth surface with my fingers.

A crewman was working on one of the wall-mounted holographic schematics of ship's systems that were throwing out a hologram. Large sections of the hologram were missing and he smiled absently as we passed, talking to himself intent on his work.

We must have looked a strange sight; Ko-Yo-Na was nearly a foot taller than me. Her hair, a single strand, reached halfway down her back. Apart from that her head was bald. The tattoos on her neck represented her family group. They didn't go beyond her shoulders, a question I had asked. Her teeth fascinated me. They were completely black, perfect but black. I looked like a sparrow next to a peacock.

Her rooms were on the seventh level and I had wandered down there, which was a hike using a combination of hydroponics and the ghastly lift shafts. She invited me in and I looked with undisguised curiosity at the personal effects that decorated her living area. Lots of holograms of ship's systems sprang out from the walls and ceiling, and the couch was covered with bits of machinery. Not much in the way of comfort, but if I'd been given a starship engine to chew on when I was three, maybe I wouldn't have been so interested in shoes. This was someone who lived their job.

I still didn't recognise most of the people I saw on board, but some faces were becoming familiar and what was different didn't seem so alien. I missed the sound of the wind in the trees, but if I stood on level three of hydroponics and looked up, the effect was nearly the same and if I closed my eyes I could be home in a second.

I asked her about Commander Stirzeker. She was remarkably uninformed.

"Are you 'interested' in him as a partner?" She asked politely but with a slight air of disapproval.

"No," I said, the memory of the last lesson in the SSV fresh in my mind, "But," I added rather stupidly and for no reason I could think of, "I wouldn't mind kissing him."

A voice from behind me said quietly, "It could be arranged." I stopped dead in the corridor, put my hands over my eyes and waited.

"Has he gone," I asked?

"Yes," said Ko-Yo-Na. I uncovered my eyes in time to see Zeke disappear around the curve of the corridor towards the briefing room. "I would like to be present at your next flying lesson. I imagine it will be very embarrassing."

I nodded in serious agreement. "It is much too easy to sneak up on someone around here."

"I'll speak to the maintenance engineer and express your concerns."

My friendship with Torriff developed around food and he was lonely. I had an antenna for loneliness. We also seemed to have a sugar low at around the same time so we saw each other almost every lunchtime, until I expected to share food and conversation with him and missed him when his duties took him elsewhere.

He had an office next to the captain's just before you got to the bridge. I wasn't sure what he did on-board, something like having a Soviet sailor on an American aircraft carrier during the Cuban missile crisis. I guessed he was the liaison officer for the Vanerians. He always seemed to be alone with his reports. I wondered if there was some poor schmuck on a ship somewhere out there doing exactly the same but the other way around and if they were as lonely.

"Hey Torriff!" I threw myself into a chair, and two plates of food down on the table. He looked amused. "What?" I asked, trying not to speak with my mouth full.

"Are you breeding?" He indicated the double servings with a delicate hand.

"Oh very witty, Rani has me straining every synapse and Pui Quan Chan has me straining every muscle. By the time I get to lunch I could eat anything." I looked down at his not quite empty plate which was more green weird-smelling slime and he grinned.

It was quiet in the restaurant, more like late morning than early lunchtime. Tariq was making something spectacular in the open kitchen. He smiled hello and carried on with his creation. Torriff came in early to avoid the forced civility of some of the crew. I had asked him about his family at a previous meal. He said his wife Kela was a biologist on his home planet and his two 'offspring' were running wild without him. You didn't need a loneliness antenna to see the cobweb of pain in the back of his eyes.

"I've brought something for you." I put a small book on the table. It was my mother's old copy of Jane Austen's Pride and Prejudice because there were some things you just couldn't leave home without. Torriff's addiction to romantic novels was a closely guarded secret known to just about everyone on-board. He said it was research; I had always done mine in the shoe sales. The warrior/scholar touched the pale blue cover with the same reverence that Father Trethowan had felt for a really juicy piece of local history.

I had started on the second plate, an incredibly sweet trifle with chocolate cream. Torriff looked at the pudding with the same expression that I usually had for his green slime.

"Thank you," he said rising, both hands gripped around the book. "I must go now." He left as a large group of noisy diners came through the doorway barely acknowledging his existence as they swept past him like water through the weeds.

I took my plate and went to sit in the casual seating near the windows. Tariq was waving at me over the heads of potential customers, which was not that difficult when you were a foot taller than everyone else. He mouthed the word 'coffee' and I nodded gratefully. I pondered licking the spoon of the last traces of sweet cream. Torriff had surprised me. He seemed pleased but there was something else there, a much stronger feeling of sadness maybe. Tariq joined me for coffee and we discussed the finer points of chocolate trifle of which there were many.

I no longer felt as if I was dreaming but the sensation of being out of place and out of sorts was strong. If there were rules maybe it was that people should live in their own time and not keep dipping in and out like reading the end of a book first. But I had always read the end of a book first.

I was so far from the exploration projects of my own time, reaching out of our solar system with country music and Earth languages, longing to catch the shape of possible planets on their own sun as they passed by, looking at the stars with interconnecting telescopes in the hope of seeing what I could now see as if the whole thing had happened in the blink of someone's eye like a film on fast forward.

Gurber and I were mapping a nebula, a necessary part of my learning curve according to Rani. I didn't really know what we were doing, but Gurber didn't seem to mind. And neither did I really. I just sat and learned, which was more sitting than learning. All the controls in astro-cartography were suited to Gurber's rather large jelly-like tendrils, which were varied and many and produced at will. Everything was up against the far wall of the room and he seemed to float along on a silent integrated hovercraft, tapping lighted keys until he found something particularly interesting. My head was filled with an endless supply of statistics and we sat inside the hologram of the nebula charting the information. I had found myself a chair by pinching one from the tech's office next door; I didn't think Gurber actually sat. Gurber charted and I said helpful things like, "This is so beautiful."

I tried what I thought was a very able verbal impression of Gurber's full name in his own language. The method, I discovered, to tackle the five syllables required nearly choking yourself with one hand and holding your nose with the other. Anyway I thought he was impressed, he rippled; either that or he was laughing at me.

The space survival suit was a tight fit, skin tight on the inside with a baggier outer layer. The fact it was possible to live in it for several days did not endear it to me in any way. The arrangements for 'waste disposal' and 'recycling' made my eyes water. "Is this absolutely necessary, Mac? Couldn't I just cross my legs?" Mackenzie Ibarra grinned back at me.

"You get used to it."

"Well," I added under my breath, "if anyone's lost a set of dinner forks, I know where they are." He spluttered a laugh and I liked the way his face and eyes laughed too. He was young and keen and earnest in his efforts to put me at my ease. He lowered what looked like a tinted fish bowl over my head and locked it into place.

"Right," he said, "Take a deep breath. That will start up the air supply and I'll explain the heads up holo/computer graphics."

"Oh good," I said, "More computer graphics. Does anything around here just have an on/off switch?" My head swam a little and I staggered as the holo/screen scrolled through its start up. It was like being inside the fish bowl with the fish still in it. He began pulling and adjusting the suit around me and looked enquiringly at my smile.

"What?"

"Well, I usually dress myself."

Mac Ibarra began suiting himself up. He seemed to have climbing into a banana skin down to a fine art. The air supply whooshed comfortingly inside my helmet and the computer settled down to just air levels and perspiration. Talking and breathing at the same time gradually became easy again.

"You're Native American, aren't you, what tribe?" I asked curiously.

He laughed, "I don't think I've ever heard anyone actually say that before."

"What, tribe?"

"No, Native American. I'm Mohawk."

"Of course," I said. "Mohawks helped to build the skyscrapers in New York. They are amazing high rise construction workers with no fear of heights. So I guess a space tech would be a natural progression."

"It's a sort of family tradition. My father was a space tech and my grandmother. I was born in space. Me and my brothers," he stopped as another space tech came in.

"Hi, sorry I'm late. I'm Tom Hatherley." He peered into my helmet and I smiled. As tall and blonde and chunky as Mac was slim and dark they were thick as thieves with the stars on their shoulders and in their hearts. He helped Mac with his fish bowl and then began suiting himself up, whistling off-key. He and Mac kept up a steady banter tormenting each other like familiar old friends. I could feel the years of shared experience between them.

"Ready?" asked Mac.

"I am really looking forward to this." He and Tom both looked surprised.

"Most people hate their first time," Tom indicated the doorway, "Into the lock and we'll do final checks." We shuffled into the airlock room and the door hissed closed. The two of them checked each other out. Head seals, air connections, com. They looked like skydivers on a jump run. Mac turned and began my safety checks. He signalled Tom like a scuba diver with a circled finger and thumb.

"Captain."

"Yes, Mac."

"Three for EVA, captain."

"Acknowledged."

The outer door opened. It wasn't like parachuting, or scuba diving. I swam on a line about a hundred yards away from the ship. Not far enough away to see her real shape just the smooth clean lines. She curved away from me like a silver arrow in a map of stars.

Mac and Tom stayed on the surface of the ship's hull and watched me. It was like falling down a long dark tunnel, a profound combination of agoraphobia and claustrophobia, creepy, but fun. I laughed as I tried to swim totally unsuccessfully in one direction.

"Use the jetpack, Bea."

"This is more interesting."

"She's not from around here, is she?" I heard Tom say.

"You've right, she's not," Mac replied.

"I heard that!"

"I thought you were," she hunted for the word, "'Married?'" said Na-Es-Yan. She looked puzzled. We had been discussing impossible relationships which were a speciality of mine. Na had been telling me about her partner, a young engineer who was from Mars and human.

I tried for a tactful question, but gave up and went with the rather rude, "Is that possible?"

"We are physically compatible," she answered coyly, "It's just that I do not understand your men," she finished with exasperation.

"We don't understand them either."

Xenobiology was a good hiding place, too many 'bugs' in jars for Rani. Gurber was working on something big, literally and Zeke was taking what he called a well-earned break from trying to improve my flying skills. I could be guaranteed at least half an hour's peace.

We were admiring a rather beautiful hologram of an amoeba, another space creature that bore more than a passing resemblance to a sea dweller on Earth. Like the space whale, very little was known about it. I speculated about the development of life on earth starting in space and Na looked puzzled again.

"But of course all life started in space," she said, "The building blocks of our DNA are carried in the interstellar dust on space winds. It is the key to all life everywhere."

My mouth must have dropped open for a moment; "I think I missed that on the info tapes."

We went back to discussing the amoeba and began trying to work out its reproductive potential which is how we'd got talking about men. Na-Es-Yan was looking at me with something that might have been curiosity. We did that little dance strangers do when they were thinking about being friends. She tried again with the fishing expedition. "Rani said she thought you were married?"

So did I once, about four hundred or so years ago. We had met parachuting over Netheravon in Wiltshire. Maxim Fiorimonte, younger than me, tallish, blue eyes, spoilt. He had two thousand jumps; I was on my first ten second delay. He tormented me all the way up to five thousand feet which was probably his idea of foreplay, but he was in the army at the time. He and his four way team had behaved like a family of chimps. The pilot looked over his shoulder catching my eye. He had a roll-up hanging out of the corner of his mouth which was not very reassuring in a fuel tank with wings. Max yelled at him, "Hey Harry, when are you going to give up smoking in the 'plane?"

"When you give up farting in it!"

Harry called 'running in' and Max stuck his head out of the aircraft doorway to check the spot for me. He gave one correction of, "Five right," which the pilot all but ignored and then yelled, "Cut!" The deafening engine noise muted slightly as the pilot throttled the powerful Porter back to 70 knots. I peered gingerly out of the doorway to check that I wasn't being dropped over Stonehenge which was typical skydiver humour and then shuffled towards the door.

Max signalled exit, by gesturing toward the doorway like a waiter indicating lunch. He had a big grin on his face. I positioned myself in the doorway, legs hanging outside and bum half in half out, left hand under my leg, right hand on the door edge behind me.

I looked in at Max and readied myself for an aggressive push off.

"Go!" He shouted and planted a sloppy kiss on my astonished face. I completely forgot to count, a heinous crime. All I could see were grinning faces, receding fast.

I yelled a swear word pointlessly and then went in for the pull.

Netheravon was an amazing drop-zone; under canopy you could

see all of Wiltshire spread out like a quilt and the big old army base sitting in the middle like a sleeping dog snoring in the sun. Masses of untidy buildings wound up in the history of the plains. I hoped that no diligent staff member had been watching my appalling exit on the telemeters. I tracked up and down the wind line enjoying the quiet and the blue sky which was just that little bit nearer for having been there.

I prided myself on my accuracy and I turned the round canopy into wind and put my feet and knees together for landing unfortunately a little too close to the packing area. A loud sergeant major's voice with a strong Geordie accent yelled, "Markam you're a frap waiting to happen!" That man had eyes in the top of his head.

Not exactly love at first sight. I thought Max owed me an apology or failing that, a drink. Four hundred or so years later, I answered Na-Es-Yan. "Yes, a long time ago I was married."

We had been travelling for several weeks mostly in star-drive apart from the initial time-jump and this was the first time we had orbited a planet. It was called Sakieen and was somewhere near Proxima Centauri, I couldn't even work out when I was never mind where.

The ship's crew were taking it in turns to go down to the small settlement. It seemed to me that it was a stopping off point for a variety of reasons, mainly trade, but also a good excuse to stretch your legs and look a little further than the nearest bulkhead.

Rani gave me some round plastic discs and said, "Go and get yourself some 'floaty' things" which was the telepathic version of eavesdropping. She explained, "The large ones are worth four of the small ones, and don't pay more than three of the large ones for anything."

I travelled down to the planet with Ko and two marines. Ko made me fly the small SSV. I didn't have eyes in the back of my head, but both of the rear seat drivers tightened their seatbelts twice. The landing was a bit bumpy and slightly sideways on but it was a definite improvement on my last attempt. I turned around to share my sense of achievement to find that both of the marines had assumed the crash position. "I thought marines were supposed to be tough," I complained.

They smiled politely as they unbuckled to leave and the taller of the two said, "Tough, but not immortal ma'am. Thanks for the ride."

"Huh," I said.

"Don't wander off," said Ko-Yo-Na, sounding dangerously like someone's mother.

There was something incongruous about being on another planet. And yet most things were the same. You walked on the bit under your feet the sky was above you even if the sun was green. Up was up again as opposed to space, where everything was down. It was as if time had taken a great big genetic spoon and stirred. The lines defining race and culture were blurred. If you didn't look quite straight the differences were barely discernible.

Still, people would find other things to fight about I thought, narrowly missing being squashed by two traders locked in what looked like mortal combat, either that or they really liked each other.

The settlement was hardly a city and was partly below ground. Dry and desert-like, the earth was red. There were no roads, everyone travelled by air. Flying craft of every shape and size were parked on the outskirts. Travellers walked in groups, or sat on the sidewalks in the shade drinking and talking, or not talking and planning and watching, eyes flicking, busy with the day.

There were shops, dark from a distance but inviting close to. I could see a few recognisable uniforms and the oddly comforting familiar face. The buildings looked like the white open-plan houses of the Middle East at home. I thought about being homesick for a moment. The sounds and smells of a vast open air market were the same but different. I was not sure that I could picture what home was any more and it seemed sad that it didn't feel more certain.

The stalls drew me with the possibility of a bargain. Most of it looked familiar, textiles, containers, every type of foodstuff, even some things that looked like weapons but they could have been children's toys for all I knew. I bargained for what I hoped was a gold and silver bracelet. It had small stones set in the hieroglyphs of ancient writing.

The trader was female, with sharp features and webbed fingers and with the benefit of no translator she made an effort to bump up what was obviously an already inflated price. We had the conversational equivalent of a one way street. Eventually in exasperation she grabbed the four small plastic discs I offered and fixed the bracelet to my wrist. I turned it, looking for a catch and not finding one. She watched me and gestured. I held out my arm. As if showing a small child she touched a small yellow stone and the bracelet sprung open. We both smiled. Me because I was easily pleased with shiny little things, her because she'd probably made enough on that one sale to pack up for the day.

The floaty stuff beckoned. I found some wall hangings that looked as if they had been made locally. The dyed colours suggested the red earth and the buildings. One even depicted the market. They seemed to be some sort of wool, I hoped it was wool. They probably came from the galactic equivalent of China, but they were beautiful. The trader offered me some small wooden boxes which were carved with animals. I looked around for trees and wondered if I was contributing to the decimation of someone's rain forest. I bought them along with the wall hangings. The trader was grinning, his teeth were stained red and I guessed he would be able to send his children to private school on my negotiating skills.

I could see Ko's peacock mane of hair disappearing between the stalls. Technically I hadn't actually wandered off and my self-appointed minder didn't seem too bothered, engrossed as she was in her own bargain hunting.

The ruins I could see in the distance seemed to dance in the heat and beckoned the closet archaeologist that lay at the heart of all of us. A short walk left me gasping and I gulped the water I had brought with me. The cloth bag of market bargains felt like a ton weight, doing anything in this heat would kill you if you weren't careful. I felt the hieroglyphs on the wall tracing the shapes with my hands, a language as silent as dust. The hot green sun cast long shadows which shimmered in the haze. A quiet, barely discernible unease crept over me, my hands still pressed to the shapes on the wall. I felt my neck muscles tense, as if I had been listening for footsteps in the dark. At first it was the silence before loud applause or a rumble of thunder, the air became heavy and thick. I closed my eyes the better to hear the voices. I didn't understand what they said, but the feelings were clear in my mind; questioning, curious and then terror.

Someone snatched me back to now, shaking and breathless my eyes opened. "Are you all right?" Ko-Yo-Na's half shouted enquiry brought her face slowly into focus.

Gasping, I said, "I won't be doing that again in a hurry."

We walked in silence back towards the SSV. I tried to quantify the experience and failed then formulated the sentence that filtered through. "Did they ever sell people here?"

"Yes, how did you know? About a hundred years ago this was a clearing place for the slave trade."

"They must be the two filthiest words in any language," I said to her back as she strode towards civilisation. It explained the fear.

Ko called out to the two marines who were sitting outside a cafe asking if they wanted a lift back up to the ship. They waved us over. The bigger of the two, they were both of them medium height, called out, "Come and have a drink with us." We wandered over and they grabbed a couple of chairs.

The waiter was an astounding shape and size, like a haystack with a dirty apron. I asked for two of the hot drinks the marines were having, thinking they were the local equivalent of coffee, which was stupid, when did marines pass up the chance for alcohol. The tray of drinks arrived and I replenished the cups the men were holding. It was hot and sweet and tasted thick on the back of your tongue.

"Sig!" The taller marine stuck his hand out in the age-old gesture. His vaguely Aussie accent seemed to be getting stronger by the minute which was another clue. He indicated his partner with a thumb. "Doz!" They seemed to have forgiven me for the landing.

I didn't remember how we got back to the Starfire. I did remember trying to teach Ko to sing 'show me the way to go home.' We left her in the corridor covered with my wall hangings. Not even the two marines could persuade her to go any further. I was escorted to my quarters and they both snapped a salute at the door and thanked me for a really interesting day, before staggering off in what I was sure was the wrong direction.

The pounding on the door was accompanied by Ollie putting a paw in my mouth. I must have been snoring. He hated that. I grabbed at my dressing gown, which was totally unnecessary as I had gone to bed fully dressed. I opened the door. It was Zeke. "What?" I said.

"It might be an idea in future if you didn't call the watch officer 'sweetie pie.' He said it was your best landing yet, I'm sorry I missed it."

"What," I said, "They *didn't* let me fly?" Zeke came into the room and began feeding the cat, who was suggesting that it hadn't been done for some considerable time.

"What do you usually take for a hangover?" He asked, handing me a large glass of water.

"Doughnuts," I said wandering back into the bathroom and turning on the shower. A horrifying thought sent me out again with a towel wrapped around me. "Is Ko all right?"

Rani had appeared and was sitting at the table with Zeke, drinking coffee. "The night shift put her to bed." She folded my wall hangings on the nearest chair. "I hope you've learned something useful from this experience."

"Yes, never drink with marines who only have one-syllable names." I stood in the shower for a really long time.

I had got into the habit of taking early morning tea with Gurber in Astro-Cartography. Or rather I had tea, Gurber had an infusion of something disgusting that he absorbed through his outer layer. Still, it seemed to have the same effect. Gurber rippled like a lava lamp, changing colours and I *felt* like rippling, but restrained myself.

We sat in companionable silence, communicating with the occasional telepathic thought which suited Gurber who was not happy with anything verbal which suited me too as it made my nose itch. Actually communicating with Gurber made everyone's nose itch it was something to do with the levels of resonance according to Ko-Yo-Na.

The massive holographic screens on each wall threw up a hologram image of the Horsehead Nebula and I sat inside drinking tea surrounded by stars and dust which was wonderful.

Rani's voice interrupted me dozing. "Can you come to the bridge Bea?"

"Of course," I said, heading for the door and adding clothing as I went. What was I going to say, 'I'm busy.' I laughed out loud startling a marine kitted out for war practice minding his own business.

"Yer right?" He said. I looked past the cam cream.

"Hi Doz."

He nodded. I didn't think I'd heard him speak before. He hopped into a lift and descended with a wide grin and an upraised thumb.

I raced down the corridor ignoring lift shafts and headed towards the nearest hydroponics entrance. It was ten minutes at a brisk walk or maybe a bit longer. I ran up the two flights of stairs and arrived at the doors of the bridge heaving for breath. I took a moment and then pressed the key on the wall panel.

Rani turned around and looked up at me with a small smile. "Did you use hydroponics again Bea?" I didn't dignify the question with an answer. The bridge was fairly empty with only six people plus the captain. Everyone turned at Rani's comment. It felt as if I had come late for a class and they had started without me. Torriff stood in the shadows and we shared an outsider moment.

"What's going on?" I said to Rani quietly.

"I'm not sure," she replied. She turned back to the forward view of space ahead. It looked as if it had once been a large ship.

"What happened?" I asked no one in particular.

"We were rather hoping you were going to tell us that," said Captain Witherspoon.

I reached out wobbly in my abilities aware of Rani just behind me and the great empty spaces between stars, the 'not ready yet' sticker emblazoned on my every nerve ending. It felt as if I was alone in a dark corridor waiting for something. I kept thinking of the practice box and tried not to look stupid.

The ship was a broken hull. There was space inside and out and no life. I looked harder. Time tipped a little bit to one side, noise, running people and fear, an explosion nearly knocked me off my feet and I was running too. The doors behind me opened and a group of heavily armed men pushed into the crowded corridor. Some of them weren't actually human and they killed everyone.

"Renegades," said the captain with disgust, after my not-quite-coherent and sweaty explanation. No one else in the room said anything but they thought a lot.

"Are they the local bad guys, Rani?" I couldn't think of another way to put it, even though it made it sound like the cast of a really dreadful film. We were walking back to my quarters.

"They are more than local and more than bad."

"What do they want?" I asked.

"Anything they can make a profit on usually." She hid her feelings like a squirrel with winter food and smiled, a ghost of fear whispered somewhere between us. Hers not mine for a change.

"Then why did they destroy that ship?"

"They are just letting everyone know they're still the most awful people around."

Commander Stirzeker came out of a doorway to one of the offices in the first level. I caught a glance of holographic screens and feverish activity before the doors slid shut.

"We're off for tea at Bea's." They gave each other one of those not-quite-glances that people who had been through a lot together had perfected, particularly if one of them was telepathic.

"Great I'm starving, have you got anything to eat?" Zeke asked.

"Tariq made me some ginger biscuits, though they're still at the experimental stage." We had arrived at the lift and I pressed the door panel. I hesitated for a moment, like an old lady with bags of shopping on an escalator timing my moment. As we stepped in Zeke looked at Rani and they both smiled. "What?" I said.

"Nothing, I didn't say anything," Zeke shrugged.

"Oh shut up, both of you."

The kettle was a touch activated hot water spout. It sensed the amount required and despite my trying to trick it at various times always filled the cups or teapot three-quarters full.

The kitchen had been programmed to my requests. The washing up had defeated me for a few days until Rani pointed out that the appliance that I thought was a microwave was in fact a dishwasher of sorts. It didn't use water it zapped things clean.

Zeke was onto his fourth biscuit when the door chimed. Before I had a chance to answer, it opened and Ollie sidled in. "How does he *do* that," said Zeke through a mouthful. I shook my head and shrugged. I took a biscuit and broke a piece off for my cat.

"So what are you not telling me?" They both made a poor effort at looking puzzled.

"The renegades remember."

Rani sighed. "There are three, maybe four main groups," she said.

"Families," added Zeke. "They refer to themselves as families. They recruit mercenaries to do their dirty work. They traffic in just about anything."

"Including people," said Rani, watching me for a reaction.

"They would love to get their hands on someone like you," Zeke said seriously. "You'd be very useful to them." He and Rani didn't look at each other very specifically.

"So what's the difference between you and them if you both want the same thing?"

"We ask nicely," said Zeke.

It seemed to me that there was always someone in every time that looked like these people, we called them different things but they survived wars and progress like rats.

"Okay." I thought about it for a moment. "Why did they kill everyone?" They did that 'look' again which made me want to scream. "Come on you two, in my time both India and Pakistan had nuclear weapons, I don't *need* protecting."

"Well," said Rani. "It looked like a warning."

Light dawned slowly for someone paddling against the tide, like me. "You mean some sort of intergalactic turf war?" I reached for another biscuit only to find the plate empty. I sighed.

"What?" said Zeke.

"I don't know. I just expected things here, I mean now, to be a little more civilised."

The expression on both their faces was 'you don't know the half of it,' which usually had the same effect on me as 'don't do that it's not good for you.'

———

No matter what I did I couldn't get more than a tepid trickle out of the shower. I went through to the main room and picked up my Com/T. "Ko-Yo-Na? It's Bea. Is there a malfunction in the power supply?"

"Yes. All the water and main power is off on half that deck." She sounded preoccupied.

"Rats!"

"What, you have rodents?" She shouted in panic.

"No, sorry, twenty-first century figure of speech. What do you have to do to get a shower around here? I'm on a starship and the shower doesn't work," I grumbled.

"I think Rani has power, you could try her," she replied, deeply insulted.

"Right," I answered, making a mental note to apologise after I'd found a working shower. Ko was obviously very touchy about the Starfire which was how I felt about washing.

Rani's room was six doors down on the same deck. It meant walking the corridors in my dressing gown with a towel. I rang the intercom on the door, nothing. It was probably late for Rani, the ultimate early bird. Commander Stirzeker's room was next door. I hesitated for about a nanosecond and banged on the door the old-fashioned way. It opened almost immediately and what passed for astonishment crossed his face.

"Err," he said, taking in my dressing gown and towel.

"Does your shower work?" I mumbled through my embarrassment.

"Yes, help yourself." He moved out of the way and I walked past him through the main room and straight into the bathroom.

"Thanks," I said, through the closed door.

"You're welcome," was the muffled reply.

It was surprisingly clean and tidy with a few interesting bottles scattered around. I was not usually so impressed with men's bathrooms, they didn't know the loo seat closed and as for what they did to the soap. I dried off and helped myself to some of his lemon scented aftershave splashing it all over me.

The main room was empty, thank goodness, also tidy, but lived in with a lifetime of pictures, holograms and interesting belongings scattered around, high quality clutter. The bedroom door was closed and I resisted the temptation to take a look with difficulty and walked out into the corridor straight into Torriff. His eyes narrowed slightly.

"My shower doesn't work," I stuttered and shuffled off down the corridor trying to look dignified in my pink dressing gown and slippers with a damp towel wrapped around my head, not too successfully.

I waited until Gurber had infused at least a gallon of liquid to my one cup of tea. It was very early. The night watch were yawning their way to breakfast and bed when I went into Gurber's workroom on the first level.

Lieutenant Commander Limbu had looked a little surprised when I said good morning to him in the corridor. He had obviously been on the bridge all night which was somehow reassuring. I couldn't imagine anyone or anything giving him trouble for too long, not anyone who had ever met a Gurkha before anyway. We, Gurber and I, sat in silence as usual. The star system in the room wheeled and danced in colours of light a mastery of Gurber's ability to program the holographic computer with technical information. Even with my eyes closed I could still see it.

It was a bit like asking your favourite relative for the family secret knowing that your parents were not going to tell you. **"Gurber, why did you give all that technology to humans?"**

"Balance." This was not going to be as easy as I thought.

"But why?"

"You are dangerous children, you are here you need help." I think he'd got humanity weighed up.

"Do you travel in time?"

"Time stands still for us." This was degree course enigmatic and out of my league.

I thought about how to ask the next question that had been bothering me for a few days. Rani had been scared of the renegades; they were just a name to me, like an ancient tribe. But an old fear for her that was part of her personality hidden behind her eyes and in the dark places of her soul. It had rumbled around in my brain like thunder, this fear.

"Raniiiii was kidnapped as a child by the renegades." Gurber was silent after that and so was I.

I wrapped a blanket around me and sat at the computer unable to sleep, my mind buzzed with the things I had heard and seen that day. Ollie climbed between the folds in his usual pursuit of a comfy space. He purred and began pawing the material and my stomach in the hope of a bit of attention. I rubbed his head and pulled his ears and his rumble took on a deeply contented tone. The blanket was as soft as cashmere but, according to Rani, made out of Teflon, a frying pan blanket.

My diary was on the bedside table but it didn't seem to have the restless middle of the night feel and you couldn't tidy on a starship. I wandered around the galaxy looking at holographic images of other worlds. They spun and danced around their suns and reflected in the windows of the room. Ko-Yo-Na's planet looked a dark and dingy place and I made a mental note not to tell her that.

My thoughts and fingers wandered home, the always of my imagination and I found that there were great gaps in what I could access. I put my name in under a search and found an empty file.

The walls of the room seemed to get a little closer and breathing became something I had to think about. I gathered up my bedding and my cat and headed out of the door towards hydroponics. The few people around in the corridors didn't seem to mind me wandering along in my pyjamas as my nocturnal travels were well known.

The door slid quietly open and then shut behind me and Ollie and I made a nest of the blankets and lay down on the upper balcony among the treetops. The massive dome above with the stars beyond gave me a feeling of quiet. The sleeping birds rustled in the branches of the trees moving over for my cat. I curled around my furry friend and we slept. I dreamed of being in my garden for the first time in ages. Ollie and I walked around the paths and I could smell lavender and the old roses that grew there.

I woke up with someone standing over me. Torriff, looking as puzzled as it was possible to be when your face was made out of old leather. It was still the middle of the night but it didn't feel quite so empty. I wondered why he was in hydroponics, if he also walked around the ship in the hope of a little peace from a troubled mind. I didn't ask. Some journeys we made alone. He helped me gather up the bedding and walked down the corridor with me without saying much. We stopped at the door and he gave a little smile and a shrug. "See you later," I said and he nodded. Ollie grumbled at the forced march and went to sulk on the table. He curled his paws and looked at me with a 'what now' face.

My rooms had returned to their normal pre-night-time state but the computer terminal still winked with blank animosity.

I woke to the sound of a child crying, a tired, hungry child. The room was as dark as the stars would allow. Ollie was also awake and listening. He hadn't moved much and was still glued to the curve of my half-asleep body. I looked around for some idea of time. It was nearly dawn according to the luminous hologram numbers dancing above the computer in the main room. The bedroom door was open so that Ollie could get to his tray without waking me up.

I tried to hear past the hum of the ship's heart and the different noises that lots of people made when they lived in a tin can. I couldn't place it.

The crying continued in desperation. It was heartbreaking. I tapped the Com/T on the bedside table. "Hello bridge, its Bea here."

"What can I do for you Bea?" I recognised Yas Molina's deep voice.

"I can hear a child crying, it sounds as if it could be right outside the door."

"Is it?" He asked.

"No Yas, it's in my head," I said, exasperated.

"Ah. What do you want me to do?"

"I don't know!"

"I can hear it too," interjected Rani's voice.

"Is it coming from inside the ship?" Captain Witherspoon said sleepily. Rani and I paused for collective consideration. There were only two Katinad children on board and I could feel they were both safe. Gentle puppy breathing, curled inwards as all small things slept.

"No," we both answered at the same time.

"Okay Yas, I'm on my way. Scan for anything interesting." The captain broke contact and I sighed, I loved my sleep and I loved my bed. Rani was already tapping on the door.

The bridge was quiet. There were two people on duty and the captain when Rani and I arrived via hydroponics. The hologram on the middle console which showed a three-dimensional view of the surrounding space looked empty. Yas looked up when we came in and grinned. He was one of the ship's pilots and wore a brown with blue uniform which he was surreptitiously trying to tidy.

The other crew member was someone I didn't recognise. "Jenny Smith," she said quietly. Her brown/green uniform was immaculate and her long straight hair was in a ponytail, she had dark orange eyes like my cat and a sweet face.

"Jenny is one of our astrophysicists," Rani added.

"Hmm," said the captain. She looked at the main view screen. More empty space. "Can you still hear it?" The sound was getting weaker, the cry of unanswered hopelessness. We both nodded, a sense of disquiet was creeping in from the edges of something and unsettling both of us.

Yas Molina was still studying the hologram. He peered into an area in the top left-hand corner and tapped a few lights on the console. He pointed at nothing, squinting. A small ship appeared.

"What is that?" I asked.

"A refugee vessel," he said.

"What does that mean," I asked. "What are they running from?"

"Poverty I expect," said the captain. "Yas, wake up the on-call crew. Let's see if we can get there in time to find anyone still alive on that rust bucket."

As Yas quietly contacted a succession of sleepy voices, Jenny sat in the pilot's seat and began tapping the lighted keys. I thought it was interesting that most of the staff on board seemed to be able to do each other's job, if you only had two of the crew on duty at night it was probably a good idea if they could both fly a starship.

The crying was feeble. I looked at Rani; she was sitting next to a lighted console over to one side looking at a small screen. I walked over to her and sat down. "Can you hear anyone else Rani?" She shook her head. "How many people do you think were on that ship?"

She sighed, "They cram them to the bulkheads. These people are fooled out of large sums thinking they are going to find a better life. Some of them end up as indentured slaves trying to pay off impossible amounts of debt and they're probably the lucky ones. Sometimes the people runners just take the money and abandon them where they're not likely to be found."

"Rani, is this the same people as the other ship?" It felt like it, there was a level of cruelty that took your breath away.

"Yes, it looks like it; Dalgety family."

"It seems as if your turf war is getting interesting." I stood up and looked at the view screen. My vertebrae felt as if I had been in a train wreck. This was a place, I thought, where worlds collide and stars were made and even here nothing challenged evil. The crying stopped.

We reached the ship which was floating as if abandoned; the angle was nose up as if the stabilisers had failed. It was small, not much bigger than an SSV.

"Rani?" Mark Limbu's gentle deep voice broke the silence. He had been standing quietly by the door. Rani looked sick. As I made to go with her she stopped me.

"No," she said, "There will be time enough, give this one a miss." I felt an overwhelming gratitude and a coward at the same time as if this was something I would never be ready for.

"Have Doctor Chan standing by," said the captain quietly. I could hear Mark talking into his Com/T as he followed Rani out of the door.

The silence was filled with small movements as if holding your breath would make things okay. All my thoughts began with 'if.' It was odd how the magic of childhood, the 'some higher being is surely going to sort this out' variety was very close to the surface. No matter when you were born.

The main intercom crackled. Mark Limbu sounded as if he had his hand over his face and I reached out only to feel gentle waves of distress coming from all of the operations team. Rani was as closed shut as a clam. That would be no for the magic.

We picked up a hitchhiker somewhere near Tau Ceti. He used a signalling device that was attached to his small craft which was not much bigger than a SSV and I thought, not capable of deep space travel. Something about this was unusual.

Rani and I had been attempting to improve my kinetic skills, *again*. I felt the pressure she felt, to prepare me for something but I was a little short on the detail.

"Would you meet the visitor in the lower docking bay, Rani?" The captain didn't wait for an answer.

"Are you coming?"

"Sure. Not because the captain wants me to, but only because I'm nosy." The whole 'something' seemed to hang in the air between us like wood smoke on a still day.

The lift shaft had the usual effect on my nerve endings and gave endless amusement to a couple of marines who were on their way to practice killing people on the same level.

The docking bays were busy. We had just taken on stores from an intriguing looking cargo ship that had docked for a matter of minutes. Anything that couldn't be grown or made was stacked in large impact resistant cylinders. Ko-Yo-Na was checking a collection against a list on a hand held computer. She smiled and waved, just far enough distance away to look small, emphasising the cavern-like quality of the bay.

I found it difficult to grasp that I could see space through open doors. A wide red line on the floor about halfway to the end of the ramp marked the point where atmosphere ended and 'out there' began. Even so several of the crew crossed the line to move a huge storage box, helped by the decrease in gravity and small face masks that distorted their features into the now familiar lupine pout. They also had safety harnesses. The language deteriorated in direct opposition to the rising level of sweat.

"Garobh! Oh sorry Rani, Bea, I didn't see you there." A face I recognised from the lunch table. Not Earth human. Kind wide eyes, pale blue skin, long arms and legs. The light green uniform an indication of Star League membership was askew with the sleeves pushed up. His home planet like Neff.P. was Des.Ra. which was somewhere near Delta Pavonis, nineteen-point-one light years from

Earth, the nocturnal trips on the computer, I felt, were finally paying off.

"It's okay, Gatt. Have you met Bea?"

"Usually she's chewing a mouthful of food." He held out a hand which was warm, sweaty and genuine. "Gatt.R.," he said.

The spaceship interrupted my response. It came into land, gliding to a dignified halt in the middle of the bay narrowly missing the large cargo box and three techs, who hopped out of the way with serious speed. "Garobh!" Said Gatt.

"Exactly," said Rani, her eyes narrowing in recognition.

Jad Lassik was a bit of a puzzle. I was completely unable to read him and he knew it. There was a quiet violence about him that made me shudder.

He waited patiently at the side of his small ship whilst a medic debugged him and seemed to be listening when Gatt. gave him advice on docking manners. He saw me looking at the side of his ship which was battered with what looked like burn marks. When I reached out my hand to touch the surface, he moved quicker than the average human being was able to, shoving my hand away with his and holding onto it a moment longer than was necessary. The craft was deceptively simple in design. On closer inspection it wasn't a basic SSV but something that had been modified to travel in deep space.

We walked in silence up the steps towards a lift shaft. Of medium height, he moved with a lifetime in space about him. Dark clothes and something that looked like an earring but seemed to be a translator disguised as a piece of jewellery. He had shoulder-length brown hair and sharp green eyes that were not human but looked like they belonged to a belligerent goat.

"Rough journey Lassik?" Rani asked with barely a polite smile.

"It's nice to see you again, Rani." He turned to me. "It's also very nice to meet you Bea Markam I've heard such a lot about you." Rani's face coiled around a swallowed thundercloud. "Now why would you think you could keep her a secret?" He asked reasonably. It felt like the first day at school, when my mother had tried to explain to me that being different wasn't the best way to make friends. A bit like walking around Piccadilly Circus in your underwear, you were not likely to go unnoticed and it made the 'something' Rani was trying to prepare me for understandable on several levels.

"What was *that* about?" Rani and I had left Lassik at the briefing room door. Only Mark Limbu, Zeke and the captain were going to be in on the conversation. We walked down the steps in hydroponics and I tried again. "I didn't know I was supposed to be a secret?"

"Not really. I was just trying to protect you until you could look after yourself a bit better."

"Rani," I said after a pause. "Does that have something to do with you getting taken by the renegades?"

She smiled; a thin, tired, no-teeth smile. "You read people really well I don't know why I worry."

"I couldn't read Lassik."

"No, he has a natural blocking chip, as well as years of training."

"What is he, Rani?" I couldn't phrase a better question, 'what' seemed rude but appropriate.

"A sort of mercenary, he works for the Star League."

"Rani, a mercenary works for money."

"Quite."

Colin the parrot interrupted us mid-thought, by trying to kill Rani and screaming, "Where's my cat," in what could only be described as a very good impression of me. We ran for it.

Later that night I wandered into the main room from my rumpled bed. I asked for low light in the kitchen area. We had sat Rani and me, earlier in the evening, drinking tea and not talking about the renegades or Lassik. Zeke had arrived at the same time as Ollie. Food scattered thoughts further away.

Rani looked puzzled at the almost touch on the back of my neck as

Zeke had left, burying her smile in orange fur and yawning cat and I had found myself for a moment looking at the closing door as he went.

The milky drink did nothing for a busy mind. So, without thinking too much, I dressed and went out into the quiet corridor. The ship did night and day, which suited nearly all of the species onboard, except Gurber, who thought it was a waste of time. I was not sure what his idea of sleep was, three times around the Horsehead Nebula probably.

I found myself in a lift shaft heading towards the lower docking bay without much trouble. There was no one about. The bay was dimly lit and shut down for the night. A few creepy shapes and dark corners made me laugh with a sort of quiet nervousness that came from walking backwards into dark rooms, not something I usually spent a lot of time doing.

I walked over to Lassik's ship. The burn marks looked worse in the half light. As I walked around the craft I could see more damage. Something creaked and I jumped, holding my breath listening inside and outside my head. I put my hand on the burn marks and closed my eyes. Everything had a voice. It was like a badly played record and sometimes it could sound like a muddle, but this was clear and fresh.

The craft lashed about avoiding a vicious onslaught of firepower. I could see Lassik's face, bleeding and bruised. He was fighting to maintain control and there was another stinging volley of fire. The com buzzed.

"Come on Jad Lassik, we just want to talk."

"Of course you do." I could just see the other ship as it came into focus, then my hand was suddenly snatched away from the side of the craft and I fell backwards into now and into Lassik.

"Well what a surprise." His face was close, dark and empty, like a clown with half the makeup wiped away. "I thought I'd find you here." He moved his free hand down my back in a lovers caress that felt obscene. He was strong. Danger was like smoke it curled around you and filled up your lungs so you couldn't breathe. This felt like the old paths at home much better left un-walked.

A voice moved in from the dark edges, "Leave her alone, Lassik."

Zeke walked up from the shadows. There were enough people here for a party I thought, so much for sneaking about in the middle of the night.

"Do you have prior claim?" Lassik looked me up and down like a horse at a fair. He still had a hold on my wrist that was beginning to affect my circulation.

Zeke hesitated before answering, "Yes." I couldn't see his face. Lassik let go of me and I sidled over towards Zeke.

"You should keep a better eye on her."

"I'll remember that." He put an arm around my waist and walked me towards the lift shaft. I looked over my shoulder. Lassik was still staring at me. We walked towards my quarters in silence.

"How did you know I was there?"

"Rani called me and said you'd be thinking about it."

I staggered a bit because without sleep I was always clumsy. Zeke moved his hand from my waist and picked me up. I put my head on his shoulder and my arms around his neck and thought about the big spaces in my life that had made me lonely. "Good night," I said unnecessarily at the door to my room. He was already walking away.

I missed the BBC World Service. The computer had a programme that picked up news and topical subjects and ran through it from different angles depending on your point of origin. But it was difficult for me to pick up a frame of reference. One person's local economic crisis was another person's 'I've no idea what you're talking about.'

Radio 4's Today Programme was another great loss. I liked to hear the presenters torturing some politician who had thought they were there for a civilised chat. The bathroom was just not the same without them.

It was early, but Rani often came in while I was drinking my first glass of hot water. The tumbler felt cool to the touch and was made out of the same slightly jelly-like glass as the windows; they were able to take really hot water without burning your fingers. I had scalded my tongue a few times taking a big gulp without thinking. I sat curled up on the sofa in jeans and a T-shirt contemplating the universe. It was like looking into the eye of a whale, all life looked back.

The door chime went and I said, "Come in," thinking it was Rani. Torriff stood in the doorway with 'Pride and Prejudice' clutched to him. He looked embarrassed and I laughed, "Come on in Torriff." He hesitated and then tiptoed in as if walking on eggshells. "Would you like some coffee?" He shook his head and proffered the book.

"I really enjoyed this. I have read another of her stories but not on paper," he pronounced the word paper as if he was trying it on for size.

"Do you know George Eliot?" I reached up for the copy of Silas Marner from my bookshelf.

"Does he work on the ship?"

"Err."

He laughed at my expression. "Yes I have read your George Eliot."

I contemplated his lovely open face and said, "My mother would have loved you, an alien who's read Silas Marner. There's hope for us all."

"Maybe." He looked sad.

"What sort of literature do you have on your world, Torriff?"

"We do not do stories." He had sat down near the window but on the other end of the sofa. I curled my bare feet underneath me and caught Ollie by the tail as he slithered by. Torriff eyed him fondly. Ollie escaped me and jumped onto his lap purring with familiarity.

"What exactly do you mean?" My early morning brain had finally registered his remark. "How can you not have stories, no wonder you've been at war for two hundred years!"

"This is a valid point. I will go right away and speak to our prime." We both smiled and then our conversation was interrupted by Rani wafting in unannounced as usual.

"Good morning, I hear you had a busy night?"

"I must go." Torriff nodded to Rani and the complaining Ollie slid from his lap. The door hissed behind him.

Rani looked at me. "What was that about?" I shrugged and the door chimed again.

Tom and Mac waltzed in looking like the low key looters you were usually related to.

————————

Tom Hatherley and Mac Ibarra were already onto their third coffee and had emptied a box of biscuits when Mac decided to overload my brain with an explanation of Tom's home town. "Mid Atlantic City, well it makes sense doesn't it, all that space?" My face must have looked sceptical. They both turned to Rani for support.

"Back me up Rani," said Tom.

"I didn't say I didn't believe you, I just said that it sounded like one of your wind-ups." The two of them were shameless in their efforts to play practical jokes on the unwary. Anyone was fair game. I had been caught out several times with the twenty-fifth century equivalent of being sent to fetch a 'long stand.' They were merciless in their pursuit of the not mentally sharp. My head felt as if it was stuffed with marshmallow and the morning was already turning into an epic experience without being set-up by the 'terrible twins.'

"There are several underwater cities; the biggest are Mid Atlantic and Mid Pacific." Tom spoke as if to a small child. I looked at Rani and she nodded with a preoccupied smile. I wondered, in the section of my brain that was capable of speculation, what was bothering her. She went over to get a cup of tea and gave Ollie a kiss on the top of his head; he permitted her to share his chair.

Tom droned on with the geography lesson. "I was born in the most beautiful place on Earth. The city is based on a series of domes which of course is the strongest shape to resist the pressure. I think the population is about fifty thousand now; I haven't been back for some years. My parents still stay in south dome." He sounded wistful. "You live in the heart of the ocean, there's a sound, like the sea is sighing." He stuffed in the last biscuit a second before Mac could get it and chomped triumphantly. He was about to speak with a mouthful of food.

"Tom, enough!" It was going to be another spacesuit day. A part of me was looking forward to having another go; my brain which had stayed awake all night however, was not.

Mac looked at Rani as he and Tom got up to leave. "I think we'll meet you at the upper docking bay, Bea." They left arguing, partners in crime. For the first time in a long time I thought about my brother Sam. They shouted bits of biscuit at each other as they discussed the merit of different spacesuits, like a couple of California brother surfers working the next wave.

"I hear Zeke had to make a claim on you last night." She looked like a school teacher trying to get the facts of life across to a ten-year-old.

"Yes." I pulled my hair away from my face, it had lost all self-control lately, "I have no idea what that means, by the way." I looked at her hopefully. "Is it as bad as it sounds?" She did the teacher face again. "Okay," I said.

"Does the captain know?" We were walking down the corridor towards hydroponics Rani had given up on the lift shafts and me ever having a meaningful relationship.

"No." We reached the doorway as it opened. Ollie came out with what looked like a face full of feathers and a satisfied smile. I gasped and covered my mouth with a hand. Rani looked around the door in horror. A sad voice said, "Where's my cat?"

The upper docking bay was quiet. Three techs were working on an SSV with small shiny tools and long complicated swearwords. They acknowledged us with a variety of smiles and waves. The blocking chips that seemed to have been handed out with breakfast didn't stop the combination of interest and curiosity from reaching me.

My Com/T beeped and Doctor Chan's quiet, precise voice said, "Bea, when you've finished can you come to the medical bay for a check-up?"

"That woman's going to be the death of me," I grumbled.

"Is she still helping you with your fitness, then?" Rani laughed.

"*Every* morning," I said gloomily. After a pause I asked, "How long is Lassik going to be here?"

Rani looked at me in exasperation. "Can't you leave it alone?"

"What *does* the captain want with that man?"

"Sometimes you have to dance with the devil."

Pui took enough blood out of my arm to supply an emergency department but at least she didn't use a needle. The small tube seemed to suck against the skin without breaking the surface. "How do you feel?" She shone a light into my eyes, doing her doctor routine with a liberal smattering of aha's in-between taking readings.

"I'm still wobbly first thing in the morning."

She held a small device over the samples of blood and then looked at the readout. "How are you apart from that?" I looked at her and wondered for a moment whether to lie. I'd had a lot of practice and lying was a lot easier than the truth.

"Pui, it's not as if I made a lifestyle adjustment. *Everything* is different." I stopped.

"Is it about being on the Starfire, or about your illness?"

I thought before I answered, trying to quantify my feelings. "I just existed for such a long time, I think I was afraid I was never going to actually do any living again and you do things differently here."

She took out a small pointy instrument and waved it in front of my nose. "Do you mind if I take a few DNA samples?" I shrugged. She scraped and added a few hairs from my head to the collection of blood samples. She explained over her shoulder, "We might need to grow you something."

I was not sure if she'd said it to reassure me but it didn't. I had seen one of the marines with an eye replacement as he had lost one of the ones he was born with on the exercise deck in a ferocious mock battle that they did down there. It looked as if it belonged to him; it was just that he kept falling over because his brain was taking a while to process the new information; actually he had been drunk when he told me and was sitting on the floor of the coffee bar, so it could just have been a great story.

"Are you coping?" The question caught me out. She looked at me again, sitting on the edge of her desk with her arms folded. Her dark eyes were concerned. I rubbed my aching head and got up to go.

"I still feel as if I'm looking down the wrong end of a telescope, but yes I guess so."

She watched me walking away, tapping her fingernails on the untidy desk. "I think I believe that all journeys are spiritual as well as physical even if you are travelling in time and the hardest thing is to find out where we really belong."

I stood by the door and thought about what she had said and felt as if I were suffering from emotional overload. It had been that sort of day. I turned to go. "Don't forget to meet me for our exercise session." I'd so nearly made it out of the door!

I could recognise some stars, the ones from the night sky at home, the Plough, Pleiades, the North Star but I was looking through a different glass. I needed to learn to look at things from a different angle. I was in a no-mans-land of stars.

"What are the signs on this about Rani?" I pointed to the hieroglyphs on the bangle I'd bought on Sakieen. I took it off with some difficulty, the longer I wore it the harder it became to remove it, as if the catch disappeared sometimes; I wondered what I would do if one day it wasn't there any more.

She looked at it closely, turning it in her hands and running her fingers over the symbols. "It feels really old, have you tried listening?"

"Yes but the sounds are so muddled I can't make any sense of them," I said. Some things could be clear and loud, sometimes a whisper, sometimes a symphony. Telepathy didn't have a volume control an on off switch or an instruction manual.

"I don't know what this means," she touched the language that ran around the edge of the bangle. "The signs in the middle are part of an old poem, one of those myths that belong to everyone, it says,

'she walks in the stars
in quiet footfalls of light
a daughter of my gods
save me from the night.'

I can't remember the other verses, more of the same I think. It's a slave's prayer." She passed it back to me and I touched the stones, some of which looked valuable.

"It looks rather upmarket for something home-made."

"Most of the people they took had a variety of skills and a pebble on one world is a precious stone on another." I nodded and clipped the bangle back on my wrist.

"So tell me. I can see something's going on." I looked at her, my cat on her lap, tea in her hand and worry in her heart.

"Your first assignment will be in a few days. We are nearly at a planet where something seems to have gone wrong with a diplomatic visit." She picked her words carefully, trying not to make them sound more ominous than they needed to be. "So it's now whether you're ready or not."

"You don't think I am ready," which was a statement not a question.

She put her cup down hard clattering it with worry. "I think you think that it's all some sort of game and you're not really here in your heart. You're still living in the past in a cottage with a thousand ghosts in the darkness." We sat in silence in my rooms drinking tea and shadows. She was right of course and I wondered if actually being able to do something gave you enough reason for doing it.

"Altair is seventeen-point-one light years from Earth." The holographic screens on the briefing room wall showed a really bright star. I got the impression from those present, Rani, Zeke, Torriff, and Mark Limbu that this was purely for my benefit as everyone else knew exactly where we were. "We are here." The captain continued, pointing to a smaller star with a group of four planets. She reminded me of a teacher I'd had at school who always 'travelled more in hope than certainty.'

"Zeke, you and Bea will take the SSV down to the surface of the beta planet and see what the problem is. Think of this as just another exercise. These people are not advanced. No interstellar travel, no ability for space communication apart from a few satellites and one basic space station." There was almost a pause here. So much being said didn't make up for what was not said. But it sounded as if I would feel right at home. "This is what you trained for Bea and Rani says you're ready. There is no need to worry all I need to know is where the emissaries are. Everything should be straight forward. Please don't make me regret saying that, this is serious," she tapped the table with a pointed finger.

"What could possibly go wrong?" said Zeke with sincerity never having seen an old horror film.

"Are you *crazy*," I spluttered. "That's what the hero says right before he gets attacked by a nine foot monster! You'll be walking backwards into dark rooms next." He laughed. They all laughed. The captain allowed herself a small smile.

Everyone looked as if they were okay with this but they didn't feel it. I wondered if it was me they were worrying about or the situation, or something else.

There was definitely a case of nerves going around and it was having a disastrous effect on my breathing. Rani had explained over and over the role I had been given. I just didn't think I should be fulfilling it quite so soon and neither did she. I suddenly realised that Rani had no say in what happened to me and worse, it looked as if the captain was dancing to someone else's piano music. It was possible that somewhere back on Earth, a civil servant with a pot belly and bad breath had decided that now was the time I earned my keep. Of course it could have been a bureaucrat on another planet. Being a self-serving twit was obviously not just a human trait, self-serving twits, it seemed, were pretty much universal.

"Remember," the captain added, "I don't want a war on my hands."

"Don't worry, it will be fine." Rani's voice was calm but her mind was a volcano. "Everyone goes through this," she said quietly to me, though it was quite obvious that very few people went through this.

"Okay, departure in two hours." The captain stood and we all filed out.

"I hope I live to regret this." Everyone politely pretended they hadn't heard me.

"Are you coming too?" I asked as Mac Ibarra had caught up with me in the corridor on the way to the upper docking bay. His arms were full of awkward shaped bits of equipment, some of which seemed to be giving him a great deal of trouble and surprisingly for inanimate objects, were trying to escape.

"Yes, do you mind?"

"No, why shouldn't my impending humiliation be as public as possible. Here," I added, "Give me some of that." I took a few pieces from the top of the wobbly heap. "What is all this?"

"Commander Stirzeker is letting me try out my new idea." He launched into an explanation. "You see it's for possible new power signatures." My face must have given something away so he tried again. "The ship's computer can tell us about power sources we already know of but this will give us an idea of what we don't know."

"Good for you," I said. He looked pleased and excited and I shook my head. We reached the docking bay and I paused. "Here goes nothing," I announced to the opening doors.

"What?" said Mac. Sometimes it was not possible to bridge the gap.

"What are these emissaries doing here, I though that you left developing races alone?" Zeke gave me one of those twenty-fifth century looks.

"They're right in the middle of a major trade route."

"Ah, so it's about money."

We had taken off under my meagre efforts, which was Zeke not wanting to waste a training opportunity. I couldn't quite see Mac's face but I was pretty sure he was holding onto his seat strap. At least I didn't call the watch officer 'sweetie pie' this time. I sat next to Zeke in the co-pilot's seat. He had taken over the controls much to Mac's relief after my shaky but dignified exit. I looked at the briefing file. The small screen scrolled upwards displaying the faces of the two emissaries.

Chad/Ze was a small child-like female with a serious face and large expressive eyes, from a planet near Epsilon Indi called Lactarra. She had an impressive list of qualifications from a variety of educational establishments, including a master's degree in biochemistry from the University of Oxford. She also had six children. They had large families on Lactarra and she was someone's mother.

The other picture showed the pale blue, smiling face of a Des.Ran. called Mar.X. He also looked too young to be missing presumed dead. His diplomatic experience covered two pages of the screen. His partner was on another Star League ship as an engineer.

They had been invited to visit after achingly protracted diplomacy with what passed for government. It had taken several years, they had roughly the same timescale as Earth on the planet, to reach this point and I couldn't see that they had put so much as a foot wrong. But you didn't have to be a telepath to know that a politician could say one thing with their mouth and another with their actions. The next section was devoted to the locals. They referred to their planet as Restra, which roughly translated as 'home.' They were still divided into different countries but had a world senate.

The dominant peoples living on the largest continent called themselves Malathrans. They didn't seem too bothered by the 'off-worlders' and had taken the realisation of not being alone incredibly well.

The two emissaries had been on the planet for several of its weeks before contact had been lost and despite of repeated requests by the Star League, the Malathrans had been evasive in their response.

We would be meeting a small group who had been contacted by an unnamed negotiator. They were described as 'keen to maintain diplomatic relations.' They were mostly scientists and intellectuals but it didn't look good.

"So we're heading for the pre-arranged meeting site?" Both Zeke and Mac Ibarra looked up from blue-green consoles, the light reflected upwards on their busy preoccupied faces. The cabin was dim with a few key spotlights which gave it a false, cosy look.

"Are you nervous, Bea?" Mac's face looked puzzled. "Listen." He tapped a key and radio communications in a barrage of language filled the cabin.

I left my seat next to Zeke and went over to stand by Mac's shoulder. He isolated different transmissions in quick succession. Military, commercial air traffic, music, sea traffic, talk shows, it went on and on. "They don't know we're here." He looked up at me and smiled. "It's a world getting on with its collective life."

I sat back down, my hands rested on the edge of the console and I contemplated my lack of reassurance. Zeke reached over and took the hand nearest him in his. He smiled and then went back to flying. Mac made a serious effort not to have noticed. I couldn't say it made me feel better but it had given me something else to think about for five minutes.

"Captain, we will be entering the upper atmosphere in two minutes." Zeke interjected into the quiet making me jump.

"Understood, be careful down there; oh and Ibarra."

"Yes, captain?"

"We're getting some very interesting readings from your survey equipment."

"Thank you, captain," he said calmly. As he broke contact he jumped out of his seat and punched the air like a little child. "Yes!" Zeke smiled without turning around and I grinned because youthful exuberance should be shared whenever possible.

We had passed two moons in peaceful orbit one slightly smaller than the other. There was no life there yet. I speculated unsuccessfully to myself on the tidal effects that two moons would cause.

The space station was manned. We could hear three men through our monitoring but I could sense another four people asleep. The conversation was to a ground crew about re-supply. It didn't seem to be going well. The station was a crescent shape with silver sails on the inner surface. It glittered in the reflected light from the planet.

Sport began to be featured heavily on the communications Mac was monitoring. Zeke was concentrating on the bumpy atmospheric conditions; then something caught his attention. He half turned.

"What's that?" Mac tried to isolate a source. "Go back a bit," Zeke said his brow furrowed. We listened.

Mac said, "Something about a grid?"

The radio announcer's voice was high with excitement. "There were ninety successful candidates and only twenty failures."

"It sounds like a 'rite of passage,'" Mac speculated.

"Yes," said Zeke, "It does." They both looked worried.

I couldn't filter out the tension. It was as if we were all waiting on jump run. People were quiet inside and concentrated on their feelings, that was in not showing them. The flight and fight syndrome was alive and well in the twenty-fifth century. It was not a great feeling, a bit like standing on the edge of a cliff in a storm.

"Ugh," said Mac, "*Weather.*"

It was rain and a lot of it. It actually felt quite good and I tipped my face up for a better effect. It wasn't exactly blowing a gale but I thought the farmers around Exmoor would have been respectful.

It didn't smell like home, even the wind felt different. I could see the shadows of trees and the feel of grass against my legs. It was strange to look up at the stars again; someone else's stars. I wondered what sort of wild animals they had and the inside of the SSV began to look attractive again rather than claustrophobic.

We were waiting for someone. No one had actually said that but I asked anyway, "Zeke, are we waiting for someone?"

"Yes. Try not to be angry when he gets here." It had seemed an odd thing for him to say though I worked it out about a moment before he arrived. Jad Lassik.

"Oh no."

"What," said Mac.

"Nothing," I muttered.

Of course it was dark, sneaking around in the middle of the night didn't work otherwise; there seemed to be all the right ingredients; we were absolutely nowhere, cold, wet and you couldn't see your hand in front of your face.

We were dressed in the appropriate disguises. In my case something that tied up at the back and made of dark material that wrapped around in all sorts of inconvenient places. Going to the loo would require imagination. At least it was warm and fairly waterproof with a hood. Zeke and Mac had much more practical attire. Whatever planet you were on nothing changed, men always got the trousers.

"What's the perzuzz?" said Mac as he came out of the SSV. He locked down the craft with a small keypad. Lassik and Zeke were conferring quietly and I refrained from some low level eavesdropping with difficulty.

"We are going to need help," said Zeke.

"What we *need* is Andy McNab," I muttered.

"Who?"

"The SAS, preferably all of them." They all looked blank. "Never mind, twenty-first century reference."

Lassik said, "I've got some transport, it's this way."

'This way' turned into a hike of monumental proportions. The boots I was wearing began to let in water and my brain began to drift. Zeke was a few steps in front of me and Mac was walking behind me. Both carried concealed emergency packs and a small red light that gave us just enough illumination not to trip over each other; though it didn't seem to be working a hundred percent for Mac, who had trodden on me several times.

Just before my temper took over in the 'I'm not going a step further' stakes, we stopped.

The landing had been in amongst the trees and the path had meandered next to a river. I couldn't see it except for the few occasions when the moonlight or should that have been moons' light, made it through the clouds. But you could hear the sound of water over stones. In daytime and without the rain, it would have been pretty and worth the walk.

Zeke and Mac Ibarra had obviously been on the 'sneaking about in the dark' course. There were lots of hand signals and they both carried a weapon. Each of them assumed that they knew what the other was thinking; they didn't. I felt as if I was completely out of place and Lassik was too far ahead to see.

I became aware of someone else standing close by. I turned towards the nearly not quite sound. Mac shone the red light down at my feet and I spoke directly into his head. Something I'd not had much practice at. **"Someone's here Mac."**

He looked at me in the barely discernable light and mimed an exaggerated 'who?' Zeke came back to join us and Mac collared him barely whispering, "We've got company."

I muttered to no one, "I have always wanted to say that," and then tried not to stumble into other unhelpful words as Zeke squeezed my arm for quiet.

In less time than it took to breathe in and out I could feel another four or five people. I did my best to pass it on; they both winced but I couldn't help it, fear made me loud.

Lassik of course was nowhere to be seen and I couldn't sense him. As a telepath I could actually feel dread and it came in several levels. This was more of an apprehension, deepening at the edges into something prehistoric; friend or foe; flight or fight. I could also feel Zeke's dilemma. Mac Ibarra was inexperienced and a bit over keen. It looked as if Jad Lassik had indicated that things were not as they should be whatever that was and I was an unknown quantity. **"Wait,"** I thought to both of them, with something more than intuition but less than certainty. We waited. The 'uninvited guests' were almost treading on us before I thought, "Its okay." Why either of them should have listened to me I didn't know, but they did.

Lassik walked into me, grabbing hold of me by the arms to prevent both of us from falling over and I knew he knew exactly where I was standing. I was sure his eyes enabled him to see in the dark. He held on for an exaggerated moment breathing in my face. It made me cringe and I pulled away resisting the temptation to hit him where I thought his ear might be.

The small group of locals waited respectfully at a distance and Zeke went over to them with Lassik and asked a few sharp questions. He didn't sound satisfied with the answers.

They gave off an air of muddled helpfulness but they were also afraid. I whispered to Mac and he nodded. He fumbled around in the pack he was carrying and pulled out a folded jelly. He spread it out and rested it on one palm. It was about six inches square and it seemed to be a computer. He tapped away on it and got a connection and an acknowledgement from the Starfire. I was sure my emergency kit didn't contain one.

Lassik brought two of the group over and we performed a ridiculous set of introductions as if we were at a badly organised dinner party. They looked like us with the usual noses and eyes, arms and legs. There were a few interesting differences, sharp eyes under thick brow ridges and a seam of bone along the jaw line that jutted out. They looked at me with the same undisguised curiosity as I regarded them.

I could feel my feet squelching in the grossly inadequate boots. A few moments of undignified silence followed with the rain dripping off the end of my nose and then we moved off again.

The transport was car size and seemed to be a hovercraft. Mac and I sat knee to knee facing each other in the back. Zeke sat with the driver and Lassik went in another vehicle with the rest of the group. We travelled in convoy to who knew where. The journey took about half an hour which was long enough for me to get chilled to the bone. I thought about my warm bed and my bath and sighed out loud. Mac patted my knee and gave me a drink of something from his emergency kit that tasted as if it might have been made illegally. Once again I felt that my own emergency kit was suffering from an inferiority complex.

I saw a few lights from distant dwellings but we seemed to be as far away from civilisation as was possible; their equivalent of Exmoor maybe. Someone saw a few unidentified flying objects in the dark sky, heard some strange noises and lights in the trees and quietly pulled the covers over their head and tried not to know. Because sometimes it was best if you didn't; I felt as if I could relate to that.

Lassik was staring at me again. We were sitting in the counterpart of a quiet country cottage waiting for Goldilocks, though it seemed as if the 'bears' were already with us. Zeke was talking quietly with three of the scientists, who looked harmless enough.

I was still steaming gently by the fire which had been lit using something that smelled and looked disgusting. One of the men came over and offered me a drink. It was hot and didn't smell too bad. Mac took it from me and stuck a small probe into the liquid. He read the device and handed me back the cup. "It won't do you any harm, I can't vouch for the taste though," he smiled. The man was still standing there looking at us with a mixture of curiosity and amusement. He turned his back to the fire and warmed himself.

"Do you think we are trying to poison you?" He asked.

"Not deliberately," I said, smiling.

He nodded. "My name is Padrig of Arwan."

"Bea of Markam," I replied. His mind seemed open and interested and I could sense a real purpose for good. He was also troubled. Nothing about this was going to be easy. I drank a little of the liquid and tried not to splutter. It was a bit like a really hot cough medicine.

The conversation across the room was getting heated. Probing their minds I could sense enough confusion to start a minor war. In the end one of them, fed up with trying to explain the obvious, walked over to a wall and slid a shutter open to expose a small screen. She pressed a red disc on the panel at the side and stood back. The screen lit up. Waving her hand towards it she said, "Highlights of the grid are on now."

Obediently we all looked over to the screen. The writing that flowed in an upward direction looked like the football results in hiero-glyphs. A male voice was excitedly reading them out. Lassik's eyes had bored a crater into the back of my head and I turned to him in annoy-ance. "What is your problem?"

"I can't understand how such a backwater of the universe could produce such an interesting talent."

"Thanks, I think. When was the last time you were there?" I asked sarcastically.

"1962 in your years; they were strange weirdly behaved people."

"Ah, well, I think I can explain that, though not many people remember the sixties, my mother gave me a full and unexpurgated account." I didn't get a chance to explain; a wave of anger rolled around the room in tidal proportions which nearly knocked me off my feet and Mac swore in a language that didn't go through the translator. I looked at the small screen.

One thing that was difficult to quantify was your brain's habit of trying to put what you saw and heard in a recognisable and familiar context. It made it impossible to focus sometimes. So it took a few seconds to understand what I was seeing which was a war film with very short people. A moment later I realised that they were children.

"So tell me," I asked, just for the hell of it and to no one in particu-lar, "What do you people do for a heart?" I could feel their confusion, which was probably just as well as it added a nice warm glow to Zeke's anger.

"Which bit of the captain's brief about not starting a war did you miss?" He asked quietly.

They did their best to explain to the stupid outsiders about their ritual coming of age test. Mac Ibarra looked sickened though he made an effort to keep it hidden and I suddenly realised how young he was. Those of us with a dark side knew that everyday monsters went home at the end of the busy working week to their partner and the children.

We divided into our puzzled groups with a separate and amused Lassik in-between.

"Now what do we do?" I asked Zeke.

"Now we try and find our people."

"I don't think they're trying to hide anything about their culture they seem proud of it. They just don't understand why we don't understand. How come there's nothing about this in the reams of information you seem to have on them?"

"Do they know what happened to the emissaries?"

I nodded. "Yes and they're frightened of what we'll do when we find out. It's a big black hole, Zeke."

Zeke went across to the little group. They looked like us, they sounded like us. How difficult could this have been, I thought. I listened in and wondered about the rich colour and nuance of impossibilities that were people.

Zeke covered his mouth with his fingers as if adding depth to his thoughts but I could see his eyes half close as he listened. He glanced over towards me without moving his head.

It seemed that both emissaries had volunteered for a place on the grid.

The one called Elider of Magred came over to talk to me. She was afraid. It was odd, with the communicator/translator there were no language barriers but it gave a false sense of similarity that really didn't exist. They were not like us. Their evolution was based on the theory that a complex society was born out of fear and development came from conflict.

"What do you think will happen now?" she asked me, her face a picture of apprehension.

"I don't know," I said unhelpfully. I really didn't know. I couldn't see the Starfire blasting them into the middle of next week. Restra was too important; they were being groomed for the Star League. This of course was going to set them back a few hundred years. Or five minutes depending on exactly how important they were and I guessed that the two emissaries had signed the disclosure form when they volunteered for the assignment, the one which meant you were on your own. The cottage was beginning to feel claustrophobic with too many feelings in too small a space. The pictures of little children with large weapons had imprinted itself on my consciousness and every time I blinked I could see the faces. The child soldiers in Africa were a part of the collective guilt and shame of an entire world in my time so it was not as if we'd never screwed up. I couldn't think straight. Elider followed me toward the door.

"Where are you going?" She touched my arm, anxiously pulling at the fabric of my sleeve.

"I thought I'd get a breath of air."

"I don't think that's a good idea, you don't know who's out there." She looked and felt of fear.

I stopped. "Why would there be anyone out there Elider?" The conversation across the room was still quiet and controlled. Mac sat by the fire talking to Lassik like a group of old friends spending the weekend together. Oh, I thought, what now?

The back wall of the house began to buzz. I could feel it and an all consuming sense of dread began to creep up my spine like the music for a shark in a film. Elider's hand was still on my sleeve. Mac walked over to the kitchen to get himself another drink. He looked at me and signalled 'do you want one?' I shook my head slowly, completely spun out by the buzzing. He came over and as he walked towards me I silently pointed towards the wall behind him. He looked over his shoulder and then back at me, puzzled by my expression and then the back of the cottage exploded and the blast pressure hit and he flew through the air.

The silence was full of anger and fear and the air rushed back into my lungs, filling my head with echoes of death. It was dark. All the lights had blown and the room was shaped by the scattered burning embers from the fire which were all over the floor. I looked for Zeke. His elongated shadow was scrunched over fiddling for a torch from his kit. He crawled towards me; a large cut over his eye was bleeding profusely. All you could hear was the rush of wind and the rain coming in through the broken windows.

I looked at Mac. Like a child curled up for sleep, he had one hand under his head. He was covered in dust.

"Are you all right?" Zeke touched my face. His hand came away covered in blood. I wiped it away with the tattered and dusty sleeve of my jacket.

"It's not mine," I said and looked at Elider. She was lying across my legs, her head thrown back at an impossible angle, one arm was nearly detached from her body and the warm blood covered the floor in an ever spreading pool. I pushed her broken body away with a revulsion I didn't want to feel.

Mac made a barely perceptible movement and I felt a sob of relief as I went to get up. Zeke pulled me back down again. "Wait," he said, "Is anyone out there?"

I shook my head. "No, but there soon will be. What was that?"

"A sonic bomb," he said, which explained the noise.

A large hole had been blown out of the back of the cottage, nothing much was left of one whole side and the ceiling canted dangerously down at one end. Most of the furniture was in pieces, scattered about as if a giant had thrown a temper tantrum. Burning embers scorched my clothes as I knelt on the floor by Mac.

Lassik appeared from out of the clouds of dust, unsurprisingly with not a scratch on him and went over to Zeke. "That was meant to kill us, we were betrayed."

"I disagree," I said, "I think they were looking for hostages. They thought they would stand a better chance of negotiating their future with a card or two."

Zeke was bending over a now groggy Mac, checking him for injury with a small medical scanner and trying not to drip blood on him at the same time. "Here," I said, "Give me that." I staggered to my feet and took the little device from his shaking hand. I gave him my hankie and he looked puzzled for a moment, I took it back and held it to his head.

Lassik was examining the Restran's but I could have told him that four of them were dead.

"Look for Padrig, he's still alive, over there I think." I carried on checking Mac, the readings on the diagnostic device suggested shock but no internal bleeding. His right tibia was broken and would need strapping until we could get him back to the Starfire. He sat up grey with pain and dust. I gave him a hug and for a moment he hugged me back.

I stood up and checked Zeke with the device. "Don't worry about me, I'm fine." He was standing with his back against the broken wall, watching for movement outside.

"They're not here yet, I think there was a mix-up." I gestured towards Elider, "She betrayed her friends. They have her children." I'd only had a glimpse of the cauldron of despair inside her head a moment before the bomb went off and I wondered what I would have done in her place. "We need to get out of here," I added.

The red light from the torches flickered against faces dead and alive. It caught at the little movements of shock as we tried to deal with the consequences of the blast.

Mac gasped as he moved his leg. He pulled the jelly computer from his pack and attempted to make a connection. Zeke looked at him and Mac shook his head. "The sonic blast took out mine as well." He looked at me. "Can you reach Rani from here?"

"No," I paused, "We need to leave soon."

"I know," Zeke snapped, "But it stands to reason that she," he pointed to Elider's broken body, "Would have sabotaged the vehicles." I began looking around for something to use as a splint.

"Then we're going to have to walk," I said calmly.

"What is the matter with you?" He hissed.

"I don't know!" Mac looked at the two of us as if we'd gone mad. "I don't know," I said. "It just doesn't seem real."

Zeke put his arms around me squashing me with the smell of other people's blood. "We really don't have time for you to be having a twenty-first century moment," he said quietly.

Lassik came over from the corner of the room dragging a weeping and wounded Padrig who was holding his badly broken arm close to his body. A large gash on his shoulder showed through to the bone. Lassik whispered the poison of Elider's betrayal with a sadist's pleasure. Padrig whimpered, "I can't believe it, I've known her for years, we went to the grid together." Which must have been a real bonding experience, I thought, dry of emotion.

Zeke was talking quietly to Mac. He pulled some small metal rods out of his medical pack and flicked them with his finger. They telescoped out, small yellow sucker pads adhered to the swollen and blotched skin on Mac's leg, he shuddered with the pain as the rods straightened and pulled the leg back into shape. Zeke gave him some painkillers in a small spray on his tongue and then came over to us.

"What are we going to do with him?" Lassik asked, poking the poor man's broken arm.

"If you leave me here, they will kill me." Padrig addressed his words to Zeke. It was clear what Lassik wanted to do with him. Zeke looked at me which was something Lassik hated and I shrugged. I hadn't been able to get much more than feelings from any of them except at the moment of death, making anything I could contribute no more than an intuitive guess.

"Okay," Zeke said, "He comes with us."

I had always had a fear of being hunted. My nightmares consisted of running in slow motion through dark woods looking over my shoulder for something unseen behind me. Something I couldn't reason with which got closer and closer. It moved fast and I knew I couldn't get away. The terror in the back of my throat usually choked me awake.

We gave the pathetically grateful Padrig a set of the emergency splints and dosed him and Mac with more painkillers.

In the half light from the two moons we made our silent agreement. Zeke gave me a weapon. I had no idea how it worked. He clicked his tongue in exasperation and showed me the release button.

"I thought you'd had some training with this," he muttered. He and Lassik hoisted Mac between them and we paused, each of us making our own bargains with whatever deity watched over that world.

We passed the sabotaged vehicles. Padrig had checked them with

Lassik looking over his shoulder and Zeke carrying a weapon and watching for visitors. They had been efficiently disabled.

The trees closed around us and I found it difficult to breathe for a moment. I held the torch in front of my feet. The path, according to Padrig, would take us back to the river and onto the SSV. I couldn't detect any deceit but we all had had a bit of trouble as we tried to work out exactly how far it was.

Padrig had drawn a map in the dust on the floor of the broken cottage with a shaking finger, as he managed to avoid sketching in the blood of his friends.

The vehicles had picked us up and taken us on the roads, they had travelled the equivalent of three sides of a square. We were going to have to walk nearly twenty miles back to the SSV and I couldn't see us being able to cover more than two to three miles an hour. Speed marching was about six miles an hour and that was with some running. There was no possibility we would have got more than seven or eight miles before dawn.

It was winter and dark for nearly sixteen hours; the temperate climate meant rain, lots of it, but it was not really cold. Padrig was stumbling along behind us, constantly looking back over his shoulder. Zeke had carefully wiped over the dust map with his foot before we left. But it wouldn't have taken an Einstein or whoever the equivalent was, to realise where we were headed.

Our only advantage was the density of the forest which was why we had landed there and maybe the fact that they didn't know one of us was injured. Padrig said that people often disappeared in the wilderness we were in without trace, which sounded pretty good.

We walked as quickly as possible. The river was now on my right and seemed to be flowing faster in my own haste. The trees sighed and rustled but shielded us from the worst of the weather. The canopy still showed moonlight in places and a few stars and it made me feel better to know that people were up there somewhere. I wondered what they were doing now that we had missed our check in time. The contingency plan that had somehow passed me by would have been nice to know.

I looked at the luminous dial of my watch we were an hour and twenty minutes from the cottage. I could hear the laboured breathing of the men on their mad three-legged race and without stopping, asked them over my shoulder, raising my voice above the sound of the wind, "Do you want to rest yet?"

They stopped and gently let Mac slide to the ground. I went over to him and got him to lie down on the wet grass raising his broken leg up to try and reduce some of the swelling that must have been agony for him. "Do you want more painkillers Mac?" He nodded and I pulled up his sleeve and used one of the sprays against his skin. He looked grateful.

Zeke and Lassik were sat back to back. I could see the shine of sweat on Zeke's face. I got some water from the river and stuck the cleansing probe into the cup for a moment, zapping it several times for good measure then handed it to Zeke. He drank all of it and held my hand for a moment in thanks. I felt as if I were living someone else's life.

Mac was transparent with pain by the light of the torch. He sat up to sip the water, balancing his leg on a convenient rock to keep it up. I removed a twig from his hair and smoothed a few lines from his face. He tried to smile which nearly broke me. Other people's pain was hard to bear when you *couldn't* feel what they felt.

We rested for ten minutes. Padrig drank from the river and so did Lassik. The rain was easing off but the wind in the trees was making me feel dizzy, like being on the deck of a ship in full sail. Zeke lifted Mac onto his one good foot and Lassik lifted Mac's arm over his shoulder. They positioned themselves as best they could and we set off again.

The track was bumpy and overgrown from little use. I broke ground as I went, pulling branches out of the way so that the men behind me didn't have to. It occurred to me that we were blazing a trail a mile wide but we had no choice.

The forest seemed to thicken as we went further away from the river. Padrig caught up with me. "I think this is where the tree felling stopped; we may find it a little more difficult from here. These paths are used by the woodsmen and hunters."

"What do they hunt, Padrig?"

"We have several large carnivores," he said proudly. "But don't worry the people in these parts do not hunt in winter."

"What about the carnivores, Padrig," I asked out of breath with talking and walking. "Do they hunt in winter?" If I hadn't grabbed him he would have stopped in his tracks which would have caused all sorts of logistical problems for those behind us.

"Oh my sacred ones I didn't think!" He would have stopped again but I dragged him onward.

"We're well armed, I'm sure we'll manage."

"They hunt in packs," Padrig added as an afterthought.

"You're making this up!" I said, exasperated. The adrenalin was beginning to wear off and I was swimming with tiredness. Telepathy was not an exact science and if you didn't know where to look it was like sorting through a rubbish dump; which was why I had heard it the old-fashioned way above the sound of the trees and the river, a whooshing noise. We all stopped in a heap of sudden lack of movement.

"What is that, a helicopter?" The word didn't go through the translator and Zeke looked as puzzled as Padrig.

"Rotary wing," I used my fingers to demonstrate the blade's function and Padrig nodded.

"Yes, it is a hover-blade. They will have difficulty finding us in this weather in the forest." He was looking upwards to the canopy of trees and we all waited for the sound to come nearer.

Zeke said, "Padrig, do you have thermal imaging?" The local looked puzzled. "Heat seeking equipment, for detecting body temperature," he explained.

Padrig looked sick. "Yes." He sat down hard on the ground.

Mac was leaning heavily on Zeke; his face was creased with the lines of pain. He pulled at his emergency pack. "I brought a Teflon blanket with me."

Zeke looked up, head on one side. "They seem to be working a general search pattern." Lassik nodded in agreement. I suddenly realised that I could see their faces clearly. It was getting light. "We will have to move fast." Zeke helped Mac to sit against the base of a tree. "You and Bea will use the Teflon blanket. The rest of us will go into the river."

"You'll freeze!" I said.

"That's the idea; hopefully they are only working the regular search patterns. It's obvious that we would follow the river. There's nearly always a track. The only thing they're not sure of is the direction we're going in and how far we've travelled. If they just do a quick pass over us we might be able to fool them."

"What are you going to do for air? No don't tell me, the trick with the hollow reeds." I shook my head in a state of incredulity overload.

"We need to space out in the river so we don't show up as a clump of heat, and hopefully the water flow will disperse some more. We might get away with it," he added to himself.

We ran around formation panicking while the hover-blade got nearer. Padrig eyed the river nervously, but he showed the other two where to find the bamboo-like reeds that they could use. I put my hands in the water and shuddered.

"Come on," said Zeke. I ran over to Mac and covered us with the blanket.

"Is it always like this?" I grumbled, "I was expecting there to be a little more technology."

"Me too," said Mac quietly. I reached for his hand which was far too hot and dry and we waited as the machine came over the top of us.

It didn't stay around for very long and as soon as I thought it was safe I threw off the blanket and ran to the river. They were in amongst the bushes spaced about twenty feet apart completely submerged. I lay down on the bank and reached in, grabbing Zeke's shoulder.

The water streaked off them in angry showers. They had stripped off and Mac and I tried to squeeze as much liquid as possible out of their clothes while they ran around and jumped up and down, like ghostly dancers in the morning grey. I noticed that Padrig had a few odd additions to his anatomy. It looked as if the females on the planet might have been able to feed more than one baby at a time.

"Do you think we will be able to travel in the daylight?" I asked Zeke. The question was almost academic as it was nearly completely light. He and Lassik were now carrying Mac, whose head was lolling on his chest.

"Rest," said Zeke gasping, and he and Lassik stopped, putting Mac down on the ground. Poor Mac barely showed any response when I spoke to him and he was having trouble breathing. Zeke was doubled over resting his hands on his knees. "What do you think?"

"I think he could be in shock, exhausted from the pain, overdosed on painkillers, or he could have a fat embolism from the bone break."

"Can we do anything?"

"Anticoagulants bed rest and a crash team." I rubbed my grainy eyes. "I don't know I haven't been a nurse for over four hundred years."

"Sacred ones you people live a long time," said Padrig, his eyes were filled with misplaced respect.

We walked on through a spectacular sunrise. My feet were rubbed raw and my clothes steamed in atmospheric swirls. I could hear strange birdsong, something that sounded like a macaw and a few raucous calls that Padrig said belonged to a bird that was very good to eat which made my stomach compete with the rush and gurgle of the river, an odd reaction for a vegetarian but understandable under the circumstances.

A dry gasp from Zeke stopped us and like a herd of old donkeys we all slumped down quiet in our collective exhaustion. I removed my shoes and put my feet in the river waiting for the cold ache to turn to blessed numbness.

I filled the cup with water and literally poured it down their dry throats. They looked like a nest full of sparrow chicks. Even Jad Lassik looked grateful though it must have been a strain for him. We all stiffened as the sound of the hover-blade grew louder. Marking time as our primitive nerve endings stuck out like porcupine quills in anticipation. It turned at the last bend in the river and headed away from us and I breathed out.

Mac's leg looked very swollen and the pressure suckers and tube splints were digging into the flesh above the knee. His eyes were open and he thanked me for the water. I touched his forehead and it was still hot and dry.

"Mac, I can't give you any more painkillers yet can you hang on?" He nodded, his lips looked bloodless and the skin around his eyes was almost black. I sniffed the area of the bone break but apart from the ghastly smell of old dried blood it seemed as if nothing sinister was going on so I decided to leave well alone. The skin of his thigh was scraped and bruised but it looked normal.

He smiled at me. "Thank you."

"For what?" I smiled back at him, I thought how young he looked and made a bargain with no deity I could remember to keep him safe.

"I don't know many girls who would check for infection."

"It's first date basis where I come from." He laughed, which caused Lassik to look up and he scowled in our direction. It was time to move on again.

The sun had come up through the trees; it was much brighter than at home and white light rather than yellow because this was a young world. The trees had fluffy leaves like a soft pine but photosynthesis must have been universal. Not the green of Earth, not actually a green I'd seen before and I felt that Torriff had introduced me to all the new green available. I thought about chlorophyll and then gave that up.

I began to feel calmer, the calm that came with daylight; all the night-time fears of not seeing were chased away by dawn. I looked behind me to smile at the others because you always thought you were going to get out of it even when you were trapped. Their faces changed from blank exhaustion to a kind of shocked incredulity. I turned to look forward.

They came in like the shadows of hammerhead sharks. I nearly walked into the leader and they were huge. Zeke shouted a warning and fired over my head. I dropped to my knees and fumbled with the weapon I'd been given. I could hear Padrig screaming, "Behind us, look out!" They were like a pack of dogs on the hunt for easy prey. The weapon pinged into the creature with a small kickback into the palm of my hand. The monster looked like a dinosaur with a large head, big teeth, bad breath and scaly skin. It had small front legs with large claws and rested on two powerful back legs and a tail. It was fast and smart and they had us surrounded and we hadn't heard them. I hadn't heard them. I kept firing still on one knee trying to dodge as it lashed out. At first it just looked irritated then finally I could see blood, little gouts of blood. The shouting behind me gave me courage and every-thing was in slow motion anyway so I just kept pressing the trigger. It fell towards me clawing at my face. I backed up on my knees bumping into someone and tried to scramble out of reach. The last gasp of its fetid breath reached my face and it was still.

"I told you there would be nine-foot monsters," I puffed, looking accusingly at Zeke whose jinx it was.

We sat in silence. My garments were once again covered in someone else's blood. Lassik had been badly scratched on the back by a claw and the wound bled freely. He said very little but his skin looked a little green which he said, was his version of pale. He put up with my efforts to patch him up in silence but refused painkillers. "I can't take the same drugs as you." He drank some water and I helped him as he eased himself gently to the ground. He hung his head down as if he was fighting nausea.

We had killed three of the creatures which Padrig had called froudours; two had escaped to hunt another day. The dead ones lay surrounded in a cloud of small gold coloured flies.

"Is this what you meant by carnivores?" I asked Padrig.

He nodded. "I have only ever seen them in a butchers shop before. I don't think I shall be able to eat froudour meat again."

"Can we eat them?" Asked Mac, we all turned in surprise. "Well," he said, "I'm hungry."

The meat fried up nicely using one of the weapons that had looked to me like a laser. I hadn't eaten meat for a long time but it had also been a while since I walked my feet into blisters running from psychopaths. Froudour meat tasted disgusting and I went back to being a vegetarian after spitting out one mouthful, but the others liked it, which confirmed all my suspicions; some people would eat *anything*.

The day passed without much help from me. Lassik and Padrig took turns to partner Zeke. Padrig was quite a bit shorter than Zeke. Mac must have been jarred every other footfall. I tried to take a turn but the height difference was even more extreme so I went back to breaking ground. For a few hours we reacted to every unexplained noise like a herd of antelope until exhaustion settled us back into almost indifference.

We covered ground and I found myself thinking that the sunlight through trees was something created for the spirit. The stops became more frequent and the rests got longer. Mostly we sat in silence. I checked Mac's wound and gave them all water even Lassik, and then folded into a heap on the ground.

"We're close," said Zeke. I looked at him. For a minute I couldn't think what he was talking about. The journey had become my whole world. The trunk of a large tree made a wonderful back rest and it was going to be hard to get up and move on.

Padrig looked up from contemplating a blade of grass. "To the space vehicle?" He asked. Zeke nodded. The evening was creeping across the edges of the tiny clearing between huge trees. It made every outline seem hazy. That and the tiredness and hunger made it difficult for me to focus on Padrig for a moment.

He had a small halo of light behind his head and it seemed to me as if he looked like an old painting of martyrs from a dusty church.

Zeke broke the spell and I peeled myself away from my tree and Padrig's thoughts.

The hover-blade began pestering us again as darkness filled the forest. They must have rested up in the daylight. We were so close to the SSV I had begun to feel hopeful again. When you were without hope you needed courage and my resources of that had been used up at the same time as the dance with the dinosaur. The hover-blade reached the clearing with our only means of escape in it, about a micro-second after we did. The huge lights that they shone down onto us were blinding and the noise of the blades filled my head like a waterfall. We staggered on towards the opening door of the SSV. I could see the grimacing mouths of the exhausted men; they looked like those theatrical masks of laughter and sorrow.

Zeke held the computer card that had opened the doorway in his outstretched hand; it looked as if he were Moses parting the seas as the long grass flattened under our feet with the down draft from the rotor above. They couldn't land as the SSV took up all of the space. A megaphone blasted unintelligible words; the local equivalent of 'stop or I'll shoot,' the Com/Ts were not making much of an effort to help for some reason.

We threw ourselves into safety and then I turned as Padrig reached into the craft and I shot him in the chest. He fell back into the clearing and I pressed the door panel and screamed into the stunned silence, "Move!"

Most events were decided, not by what was seen, but by what was unseen.

Zeke took off at a ninety degree angle before any of us had had time to strap in. The g-force that had glued us to the floor protected our bodies from the up blast of the bomb that had been placed in Padrig's chest cavity; though the SSV bounced and ducked as if we were in the path of a great wave.

When I was able to speak I turned to Zeke, "That last megaphone message was the signal to set off the bomb." He wiped a dirty hand across an even dirtier face. I closed my eyes and added, "I'm glad you didn't want me to practice my take-offs."

"I'm glad too," Mac spoke in barely a whisper.

"Oh well, that didn't go too badly then," said Rani cheerfully. I stood there as Pui sprayed my face and snorted her opinion. I was filthy, exhausted, and covered in other people's blood as well as my own and that of the nine-foot monster. "You should have seen my first assign-ment," she added and then wandered off to check on how Mac was doing. The two medics were carrying him from the SSV on a stretcher that hovered between them. It looked like a trick from a Christmas show where the magician says 'nothing in my hands.'

An SSV came in alongside our craft sliding gracefully to a halt. I could see Mark Limbu in the pilot seat and sense another half dozen people inside. I wondered vaguely if they had been looking for us. It gave me a moment of peace in the noise of the docking bay.

Zeke put his arms around me in a very public hug and I rested my head on his chest and allowed myself the feelings of fear and tiredness and some sorrow. He had the strong silence down to a fine art and squeezed rather too hard as if making up for things not said and then looked down at me.

"Well done. Why don't you go and get cleaned up before we report in to the captain." I nodded, weary with dirt and delayed shock and I wandered unsteadily over towards the steps looking like a somnambulist in a Victorian gothic play.

The second SSV discharged its cargo and I stopped short. The group of official looking men were familiar in their air of culture; we were wearing the same clothes. They looked at me and one of the delegates from the planet walked over with a hand outstretched. He laughed in what he thought was a friendly fashion.

"You were part of the group that was on the surface, we've been trying to rescue you for hours." The lie was so blatant that it hardly tweaked my telepathic antennae. He looked uneasily at his untouched hand.

"You," I said into the un-diplomatic silence, "Are a liar." A collective intake of breath followed and I could see Zeke walking over to try and reinstate some sanity; too late. No wonder he had wanted me to go and get a shower.

The liar began shaking his finger too close to my face. I could see Rani with her hand over her mouth. She winced just before I punched the liar on the nose. He was lucky someone had already taken the gun from me.

"What kind of people are you, don't the images of your dead children visit you in your dreams at night?" I yelled. "You tricked that man into thinking he was doing something for the good of his world. Do you have any idea what a body with a bomb inside it looks like after the bloody thing has gone off, his partner won't have enough bits to bury.

The only reason you're here is because you think we still don't know. Well listen to me, make up your mind do you want to be part of the future or not?" I said, poking his chest for emphasis. "Dead emissaries and a couple of hostages are not going to give you the upper hand, get over yourself!" The whole of the upper docking bay stood in silent acknowledgement, Gatt.R. was standing next to the second craft with his mouth slightly open. The man in front of me radiated fear and loathing. He looked furiously at Zeke who had arrived and was angling me towards the steps by judicious use of grabbing my elbow and dragging me; he had positioned himself between me and the official in the hope of averting further violence.

I found myself up the steps and into the corridor with the doors sliding firmly behind me.

"You don't own the truth you know," Zeke said quietly, making me feel about two inches tall. "*Why* do you have to be so childish?" He added.

"It's just not something I've grown out of," I snapped back over my shoulder as I stalked off.

I peeled off the smelly clothes, feeling as if I was removing a layer of skin and my illusions at the same time. The recycling bag by the door was stuffed full. The small system in my rooms couldn't cope with large amounts of recycling and I would have to take a walk down to level nine to dispose of it. I wished the same could have been done for the feelings going around in my head and I could empty out the things that were too big to deal with.

I stood in the shower and scrubbed, then turned the steamer on sweating the thoughts out and I tried to balance the impossible grief in the intimidating silence. Through the misted glass I could see Ollie balanced on top of the loo seat lid waiting for me to finish.

We curled up my furry friend and I, on the sofa cushions and I let a few quiet tears damp his whiskers which he tolerated. He butted my chin wiping my face dry and his purr filled my head and I slept the sleep of years, someone else's sleep, not mine and I dreamed about dying children and monsters and running from a hidden fear.

I got up in what would have been grey dawn at home. Stretching and creaking from cuts and bruises not healed and the hangover of too much adrenaline; more hot water inside and out helped but not much. I hurried to the medical bay and crept in through the doors hoping to go unnoticed. Pui looked up and put her finger to her lips in an old-fashioned gesture. I pointed at the screened bed and she nodded. Quietly I looked around the screen. Mac was stretched out with a large yellow jelly attached to his lower leg, it bubbled and fizzed alarmingly where the wound had been but all I could see was a nearly healed leg and I felt a black cloud depart the outer edges of my mind. He was snoring gently and looked like a twelve-year-old after a scrape with a skate board. Pui tapped me on the shoulder and pointed at the door.

It was quiet when I came into the upper restaurant and still early. Tariq Azel had brought a large cup of coffee and a plate of cakes to where I sat by the windows. Sometimes only cake for breakfast would do. And here was a man who understood that. I hoped his partner appreciated him. He patted me on the back and smiled. It seemed as if the bush telegraph was in fine form. I looked up from my copy of Jane Eyre as Torriff came through the door a few minutes later.

"Something from the grass menu Torriff?" I swept my hand over the abundant display of food.

He looked over towards me. "I hear you caused an incident in the upper docking bay," he said gently, like a professor whose pupil was handing in work late. I saw Tariq wince out of the corner of my eye.

Somehow the lack of tact was reassuring. "Would you like to talk about it?"

He sat down and Tariq came over with a drink for him and something on a plate that looked like a dead houseplant. I took a bite of cake; he had a handful of crunchy leaves. We talked, or rather I talked and he made mid-galactic noises of understanding.

"Sometimes," he said after a long pause, "We bring our shadows with us."

I felt occasionally that there seemed to be far too many people on board who had done advanced enigmatic. "You mean that I need to be willing to allow my experiences to change me." He nodded, pleased with his pupil's progress. I took his hand. "Thanks Torriff, thank you for listening." He looked a little sad for a moment and then smiled.

"What do you know about Jad Lassik, Torriff?" He hissed, not a sound I'd ever heard him make before. It was as if the scholar had disappeared and the warrior had taken over. "He was our 'contact' on the planet I can't believe they trust him he's so obviously slime." Torriff measured his answer, glancing quickly at Tariq to see if he was close enough to hear. My Com/T went off loudly making both of us jump guiltily.

"Bea, please come to the briefing room." The captain's voice sounded like a blast of arctic air.

I sighed and clicked the com with my fingers. "I'm on my way Captain Witherspoon." I walked and then ran down the corridor on the first level. The floor was a beautiful yellow with sprinkles of gold, a vast improvement on the early morning colour of a pale pink.

The doors of the briefing room opened onto the kind of silence that made you realise the talking had ended with your arrival. Rani sat at one end of the table a little apart from the others and unreadable. Zeke and the captain were halfway down on one side and Jad Lassik and Mark Limbu sat opposite them. It looked like a public hanging was in order and I suddenly felt very angry with these people. It was difficult to know where the lines were at the best of times, nothing I'd ever done in my life could have prepared me for this and they knew that. Rani sighed and looked at me. I looked away.

"Well?" I said, as I sat down.

Rani sighed again, "I realise you were under great stress Bea, but it would have been better to think a bit about the bigger picture."

"I was angry Rani. I didn't want to do deep meaningful shit, I wanted to punch someone." I looked at Mark Limbu's serious face. "Were you searching for us?"

"Yes of course," he said, looking puzzled, "Did you think we would leave you there?"

"Yes," I said quietly. Captain Witherspoon looked horrified. So did Rani.

"We would *never* leave an operative," said the captain. She and Mark looked at each other, everyone else knew and they'd all assumed that I did. Lassik was enjoying it and his mean little face was drinking in the anger and confusion.

The captain got to her feet and went over to the hologram that was projected from the back wall. It showed the local star system. She traced her fingers through the planets. "This is the main route for the trade ships, so we can't leave them to it any longer. Something's going to happen and it won't be good."

"I hate to state the obvious," I said, doing just that, "But something not good has already happened."

"I have arranged for the bodies of the emissaries to be delivered to the ship," the captain said after a short silence.

"Well, check for explosives," I muttered. She turned to look at me. "These people will mess you about forever," I said, "They understand their own power struggles and will apply their own rules to what they see as a political game."

She nodded. "I know, but we don't all have the luxury of expressing our feelings when ever we feel the truth is being sacrificed." Her tone was laced with irony.

"Captain, they do not have the same attitude to death that we do, they think nothing of killing their children, what's a few offworlders?"

"They have agreed to further diplomatic contact." Rani said, looking at me. I shook my head at her.

"Stand by to pick up more dead bodies then," I said. "Look, these people don't want you here and they've got something going on that I don't understand."

Mark Limbu looked at Rani and she shrugged. "They must have a natural ability to block telepathy if all Bea could get were feelings."

"Lassik?" Commander Limbu asked.

The nasty smile curved the lips. "Not my problem," he said.

Captain Witherspoon had left the room and it was one of those occasions when the door slammed in your head if not in reality. Either way I winced at the exit. It left me with Rani who was unreadable by choice and Zeke who was dangerously quiet. Jad Lassik and Mark Limbu had left before the captain.

Zeke had barely said a word during the meeting. It was odd that the captain hadn't seemed as angry as I thought she would be, when she'd mentioned my actions in the docking bay she had sort of covered a snort of laughter with a clever use of words. She was wearing a blocking chip of course which made it impossible to read her. The better my telepathy got the more the chips were adjusted. Either Zeke's wasn't turned up very high or he was so angry the chip was going into meltdown. His fists were clenched with suppressed frustration.

"Where does it say in the contract, that I have to stand by while that *liar* spits out a monumental amount of rubbish. You know they were going to try and kill us. They think it's the only expression of power that counts. They kill their children if they don't make the grade!"

"We have rules." His voice getting louder to compete with mine, "As well you know." He looked as if he had swallowed an entire thunderstorm of cold dark clouds.

I yelled, "This isn't about rules, it's about trade routes." Rani began to exude a feeling of calm. We both turned on her at the same time.

"Okay, if you're determined to fight this out the old-fashioned way." She left quietly and the door closed behind her. I walked over to the hologram of the seemingly peaceful planet aglow with light and life its twin moons keeping a silent vigil.

"Do you realise that you have caused an interstellar incident? It's taken us two years to get them to agree to accept a diplomatic assignment."

"They *killed* the diplomats. You don't actually believe those two volunteered to take the grid?"

We were nose to nose like a couple of bantam hens all fluff and feathers. I thought for one moment that he was going to hit me and I took a step backwards coming up against the wall and banging my head. But he kissed me instead, a very good kiss, one that involved his hands in my hair. He stopped, which I thought was a shame and looked at me. "Did you have to hit him?" And then he kissed me again.

"What's that?" I asked Rani, as she put a large crystal computer disc on the table. My early morning cup of hot water was balanced on my knee and Ollie was just leaving for his first walkabout of the day. He had changed his mind when he saw Rani.

"Assignment Standing Orders, a bit late, but it might make you feel a little less like punching someone next time, though I doubt it."

She came and sat next to me on the window seats and tucked her feet under her. Ollie plonked down on her lap and gave her the cat equivalent of a kiss, nose to nose, his orange eyes a kaleidoscope of affection. She laughed. I tapped her arm. "You can't shut a cat out of your head, can you?"

She made a face at me. "You have to find your own way with all this Bea." She sighed, "There's no training manual for telepaths."

I was stunned. "How many times have you trained someone?"

"Including this time?" She asked. I nodded. She contemplated, "Once."

"I can't believe I fell for that," I said.

"Neither can I."

She lifted her feet onto the glass coffee table and Ollie settled more comfortably on her legs. Her trousers were a beautiful floaty material and the matching top seemed to mould itself to her without being tight. My jeans and T-shirt looked and felt tired.

"Where do you get your clothes from Rani?"

She looked at me and laughed. "There's a tailor on board. He's on the ninth level, in fact," she glanced at the holographic clock by the door, "He's open for business about now. Do you want me to introduce you?"

We rustled off down the corridors like a couple of teenagers after school. The lower levels of the ship were buzzing with early morning activity and the floors glowed in a pale blue.

The marines were out in force, probably off to practice the ninety known ways of killing someone with your thumb. A small squad squashed us into a doorway and as they passed a familiar voice hidden under camouflage said, "Eyes right!" Doz winked and Sig smiled a toothy grin; they both snapped a salute worthy of a text book. As they disappeared around the curve of the corridor a voice said, "Good on yer girl!" Rani looked at me as if I had been egging on the younger kids to misbehave and I wiped the smile from my face.

The tailor was tall and masculine looking and the pale blue of the Des.Rans. his long arms and legs wind-milled as he displayed the fabrics and designs. The Aladdin's cave was stacked with the most beautiful materials. For the first time I allowed myself to think about my mother, who would have loved the textures and colours from a thousand worlds. I sighed. Rani rubbed my arm and gave me a hug. "I'll leave you. Lef.G. this is Bea."

The Des.Ran. and I nodded our hello and he held out a warm hand.

"I understand that this is a greeting on your world." I took it and for a second felt the genuine kindness that his race seemed to have in abundance. "Gatt. said you punched an official?"

I gaped. "Does everyone know?" I asked him. I could hear Rani laughing all the way down the corridor.

"Don't worry, Gatt. said he had it coming." I thought very quietly that it would have been good if Rani hadn't heard *that*.

I stood still while the coloured holographic lights outlined my shape in three dimensions which was not great for the ego. It was transferred to the holo/computer which filled in the details. Lef.

helped me pick out some material and a design similar to Rani's with the loose trousers and wrap around top.

He put some more information into the computer so that I could see what it looked like. It was an unflattering holo/photograph taken by someone who didn't know your good side in clothes you couldn't remember owning. We changed material a few times, but like most really good designers I ended up with something he wanted me to have.

"You work out with Doctor Chan in the mornings?" He looked over his shoulder enquiringly. I nodded. "Would you like some self defence classes, I teach the marines in the evenings?"

I looked at him suspiciously. "Did Gatt. suggest that?"

"He may have said you could do with a little help." Nef. was smiling and I thought, not for the first time, that this was someone else's world and someone else's time.

I woke drenched in sweat fighting the covers, half in and half out of bed. Padrig's face was a screaming maw of pain and confusion that threatened to swallow me. I must have been projecting because Rani called me on the Com/T and with a sleepy voice asked, "Are you okay you were screaming in my head?" I couldn't answer and she spoke gently, "Do you want me to come over?" It was three o'clock in the morning.

I managed to whisper, "I'm fine Rani it was just a nightmare." She sighed sleepily and signed off. I lay back too frightened to close my eyes. Ollie had retreated under the table in the other room and wouldn't come back to bed.

I dressed and went out into the corridor heading for hydroponics and as near to outside as possible. The rumble in my head was a curl of small bubbles, "**Beeea?**" Gurber's calling card left a trail of effervescence that I could only see with my eyes shut.

Hydroponics was quiet and moonlit because the birds and plants needed some sort of balance for a real life. I went up two levels and then down the empty corridor. A beautiful cluster of stars and dust millions of miles away filled one window after another. Gurber's door slid open in welcome and I found myself trying to hug the large warm jelly-like shape. He didn't seem the least bit bothered about me throwing myself at him and created a few protuberances to hug me back.

I blubbered a bit and it was disconcerting to see that my tears disappeared through his outer layer.

"**Gurber I killed someone.**" He acknowledged with a mental stream of more bubbles and something that sounded like a sigh of regret.

The room was as sparse as ever but somehow comforting. I sat on the floor and Gurber squatted near the computer panels, every now and then he would tap a sequence of keys, studying the nearby star systems. Rani had said that even if they had already been mapped there was still much to learn. New worlds were found every day, though somehow I got the impression that Gurber's race had been there before.

"**Have your people been to my world?**" A long pause followed.

"**Yes.**" He tapped a few more keys and avoided my thoughts a little.

"**When?**"

"**Always.**"

The small SSV was turning in towards the upper docking bay and it disappeared out of view from the front screen on the bridge. I looked at Jenny Smith and she smiled her sympathy, this was going to be as much fun as colonic irrigation. The representatives from the planet were coming to a meeting and they were bringing the bodies of the two emissaries. I had been invited to attend.

I put off the moment to go into the briefing room and watched the techs swinging about on the outside of the ship. All the techs took a great deal of pride in their ability to scare the rest of the crew by hopping from tie to tie completely unhindered by the constraints of a safety harness. They were also deaf to the auto-verbal safety requests from the ship that preceded every decompression exit. The captain turned a well experienced blind eye.

Jenny shook her head after a really brazen leap performed by a familiar figure and I leaned across her to tap the outside com. "Tom Hatherley, you are an idiot and Jenny here is not impressed by your antics." Jenny went pink to the roots of her hair, which probably meant that she was impressed.

A laugh came over the com, "Hey Bea, hit 'em for me will yer?"

Zeke stuck his head through the doorway to the bridge. "Now is a good time, Bea." I groaned with exasperation and felt Jenny's sympathetic pat on my back as I turned to go. We stood in the corridor in front of the briefing room doors. "Try and keep it calm in there, will you?" Zeke asked. I looked at him and he sighed, "I might as well be talking to the cat."

The room was full; the captain was standing holding a cup of coffee and she looked casual and relaxed. Mac was sitting next to Lieutenant Commander Limbu; I went over to him and gave him a hug. It was impossible that it was only three days since he was lying on a stretcher in agony. "How are you feeling?" He did a turn for me and laughed his reply, oozing irrepressible youth.

The Restrans looked at me with interest, much as you would a failed biological experiment. Rani moved to my side and we sat down.

The room gradually organised itself, the Malathrans seemed to make up most of the delegation from the planet which was not exactly representative. I found myself sitting opposite the black eye of a recognisable face. He looked at me, composing his features into understanding and tolerance. He said into the settling quiet, "You have to understand that some of my people still believe that the stars are the home of the gods."

"Then they have a surprise coming."

"Bea!" I think I heard it in stereo.

"Okay, okay."

He began again, "We are sorry you fell into unfortunate company when you visited us, perhaps next time we can show you something of our beautiful world." This was addressed to Captain Witherspoon and she graciously smiled her acceptance.

"Thank you for returning our emissaries, Taget of Laswin." He nodded his head as if he had just handed her the salt, not two dead bodies.

"They died well," he said solemnly. I restrained myself with difficulty.

There were four representatives, all plainly dressed in formal, almost military clothing in a variety of dark colours. The Restrans on the planet, that we had met secretly, had been much more casually attired. These people, three men and one woman, were very obviously soldiers.

I wondered what my life would have been like if my whole world had been run by the military. Their jutting jaw line and brows gave them an additional air of aggression. In the harsh light of the briefing room their skin colour was an unkind yellowish and the deep-set eyes were shadowed.

I looked around the table at 'us.' There wasn't the uniformity of looks because our branch of humanity had been allowed to diversify. The addition of Torriff, who looked every inch the warrior and Ko-Yo-Na, who *was* every inch a warrior gave 'us' a decided advantage. Restra was a planet of conformity. We had specialised in the opposite. Rani was exuding an aura of calm but it didn't seem to be having much of an effect on the representatives. They obviously had some ability to block the telepathy. It was like looking into deep water.

"A thought has just crossed my mind," said Taget of Laswin.

"As far as I can tell, not much of a journey," I 'sent' childishly to Rani, who rubbed a smile off her face with a quick hand.

"Perhaps we can invite you to our grid celebrations," he said, "To show you we are really quite civilised."

I restrained myself again.

126

"Are you attending Lef.G.'s combat lesson this evening Bea?" Ko asked as the meeting drifted out of the briefing room. The Restrans had been escorted to the upper docking bay by Mark Limbu earlier.

"Yes, are you going?" She nodded and gave me a friendly pat on the shoulder. We walked out together. "What do you think?" I added.

She looked puzzled. "What do you mean, about what?"

I tried not to laugh. "About the Restrans, don't you think they're up to something?"

"Of course they are." She looked kindly down at me and smiled, I hardly noticed the black teeth any more. "It's just a game Bea they must have done it on your planet, in your time?"

"Yes I guess so, but this game is bigger and played by giants."

Rani joined us and gave me a hug, a present for my impeccable self-restraint.

"Rani," I pondered the possibility, "There's no possibility they could have a blocking chip?"

"No, their technology isn't advanced enough." I thought about it, we were standing by the hydroponics doorway. I could see Zeke waiting for me further down the corridor; he was leaning against the bulkhead with his arms folded across his chest.

"You know, you did your best down there," Ko-Yo-Na said.

I felt my eyes filling with unwanted tears. "Why is it when someone says that it always sounds like 'you failed?'"

"I'll see you at the combat classes," she smiled again, swishing dark hair as she walked away.

"Are you going to have a go at me because I'm not sure I'm up to dealing with it?" Zeke uncrossed his arms and gave me a hug, the kind where your nose got squashed but you didn't mind. He also kissed the top of my head.

"I thought you were remarkably restrained in there, Mac bet me that you were going to match up the black eyes. I think he was a little disappointed."

We were walking down towards xenobiology. Neff.P. had told me earlier that he and Na-Es-Yan were examining some new space life forms they had found in a nearby star cluster, nearby being a relative term. "Do you want to come and look at space bugs with me?" I asked.

"Tempting, but no thank you," he said, mocking me. "We need to have a talk about our impending diplomatic visit."

"Space bugs first," I said pointing at the door.

"I'll see you in the upper restaurant; we might as well eat at the same time." He smiled and wandered off around the curve in the corridor. As I turned to go through the doorway I heard him shout, "Don't forget to wash your hands."

They looked like a shoal of fish, bioluminescent and seemingly affected by a tide. "What is pulling them?" I asked Na.

Neff.P. answered, they did that a lot; you asked one a question and the other answered, "We think they are attracted by the magnetic flip on the nearest planet," he said.

"I think I've heard of that," I muttered.

Na-Es-Yan looked at me. "You should have, your own planet does it every two or three hundred thousand years."

"Not in my time."

We examined the hologram display which showed millions of the creatures heading towards a small planet in an unstable star system. Several of the planets that surrounded the star were volcanic and lifeless, superheated with swirling storms that covered the surface. You couldn't distinguish any land or sea and the orbits looked to be irregular. The computer added a steady stream of information so that the hologram changed and moved moment to moment. It was like watching evolution fast forwarded.

Na clicked her tongue in annoyance, tapping the keys, trying to keep up with the shoal which dipped and dived as if they were feeding. The magnetic storm was obviously causing mayhem on the planet's surface and the weakness in the magnetic shield was allowing the cosmic radiation through.

As the hologram closed in on the planet you could see that the solar winds were hitting the layers of atmosphere and an amazing kaleidoscope of colours appeared like a magnified aurora borealis.

Neff.P. managed to isolate a small group of the creatures on the screen and the hologram changed to show the detail. They seemed to have no skeletal structure and resembled the strange shaped ghosts that lived in the deep sea on Earth. The computer tried to get closer to the small shapes but was having difficulty with their speed and the great distance we were from the system. Na was cursing in several languages which sounded very exotic. I memorised a few for future reference.

The space whale was a very big cousin to this creature. You could see that the smaller 'fish' was digesting something and as it passed through its tract the bioluminescence brightened for a moment. I could hear Neff.P. grinding his teeth in frustration. The computer just couldn't get a proper lock to assimilate information. I thought Na was going to have a heart attack.

The computer chattered in with some more information and the hologram shimmered outwards much to the combined annoyance of the scientists. The shoal was behaving in a most peculiar fashion. Almost as if some vast predator had appeared. The millions of creatures began a frenzied dance, travelling hundreds of miles in seconds, darting to avoid something.

We stood there watching. "What is happening?" I asked.

Neff. shook his head. "No idea."

"Have either of you seen this before?" He shook his head again. None of us could take our eyes from the unfolding story. It was odd; the corner of the hologram seemed to be malfunctioning, all the stars were gone. I pointed to the empty space.

"I can see it, but I don't believe it," Na-Es-Yan said.

"Is *that* a black hole?" I asked. They nodded in unison.

It blocked out the stars in a small swirl of angry dark energy, the creatures seemed to be dragged towards it. The readings from the computer were beginning to distort the closer the shoal got to the event horizon. In one last surge of the invisible tide they dived and disappeared. We exhaled as a team.

"Were they sucked in or were they attracted to it?" I speculated but no one was listening. The computer spewed out facts and figures which were eagerly pored over. Na's dark hair fell on Neff's shoulder and he gently pushed it away: she was oblivious to the touch, but he noticed that I noticed and smiled at me.

I left reluctantly and their flushed excited faces paused for a moment to acknowledge my exit. "Come back later if you can," Na said. They were staring at the hologram reruns as the door slid shut.

———

The upper restaurant was crowded with lunch in full swing. I smiled hello to several people as I looked around for Zeke. I felt a bit uncomfortable as for a moment it was like being invited to a party where you didn't know the host.

Zeke stood up and waved me over to a seat by the windows. He was with Torriff and Mark Limbu. I weaved my way through the tables and noise, making slow progress.

Mac was stuffing his face and talking at the same time, waving his fork dangerously close to Tom Hatherley's nose; they were sitting with three of the ship's marines. I stopped as Tom grabbed my hand. "Take me next time I won't be nearly so much trouble."

I recognised Doz as one of the uniformed trio. He looked up from a heaped plate of food and shook his head slowly. "She's a smart girl and knows better than to go anywhere with either of you."

I refused their offer of better company than 'that lot' and made it over to the table where Zeke was still standing. "Do you want me to get you something to eat before the hordes finish it off?"

"Does the pope live in Rome?" I answered.

"Actually no, but I think I get the meaning." He headed over to the buffet tables as Mark Limbu pulled out a chair for me. I sat down in some concern.

"Mark *where's* the pope?"

"She's on the Earth's moon."

"*Why?*" I said.

"There was a slight flooding problem."

Torriff had finished the green slime he called a good meal and was nibbling some dried leaves that looked like the debris from a gardening day. Zeke arrived with two plates, pasta salad and chocolate trifle, carbohydrates and sugar, which were two of my favourite food groups.

They waited in polite silence while I ate a few mouthfuls. I knew that I ate too fast but I grew up with an older brother. I looked at them. "What now?"

"Are you okay with going down to the planet again?" Zeke asked.

"I didn't realise there was a choice," I mumbled.

Mark Limbu leaned forward in his chair and touched my arm. "We don't want to load you down here, but the Restrans have asked that you accompany the assignment team."

"And why do you think that is?" I scraped the plate for the sauce that remained. They looked at each other. "Look, I can't get much from these people but I can feel the fear and I *know* I must have said this before, but they don't want you here."

"*They* don't have a choice," said Mark Limbu quietly. Torriff nodded in agreement.

"*They* don't see it like that," I said.

I slid the plate of trifle towards me and Torriff handed me a spoon with a thin smile which lit up his warrior's face. I savoured the taste for a moment. "You have a deadline for a trade agreement and the bodies of both your emissaries in the chapel, so I can see a need for last resorts. I just wish I wasn't one of them." I paused, "How did they know you had telepaths?"

"Word gets around." Mark Limbu shrugged. "They have been visited by several different ships. The emissaries may have said something, we don't know."

"Well, they want to know whether their self-imposed barriers are working to keep me out, they are paranoid about this. Did you talk to Rani?"

"Yes." Zeke helped himself to a spoonful of my pudding.

"What did she say?"

"She said what you said." He made as if to take some more trifle and I smacked his hand with my spoon. Torriff's brow ridges shot up and he looked horrified for a moment, it was obviously a hanging offence on his world.

I sighed, "Who am I going with?" Zeke patted my hand as I shook my head. "I think I'd rather go another round with Dino the dinosaur."

Zeke and I sat drinking coffee as the tables emptied. Tariq Azel came over, bringing a large bowl of sweets that he had made especially for me and the coffee pot. Torriff and Mark had left to sort out the details of the assignment.

"You said, 'you,' you have a trade agreement." He looked at me thoughtfully, his arm was resting on the back of the chair and he drank black coffee at a temperature just above boiling point which proved that all soldiers had asbestos lined mouths. He sprawled in the chair in the way that tall people seemed to sit in relaxed mode and his legs were an obstacle course for the unwary. "Can you see yourself as 'us' one day?" He added.

I sipped the hot coffee and said with quiet desperation, "I know that I have to take charge of the past, Rani has told me often enough." I paused to quantify my thoughts and realised he was listening.

Zeke had a quality of stillness, like deep water, dangerous and interesting. He also listened when you talked, a deadly combination. I didn't stand a chance.

He thought for a moment and then said very gently, "Time in its most basic form is made up of string particles," he leaned forward resting his elbows on his knees and paused, "It doesn't hold us in one place, it can tie us to what we were and what we might have been, but it also connects us to what we could be." He must have seen the sadness, because he added, "It ties us to the people we love as well, we stay connected."

I looked out of the windows at distant stars, whole worlds away, the edge of everything in the blink of an eye. "Rani told you to say something, didn't she?"

"Did you read my mind?" he said with exasperation, touching the small bump behind his ear.

"No, I can't get through the blocking chip, its intuition."

"Ah."

I drank more coffee and so did he and we sat in quiet companionship listening to Tariq singing something in a tongue that didn't go through the translator.

"This kissing," I said to Zeke. He looked slightly panic-stricken. I smiled, "I don't think I can do anything meaningful right now, if that's okay with you?" He didn't seem bothered at all, he just laughed at me and I wasn't sure why I'd said it, but I think it was because, when you got to a certain age, love wasn't hope, it was fear.

He leaned over and took my hand, "Don't worry about meaningful, I'd hate to give up the kissing though." I could see Tariq in the kitchen as he tried not to notice us and banging pots as quietly as possible.

"Are you dealing with all this? It's only been four months since you joined us." He still had hold of my hand.

"Is it only four months? I thought it was longer than that." I thought about my cottage and my time. "Back there," I said, "I was waiting for something to break the spell. Now, well, sometimes you're not always part of where you're from. You just keep hoping you'll find a place where your life is a better fit." I ate one of Tariq's sweets, it was excellent. "Zeke, what did the explorers, Gurber's race say when they first met us?"

He laughed, stretching out again and drinking the last of his coffee. "As far as I know, 'what took you so long?'"

"Bea!" An excited shout made me jump and I spilled coffee all over the table.

"Go ahead Neff," I said trying to wipe the spillage up with my serviette. Tariq wandered over with a wet cloth.

"You have got to come and see this!" Na-Es-Yan's shriek echoed into the Com/T, both Zeke and Tariq joined me in cringing against the volume.

"I'm on my way." I ran to the door and then as an afterthought ran back and grabbed the bowl of sweets that Zeke was just reaching for. "See you later." He and Tariq looked at each other and did that universal eye rolling.

The corridor was busy and I found myself performing a rather stupid dance with several people, the one where you both tried to get out of the way and didn't. 'Where's the renegade ship' was the most popular comment which was the twenty-fifth century's version of 'where's the fire.'

I made it to the xenobiology labs without my dignity but in record time and still clutching the sweets. I was out of breath as the doors slid open. The hologram was in larger form, taking up most of the room and I ducked so as not to hit my head on one of the outer planets in the unstable system.

It was like Wagner in full flow. The planet was being dragged towards the black hole and all the surrounding area of space was in the turmoil of old music. "Look at this!" Na, shrieked, pointing a shaking finger. Neff.P. was almost obscured by the solar system's sun, but he was nodding his head vigorously and pointing at the black hole.

I could feel myself drowning in the illusion that I might possibly be able to understand some of it, as the disk of the singularity funnelled and spewed the creatures it had swallowed a few hours before.

My breath slowed and I kept quiet hoping against hope that no one was going to ask me what I thought.

"Bea," said Neff.P. "What do you think?" The computer chattered out an entire book of information before I spoke.

"Are they bigger?"

"Yes," they both answered.

"What about older?"

"Yes." This was again in stereo. They certainly looked larger and they had a constant bioluminescence in a rainbow of colours.

"They look supercharged," I said to myself. Na's good ears picked it up and she nodded slowly. We were there with the ebb and flow of the shoal. In the absence of anything constructive to say, I ate a few of the chocolate sweets and chewed reflectively on my aching inability to grasp what was in front of my eyes.

I remembered something Rani had said about the early space slave trade. The captives came from a variety of non-space faring species and were ruthlessly exploited. They exchanged cultures and beliefs as they were forced to integrate and one of the stories that had become legend, were the slaves that were trapped in time as they were taken into space. The story was a lament for lost souls travelling forever. The description in the legend talked of 'lights in the curve of space dancing to the music time made.' I wondered if I was looking at the spirits of the wandering slaves.

My bangle jangled on my wrist against the metal bowl as I put the sweets down on a work surface. I think the light from the hologram was reflecting in the stones but it seemed to hold a memory that echoed in my head. It felt as if something connected me to the slave who had made my bracelet by the thread of time travelled.

"Do you think that this could be a wormhole with an exit in another universe?" I asked Neff.P. He nodded. I didn't really know what I was talking about but something must have been rattling around in my grey matter because Na was also nodding as she looked at the computer data.

"I just can't seem to see how it could be stabilised for travel. I mean we have a rough idea how we create a wormhole for a time-jump, but the technology is the explorers, we can't do it without them." She looked up. "You know, Gurber's race." I nodded this was something to file away for later. It seemed to me that nothing much happened without them being a big part of it and I was becoming more and more aware of their technological influence on all of the Star League races.

Neff.P. was looking at the detail for the creatures that were weaving around the planets and sun seemingly oblivious to the gravitational pull of the singularity. He gasped and pointed to a line of illegible maths for Na-Es-Yan to see. They looked at each other and then looked back at the information. "Well?" I asked, with exasperation, it was my turn to have the chest pain.

"It would seem that the creatures can produce some form of Exotic Matter."

"Right," I said after short pause, "that means?"

They both looked dazed. "Well," Na said.

Neff. cleared his throat. "Exotic Matter exists as something that we speculate about. It would have to be threaded through the neck of the singularity to stabilise it, these creatures are able to produce something that has negative mass properties and is able to exert a positive surface pressure." There was silence for a moment.

"I'm glad we cleared that up," I said.

I wandered back to my rooms via hydroponics. The trees rustled in the artificial breeze and the small birds swooped and dived much as the space creatures had done. Rani had told me that the xenobiology team had to produce a selection of insects for pollinating and for some of the birds and it looked as if they were feeding in the evening light. You could hear the sounds of the tropics, that familiar buzz of frogs and small creatures. It was more like a biosphere, except that the different species came from several planetary systems. It must have been difficult to work out what would exist side by side, a bit like life.

There was always someone working on the different fruits and vegetable plants scattered around the walkways on each level. I went down the stairs and headed towards the exit on level three.

"Hey Bea, come and see this." I recognised Moi Uhara who was the lieutenant in charge of the hydroponics and all the catering. He was slim and dark and not very tall. Tariq was standing next to him, he looked like the other half of a comedy duo and they were both grinning. I walked over to a see what had pleased them both so much.

"Oh, you grew *strawberries?*" I said. They both nodded. I had been trying to persuade Tariq about the benefit a few of these would bring to his pudding selection. The sweet pungent smell made my mouth water.

"Here, try one. You can give us your expert opinion." Moi picked one and handed it to me. I smelled it first much to their amusement. The scent filled my mind with warm summers and clear blue skies and the feeling was almost a pain in my heart. I tasted it. They both watched me, like parents waiting for a baby's first step.

I sighed, "Delicious," I said. "How did you manage to do this?"

Moi looked pleased with himself. "I checked the DNA library, we have an extensive collection of plants, but it doesn't always work."

I looked at both of them and felt an overwhelming urge to cry. The best part of life was the random acts of kindness. I put my arms around Moi and hugged him, his beautiful Japanese face turned a deep pink and Tariq laughed. He picked another ripe strawberry and put it in his mouth, he frowned, his face was a study in deep consideration and he tasted it like a connoisseur of fine wine.

"Moi," I asked, "How do you prevent cross fertilisation?"

He shrugged. "The DNA patterns are written with a code preventing it. We have strict rules on mixing different plant species. The same goes for the animals and birds in the biosphere. We can't do anything without permission from the captain." He helped himself to a strawberry, but made a face about the taste.

"Are all the Star League members as strict?" They looked at each other and then Moi shook his head.

I left them to it. They were still arguing about the amount of space Moi could allot on the different levels to grow a decent crop. But not of course before I had extracted a promise for strawberry trifle from Tariq.

Ollie greeted me with the 'I haven't been fed for an aeon' routine, which consisted of winding himself in and around my ankles so as to make walking a real danger. I explained to him about my day and asked him what he thought. He was keeping his opinion to himself which was unusual for a cat; they had an opinion on everything.

Ollie glanced up and meowed a second before the door chimed. Zeke came in carrying a bundle of clothes. I groaned at the now familiar garments. They looked exactly like the things I had worn on my previous trip down to the Restran surface, except for the fact that they weren't covered in blood. "When do we leave?" I asked taking the bundle.

He smiled. "Tomorrow morning." The words hung around the room like the smoke from a badly lit fire on a still day.

"You're not coming, are you?" I sighed. He shook his head and I turned to look out of the windows at the planet and its two moons. I rubbed my tired eyes with one hand and dropped the clothes on the seating.

I could feel him standing close behind me and without touching I could feel a frisson of energy and warmth pass between us. I took a deep breath. Sometimes the right words were harder to build than a wall. For life to have a chance you had to give up the hope that things could have happened differently and move on. I had spent a lot of time trying to make the past fit what I wished I'd been.

He touched the back of my neck and reached around me and I leaned back into the strong hands and gentle shadows of his good heart and didn't mind. "What were you going to say?" He said quietly, turning me away from the window. His face was inches from mine.

The barriers were still there and the old habits died hard, but when you were tangled in that fierce possessive embrace and fitted expertly in the crook of an arm, It was important not pass up on a good thing.

"Are you going to kiss me?" I found myself thinking; when thinking was possible that he was really good at it.

Rani didn't knock, nor did she look surprised when she saw us. I didn't know whether I felt annoyed or relieved that she'd interrupted. I thought perhaps I was relieved. I wasn't sure I could cope with the feelings that came with a relationship. In fact I was sure I couldn't.

She sat down and I went over to the kitchen to make tea, putting out cups and saucers, until my overactive hormones calmed down. I put cake on plates and looked over to see Zeke nodding at the information on a hand held computer that Rani was showing him. "She's got three marines and Pui and I thought maybe Ko-Yo-Na?"

"I can actually still hear you, you know," I said, with amused exasperation.

"We need to look after you, you're special." Rani said affectionately without looking up.

I muttered, "You only have to look out there to realise we are none of us anything special."

I tipped an old piece of toast that had been lurking on the work surface since early morning into the waste disposal and asked no one in particular, "How does the disposal unit work?"

Zeke looked up, distracted for a moment. "It is based on the microbe digester system it feeds on anything, including toxic waste. The results are recycled."

"Did Gurber's race provide the knowledge; they seem to have done everything else." They both looked at me with something like interest.

"No," he said eventually, "We thought that one up for ourselves."

There was a pause in the conversation as we ate really a good coffee cake that had appeared at the same time as Rani.

"This is good," said Zeke, scraping the plate with a finger. "Are you going to Lef.'s self defence class?" I nodded. "You better have some more cake then," he smiled.

"It's that bad?" I asked Rani.

She winced a bit and hunted for something positive to say, "Don't turn your back on Pui."

The class took place in one of the cargo holds behind the lower docking bay. There were about fifteen people, mostly marines. But Ko-Yo-Na and Pui were talking quietly in a corner as opposed to the marines who were talking loudly everywhere. Pui waved me over when she saw me arrive.

We stood in rows of five with Lef.G. standing at the front and performed a series of movements something like a Japanese tea cere-mony without the tea and what felt like advanced Tai Chi for the terminally double jointed. I was sweating after five minutes.

We then moved into two rows and we began a type of kick boxing, using the side of the feet and lots of defensive hand and arm actions. Lef. came among us correcting the angles of limbs. He said quietly to me, "You'll get it eventually some of these people have been practising Tran Ni for years." I was unable to reply due to a lack of oxygen. I followed the movements of the green combats in front of me and tried not to whimper. We stopped again and regrouped to practice hand and arm actions with a partner and a large foam-like defence shield. I got Doz and Sig.

We felt as if we were friends, because if you were not before, carrying a six and a half foot very drunk Amazon would establish good grounds for friendship. I watched them for a while, which gave me time for the chance to remember how to breathe. And then Doz held the shield for me to have a go. Sig gave helpful advice in the shape of, "Kill the bastard."

Lef. came over to us and patted me on the shoulder. "Remember to keep flexible, loose movements and maintain eye contact. You'll be fighting Ko, Pui and Buffers next."

I think I said, "Eh!"

"We're gonna die," said Doz very quietly.

"Is that it?" I said as Lef. wandered over to the next group, "What happened to the how to do this?" Apparently we finished the two hour session with a free for all.

"Huddle!" said Sig. We huddled. "Can you create a diversion?" He asked me.

"I can create a scene, I don't know about a diversion." I began to giggle with suppressed hysteria and sweat.

"Okay," said Doz, "that'll have to do. We'll jump Ko, you try and do your stuff with Buffers." I looked over at the very tall man standing with Pui and Ko. He was unfamiliar.

"Who is that?"

"Buffers is a medic, he's a good man, half Tyranox."

"Then what happens?"

"Then we die because Pui is a killer."

"This is what you call a plan, how am I supposed to tackle Buffers?"

They considered for a moment. "You could stick your fingers up his nose," said Doz helpfully.

"I don't care how bad things get; I am *never* shoving my fingers up anyone's nose!"

Lef.G. came over and looked suspiciously at the two marines, "Remember you two, no actual contact. Follow the moves through and *call* contact."

I looked at their grinning faces.

Rani was right about Pui; she put Sig on the floor in about fifteen seconds. I was not sure but I think I heard him say, "What a woman," even as Doz was pulling him to his feet.

I tried my newly learned skills on Buffers, who very kindly let me practice a few moves and didn't say much more than, "Ooff," when I accidentally caught him in the stomach with a wayward foot. Doz fared better with Ko, who was half a head taller than him but that didn't save her from a few good hits. She got him in the end and we all gathered around as he tried to catch his breath.

Ko explained the move to the top of his head as he staggered to his knees. "Doz, what you have to do is explode upwards." She demonstrated again with hands and feet.

Doz didn't look as if he could 'explode,' so I added helpfully, "Or if you can't manage that, a loud pop will do."

I dreamt that night that there was a storm at sea and the seagulls were in from the coast, flying on the back of the clouds and wind. They were screaming angrily and diving at each other above the house, like overexcited party children filled with too many E-numbers. I was afraid and when I eased myself awake in the early hours, I slipped out of bed and made a milky chocolate drink and some biscuits and sat quietly dunking, which was what ginger biscuits were created for. My dreams were no better when I fell asleep for the second time, curled up on the window seat. I woke to see Rani looking down on me.

"You didn't answer the door, are you okay?" She had a small curl of worry in the middle of the usually smooth forehead. "Bad dreams?"

I nodded wearily and wandered to the bathroom while she put hot water into a cup for me and made tea for herself. I wrapped myself in my tatty pink candlewick dressing gown that smelled of lavender and old thoughts. Ollie climbed up using his built in crampons and sat on my shoulder.

"Any side effects from last night?" Rani asked, sipping her tea.

"You were right about Pui, she's a killer." We drank more liquid and I sat so that Ollie could curl up for a postprandial snooze. We contemplated the early morning silently together for a moment.

"Do you miss home?" She asked, with interesting timing.

"I miss the house sometimes and I wonder if it's still there somewhere."

She looked at me, giving nothing away but her real affection and genuine friendship, which shone out of her. "Houses have histories instead of memories, maybe it's the same thing," she shrugged, "That way the past is always with us, like a piece of music that exists to be played in different times."

"I'll take that as a yes then," I laughed, "Though I can't imagine why it would make a difference if I knew whether my house was still standing!" She looked a little startled. "Oh come on Rani, I can't access anything from my time on the computer and people are so careful what they say around me it's funny."

She looked thoughtful. "It could affect the timeline."

"I understand that." I nodded.

We sat in silence again and then she took Ollie onto her lap while I had a shower and changed into the Restran clothing. She didn't offer to leave when I began getting ready and I didn't want her to; she just sat stroking Ollie until he rolled onto his back with his paws in the air.

I was ready.

"Rani, how far had the human race got when Gurber's race came along?"

There was a long pause, she sighed and then said, "Pluto."

"So basically, we wouldn't have left our own solar system without them?"

"We would have eventually, but it would have taken another two hundred years or so, give or take a scientific miracle."

I gave Ollie a squeeze and put him on the bed where he turned around and around making a nest out of the covers. Satisfied, he curled up and began the ritual of washing. I kissed the top of his head and he grumbled and buried himself further into the bedding.

The door swished closed behind us and we headed towards the lift shaft to go up two levels to the upper docking bay. "You don't think this is a good idea, do you Rani?"

She shook her head. "Captain Witherspoon has been given orders to send you down with the assignment team. She doesn't have the final word on this."

"I understand that too Rani." We wafted up to level one and my middle ear did its usual unhelpful yo-yo. I said, "But if I wasn't going you would be?" She nodded. We were at the doors to the upper docking bay. "What does the captain have the final word on, Rani?"

"Everything else but not you," she said, as she pressed the lighted door key and we walked down the steps into the chaos below.

It looked as if it were a home game between two rival college teams. There were several techs swinging like monkeys on the outer edge of the docking bay in the low gravity area. Gatt.R. gave me a cheerful wave in-between yelling at the techs and shoving boxes of kit inside the SSV. I saw Doz stick his head out of the side door of the little vehicle and take a box from Gatt. he smiled up at me. Things were going on as usual.

The absence of Jad Lassik's space vehicle filtered through the noise.

"Where's the mercenary?" I asked Rani. She shrugged. "I take it he won't be joining us on this trip?"

"He has another assignment, as far as I know," she said.

"One should be thankful for small mercies," I muttered.

We were standing at the side of the SSV waiting for the rest of the assignment team. Sig came out to stand with us and when he saw Pui coming down the steps into the bay, a slight flush crept up from his neck. She walked over to us, trying to avoid the hyperactivity. Gatt. yelled at the techs again who were still jumping from point to point right on the edge of the gravity area, "Are you going to fix that door?" They called back like a bunch of naughty children. Gatt. growled and muttered turning away. He looked at me and his good natured eyes sparkled and he raised his eyes upwards, wherever that would have been on a starship.

Pui looked stylish in her Restran clothing, not an easy achievement. Ko came over with Buffers, both were wearing the Restran layered look and I could see Doz, his face gleeful as he came out of the SSV. He opened his mouth and Ko pointed a finger. "Not one word Doz." He smiled, but wisely said nothing.

Zeke was running down the docking bay steps. He must have come from the bridge. He made his way though the cargo crews and came over to us. "You're cleared to go when you're ready." Sig tapped his forehead in a salute and the team began to climb into the vehicle.

Zeke caught my hand. "Think before you speak." He gave me a hug which was 'not observed' by everyone on the deck.

"Zeke," I said into his uniform, "Where were you born?"

"Vancouver. Why?"

"I'm having a moment here, don't interrupt." I hugged him back for a second.

"Sorry," he said to the top of my head, I could tell he was smiling without looking up at his face. "Are you ready then?"

"As I'll ever be," I sighed. I could feel some fear lurking at the periphery of my vision but I wasn't sure if it was mine.

I suddenly realised that this was the twenty-fifth century version of frontier country; that things were raw and unknown and people were either explorers or settlers or something beyond the law. The mercy of the elements was a question again, because when you were talking about the universe there was a big difference between 'nothing' and 'not anything.'

We had hitched a ride on the advanced technology belonging to another race and out here was really the edge of what was known. But human beings were an exploring species it was what we came from. We searched for our place in the universe and it was what took us forward. I wondered if that was how Gurber saw us. I also wondered who was pulling the strings of the person pulling the strings and I again thought of Gurber.

I went to sit in the empty seat next to Doz but Ko waved me into the pilot's chair, to collective groans from everyone. "Zeke says you need the practice," Ko-Yo-Na smiled.

I turned around and looked at him as he went out through the closing door. "Oh, does he, thank you," I said. Through the sarcasm he smiled his worry and was gone.

"Permission to leave the docking bay, bridge"

"Permission granted Bea and good luck."

I recognised Yas Molina's voice. "Thank you, Yas."

The alarms for 'exit' were sounding and everyone moved over to the safety barriers around the edge of the bay. I could see Zeke his arms crossed his face strained, standing next to Rani and Gatt. as I eased the SSV into a raised turn. I scraped the edge of the bay doors slightly and winced at the sound of metal on metal. I heard Tom Hatherley's voice on the main com, "Zudlocs Bea, I just fixed that door!"

"Well that wasn't too bad, was it?" I said to the captive audience behind me as we fishtailed away from the ship. I set the course in the computer as Ko read it out to me.

"Does it help if you stick your tongue out while you concentrate?" she enquired politely.

"Don't put me off, I might steer us into that nebula."

"Hey, we're loosing confidence back here!" I turned around as Sig released himself from the seat strap. It was odd how Doz and Sig's Aussie accents increased exponentially in collusion with their anxiety levels.

I was sitting reading through the information on the Restrans. Ko was checking the emergency packs with Buffers, and Doz and Sig were doing something with what looked like weapons. Pui had curled up on one of the pull-outs in the back of the SSV. She said she had been up most of the night looking after an ill Katinad crew member.

There were no more than a dozen Katinads on board the Starfire, they had a very pale green tinge to their grey skin and grey hair. I had thought that they were female and male like Lieutenant Commander Sofred who worked in the engineering department, but Pui told me that an endocrine disrupter organ kept them androgynous until they were ready to have offspring, after that they then had a male cycle. The Katinad uniform was a dark red and looked awful with their skin tone.

Sig left the weapon he was cleaning and gently covered the sleeping doctor with a blanket. I looked carefully away as he came back to the main cabin. It seemed to me that he would have been embarrassed if he had seen me noticing. I thought it was interesting that Doz hadn't teased him about it.

I went back to reading the information on the hand held computer screen. It was quite detailed about things like the main fuel sources, a type of methane hydrate, which was a compound of methane gas. I knew we had pockets on Earth on the ocean floor and it apparently looked like icy snow except that it was flammable. I didn't think it had been resourced on Earth in my time but these people had found a way to extract it.

Even music was covered in some length, but nothing of any interest about the military oligarchy that ran the planet and not one word about the grid except what we had added since the last visit. I wondered how it was possible to get something so wrong. But if you were doing a 'Captain Cook' in outer space maybe those things happened all the time.

There was information on the vehicles, dress, on geography, population density, vegetation and land use, even a detailed account of the commercial fishing in the main ocean. I was none the wiser and I felt as helpless as the moment that Dino the dinosaur decided to take a bite during our flight and fight.

The space station looked as peaceful as the last time I'd seen it and I pointed out the intricate patterns on the surface of the moon that made it look as if it might once have had water and therefore an atmosphere, to a disinterested Ko. Buffers and the two marines were sleeping in their seats which had obligingly turned into recliners. They did what soldiers had done in all times and slept while it was possible, in anticipation of the fact that sleep might not be possible soon.

The computer beeped for a course adjustment and I stuck my tongue out to assist the calculation and input of the new details. Ko laughed at me, it was an easy laugh, but it made my heart ache because old friendships were hard to find and new old friendships even harder. For a moment I felt the shadow of loneliness creep like damp through my bones, like walking through an empty hall after a party.

You could get swallowed by sorrow, it subsumed all light and the dead were silent, you couldn't hear them, I couldn't hear them and I had tried. This was a good place to let things go, on a journey to a planet near Altair and watch the sorrows drift like smoke out into space. We were made of stars and we should by rights return to them. I fixed my eye somewhere between the swirl of a nebulae and a star cluster, to the small hot core of a collapsed red giant, its stellar wind streams of charged particles rushed outwards in opposite directions in a display of bipolarity and I thought to the pinpoint of light at the centre, "**Goodbye.**"

"What's the matter?" Ko asked with some concern. I jumped and turned away from the windows to see a group of anxious faces looking my way. Even Pui was up on one elbow.

"Was I projecting, I'm sorry." I smiled a watery smile.

"If that means do I feel like I just lost the volleyball finals," said Doz, "Then yes, you zarling are."

"This is the Starfire, please confirm your status." We all jumped like a bunch of teenagers caught smoking behind the bike sheds during morning break.

I looked at Ko and shrugged.

She tutted. "Everything's fine Starfire," she looked at the computer readings, "We will confirm our descent in twenty minutes."

"Thank you Ko," Yas answered.

We went through the kit we had in the emergency packs for my benefit and Sig asked me for the third time if I had read the Assignment Standing Orders.

"It would be good if I actually knew what I was supposed to be doing here at some point," I grumbled, whilst putting back the contents of the pack.

"Why should you be any different from the rest of us," Doz answered.

"It was just a thought."

We set up for our descent through the bumpy atmosphere which was no better than the previous time, even with a daylight drop-zone. Ko sat in the pilot's seat, much to everyone's relief and we came down in an airport, there were flying craft of all types scattered around all a uniform dark yellow colour. It looked like a military base.

A group of people, headed by my favourite punch bag, was making its way over to the SSV as we gathered ourselves into hopeful heroes.

Ko was giving the Restran clothing a fight to the death and swearing quietly. She tapped into the Starfire on the main com. "We are down and about to meet the deputation."

"Understood Ko," the captain replied, "Keep us informed, Starfire out."

"That's if I can get this bloody outfit to cover me!"

"Ko, you used an English twenty-first century swearword."

"I pride myself on learning new languages, even ancient ones," she smiled smugly.

"I think I'm flattered." I shuffled behind her and smoothed the fabric which had been caught up on the pilot's chair. "You should try fighting a dinosaur in it."

The marines and Buffers were also in Restran clothing but with a few additions of their own. The weapons were concealed in plain sight. Doz and Sig had undergone something of a transformation, both of them were big and I found the fact that they looked rather mean strangely comforting, Buffers was half Tyranox and did intimidating as something of a birthright.

The hatch opened and Taget of Laswin came aboard, every inch the prime followed by the rest of the delegation and a good few guards. I ground my teeth into a smile.

"Are you okay?" Doz asked anxiously.

"I was just thinking about shoving my fingers up his nose," I whispered through the grimace that was me trying to smile whilst not growling.

"I'm going to regret saying that aren't I?" He whispered urgently. Doz stood back while I shook hands with the prime and the delegation, I then introduced the team, using what I hoped was their full name and title. As I came to Doz and Sig I realised that I didn't actually know their ranks.

Doz stepped forward and snapped off a salute. "Major Dizel and Captain Sayer Star League Marine Corps sir!" Taget of Laswin staggered back at the ferocity of the words.

"They are really very sweet when you get to know them," I said helpfully.

"Yes we are," added Sig in an out of the corner of the mouth whisper that was only just loud enough so that it gave one person a fit of the giggles.

The prime pretended he hadn't heard and waved us towards the airport terminal. "We thought you would like a guided tour of the facilities and some food before we begin the meeting."

The sky was almost all cloud cover but was still too bright. Ko and Buffers had been issued with protective contact lenses to prevent damage to their sensitive eyes. Tyranox daylight apparently looked like dusk. Ko had grown up there and Buffers had inherited the genetic propensity from his mother even though he'd grown up on Mars with his father.

I'd asked him the previous evening during the self-defence class about his family, because it had seemed rude to be kicking someone without getting to know them first. The lenses gave them a sort of blank look because you couldn't see the pupil and I wished for a moment that I'd been in the queue for them, but my eyes adjusted very quickly and the levels weren't dangerous to the rest of us, according to Pui.

We arrived at the entrance to the airport building to meet a large group of uniformed and decorated Restrans. Introductions began again. Each handshake was accompanied by a feeling of curiosity coupled with revulsion. Sometimes the revulsion won. The sense of self-importance was ballooning into epic proportions. A small creepy little man introduced himself as Sarwed of Naswell, he gave me a limp wet handshake and he seemed to me one slimy bureaucrat too many. "You're the telepath?" He hissed.

"Do I have a sign?" I snapped, my temper getting the better of me.

The sky seemed to darken in a moment and a heavy rain was followed by rumbles and jagged flashes of light. The creep still had a hold of my hand, which I removed with some difficulty. Doz moved quickly and stood next to me. Sarwed the slimy said, "Every time I see thunder and lightning I think about a higher power, don't you?"

"No, actually I think about my wet feet," I replied.

"Please come this way." We moved en masse into the building and out of the rain which was now lashing down.

"Ah, I see you have met our spiritual advisor," said Taget of Laswin with false joviality. I could imagine that the man handed out spiritual advice in much the same way as the Spanish Inquisition had.

We were followed by a large contingent of armed men a fact which hadn't escaped the two marines. I made a real effort not to look around but my neck muscles were going to need one of Pui's unrelenting massages. Doz gave me a quizzical look and I said very quietly, "No open hands here." He nodded and something intuitive passed between him and Sig.

The 'facilities' were uniformly dull and the civilians I was introduced to had been carefully picked and had, as far as I could tell, paid too high a price for their loyalty. We saw the latest vertical take off aircraft; they didn't seem to have anything that glided and a display of synchronised marching which made my face ache due to the fact that it was done outside in the pouring rain. There was wet and then there was really wet.

The conference room was set out with large plates of food on an oval table; the seating arrangements would have meant that we were each separated by at least two Restrans. Sig said a very quiet, "No," when someone tried to sit down next to me. He and Doz sat down either side of me and Buffers sat facing us, presumably so he could watch our backs. Pui and Ko chose seating to cover the other two points on the clock.

The plates of food were passed up and down the table and I watched what the diners did and took my food as they did one piece in each hand. No plates, no cutlery. These people had made a VTO aircraft but not a fork. I could see Pui nibbling politely on something that looked like black bread: no one put anything on the table. I ate, hoping that the food didn't taste as bad as it looked.

Sarwed of Naswell cleared his throat and smiled at me, it was a smile that reminded me even in my dreams that I was walking alone. "You don't look like a telepath, I've always thought of telepathy as powerful and dangerous." There was a silence as the eyes slid over to me like an audience in a tennis match.

"I think if you vilify someone it says more about you than it does about them." There was an audible sigh as if the point that was scored had approval. The ancient and evil eyes of Sarwed were however, narrowed in hate.

It was only a matter of time before the food was removed and the fun began. Not much had been said by anyone after the first shot across the bow but a few polite comments. If the obscurity of talking about the weather to someone living on another planet crossed my mind once I tried not to let it ruin my appetite. The need for chocolate cake however, was reaching the point of a medical emergency.

It was quiet. Taget of Laswin got to his feet and cleared his throat nervously he glanced over to Sarwed the slimy and began. "We welcome our distinguished visitors and look forward to an informative meeting."

The table was tapped with a wave of polite fingers. I nodded in what I hoped was agreement and then stood. I was sure that the reason I was down here was because I would be the antidote to diplomacy.

"Usually we get to decide ourselves where the line between past and future is. You don't have that choice." The faces around the table looked a little shocked. I went on, "You've been told that your planet is in the middle of a trade route, soon people from all over the galaxy are going to be turning up on your front doorstep wanting to do business, some of them won't ask nicely."

Taget of Laswin interrupted, "What is it that you want?"

"What do we want?"

"You must want something," Slimy Sarwed added, bringing new meaning to the words 'dripping with sarcasm.'

"What we want is for you to grow up, you don't seem to realise how vulnerable you are."

"Are you threatening us?" Again Sarwed spoke.

"Does this man speak for you, or can you ask your own questions?" I looked directly at Taget. His yellow skin flushed a deeper colour.

"He speaks the truth," Taget added, licking his dry lips.

I thought the slimy idiot couldn't have found the truth if he was looking with both hands, but I ploughed on.

"If you join the Star League you will be given protection and technology." I could see Pui and Ko wincing at that.

"And what do you want in exchange?" Sarwed asked. I looked and felt the reality of the situation falling around me like quiet dirty snow.

"What did they offer you?" The only faces that looked puzzled were the Starfire crew. The poker players at the table kept the cards to themselves.

All I could get was a sense of utter hopelessness and I realised that there wasn't a person at the table who didn't have some sort of blocking chip. Where the technology had come from was someone else's problem.

"I think I'm probably wasting my breath talking about trading rights, you seem to have made your decision, I hope it's the right one." My right foot touched the tip of Sig's boot and he moved slightly away from the table.

The meeting was over in the best sense, really before it had started, which left me with one or two questions as in why they had asked for a meeting in the first place and what was actually going on. Maybe they were hoping for a better deal. If they were, someone else would have to sort it out, but my intuition took over where my telepathy couldn't go and I was listening so hard for the other shoe to drop that my ears were ringing.

Taget of Laswin stood and looked nervously over to Sarwed, who nodded. "We will arrange an escort to take you back to your surface ship." The prospect of more soldiers than the already obviously considerable presence was making Sig look grumpy.

"What was that all about?" He asked me quietly.

I shook my head. "The Restrans have made a deal elsewhere," I replied. He looked so shocked that it made me smile.

"That's not possible!" I shrugged, it meant nothing to me. He added, "No one is supposed to make contact with a non-space faring race, it's against the law." I shrugged again. Whoever it was didn't seem to care much about the rules. Doz was almost stepping on my heels and Pui and Ko were behind him with Buffers bringing up the rear. It made me smile to think that I had been surrounded by people who could fight though I wasn't supposed to have noticed.

The tension was making it difficult to breathe and it was embarrassing how quickly we were moving towards the SSV, a troop of guards had broken into a trot to keep up. The bad feeling that had begun hissing in my ears at the meeting table was now a swarm of angry bees.

I looked around in some concern and caught the expressions on the faces of Taget and Sarwed, their ceremonial robes were flapping and rain soaked. The political leader was all fear and the spiritual advisor looked like he'd swallowed the devil. Doz leaned towards me. "Just how bad is this?"

"I think, just about as bad as it could be." I saw him reach for some sort of throat mic which was attached to his Com/T. I hoped that it meant the cavalry was on the way.

So much of telepathy was peripheral vision and out of the corner of an inner eye the whisper of something made its way through an army of anger and fear, a creature that moved like hidden thought. If it was about anything it was about making a connection and believing in it.

"Sig, we're going to get hit." He was slightly in front and Doz was still stepping on my heels. We were about a hundred yards from the SSV. Doz spoke into his throat mic again and at the same time he signalled to the three walking behind him by twirling a forefinger.

The door of the SSV slid open and the trotting delegation were almost alongside. A small hand touched my clenched fingers and I turned slightly to see bright gold eyes, she smiled and said, "It was a pleasure to meet you." I saw Sarwed snarl an order and she was pulled away back into the group made up of soldiers and politicians. We were going to make it to the door and I felt a sigh of relief as it worked to escape the collective tension.

I didn't know where it was coming from but I spun around, looking at the Restran guards, their puzzlement, the obvious machinations of the leadership and then around at the grey buildings. They were here somewhere, whoever 'they' were. This wasn't much more than a set-up, more fool us. My hands reached out towards Sig and I gave him enough of a push to make him stagger sideways. He turned and looked at me with a 'what was that for' expression. I walked into his space for no more than a second.

A sharp pain much like a stitch caught me and I put my hand against my right side to help the ache. I looked down, my hand was covered in blood and it was seeping through my fingers. "Sig," I whispered, he turned again and I showed him. My knees buckled and I pitched forward and for a moment the face that swam before me was unrecognisable, an almost feline puzzled sharpness, with eyes from another time. I could hear Doz shouting and I could feel his hands bunching on my clothes as he hoisted me in front of him using his body as a shield. I couldn't move, my limbs were ragged, Pui held my face, trying to keep my airway open, which was not hugely successful and they moved towards the door of the SSV.

Taget's clown-like grimace appeared in my line of sight and Sig shoved him away with one hand, walking backwards, his gun held out, Buffers and Ko were either side of him.

Taget and Sarwed were shouting, "It's the rebels, they managed to get through our security." Then, "Let us help, we have a medical team, our facilities are just here." The Restran politicians were desperate to keep me on the planet. They were frightened because making a pact with the devil could do that to your nerve endings. But when it came to demonstrations of power the 'others' had won hands down. I wondered why I couldn't speak and I tried to think at Ko, but her mind was closed with tension, although she looked at me and seemed to realise that I was trying to contact her.

The rain seemed to be falling in slow motion and each drop was a rainbow of colour. Wisps of history filtered in and out of my head and momentary flickers of the past ran like an old film, interspersed with the present snapshots of reality.

As the door of the SSV closed, I saw the cavalry, in the shape of two heavily armed space-runners from the Starfire, the sound of small arms fire and then a booming noise which must have been the runners getting us clear. I reached out to feel a furious Mark Limbu and tried to get him to throttle back on the damage. He wouldn't listen; telepathy meant people could still put the phone down on you. I could feel Pui ripping clothing and see the blood on Doz's uniform, the lift-off had both of them swearing and clutching onto the side of the pull-out that I was lying on. "It was a sonic bullet." Pui looked into my eyes. "It just grazed you..." Her voice trailed off.

Sig came over and his anxious face tried to make contact with Pui. He put his hands on my shoulder. "I think you tried to save my life, they would probably have killed me."

I tried my voice, "You're not going to tell me off are you?" I whispered.

He croaked a hollow laugh, "I was going to say, thank you." He was radiating a sense of failure and I didn't have the strength to reassure him. He and Doz were both very angry.

The speed at which we were returning to the Starfire was sucking the gravity from the SSV and the view from the windows was blurred. Or maybe that was just me. Pui seemed to be doctoring, most of which was uncomfortable and Buffers was trying to attach the emergency equipment, he smiled at me, his teeth were black like Ko's. I could hear her talking to the Starfire and to the two space-runners, who were following us up from the planet.

My ability to breathe became something of an option. Buffers said, "Pui!" and the room spun a little. Doz and Sig were standing in the doorway. Doz still had my blood on his clothes. I felt like a lone sailor in the dark and I tipped backwards into other places.

Rani looked awful, she had blotchy eyes and her pale face had a green tinge. I could see the ceiling of the corridors moving at speed.

"Rani," I whispered. She looked at me. "Next time someone has to go down to that planet, you go." I got hold of her hand and we held on tight because one of us was drowning.

My body was covered with small jelly packs which suckered onto my skin in relevant places. I could feel that something was helping me to breathe and there was a yellow cover over the wound site which bubbled in and out alarmingly. The stretcher acted like a hovercraft and it was similar to the one that I had seen Mac on when we returned from our last visit. It moved silently of its own accord and without wheels. I thought that I must be feeling dreadful as the technicalities of it didn't intrigue me for more than a second or two.

I had managed to hang on to the small crumpled piece of material in my fist and I showed it to Rani, she looked puzzled, but my voice gave up when I tried to explain. **"What is it?"** She thought.

"I need to speak to the captain."

She nodded and tapped her Com/T. "Harriet, can you come to the medical bay?" I thought peevishly about the fact that Rani was on first name terms with the captain.

"I'm on my way."

"Will you stop doing that," Pui said crossly as we flew through the medical bay doors on level one. "Your 'vitals' go through the roof every time you do." Rani stepped back as the medical team surrounded me. I recognised faces and voices and gentle hands full of concern and I felt my apprehension slip into unease.

The sensation of the wound leaking blood was making me queasy although the fluid was being recycled as fast as the emergency kit could manage it. Pui was sending out waves of tangible relief when she had me transferred to the more sophisticated bed in the medical bay. "Are you in pain?" She peered into my eyes with a small scanner. I nodded. She tapped a few lighted keys on the console at the side of the bed. "This will alter your body's endorphin levels." The impossibility of breathing in and out seemed to ease almost immediately.

The door swished open and the captain came over to the bed. She looked at Pui and they exchanged the unspoken words of question and answer between people who had worked together for a very long time. Then she looked at me. "Well," she said, "That's it." Her lips tightened, "They had their chance."

"What happens now?" I asked.

"Now, they're on their own."

"These people are bad but we both know that there's worse," I said.

She shrugged. "Do you think you will be able to tell us who they've made a deal with?" Her eyes looked tired and she was upset and angry at the same time. I realised that she was holding my hand and my eyes filled with tears. Her telepathic blocking chip meant that I couldn't read her mind but the feelings still came through.

"I got the impression of someone right at the moment of the shooting." As I described the person I had seen a sense of incredulity crossed just about every face in the medical bay, even the ones who were pretending not to listen. "The Restrans had blocking chips and I was aware of other technology that was in place that didn't belong there." She looked horrified.

Rani moved over within eyesight. "You could sense that?" She looked impressed.

"Yes, it sounds a little like music played off-key. I think they were trying to work out how to use it." I smiled. "One of their technicians was suspicious of the blocking chip and didn't turn it on."

"What about this spiritual leader?" The captain asked.

"Well I thought he was slimy, small-minded and evil!"

"I take it he's now aware of that fact?" She said dryly.

Pui interrupted, "Yes, though it was hard to get Bea to come out of her shell." I handed the scrap of material to the captain.

"What's this?" She asked.

"It says, 'don't forget us, we are not these people?'"

Rani took the scrap from Captain Witherspoon.

"Can anything be done?" I asked. The captain took hold of my hand again as she shook her head. I closed my eyes on the tears and thought of the woman who had given me the scrap like desperate people everywhere and in every time, who made the most of nothing and who lived in hope.

The room was quiet and for a medical bay it was gentle on the eyes, there were lots of plants and pictures. A really pretty statue of a child stood next to a small stone waterfall. The lighting was in pools over the beds and the overall colour was a peaceful blue. It looked more like a health club than a hospital.

I could see Pui in the little office area. Rani was asleep by the bed in a reclining chair she was curled up like my cat with her hands under her chin. Her eyes opened and she smiled. "I thought I could hear you thinking, and I don't look like your cat!"

"Well not the fat orange part anyway," I thought to her. She smiled a pale watery smile.

Pui came over when she heard Rani talking to me and began checking the computer readings on the side of the bed. The breathing apparatus was gone and so was most of the pain. Now it only hurt when I moved not when I breathed.

"Rani, do people shoot at you on assignments?" Pui did one of those descriptive oriental snorts.

"Not usually, no."

"I think maybe I need more practice then."

Pui went back to her office and the door of the medical bay opened. Ollie came in followed by Sig and Doz. "How does he do that?" Doz asked, looking at my cat with a puzzled expression. The room gave a collective shrug.

The marines were carrying a mixture of chocolate cake from Tariq and flowers from hydroponics, both slightly crumpled looking. My cat jumped onto the bed and after coming up for a nose kiss he curled against my side purring. I rubbed his head and felt an internal ache ease away as if I had been waiting for something.

I could see Pui's face as Sig and Doz came over to the bed. "Sig, you've got problems."

"No I don't," he looked puzzled.

"Trust me Sig," I said, "You do."

In a voice that could strip several layers of paint from old tin, Pui said, "Captain Sayer, could I have a word please?"

Rani and I cringed and Doz was out of the door and gone, he looked as if he'd had some practice at quick exits. Ollie yawned. The conversation was one-sided and consisted of some serious chest poking by the short doctor. The six foot plus marine just looked at her with a bemused expression on his face. Rani and I pretended not to be eavesdropping and did our best to shut out every telepathic thought.

But the gist of it was that she blamed Sig for my accident. He added his own feelings of failure to the guilt Pui was loading on him and his face closed down. He apologised stiffly to her and nodded to me as he left through the medical bay door.

I felt terrible about it and was going to say something when Rani shook her head. Pui looked stunned for a moment and then shot out of the door after Sig. "Did you do something Rani?" I asked incredulously. She held up her thumb and forefinger about half an inch apart and shrugged.

"Zeke's down on the planet isn't he?"

Rani made a face. "Not on the planet exactly, he and Mark Limbu are looking for the shooter."

"Is that possible?" I arranged myself around my cat.

"They had to get here in something."

"Who are they?"

Rani made an 'I'm not sure we're ready for this conversation' face. "Do you remember we talked about the renegades?" I nodded. "Well, it looks as if one of the families has moved into planetary development."

I thought about that for a while and about being shot. "So, the Restrans made a deal with one of the families to somehow hand me over." Rani nodded. "Not much of a deal," I said. We sat in silence except for Ollie's purr which resonated against my abdomen. "Restra means 'home' and Restran means 'the people' in their language." Rani nodded again, hearing what I didn't say. "I bet Zeke was angry," I smiled.

"He was furious," Rani said. "I found him kicking the back of the SSV."

"Did it work?"

"He said it did."

I thought for a bit. "I might try that, I'm angry myself."

"I'll just bet you are," Rani answered.

Pui came back in dazed and slightly rumpled it looked as if she'd caught up with Sig. I wondered if we were going to get any details. After checking the readout on the side of the bed she went over to her untidy office space and sat. Rani looked disappointed and kissed me on the head as she wandered out the door promising to bring more cake.

I became aware of a whispered conversation and opened my eyes to see Torriff with Pui. He looked dreadful. Ollie was on his usual morning walkabout, which included the several places on the ship that did food. His tummy had begun to scrape on the ground when he walked.

It was day two of my enforced visit to the medical bay and I could feel the 'living in a box' sensation which had crept like damp into my waking. The bed was gathered around me in a series of coils and form filling lumps. Not uncomfortable just intrusive.

I stretched and the two conspirators jumped guiltily. "Whatever is wrong with you?" I asked mid-yawn. Torriff sighed and came over to me. "Torriff!"

He tried to look dignified which was not easy when your skin was hanging in shreds like an old snake.

"I'm having my annual shed," he explained. "I don't usually leave my rooms," he paused and shuffled a bit like a nine-year-old meeting distant relatives for the first time, "I wanted to see how you were."

"I told him to use the holo/vid," Pui said with exasperation.

I leaned over to Torriff and gave him a hug and a kiss. "I'm fine; it's nice to see you even if you are shedding all over the floor." His face deepened by three shades and he shuffled even more. From behind his back he produced a copy of Sense and Sensibility. It was beautifully bound and must have cost him a fortune, a collector's item at a time when most books were in private collections, museums and libraries.

He stayed for a while chatting on about the different authors and we agreed to disagree about romance being a reflection of the social development of species. When Tariq arrived with a large slice of chocolate cake and a mug of coffee, Torriff sidled out. I watched him go and so did Pui. The shades of unhappiness had drifted for a moment from his heart, but not for long. Loneliness was an illness without a cure.

"When can I get back to my own room?" I whined at Pui, restless in my immobility. Tariq looked embarrassed and fussed around the food he had brought, rearranging the fork for effect.

"When your liver finishes growing back," Pui said absent-mindedly, searching through the mess on her desk.

There were several different types of incredulous silence and this one fell into the category somewhere up the top end of the Richter scale. She looked up, tiredness and exasperation fighting for supremacy on her face, exasperation won. "Please tell me you're not going to go all twenty-first century on me?" She bustled over to the bed. "We use a stem cell therapy and a repair system, don't panic," she added, as I lifted the covers on my wound area. Tariq left in a hurry; looking pale but I had managed to grab the plate before he launched himself towards the door.

I could see the large damage site through a jelly pack and wondered why I hadn't looked before. "Pui, did you get Rani to do something?"

"You'll be out of here in maybe two days."

I didn't know why I was surprised, but I could understand why I was angry. "Why didn't you just tell me?" I felt like sulking but there was no one but Pui to see and she looked devastated.

"We didn't think you'd handle it well."

"I don't handle being handled well Pui, everything else I think I've been okay about."

"Yes," she said quietly, "You have."

I looked at the cake and sniffed a bit in self-pity. "Do you want some of this?" I pointed at the chocolate cake with the fork. This was a peace offering on my part.

Pui smiled a tired smile and perched on the end of the bed. "Can I have the top layer?"

"No, you get the bit *without* the icing."

I didn't know how old you had to be before you spent more time looking back than looking forward. The medical bay was quiet; Pui had gone to get some sleep and one of the other medics was on duty. He sat in a pool of blue light over at the desk. I must have been linked up to something that told him I was awake because he came over to the bed.

"How are you feeling?" He smiled. His face looked familiar but I couldn't remember his name.

"It's Couzins," he said, as if anticipating the question, "Can I get you anything?"

"Have you got time for a chat?" I didn't want to be alone with my thoughts.

He looked around the empty medical bay. "I think I might be able to squeeze you into my busy itinerary." He settled down on the reclining chair by the bed, leaning forward slightly, so that his elbows rested on his knees. His pale face and grey eyes were earnest and young.

I sighed, "I miss the World Service it's the only thing that gets me through the night at home."

"We still have that."

"You do, I mean we do?"

"It's called something different where I come from."

"Where was that?"

"Ganymede, Jupiter's moon, my father was a biologist for the Space Trawler Service, the same place as Sig and Doz, except Doz Dizel's family worked on the tankers."

I needed to think about this information. The most the marines had said was that they were part of an Australian space colony. Apparently it wasn't uncommon two hundred years ago, in the twenty-third century, for whole towns to up and move. They were encouraged to immigrate out to the colonies in the solar system, as in the Middle Ages when the crusaders persuaded the population of England to travel across Europe to the Middle East, in some misguided religious belief.

"I know there's lots of rock and ice on Ganymede but what do you do for an atmosphere, do you live underground?" He hesitated for a moment, looking partly insulted over his home being referred to as a rock and partly impressed that I might know anything about Jupiter's largest moon.

"We have biospheres, huge, big enough to hold a town."

"Like the ones under Earth's sea?" He looked surprised again.

"Yes, not quite as big as Pacific or Atlantic City, but it's the same thing."

"Tom Hatherley was born in Atlantic City."

He looked as if he hadn't known that and I felt as if I had scored a point, which was pathetic.

"What do they call the World Service now?" I asked.

He smiled, "The Solar Service. It's based on Earth's moon, they transmit to all the planets and colonies it's my mum's favourite broadcast. I prefer something with interaction. A holo/transmit is a bit one-dimensional for me."

"The World Service is now a hologram?" I could sense correspondents spinning in their graves. We sat in silence for a while, both thinking about home.

He got up to go. "I could get you some holo/discs to look at?"

"Thank you, I think I'll pass." I reached for the book that Torriff had left me. Jane Austen was a good way to spend a long night and turning pages had a healing magic. Couzins wandered back to the desk in the corner after checking the readings on the side of the bed I was in.

"How am I?" He nodded and gave me the thumbs up sign.

We both started as the medical bay door slid open. A tired and dirty Zeke came over to me. He looked at me for a minute and then he reached down and wrapped his arms around me, in one of those, 'I don't know what to say' hugs. It was smelly but good. "You know you're as tough as a Parnian Warthog." He threw himself into the chair by the bed exhausted and scrubbed his face with his hands. Couzins sitting in the lighted desk corner snorted with suppressed laughter.

"I think I'm going to be insulted, but not tonight." It didn't look as if now was a good time to ask about his trip back to the planet. I sighed, "You should be in bed." Couzins tried to disappear unsuccessfully, into his desk drawer. Zeke nodded and got up to go weaving with tiredness and kissed me. Poor Couzins was doing an impression of a nine-year-old forced to watch a soppy film. "Come back in the morning, I've got some gossip."

"Is it good?" Zeke asked, perking up considerably.

"Oh yes," I said. He left, almost somnambulistic. I went back to my book and my thoughts and Couzins stopped hiding.

We did patient and medic for a while and I settled back and closed my eyes. I was actually quite good at being ill because I'd had a lot of experience and it was not about how you felt, but how you felt about what was happening to you.

"Can I ask you a personal question?" I opened my eyes, expecting something about Zeke and wondering what I was going to answer. I nodded. He paused, the shadows around him easy for a change.

"Why did you come, I mean, it must have been really hard to leave," he paused, "Your own time?" It was a good middle of the night question.

"Well one of the things that scares me is not finding 'it.'" He looked puzzled, as well he might.

Finally he said, "What's 'it?'"

"Ah, that's another thing will I know 'it' when I see it?" He nodded as if he understood.

I sighed, "I wish this room had a window."

He turned, looking pleased. "We can fix that." He tapped a few keys on the wall and a hologram of a window appeared right by my bed. I rippled my fingers through the space and stars. "What are you doing?" He smiled.

"I'm touching eternity."

"If you don't let me out of here I am going to start breaking things!" I tried to outstare Pui. She looked steadily back at me. "You said yourself I'm doing well and I'm not linked to the bed." I sidled onto the floor and walked a few paces towards the door feeling the sweat beading on my face. "Please?" Rani arrived just in time to stop me falling over. She helped me over to the recliner chair. I felt like a wet lettuce, all limp and soggy around the edges.

"Do you think you're able to walk back to your rooms or shall I get a hover-chair?" Rani asked me. I looked at her and then back at Pui. The doctor was smiling.

"You let me whinge on and you were going to let me go anyway, what is wrong with you?"

Pui came over and looked at me then she leaned down her face inches from mine. "If you don't rest I will know and you will be back here in a nanosecond." It felt as if freedom was just the other side of the door, so I meekly nodded my head. Rani had brought some clothes and I changed as quickly as I could which was at a snail's pace, behind the holographic screen. "Make sure you're back here tomorrow, I need to give you one more scar tissue treatment."

The whole world for the previous four days had been the upper medical bay, so it was really strange to see the corridor stretching away from me and the distance made me feel odd. Rani hooked an arm around my waist and we walked like a pair of old friends, talking about nothing much. I stopped at a window in the outer corridor and touched the surface, drinking in the vision of a dying sun surrounded by interstellar dust, the remnants of its red giant stage blown outwards, obscuring the hot centre. There was something about space that reminded me of the oceans on Earth, an entirety of change and sound. I could feel the movement like I could feel the waves on a beach inside my head. As there was not a chance that I would use the lift shafts we walked slowly towards hydroponics on level one. Rani put her arm around my waist again and I leaned heavily against her, glad of the nearness of her strength and the warmth of her friendship.

The corridor was empty, but I could feel the buzz of busy people behind each door we passed. Hydroponics had the desired effect on my frazzled nerves and we sat for a moment on a bench sniffing in the rich scents of the exotic flowers and plants. I looked up to the dome and listened to the birds squabbling overhead. Colin the parrot was up to his usual tricks, chasing the smaller birds with vindictive glee. They made me feel dizzy in their rush from branch to branch. He seemed to have had some more tail feathers grafted on to replace the ones that Ollie had removed.

I sighed, "This feels so good." Four days in the medical bay had felt like a lifetime, even with the mojo Rani had used. She cleared her throat and her face had that 'I'm going to say something important' look.

"Tell me we're not going to discuss the meaning of the universe?" I asked in panic.

"No!" She looked at me with exasperation.

"Thank you."

"I was just going to say that these people were not what it's usually like out here." We paused for collective thought and a bird, hopeful of some strictly illegal lunch crumbs, landed on the arm of the bench.

"They were civilised in their own minds," I said.

"I suppose it depends on whether you believe conflict or curiosity drives science." She reached out to the bird and it hopped onto her hand and then flew away in disgust at finding nothing there.

"We have had a bit of difficulty with that one," I said.

She looked pale with anger for a moment and said, "They shot you Bea, they made a bargain with murderers and they shot you!" I nodded. She reached for my hand and we shared some guilt and fear in the seconds between the flutter of a bird's wing and then resumed our slow walk down the two levels and out into the corridor.

The door to my rooms slid open on a sense of relief. It had felt like the first ascent of Everest on a bicycle. "I am starving!"

"I heard you were on half rations in the medical bay," Rani said dryly. She indicated the table. "I think Tariq has left you a little snack." I walked over to the table and smiled at the plates of food. Chocolate cake, with butter cream filling, ginger biscuits, strawberry trifle, in fact everything you needed for a speedy recovery.

The door chimed and opened and Ollie walked in closely followed by Mac Ibarra and Tom Hatherley. "How does he do that?" Tom asked, looking at Ollie.

"Have you got any scars?" Mac looked hopeful as he put his arms around me and squeezed. I showed what was left after Pui's treatment, a few faint puckers, but they both nodded, seriously impressed. "You should keep those don't let the doctor zap them all away," Mac added as he sat down.

"I'm shattered," Tom said kissing me on the top of my head and rubbing his eyes as he threw himself into a seat and pulled the plate of biscuits over towards him, "Zeke has had me chasing interstellar dust clouds all over the quadrant." He got an elbow in the ribs from Mac. "What," Tom choked, his mouth full, "How's she not going to know, she's a telepath!" Rani had started making tea, 'no comment' written all over her shoulders and I began to laugh. I reached for a spoon and stuck it into the trifle, helping myself to a huge mouthful of the sweet sticky cream. Tariq had a really creative gift with anything that wasn't technically good for you.

The talk around the table was of work and the grumbles were the kind that people who appreciate every day the job that they do, made when they were tired.

The door chimed again and Zeke and Ko-Yo-Na came in, both looking exhausted. "I heard you had been released," Ko said, as she smothered me in a bone crushing hug, "Oh good food that's bad for you."

Zeke was pressing a corner of one of the cupboards and removing two objects which he twisted into spare chairs. "I didn't know they were there," I muttered. No one was listening. "So have you found anything in the interstellar dust clouds?" I asked Zeke, who gave Tom a really filthy look. Tom shrugged mid-biscuit.

"We could talk about it later," Zeke said tiredly.

"Or we could talk about it now," I replied helpfully.

Rani sat down next to me, she had Ollie tucked under one arm and that look on her face. She put her hand on my shoulder. "We have found a few things but not any trace of the family that we think put the Restrans up to trying to kidnap you." She stopped and looked at me, working out what to say next.

"I'm Okay Rani," I reassured her. The feelings of the others around the table were muffled as if their blocking chips had been turned up a notch or two. It took me a moment to realise that was exactly what had been done and I wondered if Rani had told the captain that my abilities had improved.

"We found a small SSV that was in orbit," she continued, "It had been abandoned and I wondered if, when you were feeling stronger, you could take a look and see if you can get anything from it." All eyes were on me as if waiting for some extreme reaction. I shrugged, these were not my fears my own nightmares were made up of other things belonging to other times.

"Sure," I answered.

We talked and laughed and ate and pretty soon most of the food was gone and I was falling asleep at the table. The psychology of trifle as a coping strategy probably needed some more research but empirical evidence suggested it worked.

Rani gave me a hug and left with Ko and the boys, which was how I saw them; they scooped the last of the cake and went, sticky with tiredness and irrepressible youth. Zeke gave me a hug at the door, like a high school sweetheart wrapped up in the body of a warrior. He started to say something and I interrupted him, "I'm fine. Don't beat yourself up about it." He looked really annoyed and held my arms and shook me gently.

"You can't live your life carrying the weight of what other people expect, it's not weak to need people, let it go."

"I can't, not yet." He sighed with exasperation, raising his eyes, and then kissed me on the nose and left.

I sat waiting for nothing, looking out at the universe and trying not to think too much about anything. Once in the middle of the night at home, I had heard the survivor of a concentration camp talking about how he had lived, when so many of his friends had given up and died. He said 'never give in for a moment, because a moment is forever.' The trouble with this was sometimes when you needed to stop fighting you couldn't.

It didn't seem much of a surprise to be out in the corridor and heading for Gurber's room. I think he had a way of contacting you that had nothing to do with the layers of speech and thought with which we surrounded ourselves. Gurber was strangely quiet, he glowed a little around the edges and we sat looking at groups of stars in faraway places, they swung in and out of view and I felt as if I was flying through space, on a journey, or maybe he was looking for something. Either way I felt calmer than I had for days.

"**People get so far into darkness.**"

I didn't think I had asked a question, but if I had done, that would have been the answer. **"I'm not sure it's about the Restrans."** I thought back.

He was still taking us through stellar fields and he bubbled a bit and then settled into silence. I had got up to go, tiredness wining over restlessness for once when I heard him say. **"We were alone."** That had to be something I would think about later.

Ollie was pleased to see me when I got back to my rooms and he sat on the loo seat lid while I had a bath, purring and patting the odd froth bubble that I blew his way. I made a nest of the bedclothes and pillows and like refugees safe from the storm, my cat and I curled up and slept.

The ship was a small SSV of a type I had not seen before. Ko and the engineering team were working on the computer systems which looked as if they were fried. "Is it strange that they abandoned it?" I asked Rani. She shrugged. I touched the battered surface, getting ripples of sensation from the damage.

Rani leaned into the vehicle. "Can we come in now Ko?"

I didn't hear the muffled reply, but the engineering team came out talking and laughing, they smiled at me and four of them wandered over to talk to Gatt.R. leaving Ko standing by Rani, both of them looked expectantly at me.

I climbed in through the hatch door and glanced around. The ship's set-up was similar to the Star League SSVs, as there was only so many places you could put a seat and a few computer keys, but everything seemed to be made for much larger people, more Ko's size. Rani indicated one of the pilot chairs and I sat, feeling like a small child with my legs swinging above the floor. The configuration of the flying controls seemed strange and I couldn't read the hieroglyphic script that was all over the console.

I was aware of the docking bay crew looking curiously at me through the forward viewing windows. The noise of busy minds began to recede and I put my hands on the pilot controls breathing in the feeling and the spaces in-between.

It always felt like a combination of putting on someone else's badly fitting and smelly shoes and being sucked into an unwanted dream. I was conscious of Rani hovering about in the background trying not to influence me with her own thoughts.

The awareness of fear and the sensation of another person sitting in the seat next to me were superseded by the huge and frightening figure coming into focus and I looked at the face I had seen when the shot was fired on the Restran planet. The features were clearer, still feline but rougher and the mouth was screaming orders. The SSV dipped and weaved into the dust clouds and a larger ship loomed out of the shadows. Zeke would have been furious if he knew just how close he had come to catching them.

The face I saw reflected in the luminous surface of the control panel was human, Earth human, a frightened young man. His hands became my hands and his fear was metallic in my mouth.

Evil wasn't a long dark tunnel, or a place without a heart. Sometimes it was just the flat blank darkness at the centre of an eye. I could remember looking into the face of a little old lady in some town in the mid-west of America and finding my thoughts frozen. Some people were born evil. I watched through the feeling, as the SSV docked in the larger ship and then gasped with shock as the young man tried to take off again when the tall alien had left the vehicle. The SSV crashed into the side of the docking bay and bounced into the void beyond.

The hatch was still open, maybe he was trying to get away and maybe he didn't care any more.

I found myself grabbing and wheeling away from the pilot seat and into Ko and Rani. The shaking subsided and I sat back down again. Somewhere out there a body floated in space.

The description I gave Rani and Ko made them both uneasy. Tall, slim, male, slightly human, smooth skin, not much hair cut in stripes back from a high forehead. I realised the impression of a cat-like quality came from his eyes which had a feline pupil and what looked like extended incisors instead of eye teeth. He was dressed in a tight fitting suit, which emphasised the muscular shape. He reminded me in some ways of Jad Lassik, something that made me feel even more uncomfortable.

"Well?" I asked. We were still sitting in the SSV, Rani was perched on one of the observers' seats and Ko was leaning against the main console, her arms folded and a frown deep in her forehead.

"It sounds like the Samura family." Rani looked really puzzled.

"Is that what you got?" She nodded. I realised she'd got the dead body too and I thought I would never be that calm about violent death, particularly when you felt as if it was happening to you which was the penalty for being inside someone's head.

The long distance clairvoyance was, for me, the worst of it. Before that I had avoided touching anything that would give me too much feedback, unless the object was very old, in which case the sensation was like a really bad black and white film on fast forward. I could usually maintain some sense of reality when it didn't matter any more.

"I don't understand," Ko shook her head. "Samura don't do this."

"What do they do?"

"Mostly drugs and planetary artefacts," she answered.

I thought about that for a moment and then thought about something that had filtered through the experience, "Rani, are they human?"

"They are third generation transgenetic," she answered almost absent-mindedly.

"Right," I said, "That explains everything."

Ko said, "It's when you mix the DNA of species at the genetic level." She spoke with a combination of contempt and something else that might have been fear.

"Who'd be stupid enough to do that?" I snorted with derision. They both looked slightly embarrassed. A flash of inspiration made me ask, "Rani, is Jad Lassik a transgenetic?" A solid wall of silence greeted the question.

"Rani this," I waved my hand around, "Isn't foolproof, could I have got it wrong?"

She shook her head. "I know, but I got exactly the same thing." It might have been my imagination, but mixed in with the worry was just a tiny bit of admiration. It was typical that I was good at something that made banging your head against a brick wall look like fun.

Buffers peered in through the hatch door and looked at me, "Unless you wish to spend the next week in the medical bay?"

"Ah!" I raced out of the door and across the cargo deck as he dodged out of the way, much to the amusement of the different crews and the engineering team.

"What's happening Bea, is someone eating your trifle?" Gatt. shouted.

"I'm late for a medical!"

He frowned. "That's not funny the doc won't let that go."

"Oh really," I answered, as I ran up the steps, out of breath before I got to the top.

I was out of that door and down the corridor and through the medical bay doors as if all the ghosts of the past were after me or the ones in my dreams anyway. And if I had damaged any crew members during my flight then they should have learned to get out of the way quicker. Actually people were very understanding when I yelled back over my shoulder that I was late for Pui, even Jenny Smith who I bowled over, laughingly said, "Go," when I had stopped to pick her up.

Pui's face was scary; she smiled at me and pointed to the clinical table. I wondered if grovelling was an option. I decided to see how it went and hold on to some dignity for the moment and if things got really sticky I could do pathetic excuses.

"Do you want to get rid of all the scar tissue?" She looked at me, her eyes deep with concentration. It actually felt like a loaded question, so I thought about it carefully.

"I think I would rather not have to look at it."

Pui put a pale green liquid into a small cylinder and pushed the tube up against the puckered area on my right side. I could feel a cold sensation spreading around the old wound site.

"How does this work?" I asked, without much hope of understanding the answer, twenty-fifth century medicine was not unbelievable, just incomprehensible.

"It's based partly on TGF Beta 3, which appears in foetal wounds and partly on stem cell therapy. The treatment will take a few days as the healing process is increased, but you won't be able to see anything soon." She added, "Did Tom and Mac try and persuade you to keep them?" I nodded and she smiled. "They are really into battle scars, they think it makes them look experienced, gives them kudos."

"Well, *I've* had about as much kudos as I can manage." I hopped off the bed and went over to her as she put her torture kit away.

"What?" She asked. I put my arms around her and hugged really hard and for a moment she hugged me back.

"Thank you," I said. There was a flicker of feeling on her face, which for Pui amounted to an emotional rainstorm.

"What about the scars you can't see, can I help with those?" She had her hand on my arm and she shook it gently, as if trying to get my attention.

I sighed, "Sometimes it's not always possible to 'deal' with things Pui, I know that. I usually do my best to avoid those kinds of memories, but its part of this job. I will just have to add it to the three o'clock in the morning list like everyone else does." She nodded, because most doctors had a fairly long three in the morning list.

"How did it go in the docking bay?"

"I think I just confirmed Rani's worst suspicions." I scowled at the thought. "Although I'm not entirely sure what that is right now, but I bet it involves more running around getting shot at." She laughed, which was good, as we both knew the experience in the docking bay had been horrible and any other response would have reminded both of us that the shadows in the corner of my mind were real.

We headed out of the medical bay door and down the corridor together. A large group of squabbling scientists were getting into the lift shaft which was weird as it looked as if we would step onto their heads if we got in after them. They were actually long gone but I still looked down and gave myself a bad case of vertigo. You could see the ripple effect between the floors as they got off. One of them looked up and waved at me as he left, I waved back. Pui was smiling as we walked on and I felt like medieval man studying an escalator.

The upper restaurant was buzzing with life and coffee, or the ghastly grey stuff the Des.Rans. drank for the same effect.

"Have you seen Torriff lately?" I asked Pui as we made our way over to the food table.

She shook her head, "No, he's still shedding, I think."

"Pui, I was just about to have something to eat!"

"Something tells me you still are."

"So Pui," I said, heaping a plate with enough chocolate cake to keep the average black hole satisfied, "How is Sig?"

Her face was turned slightly away as she filled a glass with an aromatic tea. The back of her neck turned an interesting rose pink which travelled up to the tips of her ears. She didn't turn around but said waspishly, "You'd better not be smiling."

I sat in the first level hydroponics, looking up at the dome, the sprinklers began slowly as if a summer rain was due, then worked up to something like a tropical storm. In about five seconds I was wet through. It felt wonderful. The whole thing only took about a minute but the feel of rain on my face was worth a soaking. As I got up to go and dry off somewhere I looked into Sig's astonished expression.

"Did you not hear the sprinkler warning?" He looked me up and down, taking in my dripping hair and clothes.

"Yes," I said feeling as if I had been caught poking my tongue out at the teacher. "I came in here to get rained on," which didn't sound quite right.

"Okay," he said. "Are you too wet to have a chat?" I sat back down on the seat.

"Actually, I don't think you can get any wetter than wet, if you know what I mean," I speculated.

"I wanted to say," he paused and leaned his elbows on his knees, looking sideways at me.

"This is about the saving thing isn't it?" I asked. He nodded and I sighed, "I'm sorry."

"I need to do my job; next time let me do it?" He held out his hand and I took it as if we were shaking on an agreement.

We sat for a moment and I steamed gently in the warm moist air. I put my hand on his shoulder. "Look at it this way it brought you and Pui closer together." He threw back his head and laughed a deep sound that made everyone who had heard it smile. There were several other people around because I wasn't the only one who missed rain.

"Zeke is right you are tougher than a Parnian Warthog!"

"Somehow I'm not surprised that the reference had travelled so far so fast," I said dryly, "Because you're a bunch of gossips, although I must remember to check the computer to see what it looks like."

Sig looked a little worried. "Obviously the comparison was with the hog's temperament, not the way it looks you understand?"

"It must be ugly, don't panic, Zeke is safe."

He sighed with relief. His Com/T buzzed and he listened to the closed message, saying, "Yes, on my way," in answer.

Rani came in through the doors as Sig left and they nodded to each other in passing, she sat down leaving a space between my dampness and her dryness. "Feeling better?" She asked.

I nodded. "It fulfils a need," I thought for a moment. "Did you ever," I pointed upwards at the sprinklers.

She smiled. "It has been known."

"So I'm not completely crazy, then?"

"Don't tempt me!"

We sat for a while and I fingered the material of the clothes I was wearing, it was nearly dry.

"What's this made of?"

Rani was watching Colin the parrot, who was making his way towards us by stealth mode, using leaves and other birds as cover. She looked over to me. "It's a type of Teflon. We use it for all sorts of things."

"Like the pans?"

"The pans?" She looked puzzled.

"Never mind," I said, smiling. "Time and distance; one minute your cooking on it, the next, you're wearing it."

Colin was getting dangerously close and he looked as if he had something on his mind, so we decided to leave with dignity, while we could.

The corridor was a gentle shade of blue merging into grey, tasteful, although I found the constant colour change confusing, as if you had walked into a house you used to own and the new owners had redecorated.

"Rani," I asked, as we passed a group of marines, "Is everyone wearing blocking chips now?"

She looked sideways at me. "Yes." She sighed, "Look, all these people have been security cleared and psych cleared, to a very high level."

"I don't doubt their integrity, I'm just puzzled. Is it a privacy thing?" We were coming up to Rani's rooms and she indicated as the door opened, inviting me in. She banged cups onto the table and added a large plate of cakes.

"It's as much about protecting you as it is them, unguarded thoughts are very tiring." I looked at her with that look my mother used when I was twisting the truth to suit a situation. I seemed to be able to do impressions of her without trying as I got older.

"I know I'm getting better at telepathy and I know the blocking chips are being turned up. It's like listening under water."

I picked up a cake, all icing and walnuts and licked my lips. She reached out a hand and I squeezed her fingers with my sticky ones and then we got down to the serious subjects in life, as in the latest gossip on Pui and Sig and if it was actually possible to eat three cakes without getting indigestion.

The techs were getting kitted up as I entered the EVA room on the lower docking bay. It was like being back at school in the changing rooms before sports day. That smell of slightly unwashed excitement, I felt as much out of place as I had then.

My kit was in a locker with my name on it that revolved forward as I keyed in my code, replacing one just emptied by an eager young woman. It was an efficient system that made the most of a small space. I could have done with something similar for my shoe collection.

The name on the woman's suit was Tova Gordon. I had never spoken to her before, as a group the techs tended to keep to themselves; she had the space shuffle that betrayed their job description and gave me a warm smile. "You're doing safety/rescue drills today Bea?" I nodded and she signalled good luck.

As I did my best to wriggle into the suit unassisted, I realised that they would be watching for my every humiliating mistake. It was always good to have an audience. There was a lot of joking as Mac came in. I watched the techs check each other out and in groups of six and eight they moved into the airlock and out onto the surface of the ship. I could hear them talking and laughing, the type of humour that people who did a dangerous job used for communication.

While I waited for Mac to suit up I examined the bottom of the space boots which intrigued me, I could just see a pattern of overlapping leaves like a sticky tape that wasn't actually sticky. "How does this work?" I pressed my palm to the base and pulled it away.

"It reacts with whatever it comes into contact at the molecular level." He put the boot on the floor and got the other one out of my locker together with my helmet. It sounded vaguely familiar.

"Something about gecko's feet and Van der Waals forces," I said, thinking out loud.

He sat down next to me. "Yes, did they have this in your time?"

"Not quite, but nearly, I remember reading something about how a gecko clings to a wall in one of the Sunday papers."

"Sunday papers?" It was his turn to look puzzled.

"Oh how I miss that whole Sunday thing, summer morning, fresh coffee, newspapers, out in the garden in the sun." I looked into the middle distance and sighed.

"I'm still sitting here," Mac said, gawping.

"Right gecko boots." I pushed my feet into them and attached the tiny connections to my suit. Mac checked my progress. Part of the safety exam was being able to dress yourself which was not something I'd ever failed at before, unless I counted the weekend drinking black Russian cocktails after my first free fall jump.

"We had Teflon in my time too; of course we used it to cover pans. Although I *think* NASA scientists invented it," I mused, struggling with a tricky bit of tie.

"Pans?"

"Yes pans! What am I, a dinosaur?" I grabbed my helmet and shoved it onto my head, seeing stars behind my eyes.

He looked amused. "I'm sensing a little nervous tension, are you worried about the exam?"

"Oh very funny," I said, as I sat down again, checked my boots and began clipping the helmet attachments. "At least this technology is ours and not on lease from Gurber's race."

Mac finished his suiting up, deliberately leaving some of the connections undone for me to find on pre-exit checks. "Most of the head-up displays are made of the plas-glass they gave us. It's the same stuff as the windows on the ship, highly pressure resistant." I thought for a bit as I pushed the keypad on the suit to activate the air supply.

"Why do you think they gave away the technology and encouraged advancement?"

He shrugged, which was not easy in a spacesuit. "I don't know, maybe they were lonely."

That was what Gurber had said to me, I thought, 'we were alone.'

The pre-exit checks went well, with me 'finding' Mac's oversights and I called the bridge to advise EVA. "Have a good one Bea," came the reply from a helpful Jenny Smith.

"Thank you." I muttered into my helmet not quietly enough, "*I'm really* looking forward to it."

"You know sarcasm is really a twenty-first century thing, advanced civilisations don't do much of it any more." Mac was laughing at me through the shine of scrolling numbers in his visor.

"I was going for a vintage look."

We entered the airlock and I checked the door closures and the suits one more time. I nodded my approval of all the safety checks and Mac gave me the thumbs up. I called the bridge one more time and then opened the outer airlock doors. The dive into space was like jumping into water in the first breath of cold sea. It was a completely separate element and yet like a place I remembered in the heart of each cell.

I did the shuffle hop that kept me attached to the surface of the ship and watched my safety line float away in an unseen wind, bowing between me and Mac and the ship's tie.

It didn't take him long to start behaving 'strangely.' I went over to him and asked the appropriate questions, "'Do you have a problem? Do you have air?'" It would have been much more fun to say 'what's the matter you stupid idiot,' but the bridge was listening in and I didn't think the captain would approve of me rewriting the space safety rules.

I checked the suit contacts and peered into his helmet, the usual dutiful reports from the schematics, the navigation, thrusters, computer, fuel, were all missing. Mac was making some rather pathetic expressions. I sighed and called Mayday, requesting assistance from anyone nearby. Of course the bridge replied that no one was in my vicinity though the place was full of whooping techs, all offering helpful, anatomically impossible suggestions.

Grabbing Mac by a handful of suit, I tried to bundle him back towards the airlock, it was like trying to shove a pig up a greasy pole.

He did his best to be an uncooperative lump, a role that earned him a few judicious pinches in appropriate places.

I looked behind me, the doorway to the airlock wasn't getting any nearer and I swore in exasperation. There would be no help from the techs and Mac was getting heavy.

Snapping off the safety tie attached to both of us I tapped the thruster controls and got a short burst that propelled us towards the airlock. As we gathered speed I called the bridge and asked for an emergency opening of the doors. They slid apart just as we reached them and we ended up in a heap in the corner. Mac was upside down. I think I heard a muffled cheering from outside. The bridge however had maintained a stunned silence.

I looked into Mac's upside down helmet, his legs sliding down the wall as we gained gravity. He opened his eyes. "I don't zarling believe you."

"You're alive, stop whinging!"

Torriff's rooms were on level four, I tapped on the door and a quiet voice said, "Who is it?" I tried to think of something clever, but nothing came to mind.

"It's Bea, I've got treats." The rather brown crumpled leaves apparently constituted a treat for a Vanerian, according to Tariq Azel. I was going with my usual chocolate cake. The door slid open and a tatty Torriff smiled a greeting. He didn't look quite as bad as the last time I'd seen him. We stood grinning like idiots for a few minutes. "How about inviting me in Torriff?"

"Ah!" He stepped aside and waved his hands in welcome.

The rooms were dimly lit with small hologram lights in the corners which were columns of changing colours. There were lots of reading materials in a variety of representations, parchment, books, computer crystal discs, even an old scroll.

He went over to the kitchen while I satisfied my nosy nature. I picked up a holo/picture of his family, two cute children and a serious scholarly wife. I wondered how it was possible for these people to be at war with us for so long and not for the first time, contemplated the possibility that 'we' could have started it. It was just another question that would have been evasively answered by everyone on board. "Torriff, why were we at war for so long?" He dropped a cup and it clattered a bit before it settled, but it didn't break.

"Ah, well it was the usual mess." He sighed, which people did a lot when I was around. "At first it was about territory, then politics, then misunderstanding and finally mistrust prolonged the misery."

"So it was just your usual stupid war then." He nodded and passed me a plate with the chocolate cake and the unbroken cup filled with aromatic tea.

We sat in silence for a moment, interspersed with some serious crunching on his part.

"You must be fed up with being stuck in here for days, how long does this usually last?"

He finished a mouthful of leaves and smiled. "At home it would be part of a cleansing ritual that lasts fourteen of your cycles. Here, well, I am nearly ready for company."

"Tell me," he asked after a pause, "Is it true that the doctor and Captain Sig are acquainted?"

"Why Torriff you old gossip!" He looked horrified for a moment until he realised I was teasing him. "They do seem to be acquainted," I said smiling. He smiled back, a sweet child-like expression in the face of a warrior. I tried to fill him in on the latest goings on, it seemed to me that he hadn't had many visitors and I wished I had come calling sooner.

"I hear your safety test went well?"

Well maybe he hadn't been completely without contact, I snorted, "The captain told me I spend too much time with Tom Hatherley and Mac Ibarra."

"The captain is a very wise woman," he said dryly.

We paused for more tea and cake. He looked at his books shuffling through as if trying to find something. "What was the greatest romance of the twentieth century do you think?"

I pretended to give it some consideration, but there really was only one answer, "Lennon and McCartney." He looked puzzled, as well he might. "Can I access your computer?"

He nodded and I tapped in my personal code and a thumbprint. Rani had input my music collection for me. I picked a favourite and the amazing sound of 'the long and winding road' filled the rooms and spun around my head. Torriff was having trouble containing his emotions and he got up to look out of the windows. I window gazed myself until the last of the notes drifted into silence.

I had heard people talk about exile, about the pain and the desperate need for seeing your home, your country, now I could feel it, radiating from him like a shock wave. We might have talked about it but my Com/T went off. "Bea, can you come to the bridge?" Rani asked me quietly.

I felt like questioning her timing, but she knew where I was. "I'm on my way, Rani."

I didn't have time to run up three flights of stairs in hydroponics, so I braved the lift shaft nearest to Torriff's rooms. He watched me go, like a house-proud frau, waving from the door.

The corridor to the bridge seemed unusually busy, which was never a good sign. The doors slid open onto a full house. The captain smiled hello and I walked forward to stand next to Rani. It didn't matter how many times I came up to the bridge, it still felt as if it was a place I shouldn't be.

Most of the workstations were occupied and the central hologram was lit up like a Christmas tree. Jenny Smith, who flew a lot for a physicist, nodded to me from the pilot seat and Yas Molina winked as he leaned over her shoulder. It was quiet but the undercurrent of feelings made me wince a little.

I felt, rather than saw Zeke join us, realising that I hadn't seen him for nearly two days. I wondered what he had been doing and then I realised I had missed him, which made me nervous.

The front view screen began to show a recognisable shape among the stars and as we got nearer the level of tension in the room increased, it was like descending on a scuba-dive too quickly.

The shape lurched into a ship in an all too familiar list of abandon-
ment. This was becoming a habit and I sighed with the thought of
what was next.

It was hard when you knew what you were supposed to be doing,
but not really why. I reached out about the same time as Rani and we
both gasped at the damage. Most of the inside of the ship was
smashed in a frenzy of wanton destruction, possessions were scattered
around and the smell of blood and fear permeated throughout the
empty corridors.

"Anything?" The captain asked, which made me stumble back into
my skin, Rani of course returned with dignity and barely a flicker.

"I think the ship is Dalgety family; it looks like a migrant cargo."
Rani looked puzzled as did everyone else. I didn't know enough about
the situation to actually be puzzled.

"This doesn't make sense." Captain Witherspoon got out of her
chair and looked at the ship through the view screen. I could tell what
was coming next without needing one iota of telepathy.

"Okay, take Bea with you. Mark, Rani and Bea are on their way to
the docking bay."

"Oh good, I haven't been shot lately," I said, very, very quietly. Rani
and I moved towards the doors and I thought how nice a good
grumble would be, but I kept it to myself.

"Try not to get shot this time Bea," the captain smiled at me. The
woman had ears like a school teacher.

We met Commander Limbu in the upper docking bay, Sig and Doz
and two other marines were kitted up for their version of a small war.
Doz handed me a pair of slim fitting overalls that would not go over
my trousers and top. I looked hopefully around for somewhere to
change.

Rani had disappeared to the back of the SSV, so I joined her. I
began to giggle with nerves as I hopped from one leg to the other,
trying to change quickly. The overalls did great things for Rani and
absolutely nothing for me. They were the usual Teflon protection
material with feet in them, like kiddies' romper suits. I was not sure
what they could protect you from, but the techs wore them and they

were notorious wimps. "Do we usually have time to change somewhere a bit more private?" I asked as I gathered my clothes and shoes. She shook her head with a smile and shrugged.

We walked back around to the waiting team and Gatt.R. took our clothing from both of us. Sig gave me an emergency pack and we climbed into the SSV. Mark sat in the pilot seat and I heard Doz mutter, "Thanks, I though we were going to get one of Bea's exits again."

"I'm not deaf yet Doz!"

They both grinned as they strapped in, Rani and I took the two seats by the window consoles. The take-off was text book smooth and the techs at the edge of the docking bay waved as we passed. I found myself waving back like a child on a carousel.

The approach to the wrecked ship was also smooth and we wheeled around for a closer look. It was a mess, even worse close up. I could see the impact marks of heavy fire, much more than would be needed to disable the craft. Whoever had done this had set out to destroy it completely.

Mark Limbu was taking readings and talking to Sig and Doz at the same time. He moved the SSV around to a docking bay and we glided in, narrowly avoiding some floating debris near the entrance.

"The gravity seems to be still working at the far end of the bay," Mark said, as he set the SSV down by some steps.

"Air would be good," I muttered.

Doz smiled. "You're easily pleased."

After checking the quality of the air supply outside, Mark signalled the marines and he went with them to do some sort of reconnaissance. Rani and I sat like the uninvited guests at a really bad party, waiting for the all-clear, something that made both of us feel apprehensive.

"Who is Dalgety?" I asked into the quiet.

"He's the head of a family that usually run migrants." She sighed and closed her eyes, leaning back against the chair. "I keep thinking something will change, but all we seem to be doing is the same old dance, even the players don't change." She sounded bitter, which astonished me, I had never heard her so down before. I forgave her the mixed metaphor as she looked so sad.

"So this is not the same family that tried to do away with me on Restra?"

"Samura," she said. I nodded and tried to process the information which was not possible as there were too many gaps in it.

"So what's your take on this?" In the absence of my own brain cells someone else's would do.

She shrugged, "Who knows."

We both jumped when Sig peered around the open door.

He smiled. "I've often wondered if it was possible to sneak up on you two. Now I know." He beckoned. "Okay, time to use your skills." We both stood and mentally stretched nothing if not ready.

I heard one of the other marines say quietly to his friend, "The captain must be going crazy with both of them over here." The other guy nodded in agreement. I looked at their name tags. Asguard, tall, black with green eyes and Cree, shorter and blonde. Asguard was the one who had spoken.

"Hey Asguard," I said. His head swivelled around to look at me.

"*I'm* going crazy being over here." He looked mortified and Cree roared with laughter. They went off towards the steps and did the 'looking for the enemy' procedure that marines did so well.

Rani and I split up at the top of the steps, I went off with the two jokers and Rani got the long straw with Sig and Doz. It was not easy working with someone new, but they were careful and quiet and I began to relax. Mark Limbu was nowhere to be seen as Gurkhas tended to do sneaking around on their own.

We walked down a long corridor not too dissimilar to the Starfire's. It kept passing through my mind and feeding my unhelpful imagination, that this could have been us.

A doorway loomed to our left and I paused, backing up slightly. Asguard stood just in front of me and he looked behind him, gesticulating with his chin as an enquiry. I pointed to the door and they both raised their eyebrows, Cree pointed to himself and then at the door. I listened for a moment and then shook my head.

They looked at each other and signalled with their hands and then Cree pushed me gently away. Asguard nodded a count and they burst through, making me jump with the explosion of noise.

My Com/T went crazy and I could hear Captain Witherspoon saying rather urgently, "What's happening Bea?" I went into the room after the marines and tried to fit a living breathing thing to a shape, the marines were doing their best to stand in front of me and check the room at the same time, their Com/Ts were buzzing with the rest of the team's questions.

"Just a second captain, as Dolly Parton would say, 'I'm busier than a one-legged man in an arse kicking contest.'" There was a sort of hiccup noise, which I took as an acknowledgement. "Quiet please!"

They stopped as there didn't seem to be anything to kill and we stood still for a moment. In a corner of my mind and the darker corner of the room, a blanket moved. I pointed, gently touching Asguard's shoulder. He walked over to the blanket and whisked it away while Cree stood with his gun aimed at the lumpy shape.

"Eh?" They didn't always go in for long sentences in the marines.

I walked over, Cree put an arm in front of me and we all looked. I felt like saying 'eh' as well, but one had to think about sentence construction, so I went with the classic, "What is that?" They both shrugged. 'It' was small, furry and shaking.

"Are you feeling anything?" Cree asked me.

"Apprehension."

"It feels apprehension?" He looked puzzled.

"No, that would be me." They both sighed with frustration.

"Oh, great," Asguard said, "A telepath with a sense of humour."

"Rani, do you know what this is?" I closed my eyes and tried to send her a picture. Rani must have seen something she recognised.

"It's a piggiwig! I haven't seen one for years." Her voice through the Com/T was wistful and I got a momentary mental flash of a past memory. A small girl with plaits cuddled the ugly creature before me; the sadness was throat-catching.

"Is it dangerous?" Asguard asked.

"Does it look it?" She laughed back. We looked down; 'it' was trying to disappear into the carpet. I put my hand out.

"Wait!" Cree pulled out a scanner of some kind and looked at the piggiwig through it. "It might be booby trapped." He did a thorough check and then nodded and I reached out my hand again. It was about the same size as my cat, round, tubby and covered in rather coarse hair. It trembled, shoving a flat snout into my fingers and began licking my palm.

"Well, now what?" Cree asked. The creature was not cute; however Rani's memory was clear in my mind.

"We take it with us I'm not leaving anything on this ship." They did some raised eyebrows but I had already scooped it up into my arms, where it snorted and squeaked and began sucking at a strand of my hair.

We looked around the room, the marines checking corners as if looking for a clue, where there obviously wasn't; it had been some-one's home rather than just travelling, one of the crew probably. Nothing much was out of place, there were hologram's of unattractive children, games, clothes. They had left in a hurry, throwing down a holo/story on the table. I could still feel a little of the fear that hung around the room and wafted out into the corridor, like footsteps in an empty house.

"Come on ugly," I whispered, "I know someone who will love you."

"Hey Cree, she must be talking to you!" Asguard laughed quietly, as we walked further into the ship.

"Didn't you have a dog when you were a boy?" I asked Cree who was looking at the piggiwig with puzzled distaste.

He shook his head, "No, grew up in an orphanage on Mars after the war, I didn't have my own anything until I joined the marines."

I went for irony, in the hope that it would be better than weeping over the matter of fact way he'd delivered this remark.

"You need to find your inner child Cree," I said, smiling. He looked a bit stunned but smiled back.

Asguard snorted, "He needs to find his inner something." They prodded each other with lethal fingers and then got back to the job in hand.

Some people thought that marines were so thick you had to water them once a week, but apart from the fact that they all seemed to have been issued with an appalling sense of humour, they constantly amazed me with their intelligence and humanity.

I struggled with the creature, moving it to a more comfortable position on my shoulder. It was sleeping and snoring gently in my ear. Having found a place of safety it clung like a limpet. I could have done with a snooze myself. Suppressed fear always made me sleepy.

We covered more corridors and more empty rooms. The ship had been abandoned in a hurry and all along the passageway were personal items that had been discarded in the rush. I tried not to look at a small toy, grubby in its loved sadness.

Nothing and no one jumped out at us. There was food in the canteen, cold, on cold plates and workstations still giving data to thin air. Cree tapped his Com/T. "Do you have anything?"

"No, do you," came back the echo from Sig.

"Apart from the ugliest looking 'hogdog' I've ever seen, no." Cree looked around one more empty room. "What do you want us to do Captain Sawyer we've come to the end of our rope here?"

A short silence followed. "Head back to the upper docking bay, we'll meet you there. Rani says she thinks she can sense something." A short pause followed. "It might answer some questions." Not mine it wouldn't. We turned around and went back the way we had come, the rooms were empty, but I wondered if there was something frightened cowering on one of the other levels, that needed rescuing.

"What about the other levels?" I asked Asguard, "What if we missed something?"

"Don't worry," he smiled, "If there's another ugly around here, the 'clean-up team' will find it." I didn't know we had a 'clean-up team.'

The fact that it was supposed to be a learning experience wasn't lost on me. I tried to look as if I was learning something just in case someone was taking notes, but it was difficult when you were creeping down dark corridors carrying a snoring, smelly creature. We had entered the ship about half way up, on what must have been their cargo docking bay level. The Starfire's cargo bay was on the lowest level and her upper bay on level one. It occurred to me as we went down the corridor that 'meeting' in this ship's upper bay was going to involve a trip in a lift shaft. The piggiwig whimpered as it picked up some of my rising anxiety.

The doorway cracked open with a little help from Asguard's fingers and some swearwords that didn't go through the Com/T. He leaned into the darkness and spat. More unintelligible swear words. They both looked at me. "The lift's not working; do you think you can manage some access ladders?" Cree asked. I tried to suppress a smile of relief.

Asguard pulled off the panel to one of the maintenance shafts and looked inside, it smelled even staler than the corridors. "We're using the ladders, Sig." Cree clicked his Com/T.

"Yes," Sig replied, "We got that. At least Bea will be happy," he added.

Both of my marines looked at me and I smiled in acknowledgement. They shook their heads. Asguard fashioned a sling out of the cam mesh marines always wore around their necks and slung a squealing piggiwig onto his back.

He went first while Cree checked that no one was creeping up on us in the corridor and I followed. It was not possible to climb a ladder with dignity, your knees got wobbly and your arms ached and no matter what anyone said, you always looked down.

This was a dimly lit tube with creepy openings every now and then leading into horizontal nowhere. The broken lift shaft was beginning to look good.

I could hear Cree coming up behind me, he was a shadow in the darkness below and there seemed to be shapes in the dark below him that made no sense to my eyes, but seemed to be working wonders on my suddenly stimulated imagination. I put maintenance shafts on the list of places I didn't have warm fuzzy feelings about, right up there with running about in dark forests being chased by dinosaurs.

Claustrophobia wasn't usually a big problem for me, but I could feel the walls closing in and that lid on the coffin sensation creeping up my nerve endings. My hands began to slip on the ladder.

We took a rest on one of the levels and let Cree catch up. I put my aching back against a wall and rested my arms, which were shaking with strain. Cree was almost out of breath and Asguard and I stood up slightly crouched while he sat on the edge, taking his turn at a rest, his legs dangling into the shaft. Asguard shone his torch around him, lighting up the maintenance tunnel behind us. It curved away into the centre of the ship. I followed the light with my eyes as curiosity got the better of the small spaces problem.

Cree looked at Asguard and then back down below him. Asguard shuffled. "Okay, time to go, ready Bea?" I nodded and glanced back at Cree. He was still looking down the shaft and he was listening. His gun was held pointing down the ladder. It was longer than the one Zeke had given me on Restra and the butt of it rested into Cree's shoulder. For a moment I found myself thinking how little guns had changed in four hundred years they were smaller, more powerful and still capable of making me very nervous. I could feel the fear, like a wave curling over me. My skin prickled.

"What?" I whispered. I couldn't hear anything. He shrugged and then looked up at Asguard and back down again.

I listened with the other senses I'd been given, nothing. I tried my ears one more time, no, except maybe a sort of slight scraping noise. Asguard moved suddenly, making me gasp. He climbed onto the ladder and pulled me behind him. "Let's go!" We went. I could hear Cree behind me and I turned once to see him swinging out with one hand, he flicked on a powerful torch with the other. Something glittered below us, something not us.

"Bea! Can you get anything?" He shouted.

"No," I rasped through dry lips, nothing but terror, which was definitely localised and absolutely mine.

"Okay, probably not a human then."

"Great! That makes me feel," I huffed breathless, "Great!"

Asguard was talking to Sig. "We are two levels down still and I don't want to get caught in the shaft. No, Bea's not getting anything, what about Rani?"

A spray of gunfire made me nearly lose my grip on the ladder and I screamed. Asguard grabbed my arm and hung on.

Cree shouted, "Go!" He began firing again, the bounce back from the gun up against the shaft walls made a kaleidoscope of colour and the noise deafened me. I gripped the ladder again and looked down.

The piggiwig added its squeals to our shouts and Cree's gunfire. I could see in the torch light below something reaching for Cree. It was elongated and my eyes worked to make it into something my brain could recognise. A spider came into my head and as hard as I tried, I couldn't get it out again. He fired and climbed and fired again. Asguard swore because he couldn't see through me, we were like corks in a bottle. "Swing back over to that platform Bea." He shone a light for me to step onto a small ledge. I pushed my feet up grabbed at a bar of metal that was faintly warm and balanced carefully on a space the size of a front door step. Cree was only just below us now and I reached for the wriggling piggiwig Asguard shoved at me.

Cree's head appeared at my feet, he looked shaken and a little damaged. One arm was badly cut and he had blood dripping down the side of his face. "What is that thing?" I asked, my voice shaking. He shrugged. I took out a hankie and pressed it to the wound, very low tech, but effective. It was difficult to move in the confined space and Asguard was trying to cover Cree as he came up to the same height on the ladder.

A voice from above made us all jump, one level up I could see a head in the opening, it was Sig. "Keep coming!" He shouted.

Asguard changed places with me and I climbed with the now whimpering piggiwig on my back. I could have done a bit of whimpering myself, but fear and a lack of oxygen made it impossible.

I reached out gratefully to Sig and felt a sharp sting on my shoulder. I handed him the shaking creature and I could hear Rani shriek, "A piggiwig!" As Sig passed it to her, personally I thought the description Cree had given it was more appropriate.

My arm was feeling numb and I had difficulty raising it as I tried to take hold of Sig's hands. The horizontal shaft went off at a tangent to my left and I looked to see what I had caught myself on. I could hear Asguard and Cree coming up fast from below shouting something. Sig's face seemed to be swimming out of focus.

I looked back at the movement in the horizontal shaft. It glittered and then it grabbed. In the second between fear and nothingness I could hear loud voices and feel pain. Sig's hands slipped through my fingers and I thought about the spider and a web closing around me.

I had always hated the dark. My eyes were open, but it was the kind of nothingness that pressed in on you. I suddenly developed a bad case of hyperventilation and I was able to appreciate for a moment what real claustrophobia actually meant in all its glory.

A person once said, 'sometimes there is no solution, just choices.' But I bet they'd never been in a maintenance shaft with a monster. I could feel that choking panic rising up inside me.

"**Bea, Bea?**" Rani's anxious voice was inside my head; which was a reminder that even in the dark a million miles from nowhere she was there.

"**I'm here, Rani,**" I answered. Though where here was, was difficult to guess.

"**I've been calling you for hours,**" she sobbed. "**Can you move?**"

Good question, I checked my limbs, they were still tingly with pins and needles and I flopped around a bit before some coordination returned. "**Yes I can move.**" I could hear a sigh of relief as if a gentle breeze touched my face.

"**We're trying to find you. Wait while I talk to Doz.**" I shuffled myself into a sitting position, banging my head as I got upright, warm pipes stuck in my back as I leaned against them. I waved my hand in front of me, hoping that no vertical shaft was so close that I would find it the hard way.

"**Doz wants to know what you can see,**" Rani asked, her voice was calmer, "**Something that might help us pinpoint the shaft you're in.**"

I paused to think about this for a moment. "**Rani, I can't see anything, I'm in the dark here.**"

There was the shortest moment's silence, between a gasp and anger, "**You're in the dark?**" She shouted, "**Oh no!**"

I winced. A yell was a yell inside or outside your head. The anguish I could hear in her voice was comfort and fear. I remembered again how out on the edge of everything we were, frontiers with stars not mountains and rivers.

"**Wait Bea, Sig and Mark are trying to get some emergency lighting into the tunnels. Try not to panic!**" Her voice ended in a hysterical peak. The lights came on, in a dim comfort of green and I looked up the shaft in front of me, nothing. I turned to look behind me and screamed.

Like a drunk at a cocktail party, it was an inch away from my nose. Gleaming in the half light its claws outstretched with unfinished business. I backed away, my hands scrambling for a hold of sorts on the smooth surface of the shaft. I babbled with terror. "**Bea, what's happening?**" Rani's voice reached in passed the 'beyond reason.'

"Its right here," I sobbed.

"**Bea, it's inactive. Mark was able to deactivate the maintenance robot from the bridge. It can't hurt you now.**" A very small part of me wanted to scream, 'why didn't you tell me before,' but I was still gasping for breath and the relief was making me dizzy. "**Bea?**"

I did my best to describe the part of the horizontal shaft I was in. The pipes that were warm seemed to give them a clue. I began to hear real voices, as opposed to the ones that kept telling me I was going to die and then I could see wavering shadows appearing at the curve of the shaft. Doz reached out a hand and touched my arm gently. In the confined space it was difficult to do more than crawl, but as he got to me I collapsed and did a level of emotion that would have had me cringing on other worlds. Cree and Asguard manoeuvred around me and examined the robot.

It was not easy to hug a marine; they had all sorts of sharp implements that they used for killing things which got in the way. I felt very snotty and grateful. "Let's go Bea," he smiled, "Before Rani has a fit."

"Let's go before I have one." I wiped a drippy eye on my sleeve and looked behind me with a shudder. Asguard and Cree were dragging the robot towards me. I began crawling after Doz, then stopped and looked back at the out of breath marines, each pulling on a robotic limb.

"What's going on?" I asked Cree. He looked at Asguard. Doz had stopped.

"We need to make sure it's safe." Cree looked hopeful and Asguard sighed. I looked at the bruises on my wrists where I had been dragged for some distance by the tin monster. I had had cracked ribs before and the creaking pain felt familiar.

"You know Cree; you really are a bad liar."

"Hey." He looked hurt. "I've been practising." He added, "But I just don't think you should expect to be good at everything." Asguard snorted and Doz tutted, pulling on my arm and making me wince. We travelled slowly down the horizontal shaft and across two vertical ones, which explained why I had cracked ribs. The two marines rigged a pulley to drag the maintenance robot up several levels.

I was sweating with pain by the time we arrived at the same level we had been at, a really long time ago. Sig reached in and helped me through the narrow exit into the corridor. I collapsed onto the floor and found myself enveloped in calm. Rani's face swam into focus. She hugged as much as she could without causing me more hurt.

No one really ever wanted to die alone, we all sort human consolation; I kept seeing the curve of the maintenance shaft as the lights came on. Rani cupped my face in her hands. "You were never alone." I nodded, but we both knew there was a moment there when I was just that.

Mark Limbu squatted down beside me and patted my shoulder.

"Can you walk, Bea?" I sighed and reached up for a hand, he helped Rani to get me on my feet, the pain in my ribs made me gasp a bit. Rani and I stood together like the losers in a three-legged race and I leaned heavily on her shoulder as I caught my breath.

The marines were dragging the robot through the exit, folding the arms back on it, to squeeze it out of the shaft. It took all four of them pushing and shoving until it dropped to the passageway, like a mound of spare car parts.

They paused, leaning on the bulkheads. We were all getting tired, though my watch said we had only been on the ship for five hours and I'd had a sleep. Cree was still wearing my hankie tied around the wound on his head. He smiled at me as I touched the blood on the makeshift bandage. It was dry.

Mark was talking to the bridge on the Starfire, I couldn't hear the responses, but I got the gist. It sounded as if we were all in for a lecture.

I moved the robot with my foot and then gave it a kick, which stung even through the cushioned boots.

Sig looked incredulously at me. "Does that help?"

"It works for me." I huffed and did it again, with more viciousness.

"Bea!" Sig laughed and gave me a hug which made my ribs hurt.

"Hey, I think I might join you after carting that thing all over the ship." Asguard scowled, still out of breath, his hands resting on his knees, as he leaned against the corridor wall.

Rani and Mark Limbu had a quiet conversation and then came to join us. "Right, let's go." He moved to the front, doing a silent dance with the others that I didn't understand, as Cree and Asguard picked up the maintenance robot. Sig and Doz got behind Rani and me. All designed to make me feel nervous.

"Okay, what happened while I was asleep?"

Rani sighed with exasperation, "It was the fact that you were asleep Bea." I looked around at the strained faces of the marines and at the robot, then back at Rani and with one of those rare moments of insight.

"It would have killed me, wouldn't it?"

She looked distraught and held fast to my hand. "Mark got to it in time. He was on the bridge and noticed that the maintenance system was still in full flow. Which was odd as everything else was shut down. That and the description Cree was able to give us."

Mark turned around and gave me a wicked grin. "It's lucky I can count, eh?" I snorted, but he made me feel better, it was always good to have a Gurkha around, particularly when you needed saving.

We crept along empty corners and reached the upper docking bay without doing too much damage to my nerve endings. The conversation with the Starfire became more civilised. I had even asked Jenny Smith if she wanted me to bring her back a souvenir.

I realised that I hadn't seen or heard the ugly thing for a while, I looked at Rani. "Piggiwig?" She pointed to Doz, who seemed to have put on weight around the middle. He grinned and opened his shirt. I could just see the hairy snout of the creature, fast asleep.

"That's the nearest he's had to a hot date for a while." Sig cracked up over his own joke and the others grinned in appreciation. Doz looked philosophical.

"Rani, why couldn't you use the thermal imaging equipment to find me?"

"The maintenance robot had given you a cocktail of drugs, including one that lowered your body temperature."

"It would have got Cree if it could." I thought for a moment. "I wonder why, when it had them trapped did it double back and come at me?" She looked at me with one of those, 'not right now' faces.

"You're saying that this heap of junk was programmed to get me?" She gave me another look and my thought processes moved along at snail speed. "How is that possible?

We were waiting for the combined effort of muscle and brain to open the doors to the upper docking bay, there was lots of swearing and grunting and some useless helpful suggestions from those standing back. Rani began to look anxious and then quiet.

I got hold of her hand and because I'd never had a friend before that I didn't have to hide something from, the lack of barriers and her stress made me feel strange. The doors swept open onto an empty bay and the scream that came from Rani, or maybe she didn't scream. "Look out Bea!" Too late, I sank to my knees and watched Rani, mind wide open, fall against Mark, who struggled with trying to defend us against nothing and trying to protect her from the ground. Not all evil was bright and shiny and metallic, some evil was as old as time.

The marines fanned out into the bay taking cover where they could and checking the various dark corners for signs of life. I could have told them not to bother. They shouted their procedures and went through the practices that kept them and the people they protected safe and if they were puzzled about the lack of 'anything,' they didn't let it show.

Rani couldn't tell them, she was barely semi-conscious. I hadn't been 'looking' because I was still thinking about the robot and mainte-nance tunnels and my mind was, literally, elsewhere. Rani had 'seen' and 'felt' every single death.

The stains on the floor were dry from age; whatever happened had had time to leach into the walls and fill the empty space with silent screams. I felt the instant need to walk again where I could see the sun and sky.

"What's going on Bea?" Mark's face went from blur to outline, the concern etched deep in the lines from nose to mouth. "Did something happen here?" I nodded and pointed to the patch of dark brown that Sig was examining on the bay floor.

"Lots of something," I whispered. The fear of overwhelming fear was out there and inside, the darkness ready to tear you apart, like a lion feeding. I walked over to Sig, whose face was set hard. Mark Limbu wanted me to stay where he could protect me.

"There's no one here, Mark."

"That doesn't seem to have stopped them from pinging us twice." He lowered Rani to the floor and propped her up on his knee, gently trying to bring her around. "Come on Bea, first you, now Rani, what do you think is going on?"

It was difficult to think when your ribs were creaking every time you breathed and your heart felt like a punch bag. Even with my guard fully up I could hear the rumble of death and the shock of life snatched away in an instant. I looked at the dried blood, careful not to touch it. "So what are you saying Mark, a telepath trap?"

He shrugged, helping Rani to sit up and lean against the wall, she smiled at me through the haze of her mashed senses. "That cooked a few brain cells," she said, pressing a hand to her head.

The other marines came over to Sig and did the silent debrief, which consisted of a few raised eyebrows and shaken heads.

"What are you getting, Bea?" Doz asked quietly. I had to look at him carefully and he gave me a steady unblinking stare back, the hard as nails stare. "Anything you can give us, Bea would help."

My Com/T made me jump as the captain's calm voice reminded me we were being monitored. There was a whole raft of sane complete reasons for not doing it. For a moment I felt like stamping my feet and shouting my anger but I knelt down and put a hand on the blood stain.

It was like going back into a dream after answering the phone in the middle of the night, a slow slide of muddled thoughts. I looked up; the same feline face I had seen on the Restran planet was looking back at me. He pointed as I crouched against the warm twisted bodies, all dead. "I know you're here." He looked away, nodding his head gently, as if listening to some dark music of his own. My hand rested on the arm of a young man with black hair, his blood was still sticky on the ground and the expression on his face was puzzlement. I hoped he hadn't had time to realise his fate. The blood dried as the airlock doors opened and the bodies swept out into space. I could feel the suck against my skin as it dragged me out towards the stars. I lifted my hand and looked, the blood faded away to nothing and the contact broke and I sighed with the weight of knowledge and experience.

"Well?" said Doz.

"It's the same person as on Restra, the man with evil written all over him in several languages." Doz snorted and I rubbed the non-existent blood off my hand onto my clothes.

Rani looked at me and for a moment we exchanged the appropriate sadness and I realised her aloneness and my possible future, a pawn in a game played by ghosts. "Now what?" I asked.

The captain spoke to all of us, "Zeke is going to come and pick you up, I can't see any point in springing any more traps trying to get back to your SSV, Mark can you open the bay doors without spacing yourselves?"

"Yes captain." Mark tapped Rani on the shoulder and she nodded her agreement, which made me wonder who exactly was in charge of the team.

Doz and Sig went with Mark to the computer consoles at the back of the docking bay and I went over to Rani and helped her to her feet.

"Lean on me," I whispered, "Let's face it, it's my turn." Her eyes filled with tears and she brushed them away with impatience. She looked around me to the marines. Asguard and Cree were checking the dark corners again in the hope of finding something to kill.

"They don't understand," she shook her head, as if making excuses for a recalcitrant child.

"Neither do I," I muttered.

"I didn't mean that."

"I know," I answered. "I understand Rani, don't worry." She raised her eyes upward and then gave me a hug, trying to avoid squashing my aching ribs.

Mark waved us over to the far end of the bay where they were standing and Cree dragged the robot junk over to us as the bay doors opened. Something went pop inside my head. I glanced at Rani; she was looking around her, puzzled. A small puff of smoke appeared by the edge of the doors and at the edge of my vision at the same time and disappeared just as quickly into the vacuum. I pointed a silent finger. Sig looked at me and said, "I hate that finger, what?" He looked with the others.

Mark tapped his Com/T. "Don't dock, repeat, do not dock." The smoke seemed to be gaining ground. Mark shouted at Doz, "I thought you checked the doors?"

"I did." Doz looked puzzled.

There was another pop in my head. "I think this time it is coming from another level."

"Can you 'see' this?" Sig asked me, in a voice exasperated beyond belief.

I nodded. "It seems to be another one of those traps."

Sig snorted, "Really."

"I'm just trying to be helpful," I muttered, forgetting we were all broadcasting on the emergency com.

"If you want to be helpful," shouted Cree, "Do a spell or something." He and Doz were checking the other exits in a fast but frantic manner. They shook their heads at Mark who was trying to open them from the console.

"Telepath idiot, not witch!" I shouted back. I was sure I had deafened everyone on the Starfire's bridge.

Sig went over to the door we had come through which went into the main corridor, he rested a hand on it and leaned against it, listening. He looked at Mark. "I do not like this door someone *wants* us to go through it." We all looked at the smoke which was gaining ground against space; in fact I could hardly see the stars.

Mark was talking to Captain Witherspoon; he'd tapped the private mode on his Com/T which was never a good sign.

I looked at Rani, she was staring at the floor, I looked down, it seemed the same to me, a nothing much grey metal and then I got it.

We were standing closer to the middle of the bay. Cree and Asguard were trying to open an alternative exit and Sig was still over by the door to the main corridor, which was up a level of steps. Doz had clipped onto a line and was trying to check the bay doors again.

"Err," I pointed the finger again, this time downwards.

"*What?*" Sig's face was suffused with anger and frustration.

"The floor's getting warm."

A moment's pause and I wondered if now would have been a good time to express some pent-up emotion of my own. Like fear. The ratio between angry impotence and blind panic on my part was see-sawing at a phenomenal rate. Rani got hold of my hand. "Can you hear that?" She looked around her.

"You mean can I hear anything above the hammering of my heart and the racket that the marines are making?"

"Quiet!" She shouted, not actually that loudly and they all shut up; no one had ever shut up when I asked them to. A faint tapping noise began somewhere at the edge of my recent memory.

I think I whimpered, "What is that?" She looked at me. I covered my eyes with my hands and groaned.

She must have got it because she called out to Sig, "Get away from that door!" Followed by, "Captain, whatever you're going to do, do it now."

The tapping got louder and seemed to be coming from several directions, "Mark," she slid to a standstill next to him, "How many maintenance robots does this ship have?"

Mark looked at her; his horrified face was three shades too pale for normal.

We all looked up at a roar of noise at the edge of the bay doors and then Rani screamed. I went from sweaty relief at seeing a hovering SSV, to stunned disbelief at the sight of the disabled robot we had brought with us, coming back to life. It scuttled in that creepy side-ways movement of an angry spider. I thought ludicrously of the creatures I had carefully rescued from my cat and put gently out of the front door at the cottage. I could feel the vibration of the SSV behind me but there was no chance I was going to turn around and take my eyes off the robot. The floor under my feet was almost hot through my boots and the marines were in a collective war-like state.

Doz was still over by the bay doors. I could hear him shouting to the SSV about clearance. Sig had turned his gun around and was moving toward the robot in a determined fashion. It looked about it as if checking its whereabouts and it seemed to get a fix on all of us, stalking the stalker. Mark Limbu was standing with one arm very much in front of Rani and with the other he waved me over to him, like a crossing guard with a difficult child.

We were all watching it watching us. It paused for a moment and then moved, like lightning, straight for me. Sig jumped over the safety rail and intercepted it, swinging the butt of his rifle like a baseball bat. He made contact and one limb spun off into the air. It seemed to notice him for the first time and reared up.

I backed away, casting around for something I could use as a weapon. I could hear Doz shouting at me, but nothing helpful. The tapping became more insistent. Cree and Asguard were trying to cover too many doors and Mark and Rani were working their way around the walls trying to get past the robot.

The spider gave a hefty swipe that caught Sig by the legs and knocked him off his feet. He rolled over on to his side winded and he tried to batter it from an impossible angle, but it was past him in an instant. I moved as if to go to help him but he held up a warning hand. It hovered for a moment, with sharp claws too close to Sig.

"Whatever happens here Bea," Sig spoke distinctly, "You keep going."

It looked at me and I backed up a bit more feeling the gravity begin to lift, pulling at my feet. Thankfully the boots seemed to adapt to the change by sticking to the deck. I risked a quick look behind me and saw Doz trying to guide the SSV in through the narrow bay doors; he looked like one of those people on aircraft carriers that were usually filmed with stirring music and a sunset. I noticed he was wearing a small clear air mask and I fished around in my emergency pack until I found mine.

The spider was creeping towards me, two limbs outstretched, one broken, it had looked too small to drag me all over the ship a minute ago. The doors to the bay were beginning to buckle under the onslaught of the rest of the metal maintenance team and the noise, between the SSV engines and the battering, was like being inside a bell tower at midnight.

Out of the corner of my eye I could see that Rani and Mark had caught up, they were both wearing their air masks, so I put mine on, an unpleasant sensation which was a bit like having plastic wrap over your nose and mouth. The first intake of breath activated it. Still walking backwards I felt my stomach as it began to flip where the gravity got lighter and lighter.

Sig was up on his feet and a small spread of blood had appeared on the front of his shirt. Cree and Asguard had abandoned the dented doors and were working their way up behind the spider. It swung around, lashing out, but the marines dodged the limbs. It crabbed towards me and I checked behind me again, to see Doz hopping into the doorway of the undocked hovering SSV. He made not getting sucked out into space look easy.

We danced our dance the spider and I for a few more steps, then my arms wafted outwards and my hair began to drift gently like seaweed in a rock pool and my fear was as cold as the empty of out there and a metal limb reached out towards me, as I ran out of floor in the docking bay.

An arm grabbed me fiercely from behind. Doz leaning out of the doorway scooped me up around the waist and we ended up in a tangled heap in the SSV, my half scream was barely expressed. "You know," said Zeke, from the pilot seat, "You shouldn't be allowed out without a minder." He sounded angry.

"Well, I'm not volunteering for the job," said Doz as he leaned out of the door to reach for Rani. She managed to get in with a great deal more dignity than I had.

I moved over to the front of the craft and looked out at the mayhem. The doors to the bay had given way and the maintenance robots were climbing down towards the marines.

The danger of hitting one of us had diminished slightly and Cree and Asguard were backing towards the SSV firing. The maintenance robots were happy to keep on coming minus the odd limb or two. The marines had collectively managed to stop one or two of them in their tracks, but they were still spinning in their efforts to reach us.

Mark came up behind me and said to Zeke, "We need to take that one with us can you grab it with an engineering arm?" He pointed to my companion from the maintenance shafts.

Zeke replied, without taking his eyes off the front windows, "You'll have to do it Mark, I can't take my eyes off the bay doors. I'm flying with the security protection off." Mark's eyes betrayed his surprise and even *I* knew that was not allowed.

I turned around to see Sig being dragged in through the door leaving a trail of blood on the deck; he lay there for a moment and then rolled himself out of the way so that Doz could reach Asguard. My instinct was to try and help but there was no room. I stood behind Doz and looked out. Cree was giving Asguard a push up to the door. The SSV had moved nearer to the edge of the bay doors and was higher off the ground. It was swinging around too much for Asguard to get a grip.

I turned around for a moment as Rani dragged Sig to a seat and reclined it. As he lay down she began applying an emergency pack to stop the bleeding. I turned back. The robots were closing in on Cree. I grabbed Sig's gun which was sticky with blood and I leaned over Doz's shoulder. Asguard was still struggling to get a hold and Doz was tired.

I fired, holding onto the exit handle to lean out as far as possible, aiming as best I could. There was practically no kick back and once you had the sights sorted it worked easily, I did my best but it wasn't good enough.

Yellow and orange flame was beginning to catch at the periphery of the docking bay and the smoke was making it difficult for Zeke to keep a safe distance from the walls and floor. Asguard was in, out of breath with the effort, he crawled back to the doorway and reached out a hand for Cree. Doz slumped to one side for a moment and then he took the other side from me and began firing. We seemed to be making a difference.

Cree had a hand on the door frame ready to jump in; he turned around as one of the robots grabbed for him. He hit it with the butt of his gun and it spun away into space.

Doz was coughing with a face full of smoke as he reached down to help Asguard with Cree and I shouted, "Look out!" The SSV, with the safety protocols turned off, bounced off the bay door and swung out. Cree tried to reach for Asguard again and a robot slashed at his unprotected back. I leaned out as far as I dared and fired over Cree's vulnerable body.

He was wounded and another sharp limb caught him and blood spurted, forming small floating globules in the lighter gravity. His mouth opened to say something, but it was captured in the face mask and he tumbled backward.

As Cree fell, Doz pulled me away from the door which closed on my unbelieving face. I could hear Zeke shouting, "I can't override it the air has fallen to below safety levels." Asguard and Doz tried to open it using the combined brute strength of anger and fear.

Zeke was manoeuvring the SSV back in through the smoke when the first explosion spun and rocked us back into the bay doors again.

Asguard banged on the relentless SSV door until his fingers were bruised and bloody and I slid uselessly down the wall to crumple on the floor with my head on my knees.

I reached out and touched Cree and I didn't listen when Rani shouted at me and shook my arms to try and bring me back, because no one should die alone. His mind was warm and I could feel his blood on my hands and I made sure he could feel me with him and he smiled at where I wasn't. With all my strength I touched his face and he covered my warm hand with his and I stayed for as long as I could until he went further and further away and I felt like a piece of wire stretched taut, near to breaking.

He said as he turned to go, "Its fine." A part of me wanted to go with him, but he smiled and shook his head. "Tell Asguard I can make some sense of it now. Surely," he said, "That's the thing about dying, you finally understand everything."

The shaking became impossible to ignore and I opened my eyes to see Zeke, he was holding me and shouting my name and I think he thought I wasn't coming back. But you had to, I had tried to go with someone before and you couldn't. You got lost in the in-between. A blast of light was followed by another explosion and the SSV spun out of control. Mark was desperately trying to keep a hold on the spider with the engineering arm and Rani was standing by Sig's seat with a look of stunned horror on her face, he grabbed her and held on tight as we spun. Doz was in the pilot chair doing his best to stabilise the craft in the waves of the backlash and Asguard was next to him. He looked at me with hollow blank eyes and I looked back with that emptiness which came from goodbye. Zeke had dragged me upright and he pinned me between him and the wall gripping the exit bars by the door. We rattled around like a faulty roller coaster ride in some dizzy fairground.

The silence became just breathing and we all released our grip and the com on the SSV sounded like the desperation in my heart. We paused together for a moment and then Zeke went over to the pilot station and leaned over Doz. He swallowed and then said, "We're on our way back. Can you get Pui to meet us at the upper docking bay, we have wounded." He paused again and I thought 'please don't say it, because if you do it would be real.' But he said it anyway, "Cree's dead, captain."

For the first time I heard her swear. She swore loudly and she sounded angry and she sounded as if the tears in her throat were choking her.

"So here I am again," I said grumpily, "Back in the medical bay. I don't want to complain but I've done this already." The only difference this time was that Rani was in the bed next to me. Sig had been released early due to his appalling behaviour and Pui's favouritism.

"Huh!" Said Rani, "This is nothing I spent the whole of my first year in the medical bay."

"Oh great," I muttered, "Well that's something to look forward to."

I was surprised that we'd had no visitors, not the captain, no one, but then maybe I shouldn't have been as Pui had the last word in visiting.

We looked at each other for the first time in the day and a half since Doz had docked the battered SSV and we had crawled out, as if we were the survivors from a storm at sea.

She paused before speaking, "Have you done that before?" I nodded. "Your mother?" I nodded again. She nodded; you could see a pattern forming.

"You know how dangerous that is you could have been lost for good." She sounded horrified.

"Yes," I said.

"So why did you do it?"

"He was alone." This was followed by more nodding on her part.

We both lay back again and I added sadly, "Besides I've been lost before, and it's not so bad."

She looked at me. "For how long?"

"Two days." We both shuddered. Two days 'in-between' had seemed appropriate at the time, trying to find my way out of the dark with no one to guide me. In the end I had seen a pinpoint of light and followed it. How it had got there I didn't know, I just thought I knew. The people who loved you didn't really ever leave you.

The piggiwig had been removed, squealing and shaking with fear for his appointment in quarantine and I thought Rani's heart would break.

"So what are we saying here," I asked her, "This was a telepath trap?"

"They sealed that docking bay so I couldn't read it," Rani answered.

"*What*, how is that possible?"

"Bea, that robot had some of your DNA."

"It must have taken it while I was unconscious." The silence could have been one of those pauses you got before a thunderclap. "Okay, tell me?"

"It had been programmed with your DNA before we got to the ship."

I just couldn't see how that was possible. "But that would mean someone gave them my DNA," I whispered.

Pui came in looking rumpled. She had obviously been making house calls. I wished I was a little rumpled myself and sighed. I hadn't seen Zeke since the SSV docked, he went left and I went right, frog marched down the corridor by Pui. "How's Sig?" Rani asked with a smile.

"Huh," was the enigmatic reply, as she checked the output on the side of the beds, "It's time you two left."

It was amazing how quickly you could move given the opportunity, I was up, dressed and out of the door before Rani, who had only managed a pathetic giggling second. Pui watched us go with that half smile which made you wonder about her changing her mind. I virtually dragged Rani out with me, still rearranging her clothes.

We walked down the outer corridor on level one just so I could look out of the windows and it felt as if it had been ages since I had last seen the stars. Space was like being on a mountain with the clouds below. A part of you felt you shouldn't be there and a part of you belonged.

"I thought I'd find you here." The captain's voice made me jump. I looked at her tired face and the strain around her eyes. She was suffering along with the rest of us, maybe more so. The burden of responsibility was a heavy one. I wondered if she'd had to tell someone of Cree's death. Then I wondered if she'd had no one to tell and that made me feel worse.

"Captain," I said helpfully, "You look terrible, you really should get some sleep." We walked together down towards hydroponics, Rani in the middle.

Captain Witherspoon laughed, a deep throaty sound, not something I thought she'd done for a while. "I haven't had a decent night's sleep since you got here Bea, were you always this much trouble?" I scowled, which made them both laugh.

We sat, like the three wise monkeys, on a seat in hydroponics. The trees were moist with a recent rain and the birds were rushing around on the usual mission to avoid Colin the parrot. From the look on his face, or should that have been beak, we would have to do some avoiding action of our own.

"Someone on board this ship gave your DNA to one of the renegade families." Captain Witherspoon was leaning forward with her elbows resting on her knees.

"What about the traps on the smuggling ship, Rani said they were set with us in mind?" She nodded with a careful considered look.

"What is this about," I grumbled, "Do it yourself detective work, I have to say it and then you'll tell me if I'm close?"

They looked at each other and came to some agreement.

Rani said, "Bea, there are occasions when we have, in the past missed the potential of a telepath." She added, "Only a telepath could set a trap for a telepath neither you nor I could sense anything because we were blocked."

I wasn't sure that actually applied to me, I often didn't hear things because I wasn't listening. "Okay?"

Captain Witherspoon looked exasperated at my puzzled expression.

"We think we might have a rogue telepath." I looked at both of them, sensing their fear and loathing through the blocking chips they both wore.

"I have absolutely *no* idea what that means," I said, into the dripping silence.

It was difficult to remember that we were oceans apart in time and just because nothing had changed didn't mean that things were the same. We shared no cultural reference or history and I was in a time long after most people expected to be remembered. They didn't understand Dolly Parton or Marmite and I didn't know what a rogue telepath did to the nerve endings. "Rani," I asked, without looking at her, "Just exactly what year is it at home?"

"It's twenty-four twenty-eight."

We sat for a moment and I leaned back, watching Colin planning his hit from a high perch. It was like being under the watchful eye of a feathered devil. My mind made the necessary leap.

"How long have you known about this telepath?" Nothing said it better than a really long silence.

In the tradition of some situations providing more questions than answers, I asked, "Captain, why are we having this conversation in hydroponics, where is everybody?" Another long silence followed.

"Rani did a deep scan on me to clear the possibility that I might have removed your DNA from the medical bay."

"I remember that Pui took some from me when I first arrived, there was something about growing body parts if I needed them."

"You're at a medical disadvantage," the captain said. "Usually stem cells are collected at birth these days and stored to provide anything you might need later."

"So someone walked into Pui's inner sanctum and took the DNA, how is that possible?"

"We don't really know," Rani said. "But the trouble is that everyone on this ship has been security cleared and psych tested, there should be no reason why anyone should do this."

"Rani, someone tried to kill us, it's not beyond the realm of possibility that they would lie. Who else have you scanned and cleared?" She hadn't had much time between staggering off the SSV and appearing in the medical bay and it was a really difficult procedure for a telepath.

"Zeke." She gave me a quizzical look.

"I bet that made interesting reading." We were all conscious of the fact that Colin was fluffing his feathers rather closer than he had been before.

"Let's see if I'm getting this." I stood up to pace. "Before we went over to the smuggler's ship you realised my DNA was missing." There was bilateral nodding.

"Pui picked it up on a regular weekly check," Rani said.

"You have a rogue telepath and you've got the Dalgety family," I looked at Rani for confirmation, "Getting their smuggling transports hit by the Samura family?" I looked at both of them, "So far so good."

"We don't understand why. This has never happened before they usually stay well away from each other's business." Rani shook her head, her hands pressed to her mouth in thought.

"You mean honour among thieves," I snorted, "Tell me again, what do the Samura family do?"

"Mostly planetary artefacts and some drugs," the captain answered. "It just doesn't make any sense." She shook her head. "I have no idea why either of them should want to start their own private war."

"Do you usually take on the families where you find them?"

"No, the military vessels are tasked to deal with them."

"But if you come across a smuggler's' transport abandoned and the 'cargo' dead?"

She made a face and shrugged at the same time. "We investigate and call in the big guns if necessary." She sighed, which was a deep, tired sound.

"Bea," she hesitated, "Space is vast, people stay in their own solar systems, the Star League is not that organised or integrated. We rely on trade to create a level of communication." Her explanation petered out into silence and under the enormity of what she was trying to say.

I sat down and patted her hand and the three of us waited again for a while in the rustle of leaves and the overhanging shadows of what was and what would be. "What about the maintenance robots on that ship?" They both looked at me, "I mean they're not supposed to kill people presumably; they're supposed to fix things?"

"It would have been really difficult to remove the safety protection and re-programme them," Rani said.

"But somebody did it. How many maintenance robots are there on the Starfire?" The horrified silence stretched like a bit of old string.

"The very thought of what you're suggesting is making me sweat," the captain said.

I shrugged. "When I'm from bad things happened all the time."

Rani looked smug. "I told you she'd come up with something you'd never think of yourself."

The doors swished open, making us all jump guiltily and Ollie made a grumpy appearance. He wouldn't sleep in the medical bay at night, preferring his own bed. But he missed me and he jumped onto my lap with that closed mouth meow that was actually a serious complaint in cat speak. I gave him a squeeze and kissed his ears. "Ollie." I pointed his head at the parrot. "If that thing comes within four feet of us you have my permission to remove a few more tail feathers!" He looked decidedly pleased as only a cat could when the opportunity for bird feathers was on offer.

"Bea!" Was shouted from both sides at once, intermingled with laughter.

"I suppose Jad Lassik has nothing to do with this?" Not a look passed between them but the 'off limits' flag went up as soon as I had said the words, which was just one more puzzle that required an explanation. I wondered if the boats would be abandoned by the Styx and the damned walking over ice before I got an answer.

We had however, covered more ground in an hour than I'd learned in six months, "So what now?" I asked, hearing the faint sound of wolves howling in the wind as I spoke.

"I get the feeling we won't need to go looking for them, they'll come to us," Captain Witherspoon said with exasperation.

"What did your bosses say about what happened?" I got this question in without much hope of a straight answer.

The captain smiled as she recognised a fishing expedition. "My bosses are the Space Navy and they aren't really interested in anything much to do with you."

Rani rubbed her eyes and Ollie butted her chin with a furry face.

"We telepaths are administered by a very small department in a very large bureaucracy from a very minor solar system. I don't think anyone has actually given up hope that enough telepaths could be produced artificially to fulfil the needs of commercialism." She sounded bitter and tired, "But no one has been able to do it yet and for some reason humans are the only race that has them." She added, "We are a freak of nature." A really long silence followed. I was stunned, Rani sounded like the last of a dying race who were trying to survive progress, not the beginning of an amazing possibility.

"Here you are." Zeke came in through the hydroponics doorway, once again someone who made us all jump. "Harriet the bridge staff are all hoping you'll put in an appearance." She nodded.

"Where are we headed?" I asked, wondering if it involved me being shot at or drugged.

She laughed, "Don't panic Bea. With any luck no one will shoot at you," She got up to go, "Though I can't guarantee it." As she went through the door, she added, "We'll talk again."

"I swear that woman can read *my* mind," I muttered, "Where are we going?"

"Just a binary system with a couple of occupied planets, they seem to be travelling around their own back garden quite happily and we are going to invite them to broaden their horizons." Zeke rubbed his eyes and yawned he grabbed Ollie and ticked him under the chin.

"How are you my friend?" Ollie licked Zeke on the nose and I realised I had fallen in love with a non-furry person.

The corridors were quiet and a pale green as I wandered down to the eighth level. I kept seeing the door covers to the maintenance shafts. Somehow I hadn't noticed them before but there seemed to be one every few paces. I could see myself climbing through the crawl spaces every time I blinked.

I paused as a familiar tap tapping noise filtered into the corridor. My fingers began to sweat. The door in front of me swung open and a metal limb reached out. Physical sickness became an option. The engineering tech appeared behind the thing about a second later give or take an aeon. "Hey Bea," he climbed out, tugging the spider after him and dropping it on the deck with a familiar thud. He looked at me, his young brow furrowed in concern. "Are you okay?"

"Yes," I whispered, "Yes, I'm fine."

He looked down at the crumpled inert robot and then up at me and a pale light dawned. "I'm really sorry, it's faulty. I didn't know you were there." He looked really upset.

"I'm all right," I said, firmly backing down the corridor away from him and his metal friend. I wondered just how many maintenance robots there were on the Starfire and whether I would ever be able to hear the click of an engineering maintenance claw without feeling sick and afraid.

The door still said Asguard and Cree on it. I hadn't realised that they'd bunked together. Some of the rooms on the ship were single occupancy but Rani had told me most of the marines shared. I knocked.

After an empty moment the door slid open and Asguard's puzzled face looked out. It took him a second or two to focus. "Bea. Come in," he half whispered it, as if his voice didn't work properly.

The main room was dim with only one hologram light in a curved dome shape by a chair and a small glass table was covered with holo/pictures. I could see a mixture of three-dimensional friezes dizzyingly intertwined. The sadness drifted in the air like tears on the wind.

There was not much for those of us left behind, except perhaps pictures and memories and doubt and sometimes guilt and if you were really lucky a little of the love.

I saw two bedrooms, one either side of the main room which was about half the size of mine and I felt uncomfortable that I had so much more space to myself. He rubbed his face as if trying to remove the tiredness and went to make a drink. There was something vulnerable about the sight of a person in pain trying to find cups. My throat closed with the lump of endless sadness of someone else's loss. The love between those who fought that most people didn't see had been exploited by manipulators of history for the life of wars and was inexplicable to the rest of us. Soldiers would fight for each other when they had stopped fighting for a cause, or home, or right, or even god. The love was so deep that it could make you cry if you saw and felt it. Most people didn't get to experience that kind of friendship. Most wouldn't ever have to understand. I had seen the very old still weeping for those they had had to leave behind seventy years before.

"Asguard," I said into the pain-filled quiet, "His last words were for you." He stopped still for a second and then leaned on the work surface with his head bowed, the grief hitting him like a sucker punch. I whispered carefully, trying not to add to the many layers of hurt, "He said, 'Tell Asguard I can make some sense of it now.'"

The sound he made was of an animal in distress, "I told him he couldn't understand love. We'd been arguing, I was angry with him," said Asguard weakly. "He'd never had a partner or children and I was being cruel and stupid." We stopped talking over the emotional quantum singularity that had opened up between us and he started to make coffee slowly and carefully, like a drunk after a really long night.

I sat down and began looking at the holo/photos of young people in a variety of war-like poses, big grins on their painfully innocent faces. My vision kept blurring and the tears that didn't form gave the edge of the hologram a rainbow of colours in the corner of my eye.

"That's me and Cree in Basic. Zudlocs! We were so young!" Asguard put the coffee on the table and picked up another holo/picture.

"This is my first troop." The three-dimensional group sprang into life as he picked it up, fifteen young people male and female all inter-linked by arms and smiles and shared experience. "Most of them died in the Vanerian War, five of them in one battle." He snorted, "Me and Cree, we were the last." He looked at me with dark ringed eyes and I thought, 'here it comes.' "Do you think he was okay with me not being there? You see, we said we would go together."

It was impossible to understand the guilt of those left behind. It didn't take a great imaginative leap to link Asguard to all the soldiers in history who had made it through. I reached out for his hand and he took it like the drowning man he was.

You never really knew what was in someone's heart. I could read an open mind, but a heart defines courage and strength and pain and it was a closed door to me as to anyone. We sat for a moment and I tried to think of something profoundly helpful, some great words of peace. "He was absolutely okay with it, Asguard." Sometimes the truth was enough.

It was late, or maybe early when I staggered back to my rooms. We had drunk vast quantities of coffee and then vast quantities of a really bad whisky. I had left when Asguard passed out on the floor. I put a pillow under his head and covered him with a blanket. Not because it was cold but because there was some comfort in a blanket. I had left the light on too no one should wake in the dark. Ollie did the cat version of 'where the hell have you been all night.' I made some pathetic excuses and fell on my face somewhere in the vicinity of the bed, for what was left of a really dreadful day and a really long night.

The door chime was a welcome relief from a bad nightmare, but getting up proved more difficult than it should have been. I managed a low croak and sidled out of bed trying not to make any sudden move-ments with my head. Rani had one of those silly grins on her face, the 'have you got a hangover?' type of expression. Which, had she been stupid, she would have said out loud and I could then have said she was stating the obvious. Unfortunately for my bad mood, Rani was

S PARNAM-HARRIS

anything but stupid and it was telepathically incorrect to answer an unasked question, so I settled for glowering.

I decided I would forgive her when she put a cup of hot water into my hand and fed a starving and a much too loudly complaining Ollie. By the time I had absorbed the second cup and eaten a chocolate muffin, which was a highly recommended hangover cure, it felt as if the worst was over. The door chimed again, I groaned and croaked one more time.

"Are you two ready?" An objectionably cheerful Mac wandered in.

"Please go away, or I will kill you with my death ray." Mac managed to look hurt and amused without trying. We said at the same time, "Ready for what?" and "A death ray!" Which made my head spin and the thought crossed my mind that maybe a chocolate muffin might not have been the best breakfast under the circumstances. I tried for a dramatic exit into the bathroom, but 'I may be some time' was lost on both of them as 'Scott of the Antarctic' was not required reading on a starship, though it should have been.

Boiling hot shower water and some Bruce Springsteen had made things bearable and I returned after a respectable amount of time to see Zeke added to the group at the table. I felt like saying 'uh-oh,' an expression I had never really been comfortable with.

"Okay," I said, sitting down, "Ready for what?" The door chimed for the third time and Ko-Yo-Na swept in.

"Are you ready?" She sat down and pulled the plate of ginger biscuits towards her. I wondered if now would have been a good time to bang my head on the table.

"Could those of us with a hangover have an explanation?"

Through mouthfuls of biscuit and breakfast that Rani had produced from my kitchen, Ko roughed out the planet visit. It was more of the 'check out the locals' type of meeting, but any illusions I might have had about being wrapped in cotton wool for my own protection went sailing out star-ward. No one paid me any attention. No mention was made of being shot or poisoned, or attacked by maintenance robots.

Except that Cree was dead and wherever I went it felt like a trap. I couldn't control my shaking if I passed a maintenance shaft and I looked at people that had been friends a week ago and wondered if late one night, they had used the computer in the medical bay to find my DNA. I had become telepath bait to catch a telepath. The collective bleakness of the thought dimmed the edges of the group around me.

Even if I'd wanted to the blocking chips prevented me from taking a look. I felt the sweat of an unexpected panic creep up my spine. The sensation, like a nightmare of running from something unknown, fogged my brain. Somehow the voices seemed to become brittle and loud. "Are you okay?" A hand on my arm made me jump. Rani was looking anxious and the focus stopped swimming in and out.

"I'm fine," I said, patting her hand, which was still resting on my arm. I knew she could read me but the conversation would have to wait.

We stood and the others carried on talking and laughing at the day ahead. Zeke tapped me on the shoulder and said, "Harriet needs to see you before we go." I felt like I'd been given the keys to the city, *Harriet*, not the captain, needed to see me! I could of course, look at it another way, it might not be a raise in pay, she might just think we'd better get acquainted before someone killed me.

"I'll leave your clothes for the assignment in your rooms Bea," Rani called over her shoulder. Mac and Ko had disappeared in the opposite direction. I stopped suddenly in the doorway and Zeke bumped into me.

"What?" He said.

"I didn't know there was going to be clothes," I shouted at Rani. She just laughed and for a moment I felt lonely.

"Do I get some sort of brief?" I asked as Zeke and I walked down toward the captain's rooms. He stopped and turned to look at me.

"Didn't you see your screen yesterday, it had all the information you need?" I shook my head. He sighed, "Bea, you need to check your screen every day, particularly if it's bleeping."

I tried not to look guilty, the screen had been trying to attract my attention and I had ignored it in the morning and then when I had got back from seeing Asguard, I had turned off the incredibly annoying noise just before falling into bed.

I shrugged and he sighed again. "I'm new here," I said.

"You know…" he gritted his teeth and made a real effort not to look angry.

"You mean that in a loving and completely un-controlling way?" I smiled hopefully.

We stood in the corridor and looked at each other for a moment. He said quietly, "You're not taking me seriously." I gaped. Apart from the fact that I hadn't really thought it was a good idea to mention the relationship word under the circumstances, I'd never been out with anyone who would have discussed it in front of the *furniture,* never mind in a public place.

We walked a few paces. There was no outer corridor on this level and I could have done with a few stars and a lot of space to give me a sense of perspective. Na-Es-Yan came out of a room further up the corridor and seeing us, began to wave. Something in the way we were standing made her stop and beetle off in the other direction. It was so exaggerated it made me laugh.

"Look," I said exasperated, "How serous can this be, you're at least four hundred years younger than I am!" He reached out and wrapped his arms around me and sighed so that I could hear his heart beat. "I'm not good at this," I said. It came out rather muffled because of the squashed nose.

"I can see that," he said, not letting go. It occurred to me for the first time in a long time, that here was someone who might not actually leave.

He moved and kissed the top of my head and then with a sigh let me go. I had to balance myself against the wall because I felt a bit squeezed. We looked at each other again for a moment and then he turned and checked the corridor both ways and I wondered if there were enough antacids on board to settle the carousel in my stomach. He chose his words carefully, which made me feel as if a cloud had crossed the sun. "We all have secrets, and nothing is ever really as straightforward as it seems." He was whispering, so I did too.

"I'm beginning to understand that." I paced as much as the corridor would allow. "Zeke, I stayed with that boy until the last of the blood drained him from me and the explosion catapulted me back." He nodded his understanding and I continued. "You know, being a telepath is not easy, it makes you crazy and sometimes it's painful. And now, I can't read anybody and I feel as if I have a target painted on my back." The last part was less of a whisper and more of a squeak. He looked like he was desperate to tell me something and couldn't, which made me feel worse. "What's your secret, Zeke?" I asked sadly. He radiated the devastation level of a small earthquake.

"It's not that."

"Rani said she had read you and the captain," I sighed, "Why has she only read the two of you?"

There was silence. He just stood there. Finally and far too quickly he said, "We need to follow where this goes, Bea."

"There's something wrong with that argument, but I can't think of a flashy repost right now, can I get back to you?"

He grinned. "Sure." We began to walk towards the captain's rooms and he put a hand on my shoulder.

"Cree's 'Ritual for the Dead' will be performed when we get back. I think Asguard will ask you to speak." He smiled an empty smile. "You might want to read up on what that means." I nodded, too relieved that there was going to be a 'something' to worry about a public performance of some kind.

He left as I knocked on the captain's door and I realised he had said 'we,' when 'we' get back. The flood of relief made me stop and I watched him walking away, embarrassed with the emotion. I turned to the captain's door as it slid open and I walked in past Mark Limbu, who was going the other way. He nodded to me. "See you in the upper docking bay, Bea."

"Come in and sit down." The captain looked tired and the lines of strain around her mouth seemed to have deepened. "Not much to this one." She shuffled information discs and looked at her holo/computer terminal. "Just try and keep your wits about you." I nodded, as if I had actually read the assignment details. She looked at me. "You haven't read the assignment details have you?"

I gaped, "How do you do that?!"

She laughed which was a really nice sound. "I've been at this a really long time and I used to study on the way to the docking bay when I was a junior lieutenant."

She put her hand out and I took it. "You are here because you are needed, the universe needs its mysteries; you are part of the ceremony and ritual that even scientists find necessary to remember their humanity." Her voice croaked a little with tiredness and she squeezed my hand. "Now, get going and be careful." I stood up to go and my head spun with old feelings and too little sleep and too much alcohol.

"Captain," I was not hungover enough to call her Harriet, "What if this is not about power or money. What if it's about arrogance?" I had tried to describe the sensation the transgenetic Samura had given me, when I was lying in the medical bay after we had come back. It was muzzy with my own fear then and we had left it alone to think of other things.

The frustration of not being able to 'see' better than that must have shown on my face, because she stood up and came over, shaking my shoulders gently. I felt tears at the back of my mind and then stupidity. "I *feel* as if I should be angry but I can't seem to find angry," I said pathetically.

"It can't be far, I'll help you look," she said seriously.

I came out of there sure of three things. That I would never want her decisions, her responsibilities, or her shoes.

The clothes on the bed in my rooms were practical and attractive, a jacket and trousers in a tasteful shade of blue. Boots over the ankle with a sort of clasp to hold them closed. I set the holo/computer to run while I changed.

Ollie came in and leapt onto the bed, settling down with his paws curled inward. He watched with approval as I dressed and we both agreed it was a massive improvement on the Restran's idea of fashion.

The holo/computer showed the twin stars and the line of planets circling the larger sun. It went into some detail about the effect the other sun had on the solar system, all of which wafted appropriately and literally somewhere over the top of my head. The planet had three moons all named after historical characters. I wondered why Earth only called the moon 'the moon' and if we'd had more than one would they have had really interesting names, for a species that referred to its world as 'Earth' maybe not.

The world was divided into several different countries depending on land mass and power. But on the whole they seemed to have got their act together and started being nice to each other. They had a World Council, which was more than we had had at a similar stage in development. I wondered if their complete lack of anything resembling a religion had made a contribution to world peace.

The visuals of the planet were stunning, mountain ranges along the main land mass the height of Everest, and huge uninhabited deserts, three quarters ratio of sea to land and a diversity of flora and fauna.

I wondered cynically if they were in the path of a trade route, or maybe had some new source of energy that the Star League was looking forward to exploiting. Even I could recognise a few interesting things on the list of their resources that would make them new friends. Churchill had said 'success is going from failure to failure without a loss of enthusiasm,' I felt I needed to work on that.

I tapped an advance key on the computer and scrolled down to the inhabitants. Not unattractive in a sort of pale green way. They had fashions with hair and clothes which must have been a good sign. The hologram made the local turn as if on a show cat-walk. They looked intelligent and reasonable.

My Com/T hopped up and down on the table and I picked it up.

"Bea, are you coming?" An eager Mac shouted.

I walked briskly down the corridor which was now a pale pink, to hydroponics. The rain had recently been turned on and the trees were dripping and fresh. It sounded as if Colin was picking on the smaller birds as usual. I couldn't understand why the feathered schoolyard bully hadn't been spaced, made to walk the plank, or plucked long ago. I walked slowly up a level, sniffing the 'outside' smell and early spring in alternate breaths.

"Bea." A voice made me jump and I looked around. Torriff was sitting on the half-hidden seat under some heavy green vines. He looked terrible. There was a pale line under his eyes and the gentle ridged face looked careworn. I wondered if his troubles were people, like mine. I thought, not for the first time we had a lot in common. We were outsiders trying to learn the rules in someone else's party games.

"How are you doing, old chap?" I sat down, risking a moment for a sad friend. He looked puzzled. I didn't think the Com/T could manage 'chap,' the good things of the past, like the comfort of old words, were the hardest to let go of.

"How did your meeting with the captain go?" He asked politely. It was difficult to lie to such a sweet person, but I had had a lot of practice over the years. If you wanted to survive, you had to be like everyone else and when you were not, quite a lot of lying came into it.

"Strictly non fatal," I answered glibly.

He looked at me and nodded his head and sighed, "I am not considered old for my race. Do I seem old to you?"

"'Old chap' is a term of affection, something I only say to good friends," I said. I hoped we were not in for one of Torriff's lengthy requests for explanations on my antique version of English. Otherwise Mac would have died from enthusiasm overload by the time I got there.

"I have to go," I said reluctantly. I got up wishing I could hug him, but hugging an alien could be fraught with social danger as you could find yourself committed to a fight to the death, or at least a spell as someone's mother-in-law. I settled for patting his shoulder.

I walked up the steps and stood outside the doors to hydroponics for a moment, then ran back in and called down to the next level, "Torriff?" He came to the edge of the balcony and looked up. "Do you want to come around for food when I get back?"

He smiled, I think. "Do you cook?"

"No, but I know a good 'take away' and it's in the same star system." He nodded and waved a hand and I felt better, though I could see the pain was still etched deep on his face and in the shadows around him.

My Com/T had buzzed four times between hydroponics and the docking bay. I was grateful that Rani had taught me the little trick of clicking my jaw to turn it off.

The bay door slid open and the usual chaos wafted around me. I slid down the bar to the steps and landed neatly on both feet at the bottom, I had an older brother which made banister sliding compulsory. Mac looked impressed, Zeke was trying to look angry, but was having trouble with amusement and Mark Limbu would have been tapping his watch if he'd been wearing one. I thought that a brisk salute would probably be the last straw and a group hug was definitely out of the question.

A grumpy looking Doz stuck his head out of the SSV doorway and swore a word that didn't go through the Com/T, "Zudlocs Bea. Where have you been, some of us have a life you know, I can't spend half of it waiting around for you!"

"It's good to see you too, Doz," I shouted back. He made a face and somehow it felt okay and for a moment I missed Sam, which was odd as I hadn't thought about my brother in forever and he seemed suddenly to be around.

We were all dressed in the local garb. Zeke and Mark Limbu had decorative insignia on their respective collars. Blue seemed to be a theme, it probably made it easier for target practice.

"**Hold that thought,**" Rani whispered in my head. She appeared a second after her voice. Dressed in the same shape jacket and top as I was, both minus insignia; once again I thought how good she looked in everything. She laughed at my not said words and gave me a hug.

Mark looked puzzled. "I don't see why we need the both of you on this assignment Rani, it seems unnecessary."

She shrugged. "I think Bea should have a bit more support before she goes solo again." He nodded, but still looked unconvinced. No one else seemed to care. Mac was fussing with more experimental equipment and was arguing with Doz about where it was going to fit in, which I thought was nowhere from the look of it. They pushed the awkward shapes through the small doorway and I wondered where nanotechnology had gone.

I could see Sig talking to two marines who looked as if they were coming with us; they wore the same untidy but interesting combination of adapted local dress and marine uniform as the previous assignment.

"Okay, let's go," Zeke announced. "Bea, you can take us out of the docking bay."

The collective groans gave me no option but to perform an exaggerated bow. "Ladies and gentleman I thank you. I'd also like to thank my hairdresser and my analyst." A round of applause followed as I walked to the SSV doorway.

Mark Limbu scowled. "Do you take anything seriously?" I stopped and closed the distance between us, until we were much too close and proximity warning lights were going off like flashbulbs. Everything stopped.

"You try living four hundred years into your future, Mark. Try talking in another language, being surrounded by people who don't trust you just because you're different. Try being shot at, drugged and left in dark places, give it a go Mark and see how quickly you develop a sense of humour."

The ripple of silence reached the edges of the busy docking bay in the time it took to lose your temper and I could feel tears at the corners of my eyes making blinking impossible. Mark looked horrified. "Do you have *any* idea how heavy this is to carry around?" I whispered to the collective intake of breath.

The door to the corridor slid open and a cheerful Pui came in, carrying a wriggling piggiwig. She stopped, taking in the scene and then moved quietly down the steps to join us.

"I thought you'd like to see this ghastly creature, Rani. He's finished his quarantine." The tatty and frightened animal was transformed. Someone had given it a haircut which was a distinct improvement and it had the air of a satisfied puppy. It went mad when it saw Rani and she hugged and kissed it. The atmosphere went from icy to warm in the moments that furry cuddly things could bring with them. The noise level returned to near normal and people did relief at the end of possible multiple embarrassments.

Mark reached out a hand and took mine. "Please forgive an old soldier I forget sometimes that not everyone is part of my combat team." I found the tears running down my face and he looked horrified. "My daughters tell me I should not be allowed out in good company." He used his body to shield me from public view.

"I feel as if I'm drowning," I said.

He smiled. "Not on my watch."

Several heads stuck out of the SSV. Zeke, Doz and Mac all looked hopefully in my direction. Zeke's face began to darken when he realised I had been crying. He looked around for someone to punch and I told him silently to, **"Leave it alone."**

The piggiwig squealed several decibels above safety levels, which sent all of us into cringe mode. It wriggled away from Rani and launched itself at a shocked Doz.

Mark Limbu made a monumental effort not to be militarily horrified and Pui rescued a grateful Doz, who was covered in rainbow coloured slobber.

"Are we leaving any time soon?" Sig asked. The two marines stood squarely behind him, both of them were trying to suppress a smile with great difficulty.

Rani took the opportunity to speak to me, "What is wrong with you?" she asked.

"I'm in denial, like any normal person would be," I answered, wiping what was left of a tear-stained face.

Word seemed to have got around that I was in the driving seat and the edge of the docking bay was full of people as I took off. I think if it had been ice skating, the Russian judge would have given up and gone for a cup of tea.

Rani leaned over my shoulder for a moment to wave to the piggiwig and Pui held him up and lifted one of his paws and waved back. Rani laughed like a delighted child, we all needed those stupid moments which reminded us we were capable of love.

Zeke was in the right hand seat and the rest of the team were trying to avoid being tangled up with Mac's latest idea. The swear words seemed to be reasonably light hearted, although Rani turned around at one point and said, "I'm sitting right here."

I bounced the craft a few times as we left the docking bay in the SSV equivalent of clutch trouble and then narrowly missed the main doors. Zeke buckled his seatbelt which was much too late as far as I could see and said, "It's always a pleasure, Bea." The craft shimmied as we turned onto heading and there were more groans from behind. I did the computer calculations that made it work out where it was going. Zeke nodded his head and we all relaxed for a moment.

It was a bit of a tight fit with eight of us and I was really glad that the trip was going to be a short one. Being in space, in a ship the size of a small town was one thing, being in space in a Manhattan brownstone apartment was not interesting. I closed my eyes on the endless scrapping that passed for communication by anyone in uniform. I felt Rani's hand on my arm at one point but my mind drifted.

I thought about my conversation with the captain and then concentrated on the little I had picked up about the assignment in the short time it had taken me to get dressed. Most of the hard work had been done by the emissaries and the fact that they were still alive was a good sign, not everyone out there wanted to kill you it just felt like it sometimes.

I thought I must have been still slightly hungover because the sounds in the SSV began to slip. It was like falling between one thought and another. Or as if I was having a memory from long age. It had happened quite a lot in the cottage, but never in space. There was nothing old enough to touch except my slave bangle. I tried to raise my arm to look at it but my hands wouldn't move and they felt stiff and sore as if they didn't belong to me. Fear buzzed around in the background, but I could still just sense the assignment team and they gave me false comfort. My experiences had been full of little surprises, so I just waited. I became aware of someone speaking in a low dark voice that didn't make any sense. It was more the tone that made me feel as if things were not going to be good. Like an evil old crone in a really bad fairy story, the voice sounded as if it spoke the words of a complicated spell.

Something warned me that this was the time to leave. I struggled as fear built in waves, gently at first, then they pulled and sucked me under.

My efforts made no difference and I couldn't move. I wanted to cry out and scream for help. The voice became louder and more insistent, more powerful, more dangerous and why could no one see I needed help, where was Rani?

Rani, I fixed my mind away from the voice and pulled at the threads of the echo. Like sticky fingers my thoughts pushed through the web surrounding me and I strained with every muscle, used all the power I wasn't sure I had, nothing, maybe. A tiny sound filtered through the loud malevolent cacophony. As if someone called me from a cliff top in a gale. My sailboat was close to the edge of the storm. Then I could hear, "**Bea.**" I reached out and found dry land and a hand pulled me free from the evil coil of waves. My eyes opened.

"What is going on?" Mark Limbu was looking over Rani's shoulder. She was squeezing both my hands and her face was twisted into the coin of pain and fear.

Zeke was holding me across my upper arms from behind, the sweat beaded on his forehead. "You looked as if you were having a fit," he gasped.

"What was that?" Mark asked again. "I can't do my job unless you tell me." He tapped the main com. "Captain, we've had an incident here."

"That's an interesting way of looking at it," one of the marines muttered. Sig looked away from my face for a moment and the marine, muttering an apology, shuffled in his discomfort. Mark, his dark eyes glinting, faced Rani then Zeke and something passed between them that wasn't telepathy, more a warrior code being tested.

"How bad is this?" He asked Zeke.

"As bad as it gets," Zeke answered. Mark nodded and straightened. He tapped the main com and began reporting to the captain. It sounded as if he knew he didn't know what was going on and he sounded angry about it.

Sig looked at both of them and then at me again. "How bad would that be exactly?" He wasn't expecting an answer.

"How are you?" Rani asked me in a whisper.

"I think someone got up on the wrong side of the universe this morning." My voice shook. I tried to push myself out of the seat and failed miserably. My wrist burned and I raised my hand to look. The slave bangle glowed alarmingly. Rani held my arm as we examined the thing.

"Have you taken this off since you bought it?" I thought for a moment and shook my head. It had been so fiddly to undo: we were puzzled together.

Eventually I leaned my head on my hands and looked sideways at Zeke. "I'm not sure how much more of this I can take."

"Yes," he agreed. He looked exhausted.

I had a sudden sensation of warmth of someone else's strength and support, like the moment you realised your guardian angel did exist. Rani was aware of it and I took a stab at a guess. "Gurber?"

She shrugged. I'd been waiting for an angel all my life and the fact that he looked like a jelly and broke all the rules of aerodynamics was absolutely fine with me.

"Thanks for getting me out, Rani."

She looked devastated. "It wasn't me." We both looked at the bangle; all the little stones still shone with luminosity, the silver and gold metal was dimming back to normal.

"Maybe the bangle itself has some power," Sig interjected.

"You don't really believe that do you?" I said, incredulously.

"What about the writing on it, that could mean something," Doz added.

"I hope not," I said, rubbing my aching forehead, "It didn't do Frodo any good." Sadly there was total non-comprehension from all quarters. I made a mental note to put Lord of the Rings on Torriff's reading list.

Sig moved forward and lifted up my wrist. "Hey, the zarling thing's still glowing, I'm happy to suspend reality for the moment. Besides Rani said she didn't pull you out of there."

"Maybe it's the way things are when they're made with great suffering and strength," Mark added quietly, his arms folded, head down on his chest.

"Enough," I said, getting up and stretching my tired muscles.

Doz murmured to Sig, "Are we going to know what's going on here?"

I saw Sig looking at Mark Limbu and over at Zeke who was stretched out with his hands behind his head. "Not a chance." He settled himself back down in a seat with an air of quiet resentment and a sigh of irritation.

"Saving the universe isn't as easy as it used to be," Doz said thoughtfully.

"Or as much fun," Sig replied.

"You're getting old," one of the other marines said to them. Sig looked at the two younger soldiers grinning at him. He stared them out until they shuffled uncomfortably in their seats.

I hadn't really thought much about their ages. When I looked at Doz and Sig, they seemed to me to be young, but the fact that they were both senior officers and serving on a spaceship meant they would both have had a lot of experience. They fitted the central casting description for heroes in uniform. I knew that they had served in the last war together and that neither of them treated Torriff badly because of it, despite losing what seemed to me, a depressingly large number of comrades. Once, when drunk, Sig had said, "War means everyone loses." The lack of grey hair and crumpled bits had made me miss the obvious.

"Who are these two then?" I asked, trying to bridge a gap. People knew when they were on the outside of something. "We might as well be on first name terms as you've seen me foaming at the mouth." They stood up to introduce themselves.

"Atif Yonge, I'm in your defence class, usually Lef.G. is cruelly beating me up." He posed himself helpfully, half upside down, with a look of pain on his face. He had crinkly green eyes and shaved brown hair.

"Third row back on the left," I guessed. He nodded, looking pleased. We shook hands.

The other man got up. He seemed to be unfolding he was so tall and skinny. He held out a hand and shook mine shyly. "Ben Lopez." He had black hair dark skin and blue eyes and a long scar on his neck. He looked vaguely like Tariq, the cook. "Tariq Azel's my uncle," he said, by way of introduction.

"I don't suppose Dolly Parton has something useful to say?" Zeke interjected dryly.

"No, but as the iconic Bruce Springsteen said, in what was his contemporary enigmatic period, 'maybe we're just dancing in the dark.'" Everyone nodded seriously, until Rani began to laugh. I joined her and we slid helplessly into seats watched by the bemused.

The SSV circled in the upper atmosphere whilst a voice like warm honey gave us detailed landing instructions. I was glad that I wouldn't be asked to programme the computer with the coordinates. Zeke looked at me.

"What?" I said.

"You need to input the landing instructions," he said.

Stabbing haphazardly at lighted console keys, I did my best not to put us on course for any of the large mountains or the vast oceans. The computer bleeped its protest. My language got riper, the groans from the cheap seats got louder and Mark Limbu nearly had a coronary trying not to lose it. "At last," one of the marines gasped when the computer finally accepted and confirmed my set of sweaty coordinates.

I turned around. "I think I'll wipe it and do it again for practice." I contemplated the horrified faces as all but Rani fell for it.

"Got you," I said with some satisfaction.

"She's not nice," a very small voice said as I turned back to the front view. I looked quickly back over my shoulder but all the faces were blank, except Rani's who was still grinning. I narrowed my eyes and they sat quiet as mice with the ship's cat in charge.

Zeke contacted the ground and gave them an arrival time. As he finished speaking we began to sort out our kit and tidy up clothing. It was tight enough in there to bang a few elbows even with the doors to the small back room open. "I'm glad no one's on a high fibre diet," I sighed, as I ended up doing the two-step with Mark Limbu. He laughed at my awful sense of humour and held my shoulders as we circled around each other. I curtseyed and Mark did his best to not be soldierly. He turned to reach for some kit and then turned back to me.

"Are you nervous?" He asked me incredulously. I nodded. Somehow my heart was in my mouth again. Some of my fears were going to need cupboard space they'd been around for so long. The one about being shot again had taken on a life of its own.

We shuffled into discarded jackets and the marines topped up their not-quite uniforms with all the necessary killing equipment. They joked and tormented each other like soldiers in the moments before a battle. Instead of making me feel more nervous it seemed to have the opposite effect and I pulled my shoulders out of the permanent shape of tension they were welded into.

I heard Rani 'speaking' to Zeke in answer to what must have been an eloquent questioning expression. "**I think our rogue telepath got in touch.**" My momentary calm was busted in a violent shudder of fear, enough so that everyone in the SSV stopped and looked around them at the sudden outburst of telepathic panic. The saying, 'life isn't measured by the number of breaths you take, but the number of moments that take your breath away,' had become very relevant.

Rani reached over and put a comforting hand on my arm and Mark shook his head at the fact that he still didn't know what was going on. Live in my world for a minute, I thought unhelpfully, I'd been on the 'to be informed' list since day one.

Some soldiers needed to have a sword in their hand to feel right and Mark was struggling with the sensation of trying to fight without one. We all had our own battles and chasing ghosts was going to be mine. I patted his shoulder in solidarity. He didn't get it and looked really puzzled and a little alarmed.

"Are we ready?" Zeke broke the awkward silence before I offered a totally stupid explanation that would have prompted several impossible questions.

It was jump run again except we were all strapped in for our descent through the atmosphere. The planet was blue and green and gold through the SSV windows, a good place to live. Twinkling lights on the dark side outlined coastal cities and we passed a satellite for a worldwide communications system.

The twin suns gave off some interesting readings and several of the planets in the outer system had erratic orbits and were nothing but earthquakes and volcanoes. A tousled head popped out of the small back room, Mac. I had completely forgotten he was onboard. From the look on everyone else's face, so had they. "My new system is working well." He looked grubby and dishevelled.

"Where were you hiding?" I asked. He looked puzzled then smiled.

"I pulled one of the maintenance panels off and was working in a crawl space." He looked around at the incredulous faces. "Why, what did I miss?"

"Nothing much," I answered.

One of the marines muttered, "Techs."

Mac looked a little embarrassed, like the child who didn't get the joke, so I went over to join him and asked for an explanation of his latest gizmo. I could see Zeke's horrified expression and he spun in his pilot seat in an undignified fashion, in the hopes of avoiding the mind-bending boredom that was Mac in full flood.

"Why don't you join us Zeke?" I asked with undisguised glee. His head disappeared into his shoulders and he bore the sniggers of the rest of the team with fortitude.

But as he passed me his eyes narrowed, Mac was oblivious and my brain unhooked after the first few minutes.

In-between a long and detailed account of each particle of power and the connections of technical readings, I realised he was talking about extracting water from space. My interest sharpened my concentration. "Are you talking about water?"

Mac stopped mid sentence. "Yes," then warmed to his theme, "You do know that there's water everywhere in space?"

"I think so, cosmic oceans?" Mac beamed, Zeke groaned. I felt like the 'Eliza Dolittle' of the stars.

"Well, as you know," Mac smiled in my direction, "if oxygen and hydrogen get together they produce water or ice. There are whole active galaxies out there full of water particles. This equipment will make it easier to condense it into a liquid." He beamed again and opened his mouth to explain but what came next was interrupted by a compassionate Mark who had noticed our ears bleeding.

"It's time to get strapped down for landing." Mac looked disappointed, as Zeke and I made an undignified rush to get to our seats which meant we got slightly stuck in the doorway together.

I noticed a familiar sound and it filtered through my nerve endings. Rain on the windows. Rain opened the doors to old memories; it made a dream time and created the soporific rhythm of thoughts. Rain could take you anywhere you wanted to go. We passed through the clouds and into a clear blue morning.

The SSV made a dignified landing without my help and slid gracefully to a halt in a busy airport. The main structure was bannered with patterns of welcome and brightly coloured trees and flowers filled the view about as far as I could see. The buildings were many windowed and beautifully curved in kind shapes. No 'monstrous carbuncles' here. They looked as if they had been designed by someone who actually liked people.

The air in the SSV hissed as the craft did the computer equivalent of gaseous exchange. It was good to breathe smelling slightly sweet, like fresh cut grass and it made a nice change to sweat and small spaces.

We assembled ourselves with quiet words and Rani moved into a flanking position beside me, making Mark grind his teeth in undisguised frustration. She smiled at him and he melted slightly which had more to do with charm than actual telepathy.

A group of locals were making their way to the craft with the two emissaries, there seemed to be a lot of talk and laughter. There also seemed to be something wrong with my eyesight. They were not getting any bigger as they got closer. In fact the emissaries stood a good head higher than the tallest of the locals, which was odd, because I had met a Lactarian emissary and they were small.

As the door opened I gasped. Rani elbowed me in the ribs and hissed, "Close your mouth Bea!" They were *little green men*.

It was difficult not to bend at the knees when shaking hands with Admira's grand commander. It was also impossible not to smile. These people exuded open warmth and an intellectual curiosity. I looked at Rani, she was giving a silent report to Mark, all of it positive, which made a change from closed pinched minds. Mac stuck his head out of the back room on the SSV and was elbowed backwards by Mark Limbu. I heard his 'oof' of surprise as he made a few involuntary steps. The main doorway was becoming impossibly crowded with grinning green faces, all about shoulder height on me. The marines towered over the locals.

The grand commander banged the Com/T he'd been given. "Is this thing working?" He still had hold of my hand and I realised that I hadn't spoken in answer to his welcome. I introduced myself and he tapped the back of my hand. "You're the telepath, how fascinating." He grinned, showing small, even teeth.

He had strong features and up close was handsome and powerfully built, his green eyes sparkled with intelligence and it made me think for a moment how humour seemed to be universal, if you just knew where to look.

Mark was really worried about the lack of potential for any real security. I could hear him heavy breathing down my neck, which under normal circumstances could have been quite nice, but was becoming unhealthy; every assignment was a balancing act between making friends and keeping from getting shot. It constantly amazed me how haphazard the process was, but then I didn't think back episodes of Star Trek were available for reference.

Everyone paused as the grand commander raised both hands; we were half in and half out of the craft, in a rabble that would have given any leader's press secretary on Earth, a fit. It went quiet. "Welcome to Admira, we are pleased to be making new friends and look forward to our learning much from each other. We have a saying," these people had a saying for everything, he paused, we listened. "Great things can come from peace and imagination can remove barriers." He bowed and the crowd murmured a positive response. "Please." He held out a hand, a politician and a philosopher which was a dangerous combination, if not an oxymoron.

We walked towards the building in impossibly bright sunshine and a small group of military men in smart uniforms joined us. I heard one of the soldiers asking Sig, "Who was that man in the back of your craft that your chief soldier pushed out of the way?"

"A tech, he's just along for the ride, some new equipment he wanted to test."

"Are techs as boring on your world as they are on mine?" The soldier added with a smile and Sig grunted his agreement.

We moved on in the disorganisation of old friendships rather than self importance and diplomacy. Rani stayed close to me and I could feel Zeke behind me well within grabbing distance which was somehow claustrophobic and reassuring in equal measure.

The grand commander waved us inside the building and we proceeded down wide corridors into a hall filled with food and speeches.

"What do you call your own planet?" Desi:Tig asked me. We were sitting in casual groups with the noise level close to my pain threshold. The official introductions over, the grand commander and I were well past titles.

"It's called Earth," I shouted, hoping to be heard. He looked puzzled and wrinkled his nose. I think it must have through the Com/T as dirt or mud, or maybe something worse.

I pushed back my hair with a sweaty hand and he caught my wrist and looked with surprise at my bangle. "Where did you get this?" I could see Rani heading in my direction, processing the alternatives for a diplomatic incident with Zeke who was somewhere behind me.

"I bought it at a market stall on a planet near my solar system." It was the second time that day it had caused trouble, if I could find the catch it was going to be spending more time with the cat.

He shouted, "Civil:Moi!" A local looked around at the sound of his name and came over to us, smiling a greeting as he sat down. I could feel Zeke's hand on my shoulder and I felt like leaning on his arm. I ached with noise and too many curious people. Rani hovered a few feet away, talking to Asa/Et, one of the Lactarian emissaries. "This is our chief scientist."

The older man nodded and tapped the back of my hand. "It is good to meet you, Bea." His face shone with the goodness of genuine interest and his bright button eyes looked hopefully into mine, my tiredness went up a notch. He wasn't wearing any of the insignia that the soldiers and politicians seemed to have in abundance and like all good scientists he had dressed in a hurry.

"You speak the old tongue?" The grand commander asked him. He nodded. "Look." He pointed to my held arm and the writing on the bangle.

If Civil:Moi was surprised he didn't show it, but looked carefully at the words around the outer rim of the bangle. He looked back at me again. "May I?" I nodded. He touched the edges and circled it, reading the markings. "The verse is not our language it's some sort of hiero-glyph, but this says 'we have our hands bound heavy, but our hearts are free.' This is very old."

He looked at me and registered my anxiety and the proximity of Zeke. "Our people have always known they came from the stars. We are a colony of sorts."

Desi:Tig leaned in, looking from me to Zeke. "But one without a home, our written history only goes back two thousand years, but before that?" He raised his hands. "Asa/Et has been making some enquiries for us to see if we have relatives anywhere."

Asa/Et came over at the sound of her name and Rani joined us. I sensed with the expression on the emissary's face, that the enquiries would depend on the planet's entry and establishment into the Star League.

"If your bureaucrats are like ours we will have something of a wait." Desi:Tig laughed with great prescience. "We have a saying, 'middle management people make small problems big ones as it means you keep your job.'"

"Okay," I said, "Its official, bureaucracy is universal."

I patted the hand resting on my shoulder. I could sense that there was nothing but curiosity coming from both of them, the scientist and the politician. In fact, it was strange but they reminded me of us more than any other race I had met so far. Rani smiled, catching a thread of my thoughts and agreeing with me.

We were both shadowed with the exhaustion of listening for the usual trouble and the unknown crowded in to add a layer of anxiety, like a Sunday night before an impossible Monday exam. I sat with the chief scientist as the others drifted off to rearrange the pattern of things to come, glad to have my mind out of the mix for a moment.

"Is he your partner?" The scientist was looking at Zeke. He then directed his gaze at me.

"No, not really," I finished lamely.

He laughed, "Does he know that?" My face radiated with embarrassment. He tried unsuccessfully to hide his fascination with my now red countenance. "I'm sorry we are very open about our feelings, a little too much perhaps." He sighed, "Asa/Et has told us we must learn to..." his brow furrowed, "play poker?"

I laughed as he said it and nodded. "It could prove useful."

"Some of us are too old to learn new things," he sighed again, his eyes twinkling.

"You flirt!" I tapped the back of his hand in the way of these people. His smile broadened in appreciation of my gesture. It was, as I understood it, a symbol of friendship as well as a greeting.

He looked at me, head on one side in quiet contemplation. "You are I think very tired? Some of our people fantasize about a telepathic life.

I cannot imagine living without the only real privacy most of us enjoy, the place inside your own head." He stunned me with his observation.

"Do you dream?" He asked me. I nodded. "How do you know they are your own?"

"Well," I said carefully, "If it's a good dream, I tend to think I've borrowed it and if it's a nightmare, it's mine."

He tapped the back of my hand several times and sucked a breath in, like a grandfather who disapproved of the way his children were doing the job of rearing their own. "I would be afraid to go back to a time when I had dreams."

The sky had turned from blue to green which I needed to ask Na-Es-Yan about and then to a deep gold and the halls opened onto the gardens as people spilled out, still talking and laughing and eating.

Asa/Et came over to us and passed a message to the scientist, who tutted and took his leave of me in a warm and friendly way, with much tapping of both of my hands. The emissary tucked her arm into mine and persuaded me to walk outside for some fresh air. Her beautiful even features and dusky skin made her look like a teenager, though I knew she had several children all out in the universe getting the Lactarian idea of a good education which meant a lot of it. The perfume from the flowers wafted on each welcome breeze and I tried to stave off the waves of tiredness that threatened to engulf me.

"Not long now," she said as she rubbed my knotted shoulders gently.

"I don't mind, this place is just about perfect."

Her eyebrows shot up in surprise. "Nowhere is perfect Bea, not here, not anywhere." It sounded a little sharp for a Lactarian, a people who practised understatement from childhood.

I sat down on one of the well placed chairs. "What have they got in their skeleton cupboard then?"

She looked puzzled for a moment; I could hear her Com/T buzzing with frustration. "Well, they have bandits in the mountains, a nice little epidemic in the islands and a bad habit of putting off the difficult decisions."

"It sounds just like home," I muttered.

I could see Zeke, half in the shadows walking towards us he was leaning down to catch the words of a local soldier. They both smiled. The scene drifted for a second and I could hear the words in the distance and I thought it was them, but it became a chant and instinct made me look at the bangle on my wrist which was glowing again and I could see Rani turn sharply, a look of panic on her face as she pushed someone out of her way and ran and ran. The gold evening folded around her and her flowing clothes like wings.

Mark grabbed her as she passed, his face moving from conversation to fierce in a moment and she mouthed one word and he looked my way.

I felt a calm as the chant took over and I dreamed of quieter times and strangely again the sea, but without the drowning sensation from before. They were straining with the speed, pushing and pushing, mouths open. Zeke appeared at the edges of my vision, shouting silently. I seemed to be surrounded by warmth and light and I looked up to see specks like stars, spinning in a frantic dance.

Rani screamed and I watched Mark in slow motion launch himself at me in a rugby tackle worthy of a Welsh prop forward, the impact sent us both into the flower beds and all the air left my lungs. I would have laughed at the indignity of it but breathing seemed more important.

Mark was lifted gently away from me, the skin on his face was burnt bright red and his clothes were shredded. He was still alive but barely conscious and in some pain. It was difficult to process the information getting to my brain. "What was that?" I gasped. Rani was crouched in front of me.

Zeke had propped me against him and his arms were around me in a panic. He was reassuring himself and muttering. "I've never seen anyone do that," he said, his voice shaky, "I thought it would kill both of you."

"What was it?" I tried again.

"Some sort of transportation device," Rani whispered.

"I didn't realise you had something like that." I shivered, leaning into Zeke for a moment.

"We don't." He squeezed tighter as I shuddered, the shock taking over from numbness. Asa/Et was doing her job of deflecting the interested and curious.

Zeke motioned the local soldier over to us and gave him some instructions. I could see Sig and Doz moving quickly in our direction but most people didn't seem to notice, I think they thought one of the 'visitors' had had a bit too much of the local brew.

I looked at Rani, the sweat was beading on her forehead and the strain made her eyes look dark.

"Are you doing that?" I asked her incredulously, blocking a whole group of people she had to be superwoman.

Mark was gently lifted by Sig and Doz, after they had sprayed him with a plastic dressing. I giggled he looked like a salad ready for the fridge. "Do you want us to do Bea's wounds Zeke?" Doz asked quietly.

My wounds, I looked down at my hands and up at Rani. "Are you blocking this too?" The spray was cold and shiny when it touched the skin; my hands looked like uncooked sausages and the burns flashed up my arms in swirls of red.

"Close your eyes, Bea." Sig held my face carefully, coating it with an even dressing. He put some drops in my eyes. "It's the same substance Bea, just more of a liquid and it might make your vision a little blurry." His features disappeared behind a thin curtain. He patted my shoulder, the one place that hadn't been blasted.

Zeke did an impression of a white knight, picking me up and carrying me back to the SSV and we had a small puzzled escort of local soldiers. Rani went with Asa/Et to finish up the evening with some appropriate diplomacy.

The door of the SSV opened and Mac stuck a tousled head out.

"Did you bring me any food? I hate the packaged..." His voice tailed off as he took in the sight of Mark, unconscious between Sig and Doz, and then Zeke carrying me. He scowled. "What's Bea done *now?*"

We waited for Rani to join us before taking off without fanfare, or the fuss that had marked our arrival. I wondered what they had told

Desi:Tig, but mostly I thought about my burns and if Mark was going to be okay.

The SSV got back to the Starfire in about half the time of the outward journey. Rani sat close to the pull-out emergency beds. Mark had an airway put in by Sig, whose medical skills were apparently the best, because all the marines and Zeke had argued about not doing it until Rani shouted at them. I was quite sure none of them had ever heard her raise her voice before.

The clear bag over Mark's face breathed for him, but Sig had spoken to Pui about the possibility of the burns in his throat swelling.

I closed my eyes and let the tears seep out quietly. I felt so tired.

"What's to stop them from trying again?" I asked the captain. The medical bay was full of plants and flowers; Moi Uhara had taken pity on my restless state and brought hydroponics to me.

"We have a regenerating protection field around the ship."

"How did the transportation device work?" She sat down by the bed and helped herself to an apple from a bowl that Tariq Azel had left that morning. The chocolate trifle was long gone. I sighed.

She answered, "It changes matter into energy and back again. How they store the pattern, I don't know."

"That's particle physics, isn't it?"

She chewed on a mouthful of apple and mumbled, "Thys goo!" Swallowing, she contemplated the half eaten fruit. "How much do you understand about transgenetics Bea?" It was going to be one of those conversations.

Mark shifted in his sleep and we both looked towards the bio-bed he was on. A clear dome covered his body to keep a sterile field for the burns to heal. He was heavily sedated. The new skin Pui had grown for him was hardly distinguishable from normal, but it had been the damage to his airway that had kept Pui up for three nights. I was just itchy.

We were alone with the emergency sensors and an unconscious

S PARNAM-HARRIS

Mark. Pui had gone for some much needed sleep and the captain had given the duty medic permission to go and get some coffee.

"He's going to be okay captain," I said gently, as much for myself as for her. She nodded. I lay back on the bed. "Right, as we're not going to talk about the event horizon transportation device then transgenetics will do; a really clever idea, fraught with danger. We were doing some experimentation in my time. I remember something in a newspaper article about making a spider silk strand as strong as steel and of course there were the 'Frankenstein foods.'" From the expression on her face the Com/T was having a moment.

"A while ago, oh nearly a hundred years or so, we mixed up human genes with some other genetic species." She shrugged her embarrassment.

"Why would anyone do that? I would have thought that just knowing you could, would make it a bad idea."

She spoke quietly as if trying to reconcile herself with the past, "There was a war, a long stupid war we were losing, or I should say we were on the losing side. Someone thought it would be possible to make a race of fighters. So they did."

"The Samura family are descended from those fighters?"

"There was nowhere for any of them to go after the war, no one wanted them. No one wanted to be reminded of what they had done. Or what we had done."

"Where are we going with this?" I plucked at the light cover nervously.

She carried on. "They hired out and went to die in far off wars." Her eyes filled and mine did too. "A small group tried to set up a colony on one of the planets in the Epsilon Eridani system."

"'Swords into ploughshares,'" I whispered.

She nodded. "But fighting men don't make good farmers. Anyway," she straightened and took another bite out of the apple, "Eventually they took over a small corner of the smuggling market." She shrugged and looked at me.

I thought for a moment. "You know, I was hoping the future would be tidier, everywhere I look there are dark corners." She snorted and threw the apple core in a wide arc; it hit the recycler and disappeared. "Did they make female fighters as well then?"

"Yes." She made no eye contact. "But they were very careful to make sure the fighters were unable to reproduce naturally."

"So how is it possible they have descendants?" She raised her eyebrows. "Oh," I nodded in understanding. Of course it would have been a whole lot quicker if she had just told me, but whoever had made the rules put paid to that; the guessing game would have to continue.

"Right, so you think that someone thinks, I might make an interesting addition to their gene pool?" She nodded. "But I thought we had established that it was not possible to reproduce a telepath in any way in any time."

"What we know about this could be coded on a..." she looked around for a suitable object.

"Postage stamp," I added helpfully.

"Is that really small?"

I nodded, holding up a finger and thumb.

Pui stuck her head in through the door, making both of us jump. "Is everything okay in here?"

"I'm not speaking to you," I muttered, we'd had a slight disagreement about my going back to my rooms that morning.

"I don't know how I'm going to be able to live if that's the case." She marched over to Mark's bio-bed and checked the readings, "Back in a minute." She smiled and went out through the door.

"That woman is spending far too much time with Sig, I preferred her when she was enigmatic."

The captain looked stunned. "Sig?"

"Yes." I nodded. "You know, spending time," I winked helpfully. "Also, Doz is sweet on Ko-Yo-Na, in a warrior queen sort of way and that nice xenobiologist Neff. Is in love with Na-Es-Yan but of course," I added, "She doesn't know."

The captain swore something through the translator that ran to three syllables and sounded like a cough. "The substance I'm putting in the food clearly isn't working."

"You don't get out much do you, captain?" I said with some satisfaction.

"I don't suppose Dolly Parton has anything helpful to say?" She looked slightly dazed.

"Well no, but Miss Piggy, another twenty-first century philosopher, once said 'never eat anything you can't lift.'"

"I can see why you're such a well balanced person, Bea."

We sat in silence, listening to the hum of the bio-bed that kept Mark safe and for some reason tears started welling in my eyes and in a moment were running down my face. She reached out a hand and we looked at each other and I could see fear in her eyes. There was a saying about 'time making us all cowards in the end.'

"Even in my time," I whispered, "I knew people would be interested in what I could do. I learnt to avoid the ones who felt dangerous. But there were stories." I shook my head. "If *you're* scared, Harriet," it felt like a Harriet moment, "I think I'm going to lose it."

"I won't give you up without a fight." She squeezed my hand and made me look at her. I nodded, but we felt like people lost on a mountain calling through the clouds.

Pui came in with Zeke, I wondered if they had been waiting outside the door. "You're sprung," she pointed a thumb at the corridor and I leaped out of the bed, grabbing my dressing gown. I wobbled a bit and Zeke held my arm, I grinned up at him.

"Quick, before she changes her mind!"

We did a sort of three-legged race back to my rooms, I wouldn't let him carry me, so that left me leaning on him and I managed to smile nearly all of the way. Things were getting a bit difficult by the time we got down to level three, one more 'how's it going Bea' and the Com/T was going to be spinning with unsuppressed Anglo-Saxon.

"If you would just use the lift shafts we could have done this in no time," Zeke grumbled. He tutted in exasperation at my grey face and picked me up.

I would have lodged some kind of protest, but the pain from just-healed burns and the sensation of recently unscrambled DNA was making me feel sick.

"The captain told me about her gene pool theory," I said quietly. The words bounced around the empty corridor, which made both of us nervous. "Though," I added, "I don't think these people can have come from the deep end, if they think I'm going to make a difference to the genetic soup." The Com/T must have been having a good day because he laughed. We paused at the door to my rooms and I pressed the keypad with my thumb.

Ollie was curled up on the sofa, he opened one eye and then went back to sleep. Zeke still held onto me and I could feel the panic radiating from him like heat. He didn't say anything but swallowed hard a few times. I didn't dare look at his face for a moment. I had the impression that Zeke usually played by his own rules. So something was clipping his wings, or someone and I hoped it wasn't me.

He put me down and I stood by the window, a large spiral galaxy with the visible dark equatorial dust lanes, millions of miles away, filled centre stage. It made me wonder if everyone looking out saw something different, as in life. The silence, as with everything between us, was coloured by the things we didn't say.

"Do you know how to make toast?" I staggered over to the sofa and my cat. "I could just eat toast and marmalade." Zeke's Com/T made the usual whizzing noises.

"Could you give me directions? If I can strip, clean and reassemble an SSV engine I think I could make some ancient Earth dish." I explained. "Okay," he said, "Let me just get this straight, you want me to *burn* the bread?"

I woke up with a jump and half-remembered dreams swirled around in my head. I was still on the sofa, covered in a rug, with Ollie curled against my stomach. A plate of cold toast sat on the glass table and the mug of coffee had an unhealthy sheen on the surface. The holo/clock said it was still the night hours.

Zeke slept stretched out at the other end of the sofa with his feet on the table. His jacket was off and he was wearing what looked like a sleeveless vest. I usually looked at men like Zeke from a safe distance, as if I was watching really dangerous wildlife. Proximity was making me careless.

He'd taken off his boots and his feet were covered in different coloured socks. His Com/T rested on the table beside the cold toast. I realised his eyes were open and he was looking at me as if I had been out of focus before that. There was that trust problem again, hanging in the air along with the save your life secrets. I shuffled around and found my Com/T squished under a cushion. I left it there as one more barrier between me and the future.

The grey eyes dark in the half light, somehow different, made me nervous. I had one of those three in the morning moments. "You don't really work on this ship, do you Zeke?" He looked horrified. He touched the patch behind his ear where the blocking chip was still there under the skin. I knew now with absolute certainty that this was not a person who took orders this was a person who took chances.

He sat up, reaching out a hand and placing it on my leg. "There is nothing I could possibly say now that would be the right thing."

The fact that I could understand him without the Com/T was somehow reassuring, hopeful even. Basic was still English, with some Spanish, which I understood and some Chinese, which I didn't. I still found it disconcerting to see someone's lips move and a different word come out, like a really badly dubbed film. This was somehow better.

"Everything I've done since I got here is stumbling around in the dark. I mean how bad can this be? You know I once jumped off a bridge with a parachute," I paused for a second, "Actually that wasn't as much fun as I thought it was going to be, so bad example."

He cut in, "I can't tell you anything." Rubbing his face, he stood and went over to the kitchen area, setting up cups for a hot drink, in the age old need for the process to ease the tension.

"Sometimes," he said half to himself, "Things get blurred and the difference between the good and the bad is not as well defined as it should be."

"What does that mean? I hate enigmatic. Rani does it as well, it drives me completely crazy!" He looked puzzled for a moment and came over to put the Com/T back in his ear. I moved it out of his reach. "Don't do that, you understood what I said perfectly well."

"Look," he said with undisguised exasperation, "There is no grand plan and I'm not fighting for a cause here. I'm just doing a job."

"I understand." I touched his hand and he sat down next to me.

"Maybe when I first got here I thought that this was a more complicated place. But I understand 'nothing much has changed.' Life is looking for work and staying out of trouble."

He smiled, "It's still like that, just bigger. We are a part of an economic frenzy. The industrialisation of space," he added bitterly.

"So what is the problem?"

We sat quietly, so much so that I heard Ollie, somewhere in the shadows, washing a knotty bit on his furry belly.

Zeke shrugged. "We're supposed to be the good people." I nodded and he went back to the making of milky coffee and burnt toast.

I did some more thinking and thought of something else. "But why did you take this job?" He came over with the coffee and sat down close to me.

I sipped and he stared. "I saw a picture, a hologram." He put his hand on my face, turning it towards him. Whatever I was expecting, it wasn't that. I mean I was quite interesting in the right light, but I was not, nor had I ever been, photogenic. Our faces were inches apart again. I tried not to make one of those inside your head promises as they were the hardest to break.

"Can we do this next door? My days of sofa sex are well over." He lifted me gently to my feet. And removed the cup of hot coffee I had been clutching as a barrier. I contemplated for no more than a moment, the comforting fact that even in the twenty-fifth century uncomfortable sofa sex could still be had.

The horrendous noise sent all three of us into orbit. Ollie had been asleep on Zeke's bare back and so had left several claw marks in his haste to get away. Zeke cursed in a language I vaguely recognised, reaching for clothes and finding mine. "Agh! Xon Dah!" He said again.

"I'm not sure but I think we already did that."

"What?" His voice was muffled by the vest he was trying to get into.

The natural light that was programmed into the rooms to come on when 'night' had passed was not in evidence. The holo/clock said five am. "What is that?" I turned the bedside light up a few notches.

Zeke was nearly clothed and looking hopefully around for his boots, I pointed to the other room. He had scrambled into his jacket and had one boot on and his Com/T when I came through in my dressing gown with my hands over my ears. "It's the emergency alert Bea. Which," he added sarcastically, "You would know if you had read the drills Rani gave you."

"What am I supposed to do then," I said hoping for a hint. "Report to someone, or something?" I was grouchy with lack of sleep and the apprehension that went with loud unexplained noises in the dark.

"Yes," he laughed, "Me!" As an afterthought, and just before he went through the door, he kissed me on the nose and shook me gently out of my torpor. "Get dressed and find Rani and be careful."

I walked through the steam part of the shower for ninety seconds and put my clothes on. Nothing would have persuaded me to go to my death without a wash. Ollie was under the bed and I contemplated joining him.

I put my Com/T in my ear and was just opening my mouth to ask Rani where she was when the door slid open and she swept in.

"What now?" I asked.

"It looks like renegades."

I paused for a moment in the hope of something insightful. "Why?"

We were out in the corridor by now and it had weird lighting low down close to the floor. Presumably so that when you were running for your life you didn't trip over a shoe lace. But it made the faces we passed look like empty masks. "I can't imagine that they would be stupid enough to attack a 'League ship,'" Rani huffed.

"Have you 'looked?'" I asked.

"Not yet."

I turned to face her. "Is this about me?" She shrugged, which was better than a thousand words. One more piece in a puzzle I didn't have the key for.

Rani didn't even try to make me use the lift shafts and we ran towards hydroponics and up the steps. The awful noise stopped abruptly and so did I. "Does that mean I can go back to bed?" I asked hopefully. She grabbed my arm and half laughing, half-exasperated shoved me in front of her up to the first level.

The bridge was dimly lit. A dozen people manned the various work consoles, and the reflected light shone upwards onto shadowed faces. The holograms of different views from the ship were dotted around. Zeke and the captain were in quiet conversation. The door behind us slid open again and Mark Limbu came in, looking as if he still hurt in a lot of places. He nodded at Rani and patted my arm as he went over to join Zeke and the captain.

Jenny Smith was sitting in the pilot seat again, either she was really good at flying or always in trouble; she smiled a distracted smile at me as I came over to look out of the bridge windows.

There were sections of the brain that just identified motion, predator prey or mate. The ship in the forward windows fell into the first category. It menaced. Its grey looming presence seemed to suck the darkness from the space around it. Like a large crab waiting for lunch to come out of a hole. For the first time the Starfire didn't look quite so comforting in her size.

The captain spoke to Yas Molina. "Do they want to talk yet?"

He was about to send a message when a blast of sound and fury hit the Starfire, sending us reeling into each other. I heard Jenny mutter quietly to herself, "That would be 'no' then."

I could sense a feeling older than curiosity, like the creatures I had encountered on scuba-diving trips in Australia, in the deepest part of the ocean. Without seeing them I was aware of their presence and they were 'seeing' me. I shuddered.

Another blast had the captain swearing in frustration. I intercepted a look between her and Zeke that seemed to say 'what now?' somehow more unsettling for the fact that she was asking him. I voiced my nervousness, "I sincerely hope we have more large bangs because that is a mean looking ship." Jenny snorted in appreciation.

The captain looked at me. "We would have to drop the protection field to fire." Just about everyone in the room looked puzzled at this 'unnecessary' explanation, except Zeke and Rani. We couldn't fire back just in case I got whizzed into eternity.

The ship waited. Then a face appeared on the holo/view screen in the middle of the room. It was oriental with sharp dark features and a smile to freeze the soul. "Captain," he said and he turned slightly as if listening to a far off voice and I could see a long ponytail at the back of his head. He turned back to look at us with an over the top smile back in place. "We both know why I'm here. Hand it over and we'll be on our way."

The captain did that 'cut throat' gesture, with an aggressive finger. Yas Molina suspended the communication link.

Once again everyone in the room was puzzled except the four of us. I was reeling from being referred to as 'it.' Later, after the fear had left my dry mouth, I would try and be angry, if there was a later.

Jenny turned around in her seat and looked at the frozen hologram, then at the captain. "What do we have that he could want so badly?" No one answered. She turned back shaking her head. No one looked at me.

The captain signalled Yas to turn on the link. "Yamuti/Chet," she smiled her own brand of 'don't mess with me' through gritted teeth. "You're a long way from home." Another blast shook my teeth inside my head and knocked me into Zeke. He held onto my arm a moment longer than necessary.

"Captain, we're taking damage," a voice from behind us said quietly, a little out of breath. I turned to see Mark wincing as he picked himself up off the ground.

"Sig," Zeke spoke into his Com/T, "Get up to the bridge." He added, "Bring Doz." Something that I thought was totally unnecessary as they were usually stitched at the hip.

"What is Yamuti/Chet doing," Rani asked the captain, adding her own layer of exasperation to the cloud hovering over the bridge, "Do you want me to have a look?"

"I don't think that would be a good idea," the captain glanced at Rani conveying unspoken significance and boiling frustration. More puzzled expressions followed this remark. Mark Limbu was looking at me with the 'I think I might have worked this out' light dawning in his eyes. But then he had been nearly pulled into next week with me and the pain of third degree burns would sharpen anyone's senses.

I got the distinct feeling that this 'encounter' was not going according to the usual procedures and the fact that Rani was not out there doing her job was a big sign something was 'up.' Both Yas Molina and Jenny Smith had that crumpled forehead look.

"For those of us who are still in bed and having a really bad nightmare who is this," I whispered, not expecting an answer.

"Well," said Jenny, who had recovered first from the Com/T's inept buzzing, "Basically he's nobody and the last time I saw him he had a third rate ship and was scraping crumbs from the likes of Fliss Dalgety."

"Well I don't see any crumb scraping now."

She shrugged her agreement.

Rani came to stand next to me and I touched her arm for comfort, breathing in her sanity. Doz and Sig swept in through the bridge doors looking appropriately warlike and fierce, except for the big grins. "So what can we do for you, commander?" Sig snapped off a salute. Zeke pointed at me.

"Great," said Doz, "We're here to save Bea."

"Again," Sig mugged disappointment for a stunned audience, "But we've done that already."

"Take Bea down to the engineering section, get as close to the core as possible and do not break physical contact with her for any reason." They nodded and Doz gave me a sympathetic smile, their seriousness making me so much more afraid.

For a moment my brain couldn't comprehend why I should go and stand next to the most dangerous thing on the ship when some crazy idiot was firing at us.

Rani leaned in towards me. "The core of the engine has a strong electro magnetic field," she said very quietly.

The rest of the crew on the bridge had fallen into 'ours is not to reason why.' I hoped we wouldn't get to the 'do or die' part. But no one in that room could have been in any doubt as to what 'it' meant.

The captain reached out a hand as I passed her and squeezed mine. "We're going to make a run to the Ross 154 Space Station." I nodded, even though I had no idea what that meant noting that Jenny Smith's mouth had dropped open. There was that feeling when you realised you were the only one who was out of step and you wondered just how long you had been marching to the beat of your own drummer.

Sig gave me a tap on the arm and we went through the doorway. I didn't look at Zeke because the chances of pulling off a decent exit would have been halved.

We did a sort of six-legged race with Doz slightly in front. One more blast had us thrown sideways like rag dolls. Doz swore as he pulled me to my feet. I could smell smoke and my head ached from where I had smacked into the corridor. Sig rubbed my back, the way you would calm a nervous horse or frightened child. I smiled my gratitude as speaking was out of the question.

Torriff came through a doorway on the forth level, we slammed into each other and held on for balance and his eyes widened as he focused on me. "I thought you were on the bridge?"

"We're heading down to engineering," I said, out of breath.

Sig was pulling on my arm. "Come on Bea." Doz got the other side of me.

Torriff looked puzzled for a moment and then nodded his head. "I will go to the bridge I must see what I can do to help." He put his hand on my face and nodded. "Evil sleeps very lightly, it is easily roused."

"Bea. Now please." Sig manhandled me away and I found myself looking back at Torriff, until he turned and hurried off in the other direction.

We headed for the back of the ship and tried the lift shafts. They were still working. Before we stepped in Sig attached a line to me and hooked it through a karabiner on his own kit, then attached it to a loop on the outer corridor. He opened his mouth to explain. I interjected, "Don't say it don't even go there." He shut his mouth and looked bemused. Abseiling could have been part of a good day's rock climbing but it had lost its charm in the case of a lift failure. The look on Ko-Yo-Na's face was almost worth the trip through darkened corridors and swirls of clouded apprehension that seemed to suck the heart out of me.

As the doors swished open, a wave of frantic activity and noise washed around us. We were met with a barely concealed incredulity from the engineering staff and a barrage of helpful suggestions from Ko about what to do if there was an explosion in the core. The gist of which was on the 'say goodbye' end of the solution scale. The blast was preceded by a second's warning which was not enough time to grab hold of something but aeons of time for your mouth to dry in fear. I skidded across the floor, cracking my elbow on one of the barriers that surrounded the engine. Doz rolled back onto his feet and I noticed Ko distracted for a moment, checking that he was okay. We had feelings above fear and survival sometimes.

Sig had managed to keep a hold of me as the ship tipped and the floor angle changed. I had been in an earthquake once in Los Angeles. It was difficult for your brain to comprehend that the ground beneath your feet was moving, no longer a safe constant.

"Try not to lean on the casing!" Ko shouted. "It has the capacity to burn your skin off."

Sig spoke into his Com/T, raising his voice above the noise, "Captain, we're here."

"Thanks Sig," was the short reply.

A siren sounded, it was a different noise from the wake-up call that morning, but just as disturbing for the nerve endings. Ko talked through her Com/T and to Lieutenant Commander Sofred at the same time, using the good old-fashioned method of waving her hands around in the air to attract his attention. I couldn't hear what she said.

A rumble of thunder was greeted by the crew with serious, silent, satisfaction. Lieutenant Commander Sofred, who was standing at the console nearest me said, "About zarling time!" He wiped a trickle of blood from his forehead and smiled at me. I had never seen a Katinad smile before, never mind swear, it was somehow reassuring.

"We're firing back," said Doz. He looked at Sig and closed his hand over my upper arm. They braced themselves against the barriers and we sat, squashed together half squatting in some discomfort.

The core behind us hummed for a moment and seemed to dim in power, I was waiting for something more spectacular to happen. "Is that it?" I asked Sig.

He looked bemused. "All the good stuff is happening at the pointy end, Bea." He still held onto my arm, a sensation which was fast heading in the direction of claustrophobia. I felt like smacking his fingers, hard. The universe was carefully divided into those who cared why things work and those who only cared that they do work. I was not above reading the manual but I wouldn't go overboard about it. Sig however fell firmly into the first category and began a fairly detailed account on how the sonic weapons worked. "Are you listening?" He shouted above the constant battering noise around us.

"I'm losing the will to live, but yes," I shouted back. Actually I was beginning to feel sick as if everything was slightly out of focus. My forehead felt sweaty and I wiped the palms of my hands on my trousers. Doz reached out a hand and squeezed my arm again as the core dimmed for a second time. "Are we getting anywhere with this?" I asked hopefully. They looked at each other over the top of my head.

Ko was moving around the engine room like a bee with honey. She talked constantly through her Com/T and to her crew. I watched Doz follow her with his eyes and he caught me looking. A moment of deep sadness filled the tiny space between us because some things were just not meant to be.

A small sound infiltrated my brain, which was odd because the possibility of anything less than a bellow attracting my attention in the maelstrom was unlikely. So it was a fair bet that it was an 'inside' noise. "Sig, I think something is happening."

He looked exasperated as he and Doz both turned at the same time. "Could you be a little more specific Bea?"

I listened very carefully as the sound manifested itself as a rather irritating buzz. I looked behind me. "Well, it seems to be coming from this." I pointed to the engine casing.

They did a non-verbal communication on a par with Congress and in a second Doz yelled, "Ko, check the core readings!" She was puzzled which was odd without the eyebrows and went to the nearest console. Shaking her head in our direction she did some more checking. Lieutenant Commander Sofred came over to look at the readings with her, nothing.

"I don't have time for this right now," she said with exasperation. Doz looked at me. I was cringing with the noise level which felt more and more like fingers down a blackboard every second.

Lieutenant Commander Sofred leaned across and pointed to something, they both looked closer as if trying to make sense of a crossword clue. Her eyes did a yo-yo and she battered at the keys as if for confirmation.

"Sofred, get up to the third level and tell me if you get the same readings." He clattered up the steps, taking two at a time and I watched until the spiral curved away from me.

"How did you know?" Ko squatted in front of us. Doz shrugged and pointed at me. I was listening for a change. There was still an excruciating racket. A blast caught us all off guard again and we jostled together like trees in a tropical hurricane. Doz caught hold of the engineer to stop her from being battered by the floor. She thanked him and I saw a flicker of recognition pass between them, a comprehension of strength understood.

"Sofred, what's going on up there?" She yelled into the Com/T, making me wince. "Is the noise getting louder Bea?" I nodded.

Lieutenant Commander Sofred's quiet incredulous voice answered, "There seems to be some sort of device Commander Ko, attached to the underside of the console. It's been integrated with the casing coolant system."

Fear had a stimulus that imprinted itself on our visual cortex and acres of DNA are alerted before our brain processed the information. Fight or flight, but that was if you had a choice. It was the first time I had seen Ko look frightened and it chilled me to the bone.

"Can one of you go and look at that device?" Her voice betrayed her feelings. "I need to try and find an alternative solution to keeping the core casing cool." Doz released my arm and went up the steps as if an event horizon had appeared behind him.

"Has he done this sort of thing before?" Even I could detect the note of fear creeping in to my voice.

"Well no, but he can cook a mean curry," Sig said helpfully. I think my edge of reason expression must have been showing because he added gently, "He's really good at this Bea, if anyone can do it, he can." I leaned my head on his arm and he tried to pat my face and we sat there in the midst of the madness with a drift of smoke coming through from the corridor and I thought about my brother Sam who used to comfort me in much the same way after one of my learning to fly episodes from the garage roof.

The noise level began to contain a note of panic. I could feel the sensation radiating around the ship as the news of the problem permeated the walls. There was no need for an announcement over the Com/T as gossip was much more effective and faster than being swallowed by a black hole.

Ko-Yo-Na kept moving, checking readings, shouting at crew, talking to Sofred and Doz though I couldn't hear what they said and 'jury rigging' a group of portable coolers from the lower docking bay that Gatt.R. had brought up.

He looked at Sig and me sitting by the engine core and literally did a double take. I couldn't even muster a smile. "Ko, Zeke suggested I go and see if I can help," he pointed up two levels, "I had some experience with bomb disposal after the war," he explained to no one. Ko nodded her distracted agreement and went over to the coolers, shouting at different crew members to leave their tasks and assist.

I could sense Sig's growing frustration with his forced inactivity. My stomach churned with fear and noise. The incoming blast shook the ship to a standstill. People were thrown about like an invisible giant with a really bad hangover had swept them aside. My teeth felt loose in my head and my bones ached from the inability to land on anything soft.

People flew through the air in the middle of a really bad action film and everyone got up after the smoke cleared but in reality, the smoke didn't clear and people stayed where they fell.

Sig groaned and rolled onto his back, he sat up suddenly looking around. "Bea." He crawled over to me. "Can you move?"

"Do I have to?" I tried each limb carefully and slowly, checking for any pain, then looked around at the chaos. Bits of the fabric of the room were leafing down from the ceiling like a gentle snow and smoke hung in the middle layers. I could see Ko staggering to her feet and back to the nearest console, she heaved a crew member upright and he began to check the very still body lying close to him.

"Sig go and help, I'm okay." He looked doubtful for a moment. I shooed him with both hands. "Go." He scrambled away checking people for injuries, calling for medical teams and helping people who could move into more comfortable positions than the ones dictated to them by gravity. Pui came in through the doors with a group of three medical techs, all carrying kit. They looked dirty and dishevelled. I didn't think I would ask right now how things were going at the 'pointy end.'

Buffers staggered over to me. "How are you, Bea?" He helped me up. "Zeke," he looked embarrassed as he spoke, "Was wondering how you were." A whimper made us both turn. Curved at an impossible angle against the back of the core casing was a young engineering tech. Her overalls were soaked in blood.

"Oh please no!" I ran over to her. Kneeling in the debris, I pressed my hand over the pumping wound in her leg.

Buffers pulled a pack from his kit and covered my hand and the wound, nodding for me to let go. It sealed with a sucking sound and I wiped my sticky hands on my trousers and checked the name on her top; I had to clean the blood away before I could read it. Ravenscroft. I remembered her first name now. "Dana, I whispered," as I tried to get a response. Buffers did something with what looked like a stethoscope and a button sized disc was placed on the chest wall. Her breathing became more erratic and the heartbeat was rapid and thready. He passed a small portable scan over her and tutted when he looked at the result.

"Bea," Sig shouted into the din, "Not so far from the core."

Buffers snorted his reaction to that too, "I would have thought as far away as possible would be the best advice right now." He carried on pulling interesting things out of his kit bag.

"It's a long story," I said.

"It always is," he muttered.

"How's it going up there," I asked hopefully, "Are we any closer to the Ross 154 Space Station?"

"We're getting the beating of a lifetime and not nearly close enough." He attached a fluid giving device to a main blood vessel in the girl's arm and began checking for other injuries. Her breathing was getting quieter. I leaned over her to confirm my suspicions.

"Buffers."

"I hear it." He shouted over to one of the other medical techs, trying to attract his attention, but the noise, that had risen to pre-blast levels, carried it and made it part of the nothingness. I stuck two fingers into my mouth and whistled. It was train stopping and just about everyone looked around. I spat out the taste of dried blood.

"Sometime you have to teach me how to do that," Buffers said, impressed.

I recognised the tech as Couzins, I hadn't seen him for ages, we nodded our wordless greeting and he looked down to assess the situation. "It's Dana." He knelt gently by her side stroking back the long blonde hair. "We're from the same biosphere on Ganymede," he added quietly. "She joined the year after me." I patted his arm, which felt like a useless futile gesture. So much pain in the air was making it difficult to breathe lightly.

Between them they fitted the stretcher gently around the injured girl and set the auto-lift so it came off the ground. It always impressed me to see the hover-bed in action. It also made a big difference to not actually be lying on it for a change.

"Bea!" Sig waved me angrily back toward the casing. It seemed to me at this point that if I was whizzed anywhere it was the least of our worries, but my thoughts were cut short by Doz leaning over the upper balcony and waving me up. A shower of dust accompanied the gesture and it whirled in a vortex of shining particles like a shooting star. Ko looked up for a moment and was caught in the dust like an actress on opening night.

The steps were so close to the core I thought it qualified as an appropriate distance and Sig nodded at me and then went back to saving lives with Pui.

Lieutenant Commander Sofred was so far under the console only his legs were to be seen. His red uniform was torn in several places and I could see a gash on his leg seeping straw coloured fluid. Doz was no better off; he had blood on one sleeve and a bad bruise over his left eye. He looked at me, counting damage and sighed, the deep sigh of tiredness after too much. Adrenaline only got you so far then it got you nowhere.

All the inner workings of the broad console were on display with not as much wiring as I was used to but small jelly-like components, similar to the computers we had carried with us down to the Restran Planet. The unit curved neatly around the shape of the core and the last blast seemed to have missed the level to a certain extent. There was not much debris lying around and no people bleeding if you didn't include the ones still on their feet.

"Have you ever 'looked' at anything like this before?" Doz asked.

I shrugged and shook my head. "What is it, bio-mechanical engineering?" I put out a hand to touch the exposed surface of the console.

Doz curled his fingers over mine and gently pushed me back. "It's 'live' Bea, you'd get a really bad punch from that."

Lieutenant Commander Sofred shouted to Doz, "Pass me that scanner." Doz slid the small unit under the console until it connected with the lieutenant commander's hand, he 'ummed' and 'ahhed' a few times while we stood half bent over trying to see what he was doing. "Try it now Doz!"

"Not while you're still under there Sofred." Doz reattached some connections as the lieutenant commander scrambled out from underneath and staggered to his feet.

"Right, let's try again. Stand back Bea." I moved out of the way and the two of them began tapping keys. The board in front lit up like a Christmas tree and then went dark again. Doz banged his hand down on the surface. He leaned forward, defeated. "I'm not sure I can fix this." They looked like boxers that had gone one round too many.

"Where's Gatt.?" I asked, just as a hand closed on my shoulder. I was not sure if levitation had reached this part of the galaxy, or if any real scientific tests had been done over the last four hundred years, but you could definitely have seen my feet leave the floor and travel some considerable distance.

"Bea, does Rani know you can do that?" Doz snorted with laughter.

I clutched my heart and turned around to see a grinning Gatt. He was filthy and his hair was matted with blood. He jerked a thumb to the open door of a maintenance shaft. "I've been trying to isolate the power connection to this console."

A thin shiny limb curled around the edge of the shaft. My heart thudded up another notch.

"That's all I need." The robot stayed where it was, but my nerve endings were dinging like church bells with a novice in charge. It was difficult to turn my back on it.

"Any luck Gatt.?" Doz asked hopefully. Gatt. shook his head. Doz leaned over the barrier and shouted down to Ko, "How long have we got?" She looked up, her face shiny with sweat and what looked like tears.

In my peripheral vision, I saw Pui pull a cover over Dana's face, her youth a blur. A small white hand fell and flopped lifelessly down in a sweeping motion of vulnerability which made it impossible to think straight. Jim Couzins gently lifted the hand and kissed it, he placed it lovingly back under the cover and along with everyone else in the room I carefully didn't notice.

"The casing's already hot Doz, fifteen minutes if we're lucky," Ko said. "I've got all the portable coolers up and running, it might buy us a bit more time." She wiped her face with the back of a dirty sleeve and I could see Doz, his hands gripping the edge of the barrier, shaking with the effort of not running down the steps to comfort her.

"Doz, do you always feel as if you'd like to thump something at a time like this?"

"Yes."

I looked back down at the covered stretcher. "I think I can identify with that right now." A groan of noise made me shudder. "What is that?"

"The sonic cannon," Sofred answered, as it was obvious Doz's thinking was elsewhere.

"Okay, captain?"

"Make it fast, Doz."

"Can we use Bea to do a sweep?" This was followed by a short silence, when I knew that she was speaking to Rani, because I tried to speak to Rani and got the telepathic equivalent of a busy signal. The fact that she could usually do two or more things at the same time meant that she was doing two or more things.

"Does she think she can do this?" I shook my head, no.

"Yes captain," replied Doz.

"What about the risk?" She asked. I put my hand over my head I had no idea what I was doing here.

"Minimal risk captain," Doz answered.

"Okay, go ahead." The contact broke.

"Do you ever lie awake at night Doz?" I asked incredulously.

"What have you got to lose?" He smiled.

I shrugged. "You mean apart from my dignity?" I snorted, desperate times called for desperate measures.

I put my hands on the console and tried to block out the background noise. Rani had taught me to look for a bead of light in the darkness. The console felt cold, a place with no human energy or spirit. I looked deep into the angles and shapes and came to a place where it didn't feel right. In the living cell of the biological fuel battery, a large, spider-like shape, it couldn't have been any thing else could it, reached into the gel. A small angry red light pulsed in the centre.

The sensation of someone looking over my shoulder nearly made me turn and the silence behind me seemed to buzz with old secrets. I felt the light touch of something like a whisper of words, the line of a song I couldn't remember, grey and old with time. The shape of the spider in front of me pulled me towards it, but the desire to turn was strong. I shivered and broke contact to see anxious faces.

"I'm okay." I gave into the sensation and looked behind me anyway.

"Well?" Sofred's voice shook with strain and the tiredness of fear.

"I don't know what I was looking at," they all sighed with impatience, "But if you go past the frying pan and the balloon with glasses, at the place where the thing that looks like a horse's head is, there's a spider with a big red eye."

The stunned silence involved Sofred looking horrified and Gatt. looking puzzled. They both had their mouths open. Doz did some quick translation in his head and then said, "I think the horse's head is the cooling processor."

"What's a horse's head?" Sofred had found his power of speech.

"It's an equine mammal from Earth," Doz said, pre-occupied. He began drawing shapes in the dust on the surface of the console.

"What about a frying pan?" Asked Gatt.

"Cooking utensil," Doz replied absent-mindedly. No one had asked about the balloon with glasses, but the desperate sounds that had been made by the Com/T were loud enough to compete with the noise of the sonic cannon. "How does this look Bea?" I leaned over his shoulder and added a few lines. Gatt. grunted his recognition. Sofred was already scrambling back into the claustrophobic space reaching for tools.

Ko shouted up to us, "I'm going to start evacuating the section Doz." He leaned over the barrier and just nodded.

Sig had left Pui who was taking the wounded through the broken doorway and he raced up the steps.

"If the core goes it won't matter much where we are on the ship," Gatt. said helpfully to no one. He passed a small scanner to Sofred's anxious hand. I sat down on the floor too tired to stand any longer, the scattering of tools beside me irritated my sense of balance and I began tidying them up, putting them back in the container next to the console.

"What are you doing Bea?" Sig asked gently.

I looked up without really seeing for a moment and thought about it. "When my life is falling apart I tidy."

He nodded as if he understood. "My father used to be like that. When the war started he went around the freighter cleaning up and making the beds." He shook his head and so did Gatt. To me it made sense.

The ship shuddered and whipped around at what felt like a right angle. We were thrown back against the wall. Fortunately it wasn't in the other direction as three levels was a long way to fall. "Are you okay?" Gatt. tried to lift me into a sitting position.

"Yes, I've always been a sucker for a handbrake turn."

"I think I've got it!" The legs under the console were animated. Doz and Sig scrambled over to Sofred. I leaned up against the wall and closed my eyes, thinking selfishly, please let this be over. Then I thought about Dana.

"Sig?" Zeke's voice came over the Com/T on an open line.

"We're still at it Zeke." Sig was pulling Sofred out by his ankles for speed.

"We're going to have to make the jump to Ross154 Station now."

Sig looked at the lieutenant commander. "Wait one minute Zeke. Sofred?"

The Katinad looked stunned. "We can't jump with that still attached, it will overheat for sure!"

"How far away are we from removing it?" Doz squatted down next to Sofred.

He shrugged. "I think I will need twenty minutes or so."

Doz shifted down on the floor. "I'll give you a hand."

Sig spoke into the Com/T, "Give us ten minutes Zeke." I think Sofred whimpered or maybe that was me.

"You'll have to give me the exact moment you get it free. We're running out of time. And hold onto something down there, it's not going to be a thing of great beauty." Zeke cut the connection.

I hoped it was not going to be one of those countdowns with red flashing lights where the clock stopped at one second to disaster, I wondered if it was a plus that I couldn't actually see a clock.

The noise from the core was reaching a fever pitch. Sig and I reached for tools on request. Gatt. glanced over the barrier. "It looks as if we're the only ones left at the party, except Ko." He waved at her and she shouted something back but I couldn't hear what she said.

The siren sounded for a star-jump, one noise I actually recognised.

"Come on Sig, we have to go." The suppressed anxiety in Zeke's voice made me feel sick.

"Nearly there."

"We need to do this now."

"Got it!" Doz scrambled out from under the console and Sig pulled on Sofred's legs. He yanked him out as fast as possible.

"It's still live, the 'zarling' thing is still live, I thought it would be safe when we disconnected!" Sofred's face was a mask of terror.

Sig grabbed the small spider like shape. "Is there an outside disposal unit up here?"

Gatt. was already running towards a wall mounted unit. "Here," he shouted, activating it.

Sig shoved the device into the disposal chute and banged the release disc. "Go for it Zeke!"

Doz grabbed me and the edge of the barrier at the same time, as the world turned inside out and I floated in coloured lights. I could see Sig and Gatt. frozen in mid air and thought that it was surely going to hurt when we returned to normal space. The stream of time was followed by eternity as it always was and then a ripple of blue and a rush of reality and I watched Sig and Gatt. as they hit the floor hard.

The silence was ship-wide. I raised my head off the floor to see if Gatt. and Sig were okay. They were both moving, albeit like a couple of beached fish.

"What was that, it wasn't the usual star-jump?" I asked, not really expecting any answer.

Sofred moved himself carefully upright, into a sitting position. "It is similar to an artificial event horizon, so it's not always the same."

He rolled down again quickly, not happy with being upright. "Do you know what an event horizon is?"

"Of course I know what an event horizon is, thanks to Samantha Carter of Stargate SG.1, every nine-year-old in my time knows what that is!" It went quiet for a moment as they all digested the information and checked for broken bones.

Doz lifted his head. "Who is Samantha Carter?"

"She's the woman who put sex into science. Sort of did for quantum physics what Mae West did for the life preserver."

Doz grunted, "I have no idea what you're talking about, I just know it's something inappropriate."

"Does Samantha Carter know Dolly Parton?" Sig asked, still lying face down, his voice muffled by close proximity to the floor.

"They're old friends," I answered without moving my head.

I fell onto the sofa by the window in my rooms and curled my legs up to one side. Ollie was still under the bed and had decided to remain there. He had growled at me when I reached for him. I completely understood. "Are you okay?" Rani asked gently.

"Yes, I'm just getting my second wind." She snorted and I closed my eyes against the spinning headache that just wouldn't go away. The dirt and dried blood would just have to wait for a while. The walk back up from engineering had taken hours. There were people injured from the fight and those who had not been able to find something to hang onto when the ship had star-jumped. The medical bay was full to overflowing and Pui had set up a triage in the corridor for anyone who could be treated by a medic and sent back to their rooms.

My petty cuts and bruises could wait. I met Rani coming in the opposite direction bringing Jenny Smith, who was leaning on her and hobbling on a swollen ankle. Her face was covered in blood from a cut on her forehead. I thought about suggesting crash helmets as part of the uniform.

"What happened after I left?" I asked them both, as I helped Rani lower Jenny to the floor outside the medical bay. A medical tech came over and took a quick look at her injuries.

"Well," said Jenny, "We traded insults and quite a lot of ordnance and did some running away so it was a bit like my first marriage contract really."

The tech came back and looked at the three of us convulsed with hysterical laughter. "I'm not going to have to sedate you am I?" He asked suspiciously.

Rani was covered in dust and had sweat streaks running down her face. I could tell by her expression that I must have looked just as bad. We wandered the corridors for a while, collecting anyone who needed help walking to the medical bay and then headed back towards my rooms.

Teams of techs and service crew were doing emergency repairs and an air of post-traumatic exhaustion hung in the smoke and damage. Tom Hatherley was working on level five with four of the other uninjured crew. He wiped the sweat dripping from his forehead with the back of his dirty uniform, smearing black marks across his face. He smiled.

"I could drink a bucket of coffee."

Rani and I went together to the upper restaurant and grabbed baskets of food and hot drinks from Tariq, who was working with a gel cast on his broken arm. He smiled in a kind of dazed shock, sweeping debris from work surfaces to prepare more food. I didn't think anyone was going to mind if it came with a bit of grit.

Working from the upper levels, we distributed as much as possible to grateful dirty hands. Everyone smiled their gratitude and at the back of my mind I wondered if anyone blamed me for the mess. It was impossible to use the lift shafts, so we travelled up and down the steps in hydroponics and used the maintenance ladders on the lower levels. Half way through the fourth trip from the restaurant, the lift shafts came back online again and for once I didn't complain about using them. On level one I paused in pouring the coffee. Mac Ibarra with his hand outstretched, looked where I was looking. "Amazing, isn't it?" He grabbed the sandwich I had offered. Out of the double windows I could see the Ross 154 Space Station.

It looked like a child's spinning toy, with a large centre ring and then smaller and smaller rings radiating out at the top and bottom. It was beautiful in its symmetry and it sparkled with coloured lights and buzzed with life. Ships were docked on the larger ring giving it a spiky look. I could see other ships either coming into dock or leaving. It seemed to be orbiting a small moon, which in turn was close to a gold and brown planet. Far away in the dark filled solar system was its star.

More than anything I had seen in the last few months the space station made me realise that we were really out here. I could hear thousands of busy minds. The passage of human exploration, that necessary time line of need to see beyond the next hill, had finally taken us to the stars.

I came back to the coffee pot and Mac. "Do you know why we're not docking for repairs?" He asked between slurps. I shrugged. I could hazard a good guess, but if the captain wasn't making a ship-wide announcement on the subject then I wasn't going to speculate.

He stuffed the rest of the sandwich in and grabbed some more coffee, giving me a hug which made my eyes water. "Thanks Bea, I'm glad you're okay."

In my head I didn't deserve it.

The sound of milky coffee being stirred woke me from a nightmare of open-eyed torpor. Rani had found some undamaged cake in one of my food compartments which was a miracle as everything else was mashed.

We had put the rooms back into some sort of order from the whirlwind that had inflicted itself on cushions and clothes and bedding. The plants needed more help than I could give them. I got up and began putting books back on the shelves. The door chimed as Rani came over to give me the hot drink. "Come in." We both croaked at the same time. Zeke was filthy, his uniform was torn and there was blood all down the front of it. I gasped, as if I had been holding onto something too hard. He came over and hugged me. Rani made more coffee.

We sat without speaking for a good long while, dirty hands reached for cake and we ate and drank through our exhaustion. Zeke cleared his throat, "I'm thinking of volunteering for the six-year run on the fuel barges to Denebola." It sounded as if it was a good idea, I wondered if they had a bunk for a telepath.

The door chimed again and Sig and Doz staggered in. "Oh great, we thought you'd have a brew going," Doz said. They threw themselves into chairs and reached for the cake and I got up to make more drinks.

"Well done." Zeke said quietly, looking carefully at both of them.

"Yes well," said Sig, "I can remember when all you had to do was ask a girl out."

"That must have been before my time," Doz looked puzzled. We laughed because it was funny and because we had to. Death forced an intimacy between those who were left. The ceremony of food shared was about life once lived and went backwards in time forever.

"I feel responsible," I said. The collective look was one of incomprehension.

"You do *know* it's not your fault though?" Sig asked. "I mean this sort of thing happens all the time." We all paused to think about this.

Doz broke first, he sighed, "Actually that's not true, I've been in wars that were more restful than the last few months."

"Yes Bea," said Sig, "If you want a quiet day tomorrow, we could maybe invade a small planet?" There was hysteria, which went well with the dirt and coffee and eventually we talked about other things. My usual ability with denial wasn't working and I was fast approaching emotional meltdown.

They wandered to their places to sleep and I curled up on the sofa again in the shipboard equivalent of the early hours. It felt safer being close to the space station somehow, like being back in your parents' house, even when you were an adult and not supposed to need the comfort.

The chin butting by a furry purring creature woke me far too soon. It looked as if I had been forgiven for making the world go mad. Ollie put a paw into my mouth to persuade me to get up. I found food for him and had a gallon of hot water as my mouth felt like a scouring pad. The water in the bathroom was back on and I stood under the shower and then turned it to steam. I was an appropriate shade of lobster when I got out.

The clothes I had been wearing were good for the recycler and not much else. Ollie sat on the bed while I dressed. We discussed the day ahead and what we could do to make ourselves useful. Ollie decided he would put his talents to washing and sleeping and curled into a nest in the pillows.

I cut a large slice of chocolate cake and sat down with coffee. At some point I would have to brave the rest of the ship and look for food that had some nutritional value, there was nothing wrong with cake, but even I had my limits. My window was on the other side of the ship from the space station, but I could still see the incoming and outgoing traffic. Ships and vehicles of all sizes came and went in the business of trade and repair and communication. They had a range of speed that went from 'gone in a flash' to 'still trucking along.' The door chimed and Captain Witherspoon walked in.

Ollie left the bed immediately and went over to her and she picked him up and stuck her nose in his fur, sniffing in a lungful of cat; something that endeared her to me, though it would usually have got her a swipe from a clawed paw from Ollie. He tolerated her homage seeming to understand the necessity for furry comfort.

"How are you?" She sat down, putting the cat on her lap.

I shrugged and tried not to be flippant. "Coffee?"

She nodded. "We have to dock on the station, don't go anywhere without Sig or Doz."

"Has Rani read them?"

"Yes," she laughed, "She said if I wanted it done again I could do it myself."

269

"They were that bad?"

"I think they were less than helpful."

I could imagine that the two of them would see it as their duty to make things as interesting for Rani as possible. No wonder I hadn't seen her this morning, she was probably lying in her room with a wet towel around her head. I wanted to ask about the lack of people being read but I couldn't think how to phrase the question.

"Are you limiting the amount of crew being read?"

"Yes."

I though that asking why would be redundant, there would be no point in going on a fishing expedition if you'd emptied the pond.

The captain leaned back into the cushions and stroked Ollie until his purr rumbled in a deep contentment. The lines of exhaustion carved time in her face. "Do you think it's nearly over?" I asked her.

"No. For a second-rate pickpocket Yamuti/Chet nearly had us." She looked at my puzzled face. "He's got some serious help."

"Has he linked up with one of the other renegade families?"

"That is so unlikely that it's probably possible. I'm going to put out some feelers and see if I can find out anything."

I thought it was certain that we would be seeing something of Jad Lassik in the near future, but I kept the thought to myself.

We sat in silence drinking coffee. A small craft passed in front of my windows, on its way to other stars. "How's Pui doing?"

"There are four critical and Dana." She looked as if the weight of it would break her and I reached out a hand and took some of the pain for a moment. "Well, I must go and see if the repairs are happening. Gatt.R. has been buzzing me all morning about docking for stores and if I don't get down there he'll have a pale blue meltdown."

A part of me would have been curious to have seen that, but I thought perhaps I wouldn't say so.

She left and my cat went back to the bed and the interrupted washing. I realised I was putting off the trip into the corridor.

It was a gentle shade of blue, floor and walls reflected back calm and there was no smoke or dust. I knew that the ventilation system had the capacity to expel unwanted particulate matter out into space and it looked as if the techs had got it up and running.

I banged on Rani's door and got a grumpy response as it slid open. She was curled up on the sofa by her windows with a drink and a scowl that was so out of character it made me think of a sad bunny. "Did Sig and Doz give you a hard time?" I asked as gently as I could, trying not to let any humour creep into my voice.

"They were awful," It was practically a whimper. She looked at me. "You'd better not be laughing."

I went over to the windows and swallowed my smile before I turned around.

"The ship seems to be moving, I guess that means we're docking. Gatt. will be pleased."

"Don't go anywhere without one of the terrible twins Bea," she said quietly.

"I've already had that speech from the captain."

She shrugged and then threw the rug off her feet. "Come on, let's go and find some real food, before someone reports my stomach rumbling as engine failure."

We used the steps in hydroponics. The plants and trees had suffered and the mess was stacked into the sides of the biosphere. The birds were rustling but silent and there was no sign of Colin the feathered demon. Moi Uhara was working on level two as we went up.

He smiled and wiped a dirty hand over his face. "It's not as bad as it looks." Good, I thought, because it looked terrible. He added, "I wasn't able to save the strawberries though, Bea."

The trough where he had been growing them was tipped upside-down and the contents strewn all over the place. In the haste to get around the ship without using the lift shafts people had trodden the plants into the floor. I couldn't remember exactly, but I thought Rani and I had probably been responsible for some of it.

He didn't seem to mind having to start again. It was what farmers had done after great rain or wild weather from all time and like people who grew things forever, he was just getting on with it. I thought I would have been jumping up and down with frustration, but Moi was a farmer in the sky and he just shrugged and went back to shifting the dark beaded stuff they used for soil.

I leaned over the balcony from level one. "Moi." He looked up. "Do you want a hot drink?"

He looked really pleased and surprised. "Some green tea would be very welcome." I nodded and Rani and I walked on to the back of the ship and the upper restaurant.

"Rani, is Gurber okay?" I wondered why I hadn't thought to ask before. He seemed to disappear from my mind on a regular basis.

She looked as if the thought had only just occurred to her. "Yes fine, I think."

The restaurant looked a lot better than it had the night before and it was literally standing room only. Tariq waved his broken arm with the cast on; he smiled and pointed to the coffee and the food which was laid out on the side tables. You had to be impressed with the man and his team, who made food for the hungry hordes under difficult conditions and without complaint. I knew they had technology on their side, but it was not as if you could press a few buttons and it materialised out of thin air. Someone somewhere had had to bang a few pots.

I looked at the people and listened to the talking and laughing, they were so different but all of them seemed to be coming from the same place. Somehow the noise polarised into a void and I felt the shivers go through me. "What?" Rani leaned towards me to hear above the chatter of tired stressed voices.

"Nothing," I shook my head. I loaded a plate with rice and some vegetable topping and took the food to a table where some techs were leaving.

Tom Hatherley jumped up and gave me a hug. "I hear you were stuck to the engine core yesterday Bea, we have got to talk!" The rest of the techs laughed. He pulled my hair in the irrepressibility of youth and I found myself choked up at the thought of anything happening to these people who felt as if they were my people. "You do know," he added, "That all the sensible people run from that section in the case of a meltdown, not towards it!" His friends laughed again in the spirit of near misses experienced by the recently saved and I smiled.

"I'll try and remember that for next time." Over his shoulder I could see Rani; her eyes told me that not everyone had got the memo about me being the reason for the mayhem or the device in the core. Some things were better left alone.

I ate a few mouthfuls of food and watched Rani neatly buttering bread and layering salad stuff from the contents of her plate for the tidiest sandwich I had ever seen.

The ship jolted and slid sideways gently and then came to rest. The windows at the back of the restaurant were full of the space station and a slight cheer went around the room. It seemed to be the signal for an exodus as people went back to cover work assignments. A stir of anticipation hung around after they had gone and the remainder seemed to be talking in hopeful terms about 'shore leave.'

I chewed for a bit. "Rani, have we found any life forms that are not carbon-based?"

She stopped eating. "Where did that spring from?" I shrugged. She thought for a moment. "The atomic elements are common to all of us, like a universal language of electrons and protons. We think most life forms would be carbon-based, the carbon element, as you know, is the one on the periodic table that carries complex structures. I mean it is possible, I suppose, but we haven't really covered much of the galaxy yet." I nodded. More chewing went on and as it was quiet I went over and filled another plate with something that was hopefully a fruit cream thing. We sat in silence.

Rani groaned, "What?"

"Me, I didn't say anything."

"I can hear you thinking."

"Apart from Gurber's race, is there anyone out there that's more advanced than we are?"

She looked stunned. "Yes of course there is, did you read any of the crystal discs I give to you?"

"Yes, absolutely," I lied.

She snorted in an unladylike and very un-Rani like fashion, pointing at herself with the sandwich. "I'm a telepath."

I ate some more of the pudding and hoped the lecture I could feel coming on was going to be short. The arrival of Zeke and the terrible two swinging into the room and swarming to the food tables made welcome relief possible.

Sig had packed a tray with all the main dishes and had added fruit and puddings, he had four bread rolls balanced precariously on the top and came over looking like a tightrope walker after a night out.

Rani and I watched all three of them eating enough food for a small country which was not a pretty sight.

"Bea wants to know if we have encountered any people who are more advanced than we are." Three pairs of eyes looked at me.

"Do you read *any* of the discs you get sent Bea?" Doz asked. I tried for a superior expression.

"There's a sort of perfection to some people's faults," Sig added.

"Anyone interested in coffee?" I asked, standing up. Four hands were raised.

Tariq was already pouring out cups for us and he helped me load up a tray with milk and sugar and biscuits. "Are you okay Tariq?"

He nodded. "For a moment there I thought we were lost," he looked pensive. "I'm not so young that I can appreciate a near miss." We thought about this for a moment and he added some chocolate sweets.

"Tariq, how have you had time to make all this?"

"There is always time to cook." He smiled a big smile and lifted the tray for me and I realised that making food would be his coping strategy, which was lucky for the rest of us.

I helped myself to sugar and a handful of sweets. "Go on then, you're dying to tell me. You're just hiding it well."

Doz looked puzzled. "No." He was eyeing the solitary bread roll on Sig's plate. "Are you going to eat that?" He reached for the roll and just missed having his fingers stabbed by the fastest fork in the marines. Sig growled and Doz made pacifying movements with his hands.

Rani raised her eyes in exasperation. "I ought to make you go and look at the discs Bea."

"But you're not going to are you," I wheedled, eating one more sweet.

"Do you know where the Perseus arm of the Galaxy is?" Zeke asked hopefully.

"As you're looking down on it somewhere to the left and further out." This was greeted with stunned silence.

"So you do read some of the discs." Sig finished his roll and I smiled.

Zeke did his teaching voice. "There's a race called the Ractor Det. They seem to be peaceful, non-violent and are far in advance of us in science and technology. Needless to say they don't want to have anything to do with us."

"What are they like?"

"Humanoid, they have a variety of interconnected species, all very similar we think. They control several planetary systems. From what we do know they travel vast distances."

"Has anyone tried to make friends?"

Doz snorted, "We are so far down the food chain it would be like us making friends with the Stone Age tribes on Kruger 2." I decided not to ask about the tribes as it was bound to cause another chorus about disc reading.

"The Nian'tu are another matter," Zeke said. Everyone nodded, including me until I realised what I was doing. "They seem to be from the Cruz arm," he added, looking at me.

"Over to the right and further in." I could tell they were impressed the lack of sarcastic remarks was a dead giveaway.

"Those people make me really nervous." Doz had a mouthful of biscuit, but like most marines he didn't let it get in the way of conversation.

Zeke went on, "They have a very advanced civilisation. Their society is very hierarchical and seemingly aggressive. We find the evidence of their punitive justice on the edges of our space occasionally. They colonise."

Doz snorted, "Usually without the permission of the locals."

"Why do you think they leave us alone?" I asked. Something about this made me nervous.

"I don't think we have anything they want," Zeke said sipping coffee.

"Like the Ractor Det they are much more technologically advanced than we are, though I think they could use a lesson in people skills." Rani added, "I don't think we pose much of a threat to them either."

"Don't worry Bea," Sig said, "They don't seem to have any need for telepaths." This was about as subtle as chewing cinder toffee through a sad film, but somehow comforting.

"And then there's Gurber's race," I added. I tried for the last sweet but Zeke beat me to it. "Do you really think they come from the Rim?"

Sig shrugged. "All we know is that we'd still be fishing in our own backyard without them." He shrugged again, "So far, so good."

I added, "Like the man said when he fell out of a multi-storey window, as he passed each storey, they heard him say, so far so good." I sipped more coffee. "None of you think they come from the Rim." No one answered. The stomach stretching sighs filled the silence for a moment.

"The space station looks inviting, are we allowed out today?" I looked hopefully at the two marines. I tried to ignore the glance that they both gave Zeke.

"Do you want first babysitting duty?" Sig asked Doz.

"Very subtle you two," I said as I thumped Doz who was sitting next to me.

He looked hurt. "Hey I didn't say that!"

"Come on," I laughed, "I'll race you to the docking bay." I leapt up.

"Whoever gets there last has to pay for the afternoon snacks!" I was nearly at the door to the restaurant when he bowled me out of the way using sneaky marine tactics, like pinching.

I raced after him, down the corridor, in through the doors to the upper docking bay. There was an undignified scramble that involved more pinching by me, as we both tried to get down the steps whilst pushing the other out of the way. Most of the crew working in the bay stopped to look.

"Come on Bea my money's on you!" Gatt.R. shouted. We arrived at the airlock door in an undignified heap. Doz pulled my hair to get in front of me and I stamped on his foot, unfortunately he was wearing work boots.

Na-Es-Yan was waiting patiently for the room to clear of the previous occupants. She moved out of the way of our jostling. Her mouth was slightly open and her expression was beyond puzzled.

The door slid open and I elbowed Doz in the ribs, he 'oofed' and I ran in ahead of him.

"Is this a private ritual or can anyone join you?" Na was leaning in through the door. Doz tried to catch his breath. I could see money changing hands on the docking bay floor. Gatt.R. gave me the Des.Ran. version of the thumbs up and I bowed.

We waited for the hiss of one door closing and another hiss as the other door opened. A barrage of noise and movement caught my 'last day of school for the summer' mood. In fact I managed to maintain the feeling right up until the moment Doz put his hand on my arm and moved slightly in front of me.

It was like being in a giant indoor market, three floors of traders all shouting. We had come straight in on the main level. I knew someone else had done all the boring 'paperwork' like registering for us to be here, I also knew we had to declare all infectious diseases and any animals on board, because Rani had told me. Nothing much changed, a port was a port. There were two marine guards on the station door to the ship on the space station side. They looked fed up as all poor soldiers did who got the job of standing around when everyone else had a three-day pass. But they saluted Doz smartly and nodded to me and Na-Es-Yan.

The place was packed. People of all shapes and sizes were doing deals and eating and talking and watching. Shops and stalls were arranged around the wheel and radiated out with small spaces in-between, so that you got dizzy trying to see both ways at once. I looked up to the dome in the middle of the floor. A large crystal hovered in the centre about the height of the second level, it radiated coloured lights, flickering slightly, making me think of a circus ring when the finale had begun.

Na said, "I am looking for a dealer who may have some old maps of the Sagittarius Arm. I think he is on the third level. Do you want to come with me?" I nodded. Doz looked around him and up, then at me. He smiled, but it was one where the eyes were thinking of other things.

"Old maps," I asked Na, "How old could they be?"

"Well, the galaxy was here and inhabited long before your people and mine came looking," she explained. "These maps were made by a race called the Ractor Det."

"I know about them!" I said.

"For the last five minutes," Doz snorted and I elbowed him in the ribs.

We were on the escalator which was a moving spiral staircase and the second level was much like the first, with perhaps more places to eat. I pointed out a small cafe with chairs on the main concourse.

"This looks like a good place for afternoon tea Doz?"

"You're scary, you know?" He was still looking everywhere at once.

The third floor was quieter and the sellers were further apart. We walked nearly half way around the curve of the floor before Na found what she was looking for. The stall was tucked along the back wall. It was fronted with boxes and tables of maps and books, like a car boot sale on a wet Sunday.

A small man of indeterminate race, who reminded me of a badger wearing a dressing gown, was sorting through a box of books, real books. I reached out to touch the cover of one and he smacked my fingers. "The acid from your hands will ruin the paper, here." He fished out a little bottle from a pocket in his dusty robes and pulling my hands towards him, sprayed my palms. I felt like a child as I held them up for his inspection. He 'huffed' his approval.

"I wasn't expecting real books."

Doz had his back to me and was looking out into the station. He did another sweep and then turned to look at the stallholder. "I wonder how many of them *are* real."

The stallholder didn't seem at all insulted by this, but smiled instead. He shrugged in the way of people forever who worked in the market of life.

I pulled a soft covered pamphlet out of a box; it seemed to be the instructions for a washing machine. "Why would anyone buy this?"

The old man looked at me with a questioning expression and then his brow cleared, which made Doz look apprehensive. "The mundane begins to get interesting when enough time has passed. Ask any archaeologist digging in a cesspit!" He held out a hand. "My name is Aaqul." I shook it.

"Bea." I carried on looking at books, although my nerve endings were tingling. I had always loved books, the shape and feel of them, the smell alone could drive you wild with desire to own them.

Aaqul turned to Na. "Are you looking for anything in particular my dear?" When she told him, he took her arm and escorted her into the back of the shop. I trotted hopefully behind and my grumbling shadow followed me.

Books and maps were everywhere and I took one at random from a shelf. The script looked like hieroglyphs. What amazed me was not just the writing but the paper. How had all these civilisations come to the same conclusion? "Paper must be just about universal."

Aaqul looked at me. "That one is not made of paper, my dear, its skin." The way he emphasised the word made me think, not what, but whom and I put the book back carefully and tried not to cringe.

A small green crystal stood on an unusually empty table. "Is it okay to touch this?" I didn't want my fingers smacked again. Aaqul came over and picked it up, twisting the top. A detailed hologram of a young woman began speaking. My Com/T was buzzing for its life so I knew the language must have been something unusual. She told the history of a long gone race, I knew they were long gone because she explained why. It was sad and bloody and short, but I found myself wanting to own it. "Can I buy this?" I asked no one in particular.

Doz ground his teeth and Aaqul suddenly laughed. "It is a fairy story for children!" I must have looked stubborn. The old man came over leaving Na to her maps. "I bought it from a ship that came in years ago. Nothing about it is real I think. But then it doesn't matter if a story is true or not, if you tell it often enough it takes on a life of its own." He pulled at his bottom lip. "It belonged to some long ago child." He looked at me very carefully. "I suppose you would be a good person to own it for a while."

Doz tutted and shook his head, I think I heard him say, "You must be the worst kept secret in the quadrant." He was still looking out at the concourse.

Aaqul opened my hand and pressed the crystal into my palm. "Here." He seemed embarrassed and waved away the money discs I offered him.

I went back to pulling books from the shelves, finding strange languages and even stranger pictures. "Aha!" Na exclaimed. I don't think I had ever actually heard anyone say that so I went over to join her.

"Is this it?" It was a little disappointing I thought, but she seemed delighted. It looked like a blank roll with pinpricks in it and faint lines. Again I was surprised that it was actually made of paper. I touched it, maybe not.

"Watch," Na said. She laid the map down and ran her hand over it. As she moved across the map a three dimensional hologram sprang up, but only where she had made contact with the surface. She then used something that looked like a pencil to point at a particular star and a small line appeared and created a route from the edge of the map to the destination. Writing appeared and I squinted, as if that would have made any difference in helping me read it.

The negotiations for a financial transaction would have had Devon market traders sighing in admiration. It also took longer than a terri-torial treaty. I went and sat on the step outside the stall and Doz even-tually came and sat next to me, still looking around. We watched the people going about their lives but for different reasons, me because I had never seen anything like it and Doz because he had to.

"What does that do?" I pointed to the huge crystal hovering slightly below us. It wasn't attached to anything, which made me nervous with all the people below.

"It's for light and warmth, like an artificial sun and I imagine it has some security cameras in it."

"It's a sun?"

"Yes, this is a space station." He looked at me for a moment. "You need a certain amount of sunlight in a day otherwise people get ill. You'll have to see Pui for the details." I nodded, it made sense really.

Na came out of the stall with Aaqul and both looked satisfied with the outcome. We scrambled to our feet, or rather I did, Doz sort of hopped up in one move which I was sure he'd been practising.

Aaqul took my hand. He looked at me curiously. "Most men would be happy to have a woman around who could read their mind."

"Yes, they'd never have to bother with having to hold a conversation again," I snapped back.

He hissed with laughter, his little pointed teeth and mottled complexion made him more and more badger-like. "Come and see me again." He patted my hand. "Just remember, some people are not ready for the future."

"I might be one of them," Doz muttered quietly.

We glided down a level, where I hustled a pre-occupied Na and a grumbling Doz. The cafe proprietor was slightly greasy looking with a huge moustache. We ordered lots of food, or rather I did, Doz just whinged a bit and Na-Es-Yan nodded over her maps, agreeing to anything.

"You know Doz," I said after a mouthful of some excellent cake, "When I think about it, we don't seem to have come that far." He nodded, not looking at me but continually doing a visual sweep of the station. "I mean, we don't really know much about anything."

He nodded again. "What's your point?"

I thought about this carefully. "How are we out here?" I waved a hand to take in the masses of people and the space station. Na put down her map for a moment. And they both gave this some serious thought then shrugged.

We finished all the food and Doz did a vacuum job worthy of a collie dog. "Okay, what now?" he asked.

"We go shopping."

"What?" His face fell like all men since time began or since shopping began anyway.

Na gave up after a pathetic effort, which is what I would call a pair of embroidered slippers and something that looked like toffee but smelt dreadful. I however, had always thought that browsing was a necessary skill. After several hours checking out the stalls on all levels Doz was whinging like a nine-year-old faced with scrambled egg. "Are you actually going to buy anything?!"

"Doz, this is a finely crafted talent, the first sweep is purely for information gathering."

He looked panic-stricken. "You mean by the 'first sweep' there will be other 'sweeps,' as in more sweeping?!"

We were both interrupted by a familiar voice. "How's it going?" Doz practically threw himself at Zeke, which was rather undignified for a marine. "I thought I'd give you a break." They did some communication without speaking, which must have been about me, the gist of which I think was the fact that no one had tried to grab me. It took a moment and I pretended not to notice. Why spoil a perfectly good day with a dose of reality. Doz was off like a man on a mission one which I think involved alcohol.

Zeke gave me a hug and we walked in-between the stalls looking at the wares on display. I found myself reaching for his hand and it felt good to have the contact. His warmth and strength were in that hand. I looked at him. "What?" He asked. We stopped.

"Sometimes it doesn't seem like the future. It just seems like the past all mixed up." He put his hands in my hair and leaned down and kissed me. I was not sure if anyone noticed, I thought people just walked around us, as if we were an island in the stream.

The door chime interrupted the unpacking of shopping and Rani came in looking much more like the rumpled angel of my old cottage. It gave me a quiet coil of fear to see her wearing the dress that she had haunted me in.

"What did you buy?" She came over and we went through the brightly wrapped packages.

"I bought this for you." I gave her a parcel and she squealed like a little girl. The material fell out in a rainbow of colours like a waterfall of light. I had bargained for the piece, but probably paid far too much for it. "Maybe Lef.G. can make you something with it, or," I added with a grin, "You could drape it over something." She made a face at me. Rani was skilled with draping things. Personally I always fell over anything that was half on a piece of furniture.

"Okay," I said, "what's up?"

"We're leaving after the stores are onboard and we're back out to Admira." She paused. "The memorial for Cree and Dana will take place tomorrow." If the sun had been in the sky, it would have gone behind a cloud. "You need to see Asguard, he's hoping you will speak for Cree." We were quiet for a while.

Ollie came in from the bedroom and leapt onto Rani's lap, curling up in the folds of her dress. She kissed the top of his head. "Zeke isn't in the Navy is he?" The silence was filled with unspoken thoughts.

"He was Navy, he's part of a specialist team. They have a flexible job description."

"A bit like a secret agent," I suggested helpfully. The Com/T looped like a dying fly.

"I'm not even going to ask," she said.

We were examining the rest of my buying spree as I told her about the badger book man. Rani nodded. "He used to be a mercenary in the war with Torriff's race." My jaw dropped over his looks having been deceiving. "Aaqul was the commander of one of the transgenetic groups." She paused for thought. "Did he ask you about anything?"

I shook my head. "I got the impression there wasn't much he didn't know."

She raised her eyes to the ceiling. "It's like trying to hide an elephant in your bathroom. Everyone knows it's there but we're all pretending not to notice."

"Thank you for the analogy!"

The door chimed again and Pui came in looking as if tired had been reinvented in several levels below exhaustion. She sat down, Rani and I could both feel the waves of sadness radiating from her. I got up and made her a hot drink, one of those herbal teas that are aromatic and taste terrible. She wrapped her hands around the cup as if I had given her a lifeline on a wild ocean.

"Things are no better?" Rani asked gently. Pui shook her head. Here was someone who hadn't read the doctors manual on detachment from your patients.

"I'm okay," she said at last. "I just needed to be with people who didn't require an explanation." We both nodded. Ollie rolled onto his back with all four paws curled, he purred loudly. Pui unconsciously reached over and rubbed his tummy thereby earning herself Ollie points.

We sat in silence for a while and gradually I realised the ship had slipped its bonds with the station and we were sliding gracefully away from the system. Small 'tugs' moved away with us and I could see someone waving from a distant window. I waved back. If you were willing to believe, then really nothing changed. People still saw ships leaving dock and said goodbye to someone they didn't know.

"We've tried *everything* over several years to reproduce the telepathic brain." Pui had her eyes closed and was leaning back into the cushions. I looked at Rani, puzzled with the sudden introduction of the subject. I thought we were being empathetic, but Rani was enigmatic again. "Medical science has checked the DNA, brain cells, genetics, you name it. It's a switch not a difference. It's not what you are, it's because you can." Pui looked drained with the effort of the most emotive speech I had ever heard her make.

I was quiet for as long as possible. "Okay," I said helpfully, "More tea anyone?"

"What do you think?" Pui's eyes were open, looking directly at me.

So very few people asked me what I thought that I was a bit surprised by this. Rani was smirking.

"I've always thought that telepathy was like the intuitive version of synaesthesia." They both nodded seriously. "It's just that instead of something like colour and sound being linked, its feelings and thoughts."

We sat in peaceful contemplation for a moment, more tea was sipped and the stars were like dust in the window again. "I hate it when they tell you they love you," Pui said this so quietly I thought I had misheard her.

"Yes," Rani answered, "Some people are just awful." We all nodded in agreement, I was wondering where the real Pui had gone.

"How is it with Zeke?" Pui asked. I spat a small amount of tea across the table but I didn't think anyone had noticed.

"Well, apart from the fact that I don't know whether to salute him or kiss him, fine, I guess." Pui nodded in agreement, Rani added more spat tea to the table. The door chimed and Zeke walked in.

"Coffee?" I asked smiling like the child with a hand in the biscuit tin.

He looked at us suspiciously. "Why do you all look as if you're up to something?"

"Important talk," I explained.

"Ah," he said. "Maybe if I sit here quietly I will learn something about the mysteries of life?"

"Or then again maybe not," I said. "We don't just give away trade secrets you know."

Pui and Rani wandered out together, Pui to go back to trying to save lives, Rani to give hidden support to the physically exhausted doctor. I leaned my head on Zeke's shoulder and he moved his arm so he could give me a hug. "I should go and see Asguard," I said, trying not to get too comfortable.

"Yes." He kissed the top of my head, and I heard him sigh. We all grieved in different ways. Zeke's was the fallen warrior pain. So it surprised me to hear him say, "In times of great madness, it seems to me we need to hold on to our rituals. It gives us some geography."

The corridors were empty; people were either working or sleeping or eating and were all just somewhere else. I heard quiet footsteps behind me and turned suddenly, slightly spooked, almost expecting to see no one. Torriff stopped as I turned. "Oh," I said stupidly, "It's you!" He looked puzzled and I waved a dismissive hand at my own silliness.

"I was going to ask you if we would be able to have our meal together tomorrow evening." His face was almost expressionless and his eyes dark. The corridor felt too empty, as if everyone had left the sinking ship, leaving me behind, I shivered and gave myself an imaginary shake.

"That would be great Torriff, I can't be held responsible for the consequences of my cooking though."

He looked puzzled and then smiled. "You're joking." He paused, looking worried. "You are joking?" I laughed and gave him a hug, he hugged me back; the warmth of his friendship like a barrier to the dark things that waited around the curve of the night hours and an antidote to the pain of the conversation I would be having with Asguard.

He turned to go and I carried on to the nearest lift shaft. I sank gracefully past the middle of the ship, testing the computers' capabilities by sticking my foot out through the doorways as I went past; it made for a jerky ride as the current of air speeded up and slowed down. I could almost hear a sigh of relief from the computer as I got out.

The eighth level was as quiet as the one my rooms were on. Everyone was bracing themselves for an emotional battering the next day. The door to Asguard's room stayed shut and a polite computer voice said, "Tim Asguard is in the level eight restaurant." I walked further down the corridor and tapped the lighted door key.

I usually spent my eating time in the upper restaurant, it was nearer and Tariq was always there. Somehow talking about food with Tariq had become a necessary part of my day. The sports computer was down in the middle of the room. It was made of the same flexible jelly-like glass as the portable ones we took on assignments, but huge. People were sitting on both sides of the screen.

I looked around for Asguard. The room was full, but the voices which were usually loud with criticism and helpful suggestions for the players were now subdued to a buzz. He was sitting in a comfy chair with his feet up on the coffee table and a bottle of beer cradled against his chest. I sat down next to him and he reached over and took my hand.

"Does this mean you'll do it?" He didn't look at me.

"Was there ever any doubt?"

"I wouldn't blame you if you didn't want to." He tipped the beer bottle up to his mouth. It was odd how some things didn't change, like beer bottles or grief.

"I would. Blame me, I mean; more beer?" I asked. Asguard looked towards the man by the food counter who was watching the volleyball game and waggled the beer bottle at him. Two more beers arrived.

"Do you want something to eat Bea?" The young man asked. I hunted for a name to match the face which I recognised from my self-defence class. He helped me out, "Wheelan," he pointed to himself.

"Of course, Sab, You were matched with Ko the last class we had." I suddenly remembered he had been out for the count by the end of that session and might not have wanted to be reminded of the fact.

He laughed, "Occupational hazard in this job, you know the captain's motto." He walked off to get the food. I nodded as if I did.

"No I don't," I said to Asguard, "What is the captain's motto?"

"'Everyone fights no one quits.'" My stomach did a greasy flip-flop.

"Cree and I were going to leave the marines and go civilian. Hire out to the war with the Nian'tu."

My mouth dropped open. "There's a war going on, when was someone going to tell me there's a war going on?"

Asguard looked a bit sheepish. "There's always a war going on somewhere, it's just not really us fighting it this time."

"Do you want to run that by me again?" He sighed, realising he was in deep water anyway so a bit more information wasn't going to make any difference. "Well?"

"The Nian'tu are a military dictatorship of sorts, they keep their people in a kind of feudal thrall." He drank more beer. "Our colony worlds are spreading nearer to their territory and there have been incidents along the border. There are several worlds looking for experienced security."

"So you and Cree were going to hire out as mercenaries?"

"Yes, we figured we could make some money, set up a stake somewhere on the outer colonies, maybe a bar or something." He laughed, "Cree thought it was too dangerous and then this posting came up and we decided to go for it."

"You get to choose postings?"

"Sure." He finished the bottle in one long desperate gulp.

Some things did change. I had been skydiving with Royal Marines who would have given their eye teeth and probably someone else's for a choice of posting. More beer arrived and so did some snacks on plates you could pick at. "Thanks Sab." He looked at Asguard and then back at me, making a movement with his hand which said he was cutting off the beer supply as of now.

"War makes things lose focus," Asguard said. He stumbled over the words, "You can't seem to communicate with real people any more, only those who know what you know. You're out of step. All these people here," he waved his free hand, "Have changed forever now," he looked at me, "You too, Bea."

"Is that what this is, a war?"

"If you see enough people die, it's a war."

A loud sigh from the late night sports fans had us all looking at the screen, the players were using all surfaces of the court including the ceiling and the camera zoomed into the floating net for the final point and then there were some close-ups of winners and losers trying to be polite to each other without much success.

The screen went quiet and was replaced with a peaceful scene of water and trees. People got up to go to bed or back on duty, as they passed most of them spoke or smiled.

"Do you know what you're going to say tomorrow?" Asguard asked, as he finished his beer.

"No. What about you?" He shook his head. "Come on," I said, "You look as if you could do with some sleep." We left and he staggered up the corridor leaning on the wall every now and then, until I took his arm and guided him the rest of the way.

"Good night, Bea." He fell through his doorway and it closed quietly behind him.

"Good night," I said over my shoulder as I walked to the nearest lift shaft. The upward air of current was uninterrupted by me. I kept my feet and my thoughts to myself. The empty feeling persisted inside and outside my head. The door to my rooms swept open and I stood there for a minute. I could tell Ollie was off on a night prowl. The room was Ollie-less.

I walked around the corridor to Zeke's rooms. I pressed the lighted key. Silence for a moment and then it opened.

He had obviously been working in the main room. The table was covered with crystal discs and his work computer was turned on, an empty cup next to it. He stood up from the sofa, his face puzzled. "Hey, what are you doing up?" His voice was middle of the night quiet. I wandered in, not sure what to say. My face must have betrayed me because he came over and gave me a hug. "I guess the conversation with Asguard went pretty well." He exuded strength, but not the arrogance some people felt they couldn't leave home without. There was also a suggestion of the blunt power of a bear with cubs. And he smelt nice.

"What are you working on?" I turned my head to one side so that my nose wasn't so squashed.

"We're heading back to Admira, it looks as if they made Star League status. You might want to read the report before we get there."

"Where's the fun in that?" Neither of us had moved.

"Would you like one of those dreadful milky drinks you refer to as coffee?"

"Yes please." I moved over to the sofa and curled up, plumping the cushions for comfort.

He went into the bedroom and came back with a blanket, tucking it around me. It felt for a moment like a place of safety, which I knew is about all you could hope for. Usually, just when you began to feel safe, time crept up on quiet wings. It never lasted more than an instant. It was always about something you remembered feeling.

"What happens next?" I asked Zeke's back. He stopped, but didn't turn around, then carried on making coffee. He didn't insult me by asking what I meant.

There is a group of people, sometimes women, but usually fighting men, who had a flexible attitude to right and wrong. They nearly always belonged to an organisation with a three letter title. I wondered if they still existed in this day and age. I looked again at Zeke and it seemed like a rhetorical question.

We sat in silence drinking coffee and I leaned on his shoulder, which felt like the best part of the day so far. "You know that instruction manual for life," I said, "The one with all the answers?"

"Yes?"

"It's a load of rubbish."

The memories came with the stillness of ghosts in the early morning. I curled around my cat and waited for the light to creep around the room in the pretence that dawn was breaking. Some things were gone forever. You couldn't bring people back by wishing and you couldn't follow where they went.

I looked in the bathroom mirror; even in the kind reflection things were not good. No sleep showed in all the muscles of your face and in that place behind your eyes where your spirit came close to the surface.

My brother used to say that people had belief patterns so they didn't have to think for themselves. I think we were all young once and sometimes on the edge of great darkness, if we were lucky, we had the possibility to do brave things. So, we had ceremonies for life and death and vows and these things held power because of balance, because there was always good and bad. We created something that symbolised the passing from time and body because we had to.

I stayed in the shower long enough to reinstate myself as a human being and did all the early morning things that made us bearable. The door chime made me jump, an odd response for someone who was supposed to have a heightened sense of awareness.

"Ready?" Rani looked as if she'd had even less sleep than I did. Zeke was close behind her. He was wearing a full navel uniform and something that looked like medals. It gave me a moment to think that in the time when I didn't know him, he had done those things that resulted in medals.

Suddenly I felt a surge of anger, the real fact of some death is often that it was a stupid waste of life.

As I had been useless with every aspect of telekinesis training Rani had tried to teach me, it was a shock to me when I 'picked up' a box of discs from the table un-handed and slammed it against the wall. They both looked at me, Zeke with the dark eyes of 'I have no idea what to say' and Rani with the usual unreadable expression. "There," she said calmly, "I told you you'd get it eventually."

The upper docking bay was full. People stood in groups talking quietly. We came down the steps and made our way over to the captain, who was standing on her own a little apart. I put my arms around her and hugged her so tightly I could feel her heart thudding. No one should stand alone at a funeral.

The walls were decked with flags and the myriad of uniforms were like butterflies in a spring garden. The bay doors were open and the ring nebula of a dying red giant glowed green and gold as its gas was cast off into space. I thought for a moment that if the gravity field failed the entire ship's crew would have been able to see the star's phenomena at close quarters.

"Who stands for Lieutenant Dana Ravenscroft?" The captain spoke into the silence.

Jim Couzins stepped forward out of a small group. "I stand for Dana." He went over to the flag-draped coffin and put his hand on the top, gently, as if he was afraid of waking her.

"I'm not sure I can do this." I looked at Rani. Her eyes were full of the tears that shone in the light of the faraway stars. Zeke moved closer to me and put his hand on my shoulder.

"Who else stands?"

Pui moved quickly from Sig and in a small voice said, "I stand for Dana." She went over to Couzins, putting her hand on the coffin, so they were stood one either side.

"Who stands for Lieutenant Martin Cree?"

My voice found itself and I spoke, "I stand for Martin Cree." I moved away from the crowd and stood alone next to the coffin and reached out a hand, touching the silky surface of the flag. I tried very hard not to let the tears fall, because I knew from experience that it was difficult to stop once you'd started.

"Who else?"

"I stand for Cree." Asguard's voice was parade ground correct and he moved to my right touching the coffin and my hand, sharing strength, as soldiers had done for all the years of eternity that they had fought side by side.

"Then speak for those who can no longer speak for themselves." The captain moved back a pace, standing next to Rani.

"I understand now the rituals of death, the long goodbye. I under-stand this for the first time." Couzins paused trying for a breath that would not come. "We are part of a clan, a group of space travellers, Dana was proud to belong to this group, her family. We are divided by the doorway of death, for now."

Pui spoke so quietly I could hardly hear her, "Dana taught me that what matters is not out there." She pointed to the space behind us. "But in here." She touched the place where the human heart is.

I stood forward. "A great songwriter in my time called David Gates once wrote 'and I would give everything I own, just to have you back again.'" I saw Gatt.R. wiping away a tear and I wondered for a moment if it was as pale a blue as his beautiful skin. "We are a part of the universe, it is in our DNA and we are made of the same stuff as the dust on the winds of space. Cree's star is out there now, a far point of light in the darkness, ever watchful. I believe we are the spirit of what we see out here and the stars are always with us." I stood back. There was a ripple of something that was an echo of understanding in a painful reflection.

Asguard bowed his head and spoke, "These people are my people." He paused. "This soldier was my friend and I wish him a dry bed, hot food and a firearm that doesn't jam and I know he will be waiting for me at the next hill and we will make our last stand together."

Every soldier in the docking bay including the captain put an arm across their chest in the age old acceptance of solidarity in death and said, "And I."

Rani had told me about the 'soldiers' lament,' but I didn't expect to be completely wrecked by it. All hope of holding on to my tears was lost. The grief experienced for most of us was often partly grief remembered.

Zeke said, "Those of us left behind can only wait and hope that they will be proud of us."

The last post rang out into space and beyond. Asguard's hand found mine and we stood away from the coffins with Couzins and Pui as the techs moved in to rig up the device that would send the dead into the heart of the nearby star.

"It wasn't enough," I whispered.

"It never is," Zeke said.

We watched as the coffins moved out into space and waited until they were no more than specks, reflecting light from the ring nebula. It seemed a lonely place to be. People breathed out and gradually a quiet buzz of voices made it through the grief. I felt like a punch bag and my face must have looked like one. Zeke put an arm around me and kissed the top of my head. We drifted in groups towards the steps; it seemed to me that I hugged more people in those few minutes than I had in all the years before.

I spoke to Couzins, "I understand." He nodded, not really hearing me. I touched his arm and tried again. "I understand."

His eyes focused through the barrier of sorrow. "Yes."

Torriff was standing by the captain. The skin on his face was tight and shiny and his eyes were haunted with undefined sorrows of his own. We walked up the steps together and I reached for his hand. He looked grateful for a second and then we went back to the pain that is our own memories of loss.

Like all good funerals, a wake followed.

The upper restaurant hummed with the words 'do you remember' and I sat by the windows watching the old star recede, leaving my thoughts out there somewhere. Zeke came over with a large cup of coffee and a small bottle of dark liquid. "Here, try this." He poured a generous measure into the coffee.

"What is it?" I sniffed suspiciously. "You know I get drunk on fumes." He gave me one of those 'I remember' looks. I sipped it cautiously it was sweet with a hint of vanilla flavour.

"It's a home brew. The Katinads make it in a distillery I don't know anything about." He put a small amount in a glass and drank it down in one. His eyes watered a little and he cleared his throat. Some slight choking followed. An empty glass appeared attached to the captain's hand.

"This better be flower dew." He nodded and poured a generous measure. "Are they running that distillery on level six again?"

Zeke did a sort of shoulder shrug that absolved him from lying, a feat he accomplished with a great deal of charm and a rather wicked grin. I thought for a moment that some things were worth changing your life for but it might have been the flower dew.

Na-Es-Yan came over with Neff.P. They looked as if they had discovered the gold at the end of the rainbow. "Can you come to the lab tomorrow?" Na spoke and Neff. nodded.

"We've got something to show you," Neff. spoke and Na nodded. Her boyfriend in engineering was going to have to get used to being on his own soon.

"Sure, that would be great. Do I get a clue?"

"Well it's an accretion disk, which you probably know quite a lot about, but this is really interesting." Neff. was speaking but Na prodded him to add emphasis. I looked hopefully at the ceiling for additional information on accretion disks, but found nothing.

"I'll be there."

Someone shouted to them and they went off into the increasingly noisy crowd, distracted by their bilateral interest in other things. Life went on, even after death. Pui sank into a chair and passed me a plate with a large piece of chocolate cake and a fork. "From Tariq," she said.

I stood up to see if I could catch his eye which was not possible. So I stepped onto the chair and waved over the heads of the crew. He saw me and bowed ceremoniously with his palms together and a smile on his gentle face.

I felt dizzy for a second and grabbed Zeke on the way down. "Are you okay?" He asked. Something like a cloud crossed the sun and the sensory deprivation was like dust on a lens. I thought for a moment that my knees were going to abandon me and I would be sitting on the floor in a heap of undignified cake. Zeke went for a more serious, "What's the matter Bea?" The grip of his hand on my arm became insistent. I shook off the feeling of intrusion and disquiet like a thunderstorm on its way.

He took the plate from my hand and put it on the table between us and I reached behind me for the chair. Crouching close, he rested his hands on my legs, warm through the material of my trousers to my skin. The level of conversation around us and the people pressing in, as they stood in groups, made me feel claustrophobic. Pui stiffened, her exhaustion a mask, holding her features in a place slightly out of focus. "What's wrong?"

I still hadn't spoken. I leaned into Zeke and rested my head on his shoulder and he curved around me, stroking my hair. Something not right was filling the space I usually kept for myself and it made me shudder. I heard him say something about Rani.

My eyes closed, I could see my mother's funeral, the coffin being raised from the bier by men in smart suits, the rows of faces and a sea of unknown tears. I didn't know she knew so many people. I didn't know so many people knew her. As they carried her out into the roaring silence my hand sought Sam's. In my dreams my brother always took my fingers and squeezed, as he had on that cold, draughty day, but this time, in this waking memory, his hand was not there. I couldn't find it.

Rani was speaking to me, I felt tired, but I raised my head. The room swam back into noise and laughter and the brittle sense of 'not this time.' I sat up away from Zeke who was still crouched on one knee. Rani looked at me and then lifted my wrist. The bangle glowed.

"Oh no," I said, "Not again."

The wake swirled around me. I ate the chocolate cake, licking my fingers, trying to shake off the sensation of sharks closing in. "Are *you* okay?" I asked Zeke. He looked angry there was nothing worse than a warrior without a sword. He took my hand and kissed the palm. I could tell that in amongst the desire to kill something was a tiny spark of fear. It made the cake difficult to swallow.

The captain and Mark Limbu came over for more flower dew, Rani said nothing and Zeke returned the captain's look of enquiry with a look of his own. They would have had to be drunk not to have realised something was wrong, but they did their best not to notice.

More and more, came the feeling that someone was playing a dangerous game, charades without the safety net. I wanted to ask, 'is it you, or is it them,' but I didn't want to hear the answer.

"I'm going to see Gurber," I said. The table was crowded with friends, people I trusted. Ko-Yo-Na came over with Sofred, and Doz leaned on the back of her chair. Pui drank with quiet determination. Rani and Captain Witherspoon were standing with Mark by the windows. Conversations were interlocking and flowed back and forth with the ease of experience. Before I was always on the outside looking in, suddenly the inside was not as good as it had looked.

The people felt sticky as I passed through the groups of talking and laughing crew. I had to stop for the questions and hugs and minds full of thoughts. It was like a web. The more I hurried, the more difficult it became.

A hand caught my arm. "Bea, what's wrong?" Tom Hatherley's face was furrowed with anxiety. I resisted the panicked urge to snatch my arm away from his grasp.

"Just this, you know." My head felt like acres of old chewing gum.

"Sure," he said and gave me a hug. The door slid open and closed the noise behind me.

Corridors stretched away under my quiet steps. Gurber was as usual, surrounded by stars in a pink haze of dust. He settled on the floor when I came in, ready for the emotional onslaught. I didn't say anything, just gave him a blast of my fear and a visual parade of worries.

Walking through the nebula clouds I reached out a childish hand trying to sweep the stellar dust into my palm. My feet paused on empty space, vertigo for the unwary. It felt restful, a distance of time between me and the next crisis.

"**Did you arrange this?**" I held up my wrist with the still glowing bangle. The bubbling was really all amusement.

"**Knowledge is in your head.**"

"I'll take that as a yes," I muttered. We sat in silence him squashed into a jelly lump, me on the floor with my back against the wall. I put my hands over my face in the age-old reflex of what you couldn't see would not hurt you.

"**Look.**" I looked. Gurber's idea of a present was to be inside the Large Magellanic Cloud, our 'irregular companion galaxy.' It was in orbit around our own galaxy. In my time I knew it was studied, because it was near enough, if you could call 190,000 light years 'up close.' It really took your mind off the little things.

It was best not to spend too much time alone in the dark with your thoughts. Peace of mind was about looking ahead, not at 'what might have been.' And if you slept exhausted at night, at least you didn't dream.

I looked at the empty room, something I'd been doing a lot, and then walked down the corridor to Zeke's. The doors slid open on slightly drunk people. It was interesting how over-indulging in alcohol had stood the test of time.

Rani came over with a small glass of the aromatic flower dew and I gave her a hug.

"Okay?" She asked, as I sipped the thick dark liquid. My throat burned and my eyes watered.

"Yes," I croaked, "Gurber always has a way of making me feel small, but in a good way. If you see what I mean?" I finished lamely.

She looked puzzled, "Go easy on that dew."

"I think he must have arranged for this to do its odd glow." I held up my wrist. The bangle was back to normal whatever that was.

She held it for a moment. "I wonder if it has some sort of power source."

I nodded. "Ah, who cares," I slurred slightly.

"*Definitely* go easy on that dew."

There were people all over the ship that night cultivating grade-A hangovers. "Who's steering this thing?" I asked Sig.

"Jenny Smith."

"Again, that woman is always at the helm. Did you weld her into the chair?"

He shrugged. "She doesn't usually drink and she likes to fly."

I asked Sofred about his sex life and we ended up talking about grouper fish, as I was sure everyone was aware they started as completely female, laid eggs and then turned into fully functioning males. I felt his life was much improved by learning this. I thought that most people were usually too polite or sober to bring up the subject, but he smiled and gave me the potted version of his life as a female. Four offspring back on Katinad. I told him how much better most men would be if they got in touch with their feminine side, I mean really got in touch. He thought that was funny.

Later on Sig tried to tell me about Pui, but I don't think I could grasp the details.

"So," I said, "Have you tried grovelling?"

"Do you think that would work?" He asked hopefully. Zeke was listening in by now, his face serious, but slightly out of focus.

"It works for me," I said. Sig nodded.

I leaned on Zeke's shoulder as he sat down beside me. He intercepted the glass I was about to drink out of. I grumbled but didn't put up much of a fight. My lips were numb and that I felt was always a good time to stop. "What happens next?"

"What do you mean?" He asked quietly, arranging himself back in the seat and putting an arm around me. I looked at the late leavers. Rani had gone back to her piggiwig and Sig had gone off to try out my advice on Pui. Sofred was talking to Doz who had his hand on Ko's knee; they leaned in like conspirators and whispered like drunks.

"Dolly Parton said, 'A bird and a fish can fall in love, but where will they make a home.'" I leaned away to look at him. He had his feet on the coffee table and his head back on the cushions with his eyes closed.

Here I was stepping on shadows again. I put my head back on his shoulder and he squeezed, reaching around me with both arms. Fear trickled through the blocking chip he wore and I could feel the darkness pour out of him, like a city building at night. It was just as well I was drunk.

The steady clattering woke me. I was curled on the sofa in Zeke's rooms, with only one eye open it made it difficult to focus. "If you continue to make that terrible noise I will kill you with my little finger." He snorted and brought over a large glass of hot water.

"Careful it's hot, oh, okay."

I drank all of it down but it didn't touch the sides. I mumbled, "I swear I can hear my brain cells dying." He took the empty glass and filled it up. "Did we sleep here, on the couch?" I asked in a whisper. It felt like it, my neck was S-shaped.

"Yes, the rest of them left when your snoring got so loud they couldn't hear themselves speak. There was also some dribbling," he added helpfully. He came and squatted down in front of me. "You look terrible."

I finished my second glass and he filled it again. "Zudlocs! You only had three glasses of flower dew you're a cheaper date than my second wife." I was on my feet at this point and making my way with great care towards the door.

"What, your second wife, there was a second one, as in after the first?" I leaned on a chair near the door.

He shrugged sadly. "My first contract partner was killed fighting in the war with Torriff's people and my second asked for an official ending because she never saw me."

"Do you have children?" I squeaked and waved a hand, nearly unbalancing myself.

"None with my contract partners, but I've donated three times." I steadied myself on the chair and gulped more water. He looked carefully at my face. "This was too much information wasn't it?"

I nodded and staggered out the door. I stopped for a moment and turned around as the door slid open again. "Do I really snore?"

"Only very gently and with great dignity," he said solemnly.

I pointed in the direction of my rooms. "I have an accretion disk in half an hour."

"You go for it."

Na was hopping from one foot to the other, like a little girl caught short in the queue for the loo. Neff. was not much better, his blue skin was flushed a deeper colour. "Where've you been?" She asked with frustration.

I had been in the shower for longer than it took Congress to make a decision on anything. Then I had had to placate my tail swishing cat about the lateness of his breakfast. I brought a cup of hot water with me.

It was still early, but Na-Es-Yan hadn't bothered to go to bed. She looked rumpled. I looked closer at Neff. he looked a little rumpled himself.

The holographic screen was up and a huge black hole was outlined, surrounded by dust and gas that was being fed by a nearby star. The blue super-giant was literally being torn apart.

"As you can see it is on a Keplerian orbit," Neff. said, pointing. He raised an eyebrow.

"That's something to do with gravity and the centrifugal force" I had put the computer on before I came out and with the cat winding around my wet, just-showered legs, tried to get a quick brief on the peculiarities of the accretion disk.

It was peculiar in its own right and as with all quantum physics you had to suspend reality.

"The phenomena are producing massive amounts of x-ray energy." Neff. was tapping keys on the computer and they both 'oooed' and 'aahed' at the readings. It did look pretty spectacular in a kind of violent 'end of life as we know it' way.

"I have never seen one that's this unstable," Na gasped.

"What?" I tried the ceiling again for help but found as usual nothing.

"The instability causes the turbulence. It's a form of magneto hydrodynamic turbulence." Neff. was at his most helpful. "It has a weak magnetic field," he added, "Sort of feeding off itself." Even without a hangover this would be dragging my overextended abilities into a new dimension.

"But this is what I wanted you to see!" Na pointed to a very small dot which the computer enlarged with the help of excited tapping fingers.

"A space whale." They both nodded. "It's inside the event horizon?" I asked and there was more nodding.

"Ah!" I said, because nothing else would do. They both looked pleased. The creature was ducking and diving like a dolphin in the waves. "Is it absorbing the energy?" Neff. looked as if he would burst with the pride of how far I had come and I thought my head was going to explode due to the combination of particle physics and home-brew.

"Listen," said Na. A strange noise was coming through the computer system.

"What is that?" I asked after we had stood in stunned silence for a while.

"B flat," I think, Na said helpfully.

We listened some more. "Do all black holes make a noise?"

"Good question." Neff. paused, about to launch into an explanation.

"I think I might need some coffee," I interjected weakly. He looked slightly annoyed but I felt the stirring of nervous nausea as my hang-over crossed with scary science.

"How far away is this?"

Na sighed dramatically, "It's too far to see with the astro-scope. We're using long range scanners."

Somehow I felt strangely reassured. It really was a boiling hole in space, sucking in and spinning anything that came its way. As if the universe had unpicked reason a stitch at a time.

"Bea?" Torriff's rich voice on the Com/T broke into my unwelcome thoughts.

"Yes. How are you this morning?"

He sounded far too cheerful. "I am fine! It is you young things that cannot contain too much alcohol without fading."

"Ha!" I said laughing, "At least I'm not so old I have to read the news to know what I'm thinking."

He snorted, "Are you coming for coffee and some of that chocolate goo you call food?" I left the scientists having one of those conversations that the rest of us think must be another language because it contained words of more than five syllables and lots of long numbers.

The upper restaurant was still quiet as most of the crew were on the early shift or nursing the results of the previous night in private. Tariq was of course cheerful and smiling, with the coffee pot in one hand and a large piece of chocolate cake in the other. "Oh thank good-ness for that, I was going into withdrawal symptoms." I swallowed a forkful.

Torriff raised an eye ridge, "I find it hard to believe that this is your first plate of goo of the day?"

"I'm pacing myself." I drank coffee and looked out onto the space that seemed to have quickly become home, mostly it was distant stars; every now and then something caught my eye. Like the gas cloud of multicoloured dust particles that was filling all the windows on one side of the ship and swirling around at the back of my mind. I thought that I could understand the scientist's attitude, there really was so much out there we didn't understand, so much to make you wonder about. It was a wonderful feeling, like the night before Christmas every day.

Torriff and I chatted like the survivors of a lousy college party with a little too much hysterical laughter and a lot of bitching. "So are you still okay for dinner tonight?" I asked.

He looked a little puzzled. "Did we arrange a meeting for tonight?"

"I thought tonight would be a good time. We're at the planet Admira in two days and I will have to do some homework tomorrow evening. So I won't be able to come out to play." More puzzled looks as the translator did a little yo-yo over the twenty-first century jargon. It obviously didn't come up with much, but he nodded.

"That would be good," he added hurriedly, "I will bring the food."

I laughed, "Don't you trust my cooking?"

"You told me not to!" We ate a bit more, me cake, him the remainder of an afternoon's gardening.

A small bleep made both of us check our Com/Ts. The captain's voice was quiet and slightly scratchy clearly someone hadn't stopped at three glasses of flower dew. "Can you come to the conference room Bea?" Two seconds later she asked Torriff the same question.

"I think this must be about the new assignment on Karnesta," Torriff said. I tried to look as if I knew what that meant, but I was just eating the last mouthful of cake and my traitorous eyebrows gave me away. He tutted, "Do you ever read your discs?"

I made a face behind his back as we got up to go. "Only if there's nothing else to do and anyway," I added, "Why spoil the surprise?"

The conference room was full of grumpy forehead-clutching crew, the complaining stopped for a moment when we came in, until everyone realised it wasn't the captain and then they went back to it with a vengeance.

Sig was sat at the table with his head resting on his hands and he seemed to actually be asleep. Doz was quietly drinking coffee with his eyes closed, stretched out in the uncomfortable conference chair. Mark

Limbu, Zeke and Rani were all standing together in one corner. Ko was sitting with her feet up on the table with an expression like a thundercloud engraved on her face.

"Hi," I said cheerfully. Doz waved without opening his eyes, Sig grunted and Ko seemed to be growling. Rani managed a very small smile. Mark looked as if he was about to cry.

"Oh, please don't be happy," he whispered. "I can't do happy this morning." He rested his head on Rani's shoulder and she patted his face gently. There was nothing more amusing than other people's hangovers. Particularly when you had escaped with a minor flesh wound.

"If I had known you were going to be here I would have brought you some cake Sig." I sat down next to him. His answer was muffled, but consisted of something that sounded like the Katinad equivalent of 'push off.'

The doors swept open and the captain came in, seemingly none the worse for a night on the booze because being the boss meant you couldn't turn up for your own meeting looking hungover.

The rest of the room snapped together in a show of organisation which fooled nobody, and we all took our places at the table. Doz passed his coffee to Sig, who swallowed the scalding brew down in one and looked pathetically grateful. "You would think that someone would have invented a hangover cure by now," I speculated.

"They have," Sig answered. My jaw dropped down in one of those unappealing looks. He shrugged. "But where's the fun in that."

The captain began. "The good people of Karnesta have requested our help they have a slight plague that seems to be getting out of hand." She paused as the door slid open and Pui bustled into the room, carrying files and discs clutched to her and then she deposited them in a disorderly heap with a clatter onto the table. Sig helped her to collect them as they swam outwards as if they were alive and trying to escape.

"Sorry I'm late," she spoke to the captain and then quietly said, "Thank you," to Sig.

"Right," the captain continued, "Now that you're here, perhaps you can tell it."

Pui took a deep breath and got to her feet, blowing a wisp of hair out of her eyes. She put a disc into the computer by the holo/screen and began tapping keys.

"Okay, the Karnestans have been experimenting with transgenetic crops for some time now, unfortunately they were less than careful with their tests and some cross fertilisation has taken place."

"Prescription medicine ends up in your breakfast," Doz said helpfully.

"Yes," said Pui, "Inadvertent drug ingestion. The environmental impact alone would have been difficult to deal with. However as you can see, they have another problem." A person appeared on the holo/screen. The face, none too friendly to begin with, was now obscured by lumpy growths that looked painful.

"They don't exactly look happy to see us," Sig said.

"We could try 'we come in peace,'" I said solemnly. I banged the table with my hand making Sig wince. "I have always wanted to say that!"

"Eh," said Doz. The rest of the crew looked blank.

"I will be holding a course in comprehending twenty-first century humour tomorrow in the upper restaurant. Attendance is compulsory."

"Something I'm sure that we will all be grateful for," the captain said after a short pause when the Com/T reached the end of its tether. Pui cleared her throat and we all turned back towards her.

"This is what they should look like." Another hologram appeared on the screen. We were all quiet for a moment.

"Um," Sig was at his most eloquent. The two incredibly ugly Karnestan men were in uniform and had an air of unexpressed menace about them. Their dark faces and strong features reminded me a little of the Restrans and they were armed to the teeth. Several weapons were actually pointed at whoever had taken the holo/picture.

"Let me get this straight." Doz was looking puzzled. "These people have asked for our help."

"They're not Star League?" Rani asked.

"They are just beginning to travel their solar system and as Karnesta is in a busy part of the neighbourhood, we have been detailed to help," Pui explained.

"Great," Sig sighed.

"Oh I don't know Sig, they look rather sweet in a King Kong sort of way," I said.

Torriff jumped in like a schoolboy with the answer to a really difficult question. "I know!" The room folded in on the stunned silence. "King Kong was a very large primate," he said with a great deal of satisfaction.

There was quiet. The captain cleared her throat. "Well, thank you for that Torriff." He sat back, pleased with himself.

"Actually I think I was just getting used to the fact that I never have any idea what you're talking about," Doz said.

"Concentrating on the subject at hand for the moment," Zeke said. "How are we going to treat these people?"

Pui made a face. "That's the problem we need something that doesn't require much infrastructure and no skills for a delivery system. Otherwise we could end up transmitting more disease."

I drifted back to the pictures on the holo/screen as the talk went back and forth. Torriff suggested a dry powder that could be ingested in solution or spray inhaled. He cited an epidemic on his own planet as reference. Pui was taking notes and nodding. Sig was wondering how it could be got out to the remote areas. The screen showed land masses and islands and the populated sections of the planet.

It was odd, what I had seen in the last few months were colony-based settlements. Even the so called advanced races were occupying very little developed land. In fact the Restrans had been the most industrialised people so far. Maybe this was about me or maybe space wasn't that occupied. It probably wasn't a mistake that I hadn't been to any of the worlds that the crew came from. We hadn't been back to our solar system either and the advanced people that existed on the fringes of our space, they were a bit like Elvis sightings, something you had to treat with a healthy dose of scepticism.

"They're very hard to reason with," Pui was saying.

"People stop listening when they feel they're being judged," Torriff said quietly. I must have missed something because the table was quiet and the underlying features of the conversation were like a riptide, hidden and dangerous.

"Well," the captain added to the silence. "Let's hope we can come up with a solution."

The restless movement of the crew and Captain Witherspoon shuffling discs meant that the meeting was over. We drifted towards the door and I hooked my arm through Ko-Yo-Na's.

"Are you going to be okay?" I asked her gently.

She looked almost tearful. "At this point I am not sure." I tried not to laugh. Her face had an unhealthy sheen and her uniform was not quite as smart as usual. I wondered if she had fallen asleep in the corridor again.

"I'm going to make coffee and marmite on toast, a sure cure for alcohol poisoning."

She looked panicked. "Does this require ingesting food?"

I nodded. Her face became even shiner and she unhooked herself from me and ran through the door. Rani came and stood next to me. "You know," she said, "That was very slightly cruel."

"Yes," I said with a grin, "Lunch?"

We walked down the corridor to the upper restaurant. Zeke was talking to the captain and Pui had rushed off with her collection of discs and notes cradled like an unruly child in her arms.

"So," I said sitting down, "We're seeing the little green men again?" Tariq had made me some sort of pasta veggie dish that was a little out of control on the fork but delicious.

"The day after tomorrow, have you read the disc?"

I covered the non-committal reply with a large mouthful of food.

She sniffed her response.

"How's the piggiwig?" This was a calculated question and guaranteed to get her to smile.

"All piggiwigs are terrible cowards and this one is a perfect example of the breed. He won't go out of my rooms and the only person he has any time for is Doz." She spoke with a great deal of affection. It practically radiated from her in waves. It was true what was said about animals, the best part of our humanity was in the way we treated our furry friends.

"I guess Doz has visiting rights?" She made a face and drank more coffee. Her lunch had consisted of soup and fruit because some people just didn't know how to have a good time.

Tariq brought over a large plate of trifle and a spoon. He was followed by the helpful suggestions of several crew, but refused all bribes. I gave him a hug and took the spoon, pausing in quiet reverence for the appropriate amount of time. I swallowed a mouthful. "Is Tariq married, because I think I'm going to give myself to him?"

She shook her head. "Bea you're not right on so many levels."

Tom Hatherley threw himself into the nearest empty chair. "Do you want to come to a screening tonight Bea, Mac and I are setting up in the lower restaurant."

"Is this another strategy to get Jenny Smith to come out with you?"

He sighed, "Is it that obvious?"

"Tom, why don't you just ask her, what do you think is going to happen if you end up on your own together?" He looked horrified. I sighed, "Who am I to give you advice, the only person who makes worse relationship choices than me is Buffy the Vampire Slayer." They both stopped for the moment that it took the Com/T to mess it up again. "No?" I asked.

"No," Tom said eventually.

I shrugged. "Anyway, I can't tonight. I'm having dinner with Torriff."

"Okay." Tom looked resigned. He struggled to his feet, sticking a finger towards my pudding and narrowly missing getting it chopped off by my carefully aimed spoon. "I hope he's cooking," he muttered, wandering away.

Rani stretched her arms above her head and groaned. "That's the last time I drink flower dew. I am going to have an early night tonight."

I stretched my legs out, leaning my face on my hand and looking out at the stars. "Do you ever get tired of this?"

"I never have yet." She paused, "What?"

"Nothing." I thought in a small quiet place that the past loneliness was sharply outlined by being surrounded by people who cared. I remembered a time when I could have killed anyone who said 'life goes on,' because for some of us it didn't and I also remembered the very minute that it changed from one thing to another.

She reached out and rubbed my arm and I realised the place where I thought my thoughts was not so empty. We got up to go. "How do they make the flower dew? Does it have flowers in it?"

"Do you really want to know?"

"How bad can it be?"

"It involves chewing and spit."

"Okay, forget I asked."

We walked along the ship towards hydroponics. "So, you're making dinner for Torriff?" Her voice was hidden behind normal sounds, but the sensation made me look at her carefully.

"People really don't like having him here, do they?"

"The war was not that long ago. Many of the marines on board fought against Torriff's people and lost."

I nodded. "I heard something the other day." I made a face.

"Swamp-eaters," she said quietly.

"Yes, how did you know?"

"I heard it too." She sighed, a deep sad sound full of the tears of impossible feelings.

We stood on the top level of hydroponics, leaning on the balcony and watching the birds.

"Well, I need to go and see Harriet." She put her arm around me and hugged. "Try not to poison Torriff."

I went down the steps to the third level and out through the doors into the corridor and into world war three. Pui's furious face was close to Sig as she poked him in the chest punctuating each word. "It's not up to you!" She yelled.

"I wasn't suggesting it was." He very bravely stood up for himself. "I just said I thought it was too dangerous."

Pui looked at me. "This man is trying to tell me my job!"

"No I'm not!" Sig shouted.

I opened my mouth, "Maybe you could..." They both turned on me. I made that placating movement with my hands that you hoped would stop you getting set upon by wild animals and sidled around them, speeding up as I reached the curve in the corridor that meant out of sight and safety. Zeke was feeding my cat when I walked into my rooms.

"He told me he was hungry," he said by way of explanation. Ollie was climbing up his leg which usually made strong men nervous. Zeke picked the stretched cat up with the bowl of food and put them both down on the table. "There you go buddy." He looked at me. "What was that about? You came through the door like a bunch of renegades were after you."

"That was a great analogy Zeke, considering that they very well might be!"

"Oh yes right, sorry."

"Actually, Pui and Sig were having a very loud bust-up in the corridor. It must be love."

"Really," he made one of those 'I don't understand this must be about feelings' faces.

"You're not going to start shouting at me in the corridor are you?" I began setting the table around my cat.

"No!" He said emphatically. "Why, should I?" He added nervously. I laughed and scratched Ollie's ears, which made him growl, he liked to eat uninterrupted. A slight scraping noise made both of us look up.

"Is that someone at the door?" Zeke whispered.

"Yes," I whispered back. "Look, you have to promise not to give me away."

I went over and tapped the open key. Zeke's face had a strange look on it, the look which Zeke's type of people used when they thought they might have to fight with their hands. For a moment it was disturbing but as I tried not to think about the possibilities in my life that didn't fit my general air of denial, I ignored the feeling of disquiet.

Tariq sidled in, weighed down with plates of food. "Did anyone see you?" I asked hopefully. Tariq smiled at Zeke in the vague wish of some support against impossible odds. Zeke's face said 'you're on your own.'

"Bea," Tariq said, "I don't think anyone on this ship thinks you're actually going to be cooking for Torriff."

"And I'll bet Torriff's counting on it," Zeke added, as he took plates from Tariq and put them on the table.

I wrung my hands a little. "Do I have to heat anything?"

"No!" Tariq looked a little shocked and removed the covers. "This one," he pointed to a dish filled with little rosettes of green stuff, "Is the main course and this," he waved a cover with something like a flourish, "Is the pudding." A noxious pond smell filled the air. He covered the plate again.

"Thank you," I said. "I owe you." He patted me on the shoulder and gave my cat, who was still sitting in the middle of the table, a kiss on the head. The mystery of why Ollie's stomach was starting to drag on the floor had been solved.

Zeke and I sat with our hot drinks and the stars of out there and talked about nothing much. He yawned several times until I gave up and ordered him to go and get some sleep. He folded me into a bone-crushing hug which made my heart hurt for the times in my life when I had gone un-hugged.

My cat followed him out of the door on the evening prowl, which probably involved a trip to the upper restaurant.

I did some things with soap and water and changed my twenty-fifth century clothes for an old pair of twenty-first century jeans and a T-shirt. Rani had been dropping big hints about them. I was going to have to give them up soon, though she would probably be able to get all of her in one leg.

Torriff knocked on the door and came in with flower dew and a large chocolate cake. I put my arms around him because it was my day for hugging people and for a moment he returned the embrace. He smelled of books and the skin of his face was warm on mine.

We argued over music, he wanted to hear more Lennon and McCartney and I was trying to introduce him to Springsteen. I won. His face as the 'dancing in the dark' track came on was worth the tussle. "This is..." he looked at me and shrugged, his eyes shining.

"I know, never mind space travel, I go through an event horizon every time I listen to Springsteen."

Torriff's uniform was a slightly different colour than the usual, it seemed extra mottled leather-like. The subtle changes in the markings were for more complex eyes than mine. "You look nice, have you got a new uniform?"

"Lef.G. made it for me." He did a little dance to show it off. I made both of us a small flower dew drink and hoped that the meeting tomorrow wasn't going to be too early, otherwise I would have to sign up for the cosmic detox.

"Come on, let's eat."

"Yes, I imagine you're starving. It must be at least an hour since you last took sustenance."

"Oh my goodness Torriff, you made a joke!"

"Was it funny?" He asked me hopefully.

I smiled and patted his arm. "It was a good joke, I'm proud of you." He glowed and his beautiful golden eyes were like a kaleidoscope.

"Can I ask you a personal question?"

He looked nervous. "Yes."

"Are your eyes like ours?"

Astonishment took over from the nerves. "Well, no, I think not." He paused for thought. "More like the octopus in your oceans. The lens in my eye moves in and out to focus whereas yours changes shape. You would have to ask Pui for the details. Also, I have the ability to see movement in bad light, much like Ollie."

"I think Jed Lassik can see in the dark, his eyes look like yours, but yours are nicer."

"I believe the transgenetic Lassik has several features that come from the Vanerian species."

I was stunned. "They used Vanerian genes?"

"Yes. Not a great moment in our history."

"For us either, I should think."

He put his fork down. "Your great scientist Einstein said 'the most incomprehensible thing about the universe is that it is comprehensible.'"

"Chocolate cake and Einstein, just as well I'm drunk!" When he laughed it was like a rusty door being swung back and forward on its hinges. It made me laugh too. "So," I said, "Before the war between Earth and Vaneria we were friendly enough to exchange genes?"

"The procurement of genes was seldom legitimate and yes, there was an uneasy alliance between your people and mine for many years." He thought about something for a moment. "The transgenetic war was nearly a century ago, I think the scientists had no idea that their experiments would still be around."

"Well they seem to be doing okay. I guess someone must be making a good living out of stolen genes."

Torriff stirred his pudding, which made my nose twitch as the smell of swamp pervaded the room. "I believe Samura family is doing very well." He paused and looked at me. "As you say, it's good business." I ate more cake and got up to make a coffee for me and an infusion of some dried pink leaves for Torriff. My head was spinning a bit and I missed the cup with the hot water the first time.

The thought filtered through my swirling brain that Captain Witherspoon hadn't mentioned Samura family trafficking genes during our last little chat in hydroponics about the renegades; drugs and artefacts, but not genes. Either she hadn't included the information for reasons of her own or she didn't know. In which case I wondered how Torriff knew. I turned around to ask him.

He was over by the coffee table fiddling with the little story crystal that Aaqul the bookseller had given me. He turned it on. The little princess began her tale of sad loss and great battles and the end of a special time.

I took the cups over to the table and sat down on the sofa and Torriff sprayed something into my face.

I floated, a not unpleasant sensation, even though there was a nagging doubt somewhere in the room that all was not well. The walls seemed to shift and move and the stars were trails of light through the windows, as if someone had slowed down the film in my mind. Torriff drifted on a wisp of smoke to stand close to me. He was speaking but the sound was under water. A cold stream flowed up my arms and through my body to squeeze my heart. "I'm sorry," he whispered, "They have my family."

I had *no idea* what that meant, only that it made him sad. I patted his face in an effort to convey my feelings, without knowing what I felt.

We walked out into the corridor, him with his legs, me using the two lumps of jelly that I used to call my legs. My whole body was on automatic pilot. Every time I moved my head, my eyes were not catching up, as if I were at a dance with a strobe light and a spinning glitter ball.

It was late, but the ship was seldom deserted even at this hour. I expected to be rescued and then couldn't understand why I would need to be.

Up two levels in the lift shaft, I put out a hand to touch the draught, trailing my fingers through a rainbow of air only I could discern. I wondered what it would be like to see the wind on the moors at home and the colour of the storms. I turned to Torriff who was silent and sweating. A tiny corner of my mind seemed to be screaming something at me, but I couldn't hear.

The upper docking bay was empty and dark, with small pools of lighting around the steps and vehicles. The shadows looked like claws. Torriff was coaxing me towards an SSV. I wondered why he was shaking, his hands cold in mine. Gently he put me in a seat, tucking my arms under the safety belt as it curled around me and his eyes were wet with tears, I couldn't comfort him. Nothing came out of my mouth, all my body and brain could do was breathe through the fog.

I heard him say, "I'm just going to do some research on the local gas cloud."

Jenny Smith's voice answered, "Off on your usual middle of the night science trip Torriff, I thought you wouldn't be able to resist it." Torriff answered by mumbling nothing much. "We're on slow speed until tomorrow so you'll have plenty of time." Jenny Smith, I thought, as usual in the driving seat when everyone else was sleeping. A small corner of my brain, the bit that wasn't feeling like chewing gum thought it was odd that she didn't say anything about me. An even smaller corner commented on the fact that I hadn't said anything either. "Opening the bay doors Torriff."

"Thank you." His voice shook.

We moved out into space and headed towards the gas cloud. The silence was full of the unspoken voices of fear and sorrow. I wondered if someone somewhere had decided that I should lose everything I loved by painful degrees. My thoughts seemed to spin in and out of coherence. It wasn't that I didn't understand betrayal, it was not that complicated. It happened all the time. I worked on one word. My tongue felt like a lump of old putty. And eventually I said, "How?" It came out as a pale imitation of human speech, like a think bubble in a cartoon.

Torriff cleared his throat, it sounded as if he was still crying. "I've never done this before. I mean kidnapped anyone." 'It's a first for me too' I thought, as the coherent part of my brain spun in again and was quickly gone. "I stole your DNA from the medical bay. I gave it to my contact. The first attempt was the empty transport ship." He gasped then shouted, "No one was supposed to die!"

The quiet curled around us in an unspoken barrier and I watched the little craft manoeuvre into the outer area of the gas cloud. It closed us in a child's cloak of invisibility, naive in its simplicity, but effective.

He began speaking again, "I thought at first your DNA would be enough, that they would leave me alone. Your bio-signature is in the story crystal. For all anyone on the ship knows you are still in your rooms."

He came over to me and tapped a small key at the side of the chair, the seatbelt tightened and he checked my hands under the restraints. He needn't have bothered my fingers were floppy and sausage-like. When I tried to move the belt became a boa constrictor and seemed to squeeze tighter. I cleared my dry throat and said, "Aaqul?"

Torriff sighed. "He is very close to the Samura family. Roshii grew up with him." I hadn't heard the name before. I found my head beginning to clear, but decided to keep it to myself for a while.

"The crew is used to me wandering off for a few days to study the science of space." He added as if to convince himself, "They will not notice I'm gone." My brain clicked into myself, my thoughts stopped spinning and my ability to comprehend cleared some more. "What makes us honourable is usually a set of rules which we try and live by." His voice was halting and full of fear. "It all goes to dust when the lives of your children are in the balance."

The place in my head that was shouting at me finally got through.

"**Rani!**" I called her, reaching out again and again but there was nothing.

"The drug is wearing off. It is the same one that the maintenance robot gave you to suppress your own bio-signature. It causes some mental detachment."

"What now?" I asked.

Torriff looked at me carefully and came over to check my belt again. "Now we wait." He spoke gently as if to a very small child, "I gave Rani a little of the flower dew. It was spiked much as yours was. I doubt she will hear you. The gas cloud should shield us from the ship at this distance, for a while anyway."

He turned to look out of the front windows, pacing a little. I tried again to work the belt loose, but it was tight enough to make my fingers tingle with pins and needles. There was a place inside all of us and for some people it was the place where shadows grew. I didn't really think that Torriff believed he was doing what was best for his children. I could tell, that in his heart, he knew the path would take us all into darkness. Something about the silence changed, it became the moment before the first flash of lightning and it went from quiet desperation to the sensation of a wild animal about to spring.

I had been thinking about methods of escape, but nothing much had come to mind. I was usually one of those anal-retentive people, who never went out to buy a pint of milk without a Swiss army knife and a compass, just in case someone asked me to take a quick detour around the Amazon. But I hadn't needed either of those things for a quiet dinner with a friend.

I just couldn't make the seat belt loosen enough to get my hands on the controls and of course it was difficult to do anything under the nose of your kidnapper. There was not much room in an SSV for subterfuge. "Do you trust these people to give you back your children?" I asked with some exasperation.

He shook his head. "I don't trust them to do anything that's remotely good." He looked at me sadly and we both shook our heads, like a well-timed comedy duo.

A shadow fell across the floor as something moved close to the little craft. The lights inside the SSV went up a few levels to compensate. The bright swirling colours of the gas clouds were no longer visible. It was huge, at least twice as big as the Starfire. It looked like a malevolent doughnut chewing its fingernails. It seemed to be in all of the windows at once. The thought of escape was replaced by the thought of actually surviving.

The SSV's com crackled and a man's voice spoke in a language I didn't understand. Torriff answered, "Please repeat that in Basic?"

"We are opening the docking bay doors." The hissing and crackling cut off the end of the sentence. The gas cloud was running interference.

Torriff tutted his exasperation, "Do you want me to dock?"

"Yes," the person replied.

It was not exactly Jenny Smith's cheerful communication. Torriff manoeuvred the little craft around to the back of the ship and in through the opening bay doors. We landed at the edge of the docking area and Torriff turned the SSV around, as if for a quick exit. His fear was making me feel sick and my head wanted to explode with anger and helplessness.

It was a replay of the day I arrived at the Starfire, except for the faces. There were no blocking chips here that I could sense. Into the pools of dread in my mind they came, with the seriousness of sharks.

"You know what Torriff," I said through gritted teeth, "What makes us what we are is not the rules you talked about, which you seem to have parted from without too much of a fight, but about being true to yourself under awful circumstances."

He nodded his face slick with horror and other emotions, among them self-loathing. I realised something else. "You don't think you're going to get out of this alive, do you?" I asked in a whisper. He shook his head slowly. "Then why" I shouted, pulling one more time at the restraints in frustration, "Are you doing this?"

"I had to try."

The faces crowded at the windows. They were the Visigoths in space, ugly with evil and that sensation that always made me feel as if I should be running somewhere fast in the opposite direction. Some people liked to watch pain from a distance; they usually enjoyed a good hanging, or poor creatures tearing at each other in some point-less mismatched fight. You saw the faces of those watchers, like the masks in a play that people hung on their walls in the misguided belief that they were fun and not art. They took their pleasure in the blood. I had hoped in this time that their time had come and gone, but here they were.

We sat in silence waiting for something. Torriff got up and unlocked my restraints. I tried not to look out. "What do you think the chances are that I'm going to get out of this alive?"

He looked puzzled. "I can't see that they would kill you. They need you."

That sounded like the really, really sinister part. The banging on the SSV door made both of us jump and we looked at each other, the fear swirling around like the fog on the moor back home, thick enough to make it difficult to breathe. I would have cried but my heart felt frozen. Torriff pressed the door key and it slid open.

In the process of bio-engineering, a little something must have been lost in the genetic soup, like a sense of right and wrong. The man who came through the door was a nightmare walking, the one where you were being chased by something you couldn't reason with. He was also the man I had seen in my moment with the blood on the docking bay floor of the empty ship. His hair was slicked back in stripes on his head and the cat's eyes were narrow and bleak, lacking human levels of emotion. He was tall, as was everyone, with overlong arms and the clothes were close fitting and mud coloured. The quiet between us was of the hunter and prey. I remembered listening to a survivor of the holocaust talking on the World Service late one night. He said he knew he was in the shadow of a great evil.

"Roshii Samura." The man who stood before me said politely. He held out a hand and I shook it before I realised what I was doing.

"Welcome to the Nine Suns, I'm glad you could join us," he said.

"It's not as if I had a choice," I blurted out, my brain telling me to shut up a second too late. He smiled and I added mad as a frog to the genetic list.

We did a stupid little dance as he tried to usher me towards the opening. I worked hard on not shuddering as I turned my back on him. He had a blocking chip, but it didn't feel like the artificial chips the Starfire crew wore. It seemed to be inside his head and it was covering only one thing, as if I was looking at a table full of pots and only one had a lid.

The faces crowded into the open door until a sharp order moved them away. I could see Torriff in the corner of my vision, he had sat back down at the pilot's seat and looked as if he was about to set up for leaving. I wondered where he would go; surely not back to the ship. It wouldn't have taken a great deal of investigation to discover the path to my current situation. I looked at my watch. Still the middle of the night, a long time before anyone would know I was missing. I suddenly felt really tired.

The docking bay was huge and filled with cargo stacked against the walls, small craft like the SSV's we used, and people. They were looking at me. There was some talking and a lot of hostility but mostly they just looked.

A vision of un-loveliness grabbed my arm. He seemed to be human with sharp button-shaped eyes, and weasel-like features. His clothes were tight to his muscular frame and he leaned much too close for good manners.

"Redig! Don't leer at our guest."

"Sorry sir, this way." He released my arm and respectfully pointed to the steps in the corner of the bay. I stepped down into the small space around the SSV door.

The crowd parted as if for someone important. There didn't seem to be a scrap of empathy anywhere. The faces were humanoid and like the people on the Ross 154 space station, some were from races I had not seen before. The clothes were clean and varied in design with not a uniform in sight. But almost without exception, if these people had curriculum vitae's they would have put 'laying waste' and 'hurting small furry things' right at the start of page one.

Roshii Samura leaned in to speak to me, "No one here is going to rescue you." His sharp pointed teeth were on display in a parody of a smile, he couldn't read my mind he was just smart enough to know what I was thinking. Psychopaths, unfortunately, were rarely stupid.

The top of the steps led out to a corridor with no windows. I didn't look back, though I could hear the SSV with Torriff leaving. We were walking towards the front of the ship. The corridors were surprisingly bright and clean, as in no severed heads lying around to trip over. There were doors off to both sides and a fair amount of activity; people passed looking curiously at me and respectfully at Roshii Samura.

No hydroponics though, no birds, no light, no hope. I felt some tears at the back of my throat, but did some hard swallowing.

Redig took hold of my upper arm again, this time without comment from his boss and Roshii Samura moved to go ahead of me through a door. We had walked nearly the whole length of the ship. It wasn't the bridge, more a briefing room with seats and a table in the middle.

Redig left and Roshii stood by the door as if to stop me from running away. Holographic screens covered one wall, the local star cluster and gas cloud filling half the room. I almost expected a friendly Gurber voice to ask me if I wanted tea. Roshii looked expectant, almost excited. I looked back to the stars inside, puzzled.

A small point of disquiet seemed to be squirming around inside my head. It could have been the hangover, but there was definitely someone else in the room, hidden partly by the hologram and partly because they wanted to be.

Something seemed to have been communicated, because Roshii Samura grunted his assent and tapping me on the shoulder, he indicated that we should leave. I was curious, reaching out to see who was there. It was like walking into a solid wall. I wondered what Rani would say if she knew I'd found her rogue telepath.

Roshii was dragging at my arm and I was propelled into the corridor. I tried to pull away. "I just don't understand," I said quietly, "If you already have a telepath why do you need me?" He looked astonished, in a cat-like way and then did a straight out of central casting gangster.

"You'll know soon enough!"

"You're an idiot," I muttered.

He wanted to hit me but he didn't. It was a difficult moment for him and I hoped it would last as the possibility of my mouth not running away with me was unlikely.

Redig took over from Roshii Samura at the lift shaft. I was praying their maintenance was as efficient as their clichés when I stepped into the empty space. Redig took his duties as sadist second-in-line seriously, as he squeezed the blood out of my upper arm.

We got out at the lowest level, which was stowed cargo and the behind closed doors equipment that made life in space possible. It looked as if the engineering section on the ship was spread around the middle, about three levels up. Down here it was gloomy and quiet. Not untidy, but a slightly musty air and something else that felt like the echo of old despair.

We stopped in front of a door and Redig tapped a code into a lighted key with a series of hieroglyphs on it. He gave me a totally unnecessary push as the door opened and it then closed behind me. More gloomy than the corridor and furnished in early student slob it was a place where the average infectious microbe would have been happy to set up home. "Okay," I said quietly, "This can't be good and the fact that I'm talking to myself makes things even worse," I added nervously.

"Well I'm here, so that's not exactly true."

I leapt out of my skin with a screech as a bundle of rubbish unfolded itself from the corner of the room and Jad Lassik stood up. "Well," I gasped, clutching my chest in the hope that breathing would be recommenced soon. "Well, bugger me!"

"I wouldn't say that too loudly around here." He stretched. "They don't have much imagination."

He went over to the door and tapped the light key, it went up a notch, just enough for me to see the edges of the room, which was not an improvement. I looked carefully at him. His face was bruised and one eye was nearly shut. By the way he shuffled his ribs must have been broken. There was no medical help for the occupants of the basement suite.

"Do you mind if we leave the lights at this level?" He sat down carefully on one of the battered seats, and easing himself back, looked at me out of the side of one eye.

"Can you see at all?" I asked, sitting next to him. The seat felt sticky under my hands. I tried unsuccessfully to avoid thinking why.

He pointed. "Not much out of this one and nothing out of this one." I looked closer at his face, it was a mess.

"Jad, what are you doing here?"

"I'm supposed to be rescuing you." I must have looked stunned, but it had been a very long night.

"How's that working out?"

"Not well."

I was still able to appreciate the irony of being betrayed by a friend and rescued by someone I had thought of as an enemy.

"Jad," I struggled with the questions that were queuing up to be answered. "Have you seen the rogue telepath?"

He shook his head. "Harriet sent me out to make some contact with the Samura family. Roshii found me first. We have some history."

"Does the captain know of Roshii Samura?"

He thought about it for a moment, than shrugged. "He was just some bad-tempered adolescent the last time I saw him."

"So Harriet may not be thinking that little Roshii might be all grown up and has got himself some new toys?" He shook his head. It was impossible to read him as the natural ability to block me seemed to be stronger than ever. I had a moment of clarity. "Is that why they beat you Jad, because you can't be read?"

He said nothing, but looked at me with what was left of his vision and tried a smile. "It really made them angry."

"Do you work for the same people as Zeke?"

"No!" He said vehemently. "I don't work for anybody."

"Then why are you here?" I thought my brain was going to explode. He thought about it and I could hear the cogs moving. I sighed, "Jad, I'm a prisoner of a psychopath, on a family ship that no one knows about. What does it matter?"

"I owe a debt to Harriet. We're related." It was obviously a night for my mouth to be dropping open.

"Related." I nodded as if it meant something.

"Slightly." He shifted uncomfortably.

"Slightly related." I nodded again slowly.

"You know," he grumbled, "It would help if you'd stop repeating everything."

I rubbed my aching head. "Just exactly how many telepaths are there out there?" I waved a hand to indicate the universe.

"That we know about?" Jad asked.

"Of course you idiot. How could you tell me about the ones you don't know about if you don't know about them?"

He shuffled uncomfortably and winced with the pain of broken bones and bruised flesh and the thought of lines not crossed.

"Okay, never mind. I know it can't be more than a dozen because Rani told me about the twenty-seven in recorded history. Mind you that included the three that went mad, which may, or may not, include me!" I shouted. He looked surprisingly relieved for a man who could barely move and I found myself leaning back for a moment on the smelly seating and closed my eyes. "I'm so tired." I rubbed my grainy face and looked around. "I don't suppose there's anywhere to go to the loo is there?" His translator, which was smaller than my Com/T, buzzed a bit and then he pointed.

A small bathroom off the main room was a horror story of epic proportions. I did what I had to do trying not to make contact with anything and then I came back in. "So let's see if I've got this, Roshii Samura somehow gets his hands on a telepath, one that's already gone mad, we assume." Jad Lassik did his impression of a nod.

"He, Roshii, sets up with Yamuti/Chet, who's a no-name renegade newcomer." He nodded again. "They then decide for some reason that they want me."

Jad's one remaining eye glittered in the dim light and reminded me that he could still make me shudder for no good reason. "You're a transgenetic Jad, how are you related to Harriet Witherspoon?" His anger filtered through the smell of old blood and unwashed fear.

"Her mother was my human female genetic donator."

"You mean that you're her brother?" I sat down on the sticky seat again, my mind spinning with the thoughts of what else I didn't know that was about to jump up and bite me on the nose. It didn't take a psychic ability to work out the possibility that I knew nearly nothing.

"Sort of a brother," he said after a pause.

"Sort of," I repeated.

"You're doing it again."

"Sorry." I think if they were measuring incredulous on the Richter scale I would have just hit a seismic eight the level at which whole civilisations seemed to disappear. "Are we going to get out of this?" I whispered.

"I think so." We might have both been working on the theory that any hope, even false hope, was better than no hope.

We sat in silence for some time and I think I dozed off, because when the lights went up and someone grabbed my arm pulling me to my feet, it was a moment before I could open my eyes properly. The room spun into Redig's unpleasant face and dragon breath. "It's time for your medical." He pulled me out into the corridor where I tried unsuccessfully to disentangle my arm.

"Redig, let go of me you moron!" He looked stunned and lightened his grip slightly. "I'm not exactly going to be able to run away am I?" I pulled a little harder and he released his grip. It surprised both of us.

Jad was still sitting quietly on the seat. He hadn't made a move to defend me, but he would have been crazy to try. Redig was the type of bully who didn't need much of an excuse to beat an injured man. We looked at each other for a moment, Jad and I, both of us drowning in our own private sea.

The door closed on the dimly lit room and I went to the lift shaft unassisted except for the occasional shove in the back, just in case I forgot who was in charge.

We got out on level three. I had counted ten levels on the way down. Somehow it helped to know where I was on the ship, though nowhere seemed to be the most appropriate description.

I took a careful look at my watch and then covered it with my T-shirt sleeve, it was early morning. I didn't want Redig to see it. At four hundred years old it probably counted as an artefact in his pea-sized brain and I needed to know the time, even if it was only my time.

The medical bay door slid open onto bright clean equipment and a smiling doctor. He looked like a keen and eager child murderer. It was the first time I had wished someone would wear a blocking chip.

I wondered what the job advertisement had sounded like, 'complete psycho required for medical position on ship, experience in murder and mayhem preferable but not essential as training will be given.' Redig said, "I'll leave you to it Gaspar." He left and I looked longingly after him, it seemed as if he'd just become my dearest friend.

I turned back to the smiling tiger. "Please sit." He pointed to a chair. I sat.

The chair suddenly grabbed me and began stretching out. The straps were like the ones in the SSV, but somehow more aggressive. I tried not to cry but the fear was making it difficult. He pulled at my clothes and began attaching gel discs to the exposed parts. I felt like a piece of meat. The grin never left his face. I didn't make eye contact, but our faces were so close, it was difficult to avoid.

We all had evil inside us; sometimes something could bring it to the surface, but this man's eyes were a cloud of darkness without a glimmer of hope. He pulled at my jeans and seemed surprised when they resisted his attempts at tearing them. I had met a woman soldier on my travels in Australia, we had got drunk together waiting for a bus that never came and we talked about our lives in the way that strangers did when they thought they were never going to see each other again. She told me rape was an occupational hazard for a woman in combat situations. I said I thought a woman travelling on her own had to factor it in as a possibility too.

He undid the zip of my jeans and pulled at them so my underwear was only half covering me. He stopped and looked into my face. I would like to have spat in his, but my mouth was so dry it would have been a wasted effort. I took a chance. "Does Roshii know you interfere with your female patients?" A flicker of something, not fear, but a kind of acknowledgement, passed between us. He turned away and picked up a large gel sensor, which he put over the lower part of my abdomen.

He collected swabs and results without saying a word and I sat passively, hoping that it would soon be over. The room was spare and cold. There was none of the gentle healing things with which Pui surrounded her sick people. I missed her so much for a moment I thought my heart would break out of my chest. The way she loved everyone, but never let it show and her strength and quiet support that made talking to her a good part of the day. Some doctors healed and some were just an extension of the machine.

I didn't dare think about Zeke or let Rani creep into the edges of my mind because I would howl like a wolf with the loss, like the place inside where hope used to be had been filled in all the corners with despair.

Gaspar walked over to a com unit. "Redig, I've finished." His voice was strangely high and squeaky, a mass murderer with a voice like Mickey Mouse.

He tapped the side of the chair and the straps released me. I got shakily to my feet and began rearranging my clothes. He leaned against the workstation and watched. I sat down on the edge of the chair and waited. Redig arrived with a hopeful grin on his face. Some slight movement of disappointment skimmed across the place behind his eyes where the bully lived. I couldn't help but see a collusion of intent.

Some men hunted in packs, some hunted alone. Either way I was off the menu.

I brushed past Redig on my way to the door. "Hey!" He hurried after me, arm grabbing again. If only he knew it, I preferred his obvious nastiness to the clinical empty cruelty of Gaspar, stupidity wasn't an excuse for cruelty but intelligence and cruelty were unforgivable.

We passed several crew members, men and women, on the way back down to the 'dungeon.' I tried for a bit of eye contact and some low level reading. What wasn't about bad was about fear. A few spoke to Redig and the curious had their fill of looking, but no one looked as if they were about to break out with a kind word. The door to the tenth floor room slid open onto a slightly lighter look. Redig didn't notice, but it made me feel better. I got my expected push in the back and then Jad and I were alone. He had braved the bathroom and cleaned himself up somehow. Even his clothes looked as if they had improved a few degrees.

"I put the steamer on in there," he pointed. "Not great, but better."

"Would it work with these?" I indicated my jeans. He felt the material and shrugged.

"The steamer is designed for the nanotech; it activates the self cleaning element. What is this?" He fingered the edge of a pocket.

"It's cotton."

I listened at the desperate attempts of the translator he wore. Whatever went through the system obviously didn't make much sense. His face twisted into a comical one sided smile.

"Eh?"

I went into the tiny bathroom. It looked less ghastly, maybe because the steamer had removed a layer of dirt from the walls and floor, maybe because I was desperate to get the feel of Gasper's hands off my skin. I turned the controls on full blast and hooked my clothes over the edge of the stall. I cringed over removing my trainers, hopping from one foot to the other, as if that would make contact with the shower floor less hazardous. I scalded myself clean, gulping the fear through the steam, until big fat tears finished falling and I didn't need to stuff my fist into my mouth to keep quiet. The dryer was efficient on my skin but not too successful on the jeans, so I put them back on slightly damp. The T-shirt was fine, a little smaller, but dry.

"Are you okay?" Jad squinted sideways at me through the good eye. I nodded. "He's..."

"Oh yes." We sat quietly for a while.

"I've never seen so much death in one person," I whispered.

"He specialises in microbial warfare."

"You can see that every time he smiles."

I tried for a moment to keep the thoughts from spilling over into my face, but it wasn't possible and a tear escaped from my resolve. Jad looked horrified and patted my shoulder, like my brother used to do when I had come to grief with some doomed plan that usually involved trying to learn to fly. It seemed to me that I was of late always thinking about him.

"Jad. Why do you think they are so interested in my uterus?" I wiped a tear from my face and looked at him. "I mean it's been a long time since I did any physiology, but I still remember where it is and those tests I had were all to do with my reproductive organs."

His battered face was expressionless, but the one open eye stared with speculation at me until I became uncomfortable and got up to move around the small room. I pushed a little pile of dirt with my foot and leapt back when I realised it had been some furry creature that had found its way in and died. I felt like hopping around and yelling really loudly but resisted.

"I can see a little better out of this eye and the other one is improving," he said. We both ignored the fact that he hadn't answered my question. More silence followed.

A sudden movement of the door opening made both of us jump. I had done my best not to use my telepathy as it didn't do to go on a fishing expedition in someone else's river, particularly, to take the analogy much too far, when you didn't know how deep the water was.

A small, pale, shabbily dressed woman passed a tray of food to us without a word. She never actually stepped into the room, just sort of reached. Not a word, not a look. The door closed. "We're not going to starve then." I picked over the metallic packets with strange unreadable labels, written in the same hieroglyphs as the ship's signs.

"This is all processed and is full of chemicals it's not a real food source. Are you able to eat it?" He looked worried in a sort of lopsided way.

"When I think of the E-numbers I consumed as a child, it's a wonder I don't glow in the dark." He shook his head in puzzlement. Shockingly there was nothing going through the translator again.

He handed me a pack and said, "Try this one." I took a bite and chewed the small dark coloured bar. It was spongy and tasted of savoury and salt. Not tasty but not so awful I would be spitting it out.

"How long have you been here, Jad?"

He looked surprised. "About two weeks in Standard Time."

I coughed and choked slightly, "How long?" The thought of spending more than one night was enough. The food bar had made me really thirsty and I went into the bathroom for water. When I walked back in Roshii Samura was standing in the doorway. He was shaking with the sort of suppressed emotion that afflicted the terminally psychotic. He pointed at me.

"Come with me."

"Have you missed your anger management classes again?" I asked helpfully. His fists closed and his colour darkened. He moved fast, I cringed thinking I was going to get beaten and I waited for the blow. He smashed his huge hands into the side of Jad's head. It was so unexpected that I just hadn't seen it coming. I screamed at him and pushed myself in-between the monster and the now unconscious man.

Roshii seemed to have calmed down now that he'd hurt someone, and he stood quietly by the door, looking on with an air of disinterest that was chilling, while I struggled to put Jad on his side, checking his mouth to make sure his tongue wasn't going to block his airway and wiping the blood from the split on his forehead. I held my hankie over the wound and pressed in the hope of stopping the bleeding. His breathing was laboured, but his 'good' eye opened and he tried to say something. I put my hand out and touched his face trying to find somewhere that wasn't bruised. I whispered, "I'm so sorry, me and my big mouth."

"Come on!" Roshii pulled me up and out of the door. We went all the way up to the first level. I didn't speak and neither did he. I was shaking with the fear of what he had nearly done and my stupid part in it. Roshii was studying his nails and muttering to himself. No one we saw made any effort to be seen by the man, as if he exuded a warning sign. It was a pity I hadn't seen it.

We walked the long corridor to the other end of the ship. I wondered if I was going to the bridge this time. We stopped outside the door of the conference room again. "I hope the reunion is a happy one." Roshii did his impression of a shark about to bite and opened the door. He shoved me inside. Nothing about the room was any different. All the stars still spun in the darkened corners and someone was still standing somewhere close, not wishing to be seen.

I felt the stirrings of impatience, no sleep and nothing with sugar in it would do that to me. I could also feel a sensation in my stomach and head like the inside of a wasp's nest. I turned slowly like an old film drama queen, the feeling of 'look behind you' was almost shouted in my ear, nothing. I turned back. He stood close. I wanted to scream, the face was blurred and hollow, as it came into focus all that escaped me was a gasp.

"Sam?" I said. It was my brother.

"Sam," I said again. I reached out with tears and my arms, ready to touch and hold, to be comforted, as if this was just one more attempt to fly from the garage roof. The shock blinded me to the age of the face and the strange twisted expression. My arms felt nothing and a hand that didn't touch me pushed me away so hard, I fell.

It was as if my brain couldn't make me understand. I kept reaching for him and he held me away with a cold, distant expression and a power that bent the laws of physics. The nightmare that you woke up from, screaming in pain with unseen wounds that went so deep it took all of your willpower to fight your way from the folds of sleep.

I was quiet. I found a chair and pulled myself into it, curling away, holding my stomach with both arms to try and stop the ache which bent me double. There was something about betrayal that was so final.

He stood behind me, close but not touching and eventually I looked up. He seemed to be much older. Once there had been only five years between us. He didn't speak, just stared; his face was lopsided as if he'd had a stroke. But his eyes were alive with dark fires and it was like looking into a volcano. "Sam what did they do to you?" My voice was raspy with the river of unshed tears that I would have to live with every rainy day until forever.

"Whatever they wanted to for a while," even his voice sounded as if it had been tortured. I wanted to reach out, but I was defeated. I put my head down on the table and cried.

He waited, without patience, without anything, standing right behind me but not close. The stars in the corners were dust and without the hopeful possibility of worlds unseen. I scraped a hand across my streaming eyes and did something unmentionable with the sleeve of my T-shirt because Jad still had my hankie on his forehead.

"So what do we do now Sam?"

A voice full of pain and longing answered, "Now we try and make a telepath out of you and me." The sense of nausea seemed to be sucking the air out of the room.

"I'm not sure that's possible, Sam. Haven't these people tried? All of them I mean, not just the crazy ones."

"There has never been a brother and sister before."

"Really?" This had never occurred to me. "I don't think it has anything to do with us being related, Sam. It must be just a fluke."

"Do you really think that?" He was still standing behind me and I hadn't turned around. Not looking at each other could work both ways, as he could read my mind better than I could scan a good book, I didn't bother to answer.

The line between good and evil needed to be redefined regularly, the people who painted in the middle of the road should come and do the moral equivalent, every time it started to get faint and hard to see. I was beginning to drift across, just out of tiredness and the pain that went with wanting someone to love you.

I stood. "Okay, how do I put this? Ah yes, over my dead body." I turned and looked at him. "Really Sam, that's what it's going to take." He didn't touch me, but the kinetic shove of fury threw me across the room and into the wall, where I blacked out. This time the stars were wheeling inside my head and I seemed to be floating. Something like relief flooded my thoughts. The answers never really came in a moment. It was usually a slow dawning. Stumbling around in the dark until you stubbed your toe on the truth and then you wished you'd remained there, in the dark. He needed my complicity.

I was lying on the smelly sofa with my head on Jad Lassik's knee and he was stroking my hair. Not something I would have recommended. I sat up suddenly, making both of us regretful, him because he looked as if he were enjoying himself, me because I couldn't focus and my head spun. My back was bruised from the fight with the wall.

"Are you okay?" He gave me a sideways look, with the good eye, goat pupil narrowed.

"Yes," I said quietly, thinking there were doors in my head I didn't want to go through ever again. "We *really* need to get out of here," I added.

He nodded. "I was hoping to be able to get a message to Harriet by now. Things didn't go quite according to plan."

"There was a plan?" I tried not to sound too sarcastic. We sat in silence while we both contemplated the plan. "I think I can get us out of here as in," I waved my hands around, indicating the room. "Would that help?"

"How?"

I sighed and thought about what I was going to say and how to say it without having a meltdown. "I don't think they can do this telepath reproduction without my cooperation." He looked stunned and a little of something else. "You must know that's why I'm here?" More stunned looks from Jad. Either he was a really good actor or he actually didn't know. I pointed upwards. "You know that's my brother up there, my brother Sam?" I stuttered over the unshed tears, "Sam who seems to be as mad as a frog and much older than he was in my time?" This was met with more incredulity from Jad. "Well anyway, I think their plan is for me to carry a combination of Sam's genes and mine."

"What exactly do you mean?" He was really struggling with this.

I sighed with exasperation, "As in a child the old fashioned way, nine months of waddling." He looked horrified then slightly sick, welcome to my life I thought. Not all women felt the need to reproduce; I'd always preferred baby things with paws and whiskers and I had wanted a zoo when I was a child, something with giraffes and elephants.

"I can't *believe* you didn't know," I said. He shook his head, the air of stunned disbelief still lingering around like garlic bread after too much pizza. "Well *someone* knew. Someone must have," I muttered, trying hard not to think about Rani or Zeke and not succeeding. My throat caught on the threat of pain suppressed.

"They obviously attempted it with my stolen DNA and it didn't work." I shuddered to think what was in the bell jars in doctor death's lab seven floors up. "Jad, you have to give me something, I'm working with nothing here."

He paused for some considerable time thinking his own dark thoughts. "About ten years ago Standard Time, no it must be more than that, the war with Vaneria was still on." He stopped and licked dry lips, struggling with some inner demons. "You have to understand it was darkness." I nodded, as if any of it made sense. He went on, "They brought forward a telepath."

"Brought forward," I interjected, "As in from my time to yours?"

He nodded. "He was only here a few days when the ship he was on was attacked. No one survived. It was found burned out and wrecked and the dead were everywhere. We all assumed that it had been the Vanerians. It was carnage and difficult to work out who was who."

There was more silence and he looked at his hands. "Things were bad, men behaving like animals," he drifted off, "The ship was called The Firefly and it was commanded by Harriet's husband, Sandred Witherspoon."

I was still *sitting* in the small smelly room, but my brain had gone into a spiral shaped shutdown. I tried to think of something to say, but could only manage an open mouth. I must have looked like one of those paintings everyone said they liked but no one really understood. Harriet Witherspoon would have had some idea of who the rogue telepath might be and the whole thing had been a hunting expedition in uncharted territory. Now I knew how the goat had felt in Jurassic Park.

"Later on," Jad said, "Things started to happen, strange things. Word got around after a few years that a telepath had gone rogue. But no one could figure out where he had come from, or who he was." He paused again. "I really didn't know, Bea."

"So what you're saying is that Sam has been here for more than ten years?"

"It looks like it."

I thought about the face of my brother, twisted and dark, full of pain and that craziness that went with the constant proximity to fear. Much more time spent in the dungeon and I would be joining the ranks of the certifiable. "Do you think that Roshii Samura has had him for all that time?"

"No," he snorted, "I would guess that this is a mutually beneficial relationship right now, no one knew where he was."

"He's been tortured, that's for sure," I whispered. I put my aching head in my hands.

"People are not..." he looked embarrassed, "Some of them are afraid of you." We sat in complete silence. I don't think I could even hear us breathing.

"What things Jad?" I asked.

He looked. "You said things started to happen. What things?"

He sighed, a sound full of aching ribs and old memories. "Well." He looked uncomfortable.

"You mean bad things?" I said quietly.

He put a hand out to touch me and then changed his mind. "It was obvious that a telepath was involved," he answered. "You can do a lot of damage with a gift like yours." Giving in and patting my hand carefully, like you would try and calm a restless horse, he eased his battered body into the tatty sofa.

I nodded. "Just how important would this be?" I waved a hand around indicating me and then pointing upwards. He said nothing, just looked. The damaged eye was beginning to open and I could see the narrow pupils focusing on my face. "Right," I said, "Stupid question."

People had stolen and lied and killed to get their hands on someone who could read minds. They had bent time and broken space, changed the past and the future. I didn't think I had ever felt more worthless. "Well." I sat up so suddenly Jad started nervously, which was understandable when someone had been using you as a punch bag for a week or two. The door slid open and the same empty faced woman pushed a tray of food at us. I caught at her arm and she looked horrified. "Tell Roshii I want to talk to him." She pulled herself away from me, saying nothing. I could work out that her mind had been damaged and I tried not to look at the ever-present suffering she carried with her. Some people thought in pictures and hers were of a hopeless, violent past.

"What did you do that for?" Jad was incandescent with anger and a small flicker of fear. He was used to making his own decisions, even those that got him into trouble.

"Do you want to get out of here?" He nodded. "Well so do I and if it's okay with you I'd rather not wait until I'm impregnated by force with an 'inappropriate,'" I couldn't think of another word that wouldn't make me cringe, "Combination of genes by that doctor!" I felt sick at the thought.

We waited. Jad opened a metal food pack and we chewed in silence, both of us contemplating. "Do you think he can read you whenever he wants to?"

"He *thinks* he can." I washed the dry food down with a handful of water from the bathroom. I splashed my face and leaned in the doorway.

"How do we get around that?" Jad asked.

I smiled. "Don't tell me the plan until you have to." Jad looked surprised, the way you would look if your dog just beat you at chess.

It made me want to grind my teeth, but we found our allies and our enemies in strange places. I tried not to think too much about Torriff.

We talked, nothing too relevant, just in case anyone was listening, though I didn't think anyone was, because they didn't care. Jad must have had a good immune system, because the damaged eye was open and the bruising didn't seem so angry. We slept a bit, me on the sticky sofa, Jad on the floor. It passed some hours.

I sat up and looked at the door, signalling to Jad. It slid open and a smiling Roshii came in. He was completely calm, which made me nervous. We looked at each other. "Well," he finally said.

"I want to get out of here," I said, equally calmly. He obviously knew we would be trying for a better escape route and we knew that he knew. People played games with each other's lives for a lot less.

I hoped I was at least holding a card or two, or rather I hoped that Jad was. Roshii smiled again and moved aside, indicating the door as an invitation. "Him too," I pointed at Jad. The smile disappeared.

We stood in silence as everyone thought through the moves they were hoping to make. I wasn't sure but I thought my brother spoke to Roshii. It felt like a ripple on the surface of my mind. For a moment the sadness of the past filtered in. Once, I could have traced the shape of Sam's mind, recognisable forever, like the hands of time had touched the craggy stone walls of a castle and you could find your way in the dark with just your fingers.

I sat down on the sofa and waited as if it didn't matter. I could tell by his face that he was going to agree, mainly because he was the sort of man whose thinking dwelled on the results he wanted and was not based on experience or understanding. It was a leap of imagination to comprehend that someone else might win. He pointed towards the door again.

Our new quarters were on the fourth level and they had windows. It looked as if someone had moved out in a hurry because a slight scattering of possessions and the ripples of old thoughts hung around; there wasn't much need for guest quarters on a ship where people stole and killed for a living.

It was a relief to see the stars. I realised I was holding my breath and I sat down close to the windows, hugging my knees in the hope of finding some comfort in the feeling. I was so tired.

"Tomorrow you will be seeing Gaspar for more tests." Roshii departed.

I opened my mouth to speak and then realised I didn't have anything to say. Jad stretched out on the sofa, a cleaner version of the one in the lower levels, he covered his face with an arm and went to sleep and I made my way into the bathroom where I turned the steamer on to full and stripped off. I only stepped out when I felt my skin begin to shrivel.

I put my slightly damp T-shirt and my underwear back on and padded quietly across the main room carrying my too-damp jeans, I had never underestimated the positive effects of being clean.

Jad spoke without moving his arm or opening his eyes. "Are you sure you were claimed by Zeke?" I felt as if I had been left lying around at Paddington Station. I went into the bedroom. Most of the bedding was on the floor, but it looked fairly clean. I picked up a blanket and went back into the main room. If he was awake I couldn't tell. I draped it over him and then went back and closed the bedroom door between us.

Wrapping myself in one of the blankets I tried to imagine my cat creeping between the folds and purring close to my chest so that the sound reverberated in my bones.

Sleep should have been impossible but I drifted in and out long enough to have a nightmare, the usual 'chased by unseen monsters just behind me.' I was trying to fly away when I turned into a butterfly trapped in the corners of an airless room, beating my wings in hopeless desperation. I woke up with a start to see Jad in the doorway. I sat up. "What?"

"You were crying out in your sleep." I touched my face. It was wet with tears.

"Does the kitchen work?" He nodded and went out. I wrapped the blanket around me and went out after him, perching cross-legged on the sofa the blanket draped like a tepee. "Just hot water will do if there's nothing else I can drink," I said.

"I don't think the previous occupant was Earth human." He held up some seeds that smelt dreadful. "These I think are from Tyranox, slightly poisonous to most of us." He checked a cup by peering in the bottom and then made hot water for me and brought it over. I put my hand on the window; the glass was the same cold jelly-like feel as the Starfire's. It gave me comfort that the stars were always there, even the ones so far away they were like dust on the surface of the pane. We were travelling slowly, in spaceship terms at a snail's pace and I could see light from a nearby cluster reflected off black clouds and gas. It looked like the aurora borealis.

Jad was about to speak, but I raised my hand and turned inward to listen. It was as if a dark mist surrounded the insides of the ship, thick and damp, like a spooky set in a really bad film. I tried not to hold my breath against the poison that crept into my lungs. The ship's crew was mainly asleep, including the lion at its centre. I came back into the room as it slightly spun to a standstill.

"If you are able to do anything, now would be a good time," I whispered, as the angry damp followed me back into my head.

He didn't look at me, but went into the bathroom and when he came out he was holding a tiny disc, it glowed and he was tapping its top surface carefully with the tip of one finger. "Can you get me our current coordinates?"

"I can try," I said, making a conscious effort not to wonder just exactly where he had been hiding the disc. I did the process that Rani had taught me about the candle lighting the way and walked up the levels in my mind. I moved through the doors of the bridge and stopped in surprise. Three people were sitting around a centre console playing a card game. They had the mixed species of different worlds; one looked like a female from Tyranox. I wondered if it was her room I was staying in. I checked her cards, the markings and faces were nothing I could fathom. The other two were men with that middle of the night expression, their yellow eyes were bloodshot and they drank something that looked like a rainbow in a cup. I could tell that one of the men and the woman were cheating; the other was too drunk or drugged to notice he was losing.

I drifted over to the main computer screen and tried to read the figures. They didn't seem to use the same holographic technology that the Starfire had and I couldn't understand what I was looking at. But I tried to memorise the shapes. Suddenly I could feel something stirring at the core of the darkness and I ran in fear, trying to fly like the creature in my dreams.

"Bea!" Jad was shaking me. He looked pale in a mottled sort of way. "You were crying again." He knelt in front of me and I leaned forward, my head resting on his shoulder. It would have been easy to bury myself in the embrace. He moved his head and kissed my face. We looked at each other as I pulled away and I made some distance between us mentally. He straightened up, his eyes hard. "Did you get it?"

"Yes," I croaked, "I think so. But you'd better hurry."

I licked my finger and drew some symbols on the window. He looked carefully as they dried.

"Did this one have a little tail?" He drew in the same way a little squiggle on the end of the middle numerical. I thought about it carefully, closing my eyes to concentrate. "No."

"That's strange." He pondered for a moment then shrugged. Tapping at the small disc, he reached over me to the window and pushed it through the glass. He had to give it a good shove, sharp side end on, but it went through and then out spinning into space. The glass closed over the gap, like a not-set jelly.

I shook my head the incredulous thoughts spilling out. "I didn't know it could do that. How is that possible?"

Jad shrugged. "You can put really small objects through, anything larger than the disc would show up as a warning on a console somewhere."

"What about micro meteors?" He looked impressed again, which I tried not to find deeply insulting.

"They're coming the other way so it would be a hull breach."

We sat in the badly lit room drinking cups of hot water until dawn. I could tell that the ship was waking up. People were reaching the upper layers of their sleep, half dreams, half thoughts, turning to the day ahead. On the Starfire it had been my favourite time of day, light and life, full of possibilities. Here it felt something like the preparation before an attack on the unprotected and vulnerable.

If we were rescued I couldn't see anyone on the Nine Suns giving up without a great deal of blood flowing. The fact that it would be the result of a child's fairytale, the one where they left a trail of breadcrumbs in the forest was even more difficult to believe. I tried not to speculate about what would need to happen for it to work. The low tech-ness of it took my breath away.

I did the exercise of putting the thought in a box and locking the lid down tight, tucking it away at the back of a wardrobe and closing the door. He would know that I was hiding something, but with any luck I would be able to hold off. All the questions I wanted to ask Sam would never be answered, but I couldn't help think about the past and the way I used to feel about him. Somehow he was always distant and it made sense to me now, at the time I just thought he found me strange and didn't want anything to do with a little sister who was so 'odd.' It was difficult not to cry but worlds could lose their magic and in time, good things could disappear.

Oscar Wilde said, 'hearts were meant to be broken.' Mine had always been a little tatty at the edges.

I washed and dressed and ate a small chewy bar washed down with more hot water. Jad and I stared at each other apprehensively. "I think this is what they call 'marching towards the gunfire,'" I said, trying to keep the protein bar from bouncing around in my stomach, where it sat like a greasy breakfast after a serious hangover. The sweeping sense of dread seemed to be getting closer and the shadows of the dark clouds were always around. I pointed. The door opened.

Roshii Samura looked terrible; carpet chewing was never a good sign in any time. He was literally foaming at the mouth and his eyes were dark and wild. I wondered if they had the equivalent of 'speed' in the twenty-fifth century, if so, the man had had a handful with his morning tea. "Doctor Gaspar is waiting." He moved away from the door. "Are you ready?"

"Well it's not as if I'm giving a speech to the United Nations on world peace." As soon as I'd said it I knew he was out for blood, he virtually ran at me, fingers like claws, stopping short as if a leash around his neck had been pulled sharply. Jad had sprung to his feet and was half standing in front of me, I pushed him back and we were like children in the lunch queue jostling for first place. Roshii wouldn't think twice about beating Jad, I was hoping my brother was holding the other end of the leash and would protect me. Even for the worst of reasons.

We stood in the 'standoff' position for a moment, frozen in place, the tiredness and fear a sweaty sheen on my face. It took me a second or two to realise that Roshii was also fearful, though his were the worst kind, those you couldn't get away from because they were inside your head.

I moved, with placating hand gestures, towards the door as if I were trying to appease a large rabid dog.

We walked along the corridor leaving Jad in the rooms, still in defensive mode and Roshii spoke quietly, "I can't stand that man."

I looked at him, it was as if we were in the real world and he was talking about a business associate rather than the kidnapped man he had beaten to a pulp. I thought of several things I would like to have said but did some serious tongue biting instead.

The door to Doctor Gaspar's lair swept open and I walked in, trying not to let my knees go to water.

"Good morning," I said cheerfully, "Ruined anyone's life today?" He looked stunned. "No," I added, "Still, it's early." There was something about mass murderers that made my tongue run away with me and like all bullies he was out of step when the victim wasn't playing the part.

Roshii left, muttering to himself, and I stood quietly leaning against a work surface covered with neatly organised instruments. I folded my arms. Gaspar turned his back on me and began setting up what looked like a large turntable, lining the one on the floor up with one lowered from the ceiling. While his back was to me, I picked up the small tissue regenerator and pushed it into my jeans pocket, moving the remaining instruments to cover the gap. It was similar to the one Pui had lent me when I first arrived. Gaspar looked around quickly as if realising something was up. I did my impression of innocence, like the child at the back of the classroom all teachers knew to keep an eye on. Gaspar had obviously never done any teaching because he fell for it.

"I'm running the test now Roshii," he spoke into the main com by the door.

"Step on here." He pointed at me and then at the turntable on the floor. Roshii Samura came in just as the machine began its programme. From my angle it looked as if everything on the inside was on display, bones, internal organs, it could have been an awful moment but actually I was fascinated. I moved my hands and feet and squinted down at myself to get the best view. Gaspar tapped some keys on a handheld pad and my hologram uterus moved out of my body and floated to one side. "Hmm," Gaspar said.

"What?" I snapped, just a second before Roshii asked him the same thing. They both ignored me.

"Look," Gaspar said to Roshii, "You have to understand these are very old eggs, if she'd been in her late teens or early twenties."

"Are you saying she's too old?" Roshii asked him.

"I'm still standing here," I was somewhere between insulted and angry, "I'll have you know that these eggs are 'vintage' not old!" They both looked at me, the psychopath and the mass murderer. I don't think they'd ever had a victim like me before. Even though I knew that they knew, I was bug material but for the floating uterus. I said into the general silence, "Is there any chance of some coffee?" I heard a bubble of laughter inside my head so going completely mad hadn't robbed Sam of his sense of humour.

Gaspar moved towards the console and the vision that was my

insides disappeared. He thought for a moment, staring at me in a way that made my hands and face go cold. I suddenly noticed the specimens in containers behind him. Some of which looked far too recognisable.

"Well," he said in his mass murderer's voice, "I'll get on and start extracting eggs then."

I didn't move quickly enough and even if I had it wouldn't have mattered, because he was across the room and pressing something into my arm before I could do much more than crack him over the head. I heard an unintelligible swearword and a grunt of laughter before the sting and numbness was followed by nothing.

I woke up with a wet cloth over my forehead, a blanket wrapped around me and a sensation like the worst period pains. I hadn't had anything since I joined the Starfire and I had got the impression that Pui thought it was barbaric. My eyes opened without my permission. Jad was sitting next to me. He looked terrible. "How are you feeling?" He whispered.

I tried to smile, but it just wouldn't happen and I could feel tears leaking from my eyes and joining the drips from the cloth. I rolled onto my side clutching my stomach, trying for a more comfortable position. "What did they do to you?" His face betrayed his thoughts. "You were like a rag doll when they brought you back and so pale."

"They didn't rape me, Jad." I touched his face for a moment. "They took some eggs from my ovaries so it just feels like rape." I pressed my stomach again. "I think they did it with a fork, mind you." I covered my eyes and said quietly, "Let's hope we get some help soon." I tried to get up and flopped back on the sofa.

"Lie *still!*" Jad said.

"Okay, I can do that." I closed my eyes again and heard Jad moving around. He leaned over me to reach the window and sent out another disc. "Where are we, Jad?"

"What do you mean?" His voice betrayed that he knew exactly what I meant.

"Come on, you have an idea of where we're going." I opened my eyes slightly to see him chewing his bottom lip in thought.

"I don't think I should say."

"I guess they're up to more than just trying to create a telepathic nightmare. I imagine all this murder and mayhem is expensive."

He made me a cup of hot water and brought it over to me. My throat was parched and I drank it gratefully. "What I wouldn't give for a cup of coffee," I grumbled. As I sat up I could feel something digging into my leg. I put my hand in my pocket and brought out the tissue regenerator.

"Is this of any use, I pinched it from Gaspar?" He sat down and reached out for it.

"It will only heal surface injury, but yes." He looked embarrassed. "Thank you."

"I'm surprised they didn't see it." Or maybe they did but didn't care which was more likely.

He went into the bathroom and used it on his face; when he came back the lumps around his eyes were yellow, not blue and red. I was looking at my watch. "Jad, how long was I gone?" I shook my wrist and listened, it was still ticking.

"They took you yesterday morning and brought you back a few hours ago."

I had been in the medical bay for nearly twenty-four hours. I slumped back on the sofa. "What the hell were they doing to me for all that time?" I looked through my fingers at Jad, who was doing his impression of a man without a mission. "I'm getting tired of this." He didn't look at me.

"I was produced from a stolen egg." The silence that followed was followed by more of the same, but only because I couldn't form a coherent question, not because I didn't have them. "As far as I understand," he was trying for a reasonable tone, "Though Pui would know for sure, they have to alter your hormones to extract the egg, if they want more than one they have to give you more drugs, I think."

He was hovering around like people did when they were wondering which way the wind was going to blow. I let him suffer for a few more minutes. "I'm going to take a shower." I unwrapped myself from the blanket and shut myself in the bathroom.

My lack of clothes revealed a variety of bruises and a small scar low down on my abdomen. It was well healed as if it had been there for some time, except that it hadn't. I felt sore and angry and a lot of other things that were of no use to me. I stood under the steamer for far too long; in the end dizziness drove me back into my jeans. I leaned on the wall in the bathroom and tried to breathe without panic; I told myself it was just the hormones that were bouncing around in my blood stream.

I walked back in with a not quite smile on my face to see Roshii Samura with his hand around Jad's throat. They staggered around like drunks dancing, each one releasing a grip to get a punch in. I flew at him, ripping his fingers away from Jad and screamed like a banshee. All three of us stood back in astonishment.

Roshii was rubbing his hand, which had my fingernail marks on it and was bleeding. "Come with me." He walked through the door, not looking behind him. I made a silent gesture at Jad asking 'what?' He shrugged an equally silent 'I don't know,' wiping blood from his face with a torn sleeve. We followed.

The trip up in the lift shaft was full of quiet menace. Something had changed, the leash was off. We went up to the first level and all the way along to the front of the ship. Not the conference room but the bridge. The doors slid open on several people in various states of suppressed excitement; they were like a pack dogs who had just seen the prey.

I looked curiously at the hologram of the system we were in and then out of the view windows at a planet; it looked familiar, all planets looked alike when you didn't know where you were, but there was something about the twin stars and the line of the other planets in the system. I looked at Jad, his face was impassive but his eyes were bleak.

Admira. We were coming into a high orbit around a totally undefended planet. The rule book had been ditched a long time ago for Roshii Samura and the chances were they had got the information out of my head. Sam must have 'read' me while I was drugged, sucked me dry of all the useful information. Now I knew why I had been in the medical bay for so long.

The Admirans must have looked like an open invitation to an 'all you can eat' buffet. The silence was punctuated by the grunts of approval from the terminally evil. I stood in misery with no additional help from my messed-about hormones.

"Your brother would like to speak to you." Roshii pushed me toward the door. I moved as if the ghost of my footsteps were walking through an old house somewhere. Jad followed. No one watched us leaving, much as they hadn't seen us coming in. The conference room door opened on the local star system and the planets moved around so that you felt as if you needed to duck when they swung towards you. Sam was standing in the middle of it all like a quantum singularity, sucking all the hope out of tomorrow.

"I don't suppose this ship comes with an exorcist as standard, but we could hire one?" I sat down on the nearest chair. Jad moved to lean on the wall, trying to be less visible. I could have told him he was wasting his time. Sam didn't care if he was there or not. In fact the only reason he was still alive was something to do with me. How long that would last depended on how cooperative I was going to be.

The silence stretched out. No one moved. I looked at Sam. He wore the layered tight clothes that Roshii favoured and his hair was shoulder length and grey. He seemed to me to be in a great deal of pain, one shoulder was much lower than the other, as if at some point his back had been damaged.

He waited for me to beg for the Admirans. Then he leaned forward and scattered a handful of discs on the table, they were the breadcrumbs that were going to lead the Starfire to us.

"Did you think I wouldn't know?" It wasn't even a question.

For a second it seemed to me that it had been a pathetically obvious way to affect an escape and then my mind recognised the fact that it was obvious and I buried the thought but too late, Sam had seen something. A massive siren tore apart the silence. We all jumped like guilty children caught in the act, which was interesting when you had counted the number of telepaths in the room. Roshii was going through the door when a blast caught the side of the ship sending me flying off my chair and into Jad. He shoved me away from him and onto my feet. His eyes glinted with the possibilities.

The open door was full of running, shouting people. Roshii staggered to his feet, holding onto the table, the only thing fixed in place. "What?"

"I don't know," Sam answered the unasked question. "It's not from the planet, it must be another ship." His face changed as he listened and his eyes turned inward and black. I wondered if I looked like that when I was 'reading.' "There are two ships!" Sam shouted at Roshii's retreating back.

"How did you not know?" Roshii screamed at him.

I could have told him, it was not easy to be doing two things at once inside your head. I would have liked to have done some looking of my own.

Sam tapped the keys on the wall console and the star system disappeared, replaced by the planet and the ships bearing down on us. His back was turned and I felt Jad grab my arm and pull me towards the door.

Sam swung around, his face dark with barely suppressed rage. He pushed. It felt like a cushion of air with the violence of a whirlwind. Before I could move my hand to react, my anger took over in a burst of kinetic energy and I pushed back. He slammed against the wall and slid down it, a look of astonishment in his eyes. I ran over to him, kneeling I used the sleeve of my T-shirt to wipe the blood running from the corner of his mouth. I wanted to say sorry, as if we were children who had gone too far in a game.

Jad pulled me roughly to my feet dragging at my arm and propelling me towards the door.

"I don't want to be around if this ends up as a slugging match!" I assumed he meant the ships, rather than Sam and me. I didn't want to be around for any more of either.

Another blast threw us against the wall in the corridor and I looked over my shoulder at my brother, lying on the floor like a broken discarded doll, the unloved toy of a cruel universe.

We rounded the corridor and ran straight into an armed and grinning Redig, who had probably been waiting for us. He grabbed at me, in too close to fire his weapon. I raked my fingernails down his face as Jad kicked him hard in the back. Redig fell against the wall, sliding down under the onslaught of uncontrolled rage. Jad, half kneeling, grabbed his neck and yanked it in a sickening crunch. He looked at my horrified face. "Killing someone with your bare hands is not," he said chillingly, "Unfortunately, as difficult as you would think." He got to his feet and pulled me after him once again. "Bea," he shouted, shaking me, "Come on."

I stopped looking at the crumpled form of Redig behind me and we ran towards the other end of the ship. I passed Jad the weapon I had picked up when he was fighting and he carried it in front of him.

Another 'whomp' of noise was followed by the air being sucked out of my lungs and we went flying. Dust and debris and silence followed for a second until the shouting and crying of the wounded began. I got up and turned to find Jad struggling to his feet. He wobbled a bit and I had blood and dust in my face and eyes. We hung on for a moment to get our bearings. I couldn't tell which way we had come.

The corridor was dark with the emergency lights dotted about.

"This way," Jad pointed and we ran. A lift shaft was open to one side and I stopped dead in my tracks.

"Jad," I shouted. He had almost rounded the next turn.

"Come on Bea." He ran back to me and began pulling at me again. I pulled back this time.

"Wait," I pointed to the lift shaft. "There's something I need to get from the medical bay." Another loud bang punctuated the air between us and Jad's face was purple with rage, he looked like the men he had been fighting. In a way the line between them was paper thin. "Jad," I shouted above the din, "I'm not leaving it here." I could see him contemplating just dragging me. We were a hundred yards from the docking bay and the possibility of escape. "I need to get this, why don't you try for an SSV and I'll meet you there."

"Yes, that's really going to happen." He peered into the lift shaft and stuck a foot in. Miraculously it was still working though there was no emergency line. We got off at the third level close to the medical bay. The corridor was empty, but we could hear people shouting somewhere behind us.

We ran for the medical bay doors. They slid apart onto an empty room. "Go on," Jad shouted at me. He stood by the door which was open a crack, jammed by the toe of his boot. He watched the corridor while I did some low level ransacking. I couldn't find anything that looked like a possibility. "Jad, I need some help here." He looked over at me and then around the room.

"Try that." He pointed at a small container that was on the work surface. It had resisted my first sweep as it was fixed into the unit. I opened the lid onto bubbling liquid. "Hurry up Bea." The noise of people, angry people, was getting closer. He turned to me anxiously. "Don't put your hand in there!" He shouted as I reached in, making me jump.

I found a spoon-like utensil and hooked out the small tubes, there was nothing much to be seen, just a few cells. Not enough, as far as I was concerned, to kill for. Someone once said not to be afraid of the things that haunted the world we lived in, only the things that haunted the human mind are worth being scared of.

I put the two vials into my pocket, wrapped in my blood-stained hankie. I turned to Jad who had his hand up in warning. He waved me to stand behind him close to the door. It was like queuing up for a bus in the rain.

The shouting came nearer. I could feel the echo of running feet reverberating through the floor, the sound of people with fear in their throats, the sweating, choking thoughts that this time you might not get away with it. The noise went past with a whirl of emotions, a vortex that could suck you in, like children in a school playground when the wind is wild. We waited a moment then Jad stuck his head out and motioned me to follow.

It was quiet for a minute, someone somewhere was negotiating. "I hope one of those ships is the Starfire," Jad muttered.

I stopped, stunned. "Who else could it be?"

He turned, pushing me on in front of him. "More renegades, hoping for a piece of you and your brother." I think my mouth dropped open as the thought had never occurred to me that the help might not be help. "Can you look?" Jad asked, checking the lift shaft for occupants and efficiency before he got in.

"I dare not," I said, grabbing him for stability, mental and physical. He looked puzzled. "It's the same reason Rani hasn't contacted me, if she's out there."

We arrived at the first level. Jad had the weapon in front of him and we sidled out of the shaft, standing still for as long as it took to see that the section of the corridor we were in was empty.

"It would be like opening the door and inviting the local vampire in for supper," I explained. He nodded, his back was to me and complete incomprehension in his every step. "Actually," I added helpfully, "It's more like a Vulcan mind meld." He risked a glance over his shoulder, in the quiet of the corridor I could hear his Com/T doing a search and coming up empty. He shook his head, muttering something that I couldn't understand. It made a nice change.

The impact knocked us both off our feet. I ended up on my back seeing red spots spinning in front of my eyes. My breath completely sucked out of my body. I raised my head. Jad had pushed himself up on one arm. He looked exhausted. "I guess," I whispered, "The conversation wasn't going that well."

He began to laugh and then so did I. We must have been a ridiculous sight, covered in dust and blood, our clothes torn and dirty. The tears ran down my face in rivulets. Jad pulled me to my feet for what must have been the tenth time. "Come on." He wiped his face with an equally dirty hand. The corridor was curved towards the back of the ship where the docking bay was. We were both wondering if it was possible to get away with this. I still couldn't hear anything that felt like my brother. Roshii Samura was another story. Maybe he was relying on Redig doing his bully work, if so, someone would find the body soon enough.

I looked at my watch; barely twenty minutes had passed since we had been sitting in the conference room. It felt as if it had been hours, which was a perfect example of Einstein's Theory of Relativity.

The rooms at the end of level one looked like their version of science and astro-cartography. Even renegades needed to know things. But best of all was an open locker attached to the wall by one of the lift shafts; it looked as if it had been broken into. The door was hanging off and a buzzer must have been sounding on the bridge, because a lighted console kept flashing a warning.

Most of the contents had gone but Jad fell on what was left, like a thirsty man with a river. He handed me the weapon he was holding and picked up a much nastier looking version. He tucked some small cylinders in his pockets and handed me three flat, saucer-sized discs.

"Don't move this." He pointed to the top red circle. I juggled them with one hand, feeling stupidly safer with a weapon in the other. We moved carefully down the corridor. All the noise seemed to be happening somewhere else. Disturbingly Jad was checking behind me virtually every other step and switching off my sixth sense was making me slightly crazy too; like a sudden hearing loss.

The door to the docking bay was open. It sounded as if it was full of people playing football, shouting and running up and down. We both peered carefully and quickly around the gap, him standing, me kneeling. We looked like the paramilitary wing of the local school gang.

"I counted ten?" He whispered. I nodded my agreement. A sudden whoosh of power and the shaking of the wall I was leaning on stopped our conversation. I raised my hands in enquiry. He looked quickly around the doorway again. "I don't think that loyalty to Roshii extends to dying for him," he said quietly. "That was an SSV taking off." He didn't really need to lower his voice the noise in the bay would have covered a herd of stampeding anything.

I mimed 'what now' as part of my new sidekick act. He held out a hand for the discs. They made a small whine as he armed them by turning the top anticlockwise. "Garobh!" He swore, "We could do with some help right now." He counted and then threw them into the bay in different directions. "Get down and cover you head!" I was getting so good at it I didn't even ask why.

Some angry yelling was followed by a succession of bangs that made my eyes spin and my ears ring.

"Wait here!" Jad shouted and ran around and through the doorway. I ran in after him.

The bay was smoke-filled and several of the people in it were now dead. I knew this because not all the bodies were recognisable as having once been human beings.

Nothing prepared you for the sight of real carnage. The thick iron smell of blood and the sense of violent death hung in the air.

A wall of unexpected weapons fire sent me flying behind a series of storage containers. I landed on something soft and in pain. A bloody hand gripped my arm and I wrenched myself away in the time it took me to recognise the woman who had brought our food.

She sat there cowering, blood coming out of her ears, her eyes wide and dark with shock. There was more firing and Jad yelled at me, "Make for the nearest craft Bea!" I looked out and gauged the distance from the boxes to the nearest of two remaining SSVs.

Three men were aiming at Jad, who was no more than twenty feet from me. They were the other side of the bay and the SSV on my side had a temptingly open doorway. The woman pulled at my arm, she shook her head and pointed at it. We were not able to speak to each other as she had no Com/T, but her message was clear. Someone was inside the SSV. She motioned for me to let her go first and brought out a small weapon. I watched her creep towards the doorway, using the side of the SSV itself as cover.

Jad had reduced the opposition to one and was preoccupied. A slight movement in the craft caught my eye and I steadied the shaking hand holding the weapon on the side of my hiding place. "Bea, get going!" Jad was making his way over to me, backing up and firing.

The woman moved quickly, jumping out and firing her own weapon into the craft. A stream of light just missed her, but the man had broken cover and was partially visible. I closed one eye and squeezed the trigger. He fell backwards as the weapons fire hit him, half in and half out of the door. I wished I could have said I experienced remorse but I just felt empty and tired.

The woman was dragging at the body, trying to get it out of the blocked entrance. Jad motioned with his hand, just dodging a line of fire and landing next to me. "Who's that?"

"You said we could do with some help."

He looked exasperated. "I was thinking of someone large and intimidating."

To get a clear shot at us, the man over on the other side of the docking bay was working his way around the edges using the stores as cover. Jad gave me a shove and began laying down continuous fire that kept the man with his head sensibly covered and out of sight.

I ran the last few feet and helped the woman remove the still-warm body. A shudder began in my fingers and threatened not to stop, my arms shook, my teeth began to chatter even though I tried to clamp them together. We climbed quickly into the SSV and collapsed on the floor. She pointed a bloody finger at herself and said, "Calla." I nodded; the possibility of her not knowing *my* name was unlikely.

"Start it up Bea!" Jad yelled. I scrambled over to the main console and began the procedures. I couldn't read the hieroglyphs but it was set out in much the same way as the SSV's on the Starfire. At least I hoped it was. There were levels of afraid and I had experienced most of them in the last few days. This particular variation trickled down my forehead into the dirt around my eyes and made them sting.

I turned the controls in one small hop so that the little craft was pointed towards the open bay doors, which seemed to have been jammed apart using some sort of jury-rigged ropes. The spaceship had a shimmering protection field holding the air in, which would have come on when the doors were opened. There must have been a console on the bridge that looked like a Christmas tree.

Suddenly increased weapons fire had the semi-prone Calla leaping to her feet; she flattened herself against the wall by the door and began firing back. I tapped keys with my eyes nearly closed, trying to remember what the sequence should be from memory.

She shouted to me over her shoulder in a language that sounded like a series of chokes and coughs and then, at my look of complete incomprehension, waved her hand in the air, signalling that we should lift off and hover. I tried for smooth, but a pregnant duck could have done it better. She was yelling again but not at me and out of the corner of my eye I saw Jad throwing himself at the doorway and clambering in. More firing hit the closing door and shook the craft as I tried to angle towards the docking bay exit.

Suddenly everything went quiet and I realised the craft was handling awkwardly. A body came into view, bumping the front window, an open mouth in a silent scream and the scratching of fingernails trying desperately to get a grip. Someone had turned off the protection field and the docking bay had filled with space.

I tried to swallow the awful feeling of not being able to breath and struggled to keep the SSV from bumping into the walls of the bay, it was swinging around as if in a brisk north wind. Jad came over to me and leaned in, taking the controls. "I've got it!" I moved out of the seat and let him take the vehicle out through the doors. Another body, this time bloated and dead came floating out beside us, it moved in the ebb and flow as if it were caught in the ship's wake. Calla's face in the dim cockpit light was a series of hard lines and set with tears and blood.

I didn't know if we were going to get out of this but if we did, rocking in the corner with a blanket as a comforter was not going to be out of the question.

"It's amazing the bombs didn't destroy the SSVs," I said, sitting down on the floor, using the wall as a back rest and propping my elbows on my knees. I leaned my head back and closed my eyes.

"The bombs are designed to kill people, not damage anything else," Jad said, not looking away from the task of manoeuvring carefully away from the big ship.

"Great. It's good to see progress." I put my head in my hands and hoped the spinning would stop. A large cloud of malice seemed to descend around me. "Jad," I screamed, "Sam's awake!" I got to my feet and went to the front, looking out I could see the Nine Suns; she was tipped alarmingly to one side. We turned towards the planet.

"We should be okay," he shouted back, "That's the Starfire!" He pointed in the other direction. There were two ships side by side, one of them I didn't recognise.

"I can't believe you said that, go outside immediately and turn around three times, anticlockwise!" My face was sweating again and I wiped my eyes with a filthy hand.

"We're on a spaceship Bea," Jad said seriously. "I don't think that would be a good idea." It was not the time to explain the karmic consequences of pushing your luck, or my small corner of the galaxy's idea of ironic humour.

I could feel a small candle of warmth at the edge of my sight. Rani. It was dangerous even for her prodigious strength to open her mind. Sam was in a killing mood. As much as I wanted to reach her, it would be a tightrope walk and in-between us was a chasm filled with hate.

"Strap in," Jad said. I moved over to a seat and let the belt reach around me, trying not to get claustrophobic with the memory of the last time I had worn one. Calla got up from her exhausted crouch and moved to the other seat as soon as she saw what I was doing. I held her hand in a moment of fearful solidarity and she looked astonished, I didn't think random acts of kindness had figured in her life up to that point. We nodded to each other and then got on with the necessary task of being frightened.

Sam prowled at the corners of my mind like a pack of hungry dogs. He pushed. I pushed back. I must have had help, but the shove I gave him was the last straw. "Look out Jad!" I leaned forward and covered my head.

"What?" Jad shouted, desperately looking around.

"Incoming!"

He turned back to the console and swore, "Zudlocs!" The little craft was spun and buffeted. The blast seemed to have been deflected away from us by the Starfire. But Jad was thrown from his seat and as he hadn't followed his own advice to strap in, his head connected with an unrelenting wall and I was out of my seat a second before Calla.

The roller coaster ride continued as we struggled to regain control, me with the console, Calla with Jad's unconscious body. I entered the upper atmosphere of Admira in an almost upright position, but we were in trouble. I hadn't been able to set up for the descent and the craft was really flying out of my hands.

There was no time to worry about who was listening now. "Starfire I think we are going in," I squeaked in a voice that sounded like Minnie Mouse. I tried for an octave and a half lower. "Starfire, we are definitely going in!"

"Xon Dah!" Calla said, pulling at Jad and bracing herself against the wall with her feet.

"Exactly," I said, as we exchanged looks of absolute terror.

A voice I thought I would never hear again came over the main com, "We're doing what we can Bea." Jenny Smith sounded just exactly what she was, a calm pool in a wild sea. "Can you turn to the left side of the console and hit all the red lighted keys?"

"There are no red lighted keys," I said to myself looking where she had indicated. Just then about seven of them lit up and a loud beeping noise began. I hit all the ones that were flashing and the noise stopped. "Okay Jenny," I spoke with forced calm, "I've done that."

"You're going to have to ride this down Bea. Take the controls and try and keep it steady."

I reached out and put my hands on the console in front of me and tried to keep the left, left, the up, up and down from not hitting us too hard. "Understood Jenny," I said, sounding like the World Service announcer for Dubai.

Calla asked a question in the same cough, choke language and her voice shook, she might have been wondering if I'd ever done any 'falling out of the sky' in a past life.

"Amazingly enough I've never actually crashed before!" She looked confused. I shook my head and she swore quietly again, bracing her legs, reaching her arms around Jad and hanging on. From the expression on her face I thought the possibility of freedom didn't look so good. Or, poor woman, she may have just been asking me if we were going to get out of this alive in which case I had just confirmed her worst fears.

I watched the readings, not really comprehending the language scrolling up on the small screen, but the speed didn't feel right and I slowed it down a few notches. "Bea," Jenny's voice seemed a little anxious, "You're just hitting the point of setting up for landing but you're coming in too steep. Try and lift up the nose a bit and increase your speed to compensate." I did that, working without figures. "It's still too hot Bea, what does the computer say?" I stopped tweaking the keys and tapped the main com.

"I can't use the computer Jenny it's in a language I don't understand."

There was a *long* pause, while those on the bridge of the Starfire were stunned into silence. That was right one of us hadn't been to space flight training. I used the moment to do some more pathetic half moves with the controls. We came out through the high cloud at the same time. Even I could see that the adjustments I had made were not enough. I tried a more radical approach, which made the little craft buck and sway. "Oops." I tried again. Calla groaned. "If you think you can do better, feel free!" I snapped at her. She made a placating movement with her hand and then went back to hanging on. "Starfire, how does it look?"

"Well it's not a thing of great beauty Bea, but it looks as if a landing is about to happen."

My feeling was that it would be more of an arrival. I strapped in. "Bea," Jenny sounded pleased, "Is there a set of three small switches on the right hand console near the upper edge?" I stopped what I was doing in the way of watching the ground come up towards us.

I looked around. "Yes." I reached out a hand to flip them to green.

"Don't touch them yet," Jenny's voice interrupted me and my fingers snapped away as if I had been burned. I sighed. "They are an emergency antigravity force field. You need to deploy them at the moment before touchdown."

"A bit like flaring a canopy," I said hopefully, there was more silence, "You know a parachute?"

"It works like the lift shafts."

I was quite sure this would have been followed by an explanation that would have defied the laws of physics, never mind my comprehension. But I cut her off. I needed to concentrate on crashing. "Do you have any idea where I should try and land?"

"Follow me," another voice came over the com. Zeke.

I could think of only one thing to say, but I didn't think 'where have you been?' would go down well bearing in mind that this part of the galaxy was listening in. I went with, "Okay, Zeke."

He tipped the craft I could see out of my front window slightly off to the left and I did my best to do the same. The ground was so close now I could make out the shapes of trees and buildings and see animals in the fields. Antigravity was beginning to sound like a really good option. I turned my head for a moment and signalled to Calla with my hand, showing her all five fingers. She nodded her lips white with fear.

I tried to keep the little craft in position slightly behind and to one side of Zeke, but I kept drifting off. It helped if I hummed the Bee Gees song 'stayin' alive.' My flying instructor at Dunkeswell, who had said I had brought new meaning to the words, 'any landing you walked away from was a good one,' used to say the middle stanza from 'the ride of the valkyries' would have been more appropriate.

I could hear above my humming that Calla was reciting some sort of prayer. I held up one finger without looking around. She was silent but I kept humming.

The chair felt as if it was restricting my breathing and the ship seemed to be sliding above the ground at an ever increasing speed. I knew this was an illusion but it made me feel like slamming on the brakes which was not a good idea even in my time so I resisted. "Bea, hit the switches now!" Zeke shouted.

I flicked all three to green and leaned back in my seat, wrestling with the controls, reciting the mantra 'flat and level' over and over under my breath until we slammed into the ground and my breath was knocked out of me. The SSV careened around one tree with no help from me and ploughed through a field full of surprised cattle-like creatures. It kept on going despite me applying full brakes. Calla and Jad's unconscious body were tossed around. I heard her cry out in pain, just before I saw the tree that hadn't got out of our way. My head snapped forward and then back and the ship slewed sideways smashing into the trunk which wrapped itself around us like a lover. I tried to cover my face, but the SSV hadn't stopped moving. It spun one more time, throwing me on my side and down into a black pool of quiet pain.

I came to with the extra pressure of an unconscious Calla lying partly on my right arm. She was wrapped around the seat I was amazingly still sitting in. The ship was tipped over onto its left side, which made opening the door tricky. The safety harness holding me to the chair had done its job and I hung in an undignified heap. Jad had not fared so well, he had been tossed around like a rag doll and had come to rest in a worrying position which suggested a broken leg at least. There was no possibility I could move, but he seemed to be breathing, in that short, laboured way of the deeply in trouble.

The shouting woke me out of a daze and I tried to shout back but the pathetic croak that came out wouldn't have alerted a sleeping mouse. I moved the arm that Calla wasn't leaning on and tried to reach the main com, which was not possible, maybe I would just sit and wait for rescue. A rush of fresh air in my face made me open my eyes again. Zeke put a hand in through the removed front window and touched my arm and I could feel the warmth of his fingers through my battered T-shirt. "Hi there," I murmured.

"Hi," he whispered back, crawling in through the gap. He slid to the floor which had been the wall and checked Jad's pulse, adding, "Pui can you get in here please."

Pui's face appeared after a few moments and she seemed to float in through the window. I thought I was hallucinating until I heard Sig muttering something about her having eaten too much breakfast. She turned around and swatted him on the top of the head. I heard an 'ooff' and it felt good to be home.

"I'm going to give you something for the pain so we can move you Bea." Pui leaned in close and her perfume reminded me of jasmine on a warm night. I was about to say that I wasn't in any pain when the ache curled up from my legs and spread over my whole body and I gasped.

The spray made me instantly woozy and I drifted in and out of my senses. I could feel something like a cold jelly being wrapped around my chest and hear Sig making helpful comments about my landing.

Breathing became easier, so some of the jelly treatment would have been for organ support, which meant more time in the medical bay.

I waited until Zeke's back was turned and he and Sig were preoccupied moving Jad onto one of the portable hover-stretchers. I reached a hand into my pocket and pulled out the vials. I handed them to a curious Pui and whispered, "These go to no one else." She nodded and her beautiful face was already in an enigmatic pose.

I knew for sure that she would never do anything that would compromise her own sense of right and wrong, whoever was in charge. The lifting and being moved out of the crashed craft passed me by and I felt my mind wander despite the warnings I had left myself. A small spiral of smoke began to appear at the edge of my consciousness and then a familiar stranger wandered over to me, leaning down with a gentle smile. He wore an old military uniform with large brass buttons and he had huge whiskers that tickled my skin as he whispered in my ear. Only the voice was different, "I'm glad you are okay."

"You were the soldier with the buttons?" I asked my brother.

Zeke answered, "What did you say Bea?" The soldier walked away, whistling quietly and old tears slid down my face. Some things were harder to let go of than others.

The sea was choppy and I was shaking with cold, my arms and legs wouldn't move for weariness. I knew this wasn't real and I was tired of the mental analogy to do with the sea. Oh for a waking nightmare that happened on dry land for a change.

"Bea?" I could hear Zeke's voice. I tried for an answer, nothing happened. I forced my eyes open. There was pain and bright lights, but it was better than being tossed around on the deck of an imaginary ship. "How are you?" He was sitting by the bed. I looked around me I was back in the medical bay again. This surely had beaten Rani's record.

I tried for the spoken word and a small croak came out, "Torriff?"

"There's no sign of him." He swept my hair from my forehead and left his hand on my face. "I..." He shrugged, giving up. Not knowing what to say was his prerogative much as changing my mind was mine.

I tried to sit up. Pui came over to me like a bee around honey and equally as buzzy. "Easy does it." She pushed a few keys and the bed did the sitting up for me. More button pushing and a grunt later and she went on her way to make her other patients' lives more interesting. I could see Jad Lassik and Calla in the opposite beds, Calla gave me a very small wave but Jad was unconscious and covered in bits of plastic and wire. It looked as if he'd broken more than a leg.

Zeke tapped a wall key and an opaque screen appeared around us. Planets and moons circled a bright blue star. They danced around my bed, making me slightly dizzy. He reached out his arms and wrapped me up in one of those hugs you'd never forget in the moments between broken dreams and loneliness.

I think my quiet tears were enough to sail the nightmare boat on. There was a lot of silence and pain involved in loss and letting go. Eventually he said, "Tariq brought you trifle." I tried not to be too hasty as it looked undignified, but the thought of a Tariq pudding had kept me going. So I disentangled myself and sat with spoon and bowl contemplating. "Are you actually going to eat it?" He asked.

"Shh," I said, sighing with anticipation, "This is a serious moment."

I began to work my way round the edge of the bowl in silent homage to the king of trifle makers. By the time I got to the bit in the middle I was thinking of a statue in his honour or maybe sonnets and a small chapel.

"I couldn't find you." The words were bleak and hollow and whispered. Zeke was leaning forward and resting his arms. The crinkles around his eyes were deeper and smudged with desperation and he tried to scrub the weariness from his face. I nodded because anything else would have lost me. The empty bowl and spoon clattered on the table by the bed and I noticed the flowers. A bunch of gentle yellow roses, I imagined from the farmer in the sky. Here were politics and planets and people and Moi Uhara, growing roses, I touched a petal.

"Roshii Samura?"

"He was killed in the initial attack. He was a bit of a surprise to us.

I think his growth had been accelerated, hence the crazy on top of psychopathic. I went looking for Fliss Dalgety and that led me to Telmar Samura."

"So Roshii was trying to cause trouble between his father and Fliss Dalgety to 'muddy the waters?'" There were lots of Com/T whirring noises.

"Yes. That would be it."

"So when you told 'daddy?'"

"Oh yes."

"Sam's not dead," I said. Zeke face changed to tense.

"Do you know where he went?" I shook my head. A place I couldn't follow. Some people travelled alone.

A kerfuffle at the bay door made me sigh, here was life pushing in whether I was ready or not. An apologetic Rani stuck her head around the privacy screen. I held out my arms. "Have I broken your medical bay record yet?" I asked.

"Not even close." She hugged me and I could feel my ribs squeaking.

"Are you up to visitors Bea?" The captain asked. Pui was standing next to her and was just about to say 'No.'

"Of course," I answered.

The spitting image of Roshii Samura walked around the screen. I felt my stomach clench on the just eaten trifle. He held out a hand.

"Telmar," he said and he bowed from the waist. I tried breathing but nothing seemed to work and I found myself gasping like a fish. Pui went ballistic. She pushed passed the captain and Zeke, shoving Telmar in the ribs and swatting Rani with a sharp hand. A small device was placed over my nose and mouth and a blast of air reminded me what my lungs actually did for a living.

Calm was established, although Pui was furious and you could hear her mumbling in a language that didn't go though the Com/T, all the way over to her desk.

"I am sorry to have shocked you." Telmar oiled his way back to my side. I did my best not to read him. Even the outer layers of his mind were Roshii memories. Just more controlled. Here was someone who kept his inner psychopath, in.

"I don't suppose Roshii was expecting to see you, Mr Samura?" I wasn't really asking as much as fishing.

"No. Not after starting a war with Fliss Dalgety," he answered dryly.

We all stood or sat in silence until I'd had as much of Telmar's scrutiny as I could take.

"Have I grown another head?" I asked politely. He roared with humourless laughter.

"You owe me, Witherspoon." He poked her in the chest. A move that I was quite sure brought him close to a near death experience. He swung past the privacy screen looking as if he'd just got a real bargain which of course he had.

"I'm sorry about your son's death," I said to his retreating back.

"Don't worry," was the chilling reply, "I can grow a new one." Quiet filled the air between us, while we all contemplated making pacts with the devil.

I touched the roses again, to remind me of what clean felt like.

"Mark Twain once said that 'if you crossed a man with a cat, it would improve the man but diminish the cat.'"

Zeke laughed and leaned back in the chair scrubbing his face with his hands again. He looked terrible. I wondered when he had last slept.

Captain Witherspoon hung around not saying something. I sighed and thought my heart would break with the weight of what I needed to know. "Did you set me up?" I asked in a whisper. It didn't seem like a question you could ask in a normal speaking voice. I felt as if there was nothing between me and eternity when I looked at her face for an answer.

"We didn't know about you," she said, sitting down on the edge of the bed. Zeke had closed his eyes against the stress. I leaned down with the spoon from the bowl and poked him hard in the ribs.

"I've just had my ovaries scraped out with a fork and I'm armed." I waved the spoon. "Don't make me angry!"

He opened one eye, "What did you just say?"

"I said 'don't make me angry!'" I poked him in the ribs again.

He relieved me of the spoon. "I mean about your ovaries." He spoke quietly, but his voice was pure rage. I realised and not for the first time, that here was someone who fell into the category of the people who made life and death decisions. The fact that Rani had sat down on the bed next to the captain and was looking rather green made me realise that I had said the wrong thing. It was too late to take it back. Behind the screen I could sense that Pui had just put two and two together. Her silence was filled with noisy adverbs.

"So what are we saying," The captain tried for some calm. "They took your eggs?" Her voice ended in a squeak. I looked at them in turn, they were all stunned and it was my turn to be surprised.

"What did you think they were after?"

"When the ship was attacked, my husband managed to get off a distress beacon, but rescue arrived a day too late." The captain had gone back to the beginning which was a clever way of avoiding my question.

"We were in the middle of a war and no one really knew what had happened, it was just one more disastrous battle for the historians." Grief filled her eyes with angry tears. "Nothing much was left of the Firefly or her crew. Your brother had been thought lost with the rest," she paused, "A few years later we noticed that renegade activity was getting more aggressive in certain sections of space. As you know they usually stick to their own 'area of expertise,' this was different. We couldn't seem to find anyone responsible. They had the capacity to disappear well before the troops arrived. The war with Torriff's race had ended, but there were still pockets of fighting. So no one seemed too surprised by it. Odd things started happening which didn't make much sense. Then," she paused again, "A Gurber was killed in really strange circumstances." I felt the wisps of fear touching the air between us, like fog on the water covering the sound of muffled oars.

"Would you care to define 'odd' and 'strange?'" I leaned back on the bed and looked sadly at the empty pudding bowl.

They all did some inter-dimensional raised eyebrows. I gritted my teeth to stop from grinding them, "I have just spent a week with a psycho and a murderer, not to mention my brother and no insult intended, Jad!"

"No offence taken," said a fragile voice from the other side of the screen as he was not unconscious after all and was clearly listening.

"So if you don't mind?"

The captain looked at Zeke and he nodded which was something else to file away for later. "Three scientists from the space laboratory on Deimos were kidnapped. The place is impregnable, but someone got in. A large power core, the type that is used in deep space travel, was stolen from a freighter heading for Alderbaran then the Gurber was killed."

I could think of a million questions, all of which would lead me somewhere I didn't want to go. The bay door slid open and Tariq sidled in. He was clearly visible from my side, but couldn't see in. He held a huge container of trifle. I shrieked, making everyone jump and sending Pui skidding around to the bed, "Tariq!" He took that as an invitation and put his head around the screen, all smiles. "I'd give you my firstborn son, but I don't have one, is there anything else you want?" He looked stunned and rather nervous.

"She means thank you," Zeke said helpfully. Rani took the bowl and handed it to me. Tariq smiled again and was gone. I wondered if his partner was the size of a small planet. There was nothing of the 'no calorie' about the pudding and three spoonfuls was an antidote to the fear.

"What happened to the Gurber?" I studied the roses carefully. Rani reached for my hand and I took it gratefully.

The captain answered, "The ship he was on was attacked somewhere near the edge of our space. They were doing a scientific project on time travel." Here it was, the key statement, I tried for calm but my heart was quite literally in my mouth.

Rani squeezed my fingers. "No one could believe that a rogue telepath was trying to bring someone forward." Rani was speaking very quietly, "We have never done it without the help of Gurber's race.

They hold the knowledge and they guard it, quite rightly, with great care."

"What made you look for me?" Both the captain and Rani looked at Zeke. They were three sides of a deceptive triangle, each with a part to play. That was the pity about human feelings they were always in the way. It made me cringe when I thought of my naivety. I wondered if it was possible to feel any more desperate.

Zeke answered, "We found some intelligence that suggested we may have missed something."

"I'll bet." I touched the roses again but they'd lost their magic ability.

"Pui," I spoke quietly, but like most doctors she had the ability to hear around corners. The lighted beds showed their patients to her in various sleep modes. Little caves of privacy from each other.

"What?" She snapped, coming over to my bed. Her face had an insincere scowl which made me think of being mugged by bunny rabbits.

"Thank you for not saying anything today." I touched the hand that rested on the bed. She nodded, never one for great speeches where quiet calm would do.

"Let me know what you want me to do with them."

She sat down by the bed and I reached for the pillow controller that meant you didn't need to plump them yourself. I added stars and space to the screen which curved around us and breathed deeply of their energy. When you looked into the heart of a star, you could be sure that it looked back at you.

"What happened to the Nine Suns?" I asked. She had pushed the captain and Rani out of the door using her doctor's prerogative and Zeke had fallen asleep in the chair soon after. Most of my questions were left unanswered and I'd drifted into an uneasy sleep myself and as was the way of ill people, had woken in the middle of the night. Pui of course was still at her desk.

"The 'Suns' was blown into small pieces by Telmar Samura. That's in spite of Harriet shrieking at him like a Katinad ottic seller," she sniffed, "I think he was just covering his tracks. Apparently the night sky above Admira was full of shooting stars. It was quite a sight."

Out here, I thought, you were a long way from any type of law and if you broke the rules of the tribe, you found yourself faced with punishment as the people around you saw fit and usually it was a rough justice that made those of us who liked to think we were civilised cringe. I cringed.

"Don't worry about Roshii; he'll be happily pulling the wings off angels somewhere." Pui had misread my wry smile for misplaced sympathy.

"Did you know Doctor Gaspar?"

"Only by the trail of misery he's left behind him." She twisted her mouth as if tasting something bitter.

"He was disappointed that my eggs weren't exactly 'farm fresh.'" As usual the Com/T did a rewind that had Pui's expression go from 'what?' to 'I see' and finally 'what a cheek' in an unusually reasonable amount of time.

"We usually store ours from an early age because there's something about space travel that makes having children a choice for later."

I nodded, thinking. "I guess it makes them easier to steal though." Her face clouded and she spoke in a language that sounded like Cantonese, but didn't go through the translator. I agreed with the sentiment.

"Did you see what happened to the other SSVs that left the ship?" I studied my fingernails carefully. She snorted again.

"Telmar began shooting at them too. Rani told Harriet which vehicle you were on and the Starfire got between him and you. Zeke was already on his way to Admira. He, Sig and Doz have been turning over rocks on every planet between here and the Ross 154 Space Station." She returned the favour and looked at her own fingernails.

"I hear that Sig had to pull him off Aquil the bookseller, though not before he had broken the little zudloc's nose!" She looked satisfied with the warrior expression that was very familiar to me from the Tran

Ni classes, usually after she'd dumped someone on the floor. I realised that I was also feeling a little satisfied and struggling to find the moral high ground.

"I suppose the creep said he had no idea about the story crystal?"

"I think he was trying to say that when Zeke flattened him." Pui leaned back in the chair suddenly looking tired. I wondered how long she had been without rest.

Her eyes closed for a moment. The silence stretched so that I thought she had actually fallen asleep. "What did your brother think he was going to achieve?" The shadows in the medical bay fell in quiet corners and the sound of painful thoughts echoed with those secrets again. I shrugged and raised my hands, because for some reason my throat was sore with unexpressed feelings.

The door to the bay opened for a second and seemed to close without anyone coming through. A shape moved swiftly across the floor and Ollie jumped onto the bed. Rubbing his chin over my face, his purr rumbled through the sense of hopelessness. I filled Ollie's ears with my tears. He flicked them away but kept his furriness pressed to me in that way of creatures who could love you without betrayal.

I must have slept, because morning was something of a shock and Zeke was standing over me. He had a smile on his face. "What," I asked grumpily, "Was I snoring again?"

"Harriet asked me to see if there was a problem with the engines, but I thought I would check here first."

"That's very funny!" I said grumpily and tried to sit up finding out the hard way that an elephant had been sitting on my chest all night. "What do you think the chances are of Pui letting me out of here today?" I gasped.

"None if she'd just seen that." He smiled again.

"You're not going to give me away are you?" I scowled, trying to do something with a severe case of bed head with my hands.

"Is your hair natural?"

"Either that or I was electrocuted at birth!" I gave up, even I couldn't get my fingers through it and nothing short of industrial amounts of shampoo would have made a difference when it got tangled.

Pui came through the bay doors, looking a little better for what must have been hardly any sleep. She went to check in with the medical tech, who whispered details about each patient in turn. As she turned I opened my mouth to whine. "Go," she said.

I flipped back the cover and was surprised to see that I had been unattached in the night to all the little tubes and jelly packs that made up twenty-fifth century treatment. My legs were wobbly but Zeke did a good job of covering my drunken progress. The ghastly pink dressing gown that made up an essential part of my early morning wardrobe was lying on the chair. I grabbed it and made for the door.

"Hmm," Pui cleared her throat. I stopped in mid-stride my head cringed into my shoulders. Zeke was still grinning, but hadn't turned around. "Make sure you get back here for a check up this evening." I raised one thumb in assent as we sailed out of the door.

"This three-legged race," I said, as we were moving down the corridor to my rooms after a short trip in the lift shaft. He was doing most of the work and as usual, I was hanging on like a bag of wet washing. "I think," I added as we went through the door to my rooms, "We're ready to turn professional."

The food fairy had left enough to keep a party of six-year-olds hyper for a week. But the best thing was my bathroom. I turned on the steamer and stripped, examining bruises that were at the multi-coloured stage. My ribs looked and felt as if someone had been playing xylophone with a sledgehammer. I caught sight of my hair in the mirror and yelled. The door opened and Zeke ran in, fists clenched, eyes narrowed.

"What," he shouted, looking wildly around.

"Oh. No." It had taken on the texture and appearance of candyfloss. His eye's rolled and then he tried to look sympathetic, unsuccessfully. "This is bad," I grumbled, "Really bad." The back of my head was matted into one lump.

"Can I do anything?" Rani stuck her head around the bathroom door and did a better job of looking sympathetic, though she'd clearly never had a bad hair day in her life.

"What is it?" Sig asked helpfully from the other room.

Any more assistance would have involved barriers and crowd control. I realised I was naked and went rapidly into the shower stall. "Go away and don't eat all the chocolate cake."

As the bathroom door swept shut I heard Doz say, "Can she see around corners?"

After half an hour of hot water and steam and a whole bottle of hair conditioner I put my pink dressing gown back on and went out into the living room. "We were just drawing straws for a rescue mission," Doz said through a mouthful of cake. "We decided even you couldn't get into trouble in your bathroom."

"Unlikely but still possible," muttered Sig under his breath.

"It's good to see you too." I swiped the remainder of Doz's cake and ate it, laughing at the stunned expression on his face.

On my wobbly return from the evening trip to the medical bay, Rani was doing a good job of tidying up after the massed hordes. I leaned in the doorway trying to catch my breath, having insisted I was fine to go on my own to a sceptical Zeke. I was the picture of 'not fine,' but fortunately he wasn't around to see. When I had left, after a timely reminder from Sig, the room was full of people doing their best to make me feel as if normal existed in the cups of coffee and plates of food. That if they hugged me enough, I would understand how hard they had tried to make it right. Near misses affected everyone. We all needed to be reassured that sometimes, however close the call, we got away with it.

"How did it go?" Rani asked. The wonderful empty corners radiated with her question and it was a good one. Not just an aside, as anyone who had experienced Pui would understand.

"Well, the ribs are okay, nearly fully healed. My back had a few dints in it that made it look like an aerial photograph of the Somme and I think I will have to have more work done on my spleen based on the series of grunts that I heard." I slid carefully down on the sofa and moved a few cushions so that my back which felt the way it looked was supported. I couldn't cross my legs without pain and the only way to sit comfortably was a lopsided lean. For a moment I thought about soaking in the bath with bubbles. A puzzled expression on Rani's face made me realise that I had been projecting a solid image of me sitting blissfully up to my neck in a steaming tub. I laughed which was a noise that sounded as if I was out of practice.

Rani finished the tidying and came over with a large mug of hot water. I drank it gratefully. She kissed me on the forehead like my mother used to do after I'd had a hard day falling out of trees, settled opposite me and waited.

"Torriff," I said eventually, my throat feeling as if it was closing over again.

She nodded. "It's what happens when a good person does something evil; it destroys our belief in ourselves."

"Did you know?" I asked carefully. She shook her head. We sat in silence while I tried to find the words. "But someone did?" I looked her in the eyes and saw that she was devastated and realised, not for the first time, that I wasn't the only one stumbling around in the dark. True understanding of a situation was many things but mostly it was lonely. People with a sixth sense shouldn't get caught out, but telepathy wasn't a constant, you still had to listen. One thing I *was* sure of, the person pushing the buttons was a few chromosomes short of a cabbage.

We both tried to say something at the same time, again.

"I've done a lot of weird things in the last few months," I said quietly, "But this last experience let's just say I'm weirded out."

"Zeke nearly went crazy when he found you had been kidnapped." We both wrestled with the word, looking at each other in astonishment as it was a word most people never experienced in a lifetime.

"I felt a little crazy myself." I struggled to my feet and went for more water. Without asking I made Rani a cup of the green tea she drank in the evenings.

"He has this 'protect' feeling he doesn't know what to do with." She took the tea and smiled up at me. I contemplated the thought of being protected and decided that actually I didn't mind.

"Your brother," she began and then gave up. Even processing the thought was difficult, quantifying it, impossible.

"I used to think that if I could just find the right words." I leaned my head back on the cushions and closed my eyes. "The special words that if said in the correct order would open the door and everything would be okay." I wiped some tears. "There are no right words."

Ollie had curled up, grumbling into a small grouchy ball as I moved restlessly around the rooms from the bedroom to the bathroom to the kitchen area and around again. I touched the old books I had brought with me and fiddled with the computer, spinning holograms out of the screen like a child who blew bubbles until they'd filled the dark corners. I turned it off and the shadows crept in. I was back to being a restless ghost in someone else's dreams. The stars of outside pressed in on the windows. In the end I put some clothes on and went down the corridor. I stood for a moment outside Zeke's door thinking and then pressed the chime. I wondered if he ever slept at all.

"Do you ever sleep at all?" He was sitting working at the small table by the window. Discs and computer spread around as usual. He came over and gave me a hug, trying to convey all the feelings that he was unable to express. "It's okay," I said to his chest, my voice muffled by my squashed face, "I understand."

"Do you want a drink or something to eat?" He moved away making clattering noises with mugs and coffee and toast. He laughed at my expression. "I'm addicted to the burnt bread. You know, you can put just about anything on it except," he added thoughtfully, "Trifle." He handed me the drink and pulled me over to sit on the sofa. The ship was still in the Admiran solar system and the twin stars were dictating mornings and evenings and time.

"Can you promise me that this is it?" I asked. He looked back with that hopeless, helpless expression of the truly warrior at heart, those people who would fight the local dragon for you but couldn't say how they felt unless you dug it out of them with a sharp spoon. His face was the shape of impossible dilemma and he tried for something, but in the end said nothing.

I suppose I should have got up and stomped out in the righteous rage of the truly wronged, but I just felt tired and it seemed to me that we were all part of something that had a beginning, a middle and an end; even if you sneaked a look at the end you still had to be part of it and you couldn't blame people for history.

"Telmar Samura is a piece of space rubbish," Zeke grunted. "He will be delighted to have the captain of the Starfire owe him that's for sure." He thought some things quietly for a moment.

"Once these thugs had family ties and an identity to bind them, now they have territories and affiliations with like-minded thugs, they cross old boundaries easily. Things are changing and I don't think we really understand the changes."

"I don't know; we don't seem to have come very far since Copernicus moved the Earth from the centre of the solar system."

"Don't give up on the human race yet." He squeezed me closer and I could feel my eyes closing. "We know when to fight, when to dive for cover, we are capable of the extraordinary and we are still here." My thoughts faltered in that moment between sleep and awake, drifting around looking for something to hang onto that would make some sense of things, but sometimes sleep was all there was. I hoped vaguely that it would be without the snoring.

I woke to the familiar feeling of 'Monday morning, late for school.' Zeke was making coffee at the business end of the kettle spout. I stretched on the sofa, encountering resistance in the form of my sleeping cat; he had taken up residence on my chest and was looking into my eyes with deep intent. Obviously this was about food and Ollie was hungry, he opened his mouth and half yawned half meowed. I put my finger on his pink tongue. He hated that, but I have always felt that it was rude to yawn in someone's face.

"Are you up to a meeting this morning?" Zeke enquired, bringing water and lemon as a peace offering. I groaned, gulping the hot water gratefully and dislodging my grumbling cat. I threw back the blanket and stretched my cramped body.

"You know, considering that we have two perfectly good beds between us it's amazing how often we end up sleeping on the sofa."

He rubbed my shoulders for me. "We have to straighten out a few things, like the fact that your brother is still available for planetary unrest and mayhem on request for a small fee."

"Maybe that's what you get if you keep prodding the karmic pudding, all that to and fro in time," I grumbled. He nodded his assent, drinking coffee and leaning against the kitchen table. He looked showered and un-crumpled in a very irritating way. I drank more water.

"Does the captain ever go on assignments?" He shook his head. "Okay, a sort of sinking ship rather than Star Trek," I thought aloud.

His incredulous expression seemed to be permanently welded to his face whenever I opened my mouth. I picked up Ollie and pointed towards the door. "I'm going to do some washing and eating." He came over and hugged me, kissing the top of my head.

"It makes me nervous that I really don't know what you're talking about, but I understand it anyway." I gave him a shove and went towards the door, my cat winding himself around my neck.

"How long have I got until the meeting?"

"Actually it started about an hour ago, but I told them Pui said you needed your sleep." He smiled, finished off his coffee and followed me out of the door, turning left as I turned right.

The trouble was I thought that it felt like home. I looked really quickly around and he was looking back at me and he felt like home too. If you scraped around in the rubbish at the back of your mind, it was usually there in the bottom of some dirty bird cage, the thought that you might love someone again.

I washed and dressed in the top and trousers that Lef. had made for me. Ollie created a nest in the sofa cushions after eating his weight in food. I finished making myself a serious plate of toast and marmalade, wandered down the corridor eating on the way and hopped into a lift shaft. I had been more amenable towards the anti-gravity force field since it had saved my life in the SSV.

I was even humming. The doors opened to the conference room and several faces looked at me, I felt like the swimmer that everyone knew was going to get chewed by the shark in the first reel.

I sat down with the remainder of the toast and crunched my way through another two pieces.

Zeke was looking at his hands and Ko had found something interesting on the table's smooth surface to study. Rani was shell-shocked, which was an interesting look for her. I transferred the rest of the sticky marmalade from my fingers to my mouth, by licking them in such a way that would have got me into trouble if my mother had seen me. I was making an effort to be badly behaved for some reason I couldn't understand, like a child wanting to push the adults into a fight, but it wasn't working. They had just put it down to my twenty-first century manners.

The captain was trying to say something but couldn't quite get the words out. There was that silence, the one that occurs between the pistol being cocked and actually fired. I sighed, "Torriff?" I said.

"The SSV is just outside of the Admiran solar system," The captain's voice was even and quiet.

"Are there any signs of life?" I asked, sounding like an actual episode of Star Trek. The sandstorm of emotion was somewhere in the room, but not mine yet.

"No," Zeke answered after a long pause. I nodded and watched the pain wash through the walls and surround me in overwhelming waves, each one bigger than the last, until I gasped. I put my head between my knees and concentrated on deep breathing.

I could feel Doz patting my back in sympathy, he muttered something about, 'swamp-eaters' and I sat up suddenly. "Don't say that, please don't say that."

Doz nodded. He and Sig were looking sadly at me. "We're going to take an SSV and go and get him."

"I want to go with you." I looked at the captain and after a moment she nodded at Doz. The walls of the conference room were full of the local star cluster and the group of people at the table seemed to have found seats in space. I felt the same sense of unease that I had experienced on the Nine Suns, when my brother had concealed himself in the hologram. It gave me an odd feeling and I looked carefully at Rani, she was looking carefully back.

As the marines and Ko-Yo-Na moved to go, it was as if they had to push through the galaxy to find the door. I sat quietly until Captain Witherspoon, Zeke and Rani were left. "Do you have any idea where your brother might have gone?" Zeke was still looking at his hands; the very idea of questioning me was distasteful to him, a fact that endeared him to me mightily. That he was doing it under orders from someone else made me madder than a wasp in a window.

I shook my head. "He is far smarter than I will ever be. He's far more 'anything' than I will ever be." I did the inverted commas with my hands, purely for the benefit of the people who weren't at the table. The sheer arrogance of it was making me unhelpful by degrees.

"You mentioned that your reproductive organs," the captain choked on the words, "Were interfered with?" If I had any doubt before that someone else had been writing the script, that question would have alerted me, either she was trying to warn me, or she'd been possessed. I went with the unseen blubber-faced bureaucrat with an overactive sense of self importance and grubby little fingers in every pie.

I leaned back in my chair, the way that a recalcitrant teenager would deliberately goad a teacher, I would have picked my teeth and spat, but I wasn't sure how you did the first and due to lack of practice, I tended to miss the floor whenever I'd tried the second. "They filled me full of hormones and scraped my eggs out." I banged my chair down because Zeke's face clearly said 'don't bury yourself in the part.'

Rani was concentrating on a small dot of marmalade I had managed to get on the table as if her life depended on it. "Sam had claustrophobia," I said, thinking aloud, "He couldn't even get in a car without the windows open, I don't know how he thought he was going to manage in a spaceship."

The captain looked puzzled, "Why do you think he agreed to come with us?" I had been giving it some thought ever since I had been able to put my mind to anything other than being kidnapped.

"Well," I said carefully. Zeke looked up for a moment noticing my tone and wondering where I was going. "I think he would have done it to keep you as far away as possible from me. Which is odd isn't it, considering you're supposed to be the good people?"

They were a combination of hurt and insulted and I had done it deliberately because *I* was hurt and insulted. The truth didn't set you free, it actually stuck in your throat and made you feel very, very alone. "Before you ask," I looked directly at the hidden observer, "The eggs were destroyed along with the Nine Suns." I knew without a doubt that Rani would know I was lying. I also knew she would not give me away.

I sat back and folded my arms and waited. Captain Witherspoon cleared her throat and eventually said, "Well, I think that covers it." I stood and made my way through the spinning stars and the dark energy that is the 'nothing' of space, to the door. Rani followed me and the door slid quietly closed behind us.

We walked towards hydroponics in silence and she took my hand and squeezed it and I reached out and gave her a hug and we both made a monumental effort not to cry, because sometimes when you started you couldn't stop.

We sat in the upper levels of the space garden listening to birds and smelling green and not saying anything until my Com/T beeped and Doz's calm voice said, "We're waiting for you in the upper docking bay, Bea."

"Okay," I said quietly.

"Take your time, no rush," Doz replied, the gentle Auzzie burr resonating with kindness made me feel even wearier.

I leaned my head back and closed my eyes, if you couldn't see than the sounds were the same as the wind in the trees everywhere, a sigh from the spirit. The hydroponics door opened and footsteps came closer.

We were sitting on a bench close to the edge of the balcony, half hidden by bushes and the rustling sweep of branches. The warm breath touched my skin a second before cool lips and I opened my eyes to see an exhausted Zeke. He sat down on the floor opposite us and sighed, scrubbing his face, "I am so tired."

"How does Earth bureaucracy fit into all this?"

"They pay the bills," Rani answered bitterly.

Nothing had actually changed, not all bad people came with a lopsided leer and a nifty set of clichés. The thought that I might, at last, have had a life of my own was something of an illusion as well.

"Would you like me to come with you?" Zeke asked, as I got up to go. I was stunned. I felt sure that no one had ever asked me that question before.

"No, I said, "But if you were here when I got back that would be nice." He nodded, his long legs stuck out so that I had to step over them. I didn't think I deserved someone to hide behind. Some things you had to deal with alone.

"I'm going to eat some of your trifle Bea," Rani announced. Zeke and I looked as surprised as you could be when the health guru took a deliberate nose dive off the pedestal. "Because, quite frankly, this day is so bad that even a toxic overload would be a welcome diversion."

I began to laugh, after the astonishment at the vehemence of the statement had sunk in and soon Zeke started to snigger and eventually Rani joined in. We rocked and shrieked with undignified mirth, Rani snorted and I thought my ribs would pop with the strain. Finally we were quiet.

"I feel terrible," I said stretching out my arms, every part of me felt cramped and strained, as if I'd spent too many days waiting for a storm.

"Well, Harriet Witherspoon is feeling worse," Zeke said. I think I must have looked surprised, because he added, "The bureaucracy were not exactly impressed that she made a deal with Telmar Samura. In fact they were 'pissed off,'" he smiled as he used the language he had picked up from me. Some bright spark must have been doing a bit of mainframe updating because the Com/T didn't have a fit.

"Usually we don't spend a lot of time with the renegades," Rani said dryly.

"Speak for yourself," I said, which started us off again.

My Com/T buzzed and Sig sounded exasperated, "Bea, when Doz said 'take your time,' he really meant 'we're waiting.'"

"Okay, I'm just going to grab some emergency gear from my rooms." I wandered down the steps and out of the doors into the corridor.

"You don't need anything Bea," Sig was impatient.

"The last time I travelled in an SSV I did." There was something of a pause while the information filtered through hard skull to several layers of grey matter.

"I understand," Sig answered carefully.

I swept up a small backpack and a sweatshirt, kissing Ollie's complaining head. Cats didn't like you to do that when they were washing. I grabbed the paw he had extended like a ballet dancer and kissed that too, was I in trouble.

I did the short trip up to the docking bay in the lift shaft and went in through the sliding door to see a busy Gatt.R. shouting and shoving a large container out of the way of the SSV. In normal gravity you would have needed a special vehicle with lots of additions. It was near the edge of the outer doors and all it took were three techs and Gatt. plus a variety of the colourful obligatory swearwords that always accompanied pushing large heavy things.

He waved at me and came over, his kind eyes trying to express a range of emotions. After careful thought, he went with, "How are you?" I patted his arm and tried not to fling myself at him and cry. One more kind word and I was going to lose it.

"Garobh, Bea! Where have you been? I'm on a schedule here we can't all sit around knitting a sad-on." Doz was pink in the face and half in and half out of the SSV doorway. His short hair was sticking up on end, as if he had pulled at it once too often. I felt the pain recede and my ability to control my emotions seemed to click in. I scowled and smacked him none too gently on the ear.

"Watch your mouth!" He grabbed my hand and hauled me into the craft. Sig was pretending to be asleep in one of the reclining chairs; I kicked him on the ankle and he opened his eyes.

"Hey, don't give me a hard time. I'm not the one having a bad day." He rubbed his eyes and looked at Doz with a grin. "Not enough wild sex, eh mate?" Doz threw a pretend punch and they began to wrestle.

"I don't want to interrupt any pre-flight rituals, but do I have to be here for this?"

"Do you want to fly?" Doz asked me. Sig and I both looked at him in silence. "No then." He did some programming with the computer and we lifted smoothly off and swept gracefully out of the bay doors.

Jenny Smith's voice came over the main Com/T, "We'll be here when you get back." I could feel my defences melting, but Sig had stolen my pack and begun rummaging through it.

"Have you got any food?" He pulled out the various things that fell into the category of 'emergency' in my world, examining them carefully and then tipping them on the floor. I grabbed the bag back and went to a foil wrapped packet of chocolate bars that Tariq had put together for me. I handed one to Sig and then passed one to Doz as he waved a protesting hand over his shoulder.

I had always had a faithful and enduring relationship with chocolate and I respected what the science said about brain chemistry and heart muscle. In an emergency would I rather have had a plug for that leaking boat, or a large bar of chocolate?

We silently munched and Sig helped himself to another snack. The Admiran system slid behind us and we moved towards the outer planets which were several ice rocks and a gas giant three times the size of Jupiter. A small shower of meteors spattered up against the regenerating protection field. Doz checked the computer and then stuck his feet up on the edge of the console, chewing thoughtfully.

The small SSV came into view before I had got myself mentally organised and my stomach lurched up against the feelings of pain and guilt. As if he could read my mind Doz said without looking at me, "Don't even think of blaming yourself for this Bea." He pulled smoothly alongside the other craft and we examined it for damage.

Silence followed as we scrutinised the outer hull of the Starfire's missing SSV. From what I could see there wasn't a scratch on it. The door was intact so space was still outside. Nothing moved as we looked into the front windows.

"Hmm," Sig said. I nodded in agreement. Doz brought the craft round so we were nose to tail and we waited until a slight clunk of the outer skin made contact, creating a seal. He began tapping the main console keys, looking for something. Sig stood by watching over his shoulder. They did the grimace and a shrug of people who walked into danger.

"Well the computer can't detect anything," Doz said.

"It doesn't mean there's nothing there," Sig answered.

"What?" I shouted a bit too loudly.

"Telmar Samura's rather keen on booby trapping his little problems, no reason to think his son's any different." Sig moved away to pick up some kit in a belt-type arrangement. He also picked up a weapon. "Ready?" He spoke to me. I nodded, but my head wasn't at all ready. He tapped the 'open' key on the door, looked at Doz and we stood to each side as the two doors slid back.

Nothing, no sound just a faint musty smell and my own breath in my ears like the waves on the beaches at home. The other SSV mirrored the one we were on. The main area was empty, but the door to the small room at the back was closed.

Sig waved me away with a puzzled hand and he stood to the side again as he tapped more door keys. I looked into the dim light of the back room and saw feet swinging. It didn't make sense. Then when it did I screamed, loudly. Sig swore, trying to prevent me from going in, shoving me with his body. I must have pushed back using my other strength, because he flew up against the wall with a loud, "Ooff Garobh Bea, I didn't know you could do that, does Rani know you can do that?" He shook his head like a dog surfacing from water and staggered to his feet.

The face was terrible. Hanging yourself must have been a painful and lonely death, as if just dying wasn't enough. I looked around for something to stand on and picked up the storage container that was on its side in one corner. "Give me a bunk-up, Sig." I put one foot on the container and Sig shoved helpfully. I nearly hit my head on the roof. "I said a bunk-up you idiot, not launch me into orbit!"

We began to laugh. I tried not to, but I couldn't hold it in. It was as if my emotions had got mixed up and were being spat out in an inappropriate sequence. I cut the line with difficulty using the penknife I had put in my emergency kit bag. I giggled some more as Sig took the weight of the body and we gently laid Torriff down. And then I sat on the floor cradling him to me and laughing as the tears streamed down my face and my mouth gulped in air that didn't seem to get anywhere near my lungs. Doz came through the doorway and he and Sig tried to move me away from him, but I couldn't let go.

They conferred for a while and Sig said he would fly the SSV back to the Starfire. He knelt in front of me. "Hang on Bea, we'll get you back." He touched my arm with his hand and then in a brief moment that I hardly recognised he kissed the top of my head, like my brother used to do when I'd really worried him.

Nothing seemed to be real. I knew that I talked to Torriff about the music he liked and some books he must read. I could see Rani's face close to me and feel her cool fingers trying to untangle mine from Torriff's clothes. But I think it was Pui who gave me something and I felt my grip relax and my eyes close. I was still trying to reach for him even as the dark came creeping in.

There were all types of sickness. It was as if the grief folded in on me and my vision was clouded with the death of my mother and the loss of Sam, who was as if he were dead, maybe the unreachable person is something worse. In my half dreams were the faces of Martin Cree, who had not experienced love, and Torriff who had loved too much.

It was not possible to explain grief, it had to be lived. All the loss spun out of control and all the questions never asked seemed to blend into a sea of misery. It was not probable to sleep without thought and there was no peace anywhere. Also, somewhere, somehow you had to be okay with your own death to be able to live with the death of others.

I woke to see Zeke sitting in the chair by my bed. He was looking at me with a hollow sadness that made me feel as if the shadows were winning. His face changed to a guarded smile when he realised I was awake.

Ollie made a purring noise in my direction and stretched in the way that cats did with every vertebra extended, along with paws and tail. He came to my end of the bed and put a cold nose in my face, rubbing his whiskers on my cheek. For Ollie a demonstration of affection that was right up there with banners and a ticker tape parade. Zeke snorted as I grabbed my cat and gave him a smothering of kisses, which he pretended to be annoyed about. "Maybe I should grow whiskers and a tail." I reached out a hand and Zeke reached back and we stayed like that for a moment.

"I'm afraid," I said. He nodded, swallowing the words he wanted to say, which cost him a lot.

"Would you like a cup of that slush you call coffee?" He asked carefully. I could see by his eyes that the fact that he couldn't do anything about whatever it was, was chewing him up inside and the fact that I didn't know what it was he couldn't do anything about was affecting me on a spectacular scale. But slushy coffee sounded good and I nodded.

Rani put her head around the bedroom doorway, "Can I come in?" The lighting was on low and it seemed as if she had a halo, she looked like a copy of the old renaissance paintings of the Madonna. Long smooth hair and floaty clothes. She sat on the bed and reached for my hand. "Do you think," she asked quietly, "You could not do that to me again?"

The coffee arrived in a large mug, suitably milky and frothy with lots of sugar. On a large plate were ginger biscuits and in the centre of the plate was a beautiful yellow rose. A large tear escaped and ran down my face. Rani looked panic-stricken. "Do you want me to get Pui?" I leaned on her shoulder and cried and she made those noises that people who had small overtired children did. Eventually I leaned back on the pillows and looked at both of them; Zeke was hovering in the doorway, trying to find a reason to break something. Rani was pale with borrowed sorrow. My cat did his best to look as if he wasn't getting as close as possible to the biscuits. In the second between the intake of a breath and a thought, Ollie had grabbed his prize, upended the plate which scattered the rest of the biscuits and he scampered under the bed where he crunched loudly and with great satisfaction.

I crunched biscuits myself and we talked of other things, managing to hide the elephant size sadness in our conversation. "We have a diplomatic visit to Admira tomorrow," Rani said, "Do you want to go?"

"Sure. There's nothing like someone else's problems."

We did some more crunching; it was amazing how quickly a plate of biscuits could disappear when one of you was a cat. Zeke sat on the bed by Rani and just kept dropping half a biscuit and sliding it with his foot. It sounded like a pig chewing cinders under the bed. The floor was decorated with crumbs and so was the bed cover.

"Tell me what it is you're not sure I'm up to hearing." Zeke fingered his blocking chip and Rani smiled a not really smile.

"There was a message on the SSV computer. Torriff had let it run, over and over." She licked her lips as if they were too dry to talk.

"Roshii had 'disposed' of Torriff's life mate and his children and sent the message to him while he was waiting to make contact." We all dealt with the enormity of this, while Ollie crunched with dignity into the silence.

"How did Roshii get hold of them?"

"He sent a coded message to Kela asking her to meet him on Ross 154 as if he were Torriff," Zeke answered. "Apparently he had Torriff's key code so there was no reason for her to think it was a trick."

Poor Torriff, he would have known where they'd gone from the second he had tried to contact them at home, whenever that was. I looked at my fingers and thought a nail file would be a good idea. "Did he leave a suicide note?"

"It said 'the guilt is mine alone, do not blame my people for my cowardice. Please forgive me.'" Zeke spoke, in the matter of fact tone of people who fought, when they were talking about people who'd given up without one.

"Do *you* think he committed suicide?" I asked.

"I would, if Roshii Samura had got hold of my family." Zeke made a face. Not answering the question.

"You don't know do you?"

"There's not much we can do about it anyway," Rani said, in that head girl voice that made you want to pull her hair. "It is, as it is."

I sat thinking, the plate was empty and Rani had put the rose in water by my bed. Zeke got up and stretched, his joints popping and his face contorted in a yawn. "You look terrible," I told him. The shape of tiredness was in a half moon under his eyes and the memories of old worries were behind them. "So the people in charge think I might have been complicit in my kidnapping?" Zeke made no eye contact with me he just shook his head wearily. "They think because it was my brother I must have been part of it?"

"You said yourself you thought he would do anything to keep us from you," Rani answered gently. "You have to understand," she added with a great deal of bitterness, "They have no imagination where people like us are concerned."

"The truth is Rani," I said sadly, "I would be the last person who'd know what my brother was thinking." I added quietly, "Some people don't just not love you they can't let you near them either." I began to experience the familiar sensation of bubbles behind my eyes, a calling card for those who listened. I was sure Rani must have heard it, but like a Victorian dowager she politely ignored the sensation, as the message wasn't for her.

Zeke pointed at the door yawning and mouthing an unintelligible, 'if you need me' and left. Ollie trotted out after him his tummy dragged, full of ginger biscuits.

Rani squeezed my hand and reached for my dressing gown, putting it on the bed. "Don't be up too long. You need some sleep." I think the whole ship must have been used to the pink dressing gown, because no one said anything but 'hi' as I wandered up to level one.

Na-Es-Yan gave me a hug which made my eyes water and said,

"Don't let Pui catch you, she's given everyone the evil eye to let you rest." I nodded that I would be careful as it wasn't a good idea to take anything that Pui said with anything less than complete seriousness. You could find yourself permanently grounded.

The doors to the astro-cartography rooms were opening as I came up to them. A dark interior was an unusual feature until I looked into the very centre of the room. My heart did some somersaults. I stepped forward without taking my eyes from the tiny puff of spinning matter. Energy and gravity fought as the matter spread, until a swirl of colour and light spun in a silent wheel of violent birth. This was Gurber's way of saying 'don't sweat the small stuff.' I inched forward; though it wasn't easy walking on stars. The glow began near my feet and a path of sorts made of interstellar dust in orange and gold led to the back of the room. I gave Gurber a hug.

"**We are order. There is chaos also. We were aware of our existence.**"

It was going to be one of those enlightening conversations where I usually came away unenlightened. I thought about something to say. "**Is chaos evil?**"

"**Chaos is a being like us, not good not evil.**" The 'being like us' was a rather a misleading statement as Gurber used 'we' and 'us' when he talked about himself and his race was obviously more than one. He began speaking again, "**We were lonely we made you from the stars, from the energy. We hid you in time. You became reborn at a higher level.**"

I think I'd just about lost track and it seemed to me he had covered all the belief systems on Earth that I could think of, ancient Egyptian 'Order of Life,' physics 'cosmic time' and Buddhist 'reincarnation.'

"**Are you the creators?**" We sat in silence while he thought for a while. I knew he was thinking because he bubbled at the edges and fizzed occasionally.

"**There is, before us.**"

That would mean what exactly? I didn't say anything as it would have been rude. I wondered if, as Gurber's 'order' was round and cuddly if 'chaos' would turn out to be craggy and rather standoffish, I didn't think I'd ask about that either.

"Are you made of the same stuff as we are?"

"We are photon, not as you are."

What I knew about physics could be written on a really small pinhead, but even I knew photons were about light and waves, they were also electromagnetic and something else someone once told me, 'light does not get old.' Photons that were around at the 'big bang' were the same age as they were then.

More silence followed. Gurber was trying to tell me something, but I hadn't a clue what it was and my head was clogged with the thoughts of the spinning galaxy at my feet. Gurber went into a still state and I wondered if he were asleep, but if you were made of the very elements that light was made of, maybe you didn't need to.

I felt my feet begin to cramp and my whole body was tired and ached as if I had been in a car crash. I crept carefully over the stardust path to the doors, which slid open without me touching anything. I turned to look at my friend, but the galaxy was in the way and all I felt was a gentle wave of warmth, like the breath of a sleeping child.

I walked down the quiet corridor and into the lift shaft. The rooms I passed by were without people, but not empty.

The steam woke me up and cooked me to a fine pink glow. I finished with a blast of cold water which was good for the spirit if not the nerve endings. I checked the bruises, the pale yellow of nearly gone. More than could be said of the bad dreams and hot drinks of the early hours.

What haunted my sleep was not so much the twisted face of Torriff as we cut him down, as all the words unsaid and the one abiding thought common to all those of us who lost friends, that I could have done something if only I had followed the signs. Of course I knew that different decisions would make no difference in the clear light of day, but in the early hours you always thought you could have changed things.

Rani was in the main room making early morning tea when I finished in the bathroom. She handed me a large glass mug of red aromatic liquid as I drifted naked into the bedroom. "You might want to wear a bit more for the meeting this morning."

"I was thinking my dressing gown?" I looked wistfully at the comfy robe and the feelings of safety it seemed to give and thought about going back to bed on a serious level.

"Is it still bad?" Rani was leaning in the bedroom doorway.

"Yes," I whispered. I used some moisturiser which I'd pinched from Pui, whose incredible skin didn't need it anyway and put some twenty-fifth century clothing on in the hope that it would cover my twenty-first century emotions; which consisted of a wrap top in clingy material and a pair of loose trousers. I scraped my hair back in a scrunchy, where it sat on the back of my head like a bundle of old wool. Ollie had long gone on his usual morning hike, which I was sure from the size of him still included a visit to both restaurants.

I shuffled some thoughts that had been spinning around in the early hours, like a really annoying song that I couldn't quite remember the words to. "Rani, why do you suppose Sam took the Nine Suns to Admira?"

"It could have been he found the information in your subconscious? He told Aquil that's where they would be otherwise we would never have found you."

"I'm sure that's part of it, but why Admira? I mean, I was thinking about it last night and I checked the holo/files. They don't have anything to offer more than any of the other unprotected worlds. And the fact that the Star League was looking at them would make them a more difficult proposition. It just doesn't make sense," I added.

"Does it have to?" Rani asked helpfully.

"I know my brother and he never did anything without a reason." We were nearly at the doors to the conference room. I stopped. "Do you think that the trip to the Admirans could have something to do with us?"

She whispered back, "What do you mean us?"

Because she had whispered so did I, "I mean you and me, us." I knew she'd got it because she began to look worried. I spoke carefully, "Has anyone done, I don't know, tests on these people?"

"Why would we? You don't have to have a DNA test, or a psych test for that matter to join the Star League. Space travel is the usual criteria. Or sitting in the path of a trade route," she added dryly. She looked carefully up and down the empty corridor, which frightened me. "Have you spoken to anyone else about these ideas?"

I shook my head. "I might be reading too much into it, but I can't think of any other reason for the Nine Suns being there, can you?" We didn't speak as the doors slid open.

The usual suspects were ranged around the conference table. The captain was drinking coffee and looking at holo/discs on a small hand held computer. Sig was talking to Pui and Doz was trying to get Ko-Yo-Na to agree to a volleyball game. She would wipe the floor with him, but maybe that was the idea.

Zeke came over and gave me a large cup of milky coffee and a smile. He looked at Rani and then back at me.

We settled down in our seats and the captain spoke to Sig, "How are we going to set this up today?"

"Well, I thought we'd bring the Admirans up here for an initial conference, go through all the legal procedures. Pui will have to do a medical assessment on all the diplomats who will be transferring to Earth." He thought for a moment. "That's it I can't see any real problems."

"Um," I said, feeling as if I should raise my hand like the child at the back of the class. "These people will want to perform some sort of ceremony. I mean they seem keen on anything meaningful." It was quiet around the table. "I'm probably trying to teach my grandmother to suck eggs." The Com/T had a serious meltdown and everyone stopped focusing for a second.

"That," said Sig, "Is disgusting! I can't imagine what that means, is that something Dolly Parton said?"

The captain was looking bemused as she watched a professional meeting deteriorate into the usual claim and counter claim that always followed. I felt very twenty-first century again despite the wardrobe. Ko was closest in her definition and interpretation and I told her so. She looked smug.

Captain Witherspoon cleared her throat, "I think a ceremony would be a great idea, Bea."

She had that way with her like the teacher that children were always quiet for, when they behaved like hellions for all the others. I wondered if she had to work hard at it. Just when I thought I'd got her sorted in my mind I ended up with more questions.

"Perhaps you could set out a plan and let me have it before the end of the day?"

"What," I said, gasping like a fish, "Me?" I had walked into that. Sig was grinning.

Rani was laughing too and she gave my shoulder a friendly pat. "I'll give you a hand we'll speak to Asa/Et she's still down on the planet."

"Right," said the captain, "Housekeeping, does anyone want to start?" Pui took out a disc and put it into the main com, it threw up a really long list and everyone groaned. She looked at us all in turn and we settled down, where you were quiet for Captain Witherspoon to please her, you were quiet for Pui because she was really scary. "You may remember these people?" A holo/picture spun towards us, the lumpy, grumpy faces of the Karnestans and everyone groaned again.

"I thought the Star Fury was going to take care of that?" Doz asked.

"Well," said Pui, "I've just spoken to the medical officer on the ship and they're not having much luck. So it's up to us to come up with something." We all looked at her. "I have one or two ideas." She tapped keys and a list of drugs and diagrams of populations hovered in the air.

I found myself blurring the room out and thought about the Admirans. Rani dug me in the ribs and I shuffled in my seat. Sometimes space travel was terrifying and sometimes it was boring, either way, I realised, I was happy to be there. My stomach rumbled and Zeke slid me a plate of cakes that had come straight from the restaurant. I took two. They melted in the mouth and looked similar to a muffin with lots of fruit and nuts. The shape of the Karnestan home world did a bit of a shimmy and Pui gave the main computer a swift blow which righted the holo/picture. When I had first arrived on the ship, it looked to me to be everything shiny and cutting edge that technology could possibly be. It had taken me a while to realise that sometimes things just didn't work and you couldn't stop off and get a spare part. The thought that we were part of some 'out there' frontier, but without the horses and wagons crossed my mind again: except that, this time it was the Mohawks fixing the 'horses and wagons.' I realised I hadn't seen Mac for what seemed like ages, or Tom Hatherley, for that matter.

I chomped on the cake and thought about the past and the future. Pui was still talking and I wasn't the only one who had stopped listening. I wondered if I could get a clean bill of health ticket from Pui and persuade Mac to take me out on another space walk.

The meeting broke up and I took my coffee out with me. Pui, Rani and I sat in the upper level of hydroponics finishing our respective drinks. Both of them tried my trainers on, fascinated with the texture and shape. It must have felt as if they were trying the clothes on in a museum. Pui got up and stretched, scattering holo/files and the medical things that all doctors carried around in case someone had the stupidity to stop breathing in front of them. She gathered up the feathers of her life and went on her way. But not before giving me a time for a medical the next day. I smiled sweetly, thinking of the space walk.

"Rani, do you trust the captain?"

Without much of a pause she said, "It's not that I don't. It's just that I know what hoops she has to jump through and what a fine line she walks. It's complicated."

"What about Zeke?"

She laughed, "Absolutely! I have no idea who he answers to and what lines he has to walk, but yes."

"Pui?"

"Implicitly." We laughed and then she asked me, "What about me Bea, I'm on that list, do you trust me?"

I paused long enough for her to look sad, before I nodded carefully.

"Then why," she asked, "Didn't you tell me about the vials you brought back from the Nine Suns?"

"Did Pui tell you?"

"Of course she didn't."

I would have been surprised if Pui had volunteered the information even under torture.

"Did you get it from me?" She nodded. "You're like a pickpocket," I said.

She examined her nails, looking like Fagin before he sent out the boys to do a days thieving. "What are you going to do with them?"

"Well, I've thought about it." I really had, long and hard and there seemed only one thing to be done. "I think I'll ask Pui to destroy them."

She didn't say anything for a while and her face barely moved, but I could tell that she was utterly and completely relieved and because she was, I was. It felt as if a very great weight had been lifted.

"Are we going down to the planet today?"

"Yes, I'll arrange it with the captain. Meet me in the docking bay in an hour. Let's go and see what the Admirans want to do about celebrating their membership of the Star League."

I said, "It's bound to involve lots of meaningful quotations."

I changed into something that was more 'diplomatic' it involved a long wrap dress made by Lef.G. which was comfortable but not practical. Then I buzzed a surprised Mac Ibarra and pleaded for a space walk. He was quiet for too long to be polite. "Let me get this straight, you want to go outside for fun?"

"Yes!" I gathered my emergency pack and another layer of clothing, just in case it got cold. There was a long silence. "Mac, are you still there?"

"Tell me I'm awake?" He answered, bemused. "Does the captain know about this? It was my turn to be silent. I couldn't come up with a good reason for my going 'outside' except that I really wanted to. "Okay, I'll think of something," he sounded exasperated.

"You're a star!" I shouted as I went out into the corridor.

"Yes," said a hollow voice, "He sits in space using up energy doing nothing, while everyone has to dance around him." It sounded like Tom Hatherley, so Mac had had his Com/T on open.

I checked the SSV and found Rani sitting at the controls. Looking out of the door again for one of the usual escorts I said, "Where are the marines?"

"It's just you and me." I thought she was joking until the minutes slipped by with her doing the pre-flight checks.

"Who's flying?" I sat in one of the back seats and looked hopeful. Rani turned fully in her seat and said nothing and I sighed, got up and stamped over like the child at the back of the class who had to do a sum on the blackboard.

The checks were done and I called the bridge, "This is Bea and Rani, we're off to the surface."

"Understood Bea," Jenny Smith's gentle voice answered and was loaded with unspoken empathy. "Have a good trip." As the last time I'd been travelling down to the planet I'd crashed, I thought it would have been difficult to have a worse one. My curiosity got the better of me.

"Jenny, are you welded to the pilot seat on the bridge?" I added, tapping keys, "I mean that in the nicest possible way." A stunned silence was followed by a shriek of laughter.

"I'm training Bea, for my spaceship licence. I have to have a thousand hours to qualify."

"That is a lot of hours," I said, turning the SSV around and catching a storage box as I swung about. "Thanks Jenny." Gatt.R. was shaking his fist at me as the huge box skittered along the floor as if it had been cardboard blown about on a windy day. It must have weighed a ton. I threw him a kiss and made my way to the bay doors in a fair impression of a drunken stagger. We cleared the ship with only a tiny scrape down one side of the SSV.

I set the computer for destination and put my feet up on the console. Out of the window Admira was doing a beautiful pirouette on its axis on a course around its sun. At the darkest point on the edge of the system, I could see a comet, its tail a stream of sparkling blue dust as if a child had painted it. The main com buzzed. "Hey

Bea can you see us?" Na-Es-Yan was speaking in breathless excitement.

"No, but I bet you're somewhere near that comet." Rani and I moved over to the window and she input the grid on the computer. The hologram sprang up showing the comet and as a tiny speck, the SSV hanging in the wash of the tail, bobbing and weaving like a creature in the deep.

"Here we are," said Neff.P., his voice full of emotion, "Stealing dust from the tail of a comet."

"You know," said Rani, "Whenever I hear those two, I'm sure I'm not getting enough out of my day."

"Take a closer look Bea. It has the most unusual surface." Na was squeaking in her enthusiasm. I wished I was with them instead of a whole day of meetings with the locals. Nice enough as they were, the Admirans couldn't compete with a comet. Rani tapped more keys and we looked carefully at the hologram of the lump of ice and rock travelling at some speed. It had tall thin spires like telegraph poles sticking up from the surface.

"How did that form?" I asked no one.

"No idea," was the reply from two voices acting in stereo. They sounded deeply satisfied that they didn't know, because that would mean there was something more to find out. I agreed with Rani that I needed to work on my goal setting.

"Come and see us when you get back to the ship Bea. We'll have some more information by then."

We signed off and I sighed, sitting down and setting the computer up for a landing as we passed the outer satellite and then the space station. We hailed them as we went by and got a grateful response from two rather lonely engineers.

The upper atmosphere was a little bumpy, but Rani, with great restraint, left me to it and I sweated out my nightmares in silence. We both knew I needed to put the fear to rest, but it was hard. The problem with facing your fear was it stunk.

I leaned back in the seat and we both sat for a moment. "Okay," I said. "It's done, let's go." Rani didn't do much more than give me a swift hug to let me know she understood.

The problem with 'ship's time' was it was calculated to run along Standard Time and everywhere you landed it was local time. So it was late afternoon when we landed and the Admirans had a twenty-eight hour day to cope with the two suns which didn't rise at the same time.

It was good to see Asa/Et again. She wafted over on a cloud of efficiency, which made me feel like a badly dressed relative up from the country. Civil:Moi was close behind her with a grin on his face.

"Bea," he shrieked, "We were so worried about you!" It would have been something and nothing from someone else, but this man really meant it and took my hand to let me know he was sincere. "Asa said you were fine but I wanted to see for myself."

I got an eyeful from the emissary, which clearly said she had not told them anything about anything. We walked back towards the main buildings and a small escort of soldiers fell in behind us. We looked like a school crocodile on a day out. We hadn't landed at the busy airport, but closer to the more political centre. No one seemed to mind. I thought about the unlikely possibility of landing a helicopter outside the Houses of Parliament or the White House. A small contingent of people gathered to greet us and introductions went with the traditional hand tapping and were lost in a sea of faces and titles.

The table was set with a mock-up of the hoped for ceremony. I couldn't tell from looking at the diagrams but Rani's face was a dead giveaway. It seemed the Admirans were happy to bury themselves in the part. I sat and watched as Asa/Et talked them down from four days of events to one. Each item on the agenda was detailed and argued for. They looked stunned with what was left. As if we'd asked for everyone to give up their firstborn, in fact they might have been happier if we had.

Civil:Moi had an expression of undisguised glee on his face. For a scientist he could be vindictive, but with a great deal of charm. He twinkled at me and roped me into his delight at the political hierarchy getting a smack on the nose. I couldn't blame him; we all liked to see our politicians with a dent in the ego.

I moved, carefully sidling towards the door, Rani looked over her shoulder and narrowed her eyes. I stopped, like a rabbit caught in the headlights. When an official, one with a very, very large ego began spluttering, I ran.

The evening was wonderful, two suns were setting and a rich red glow made the gardens and mountains beyond look like an advertisement for a holiday in paradise. I wondered how long it would take before the rest of humanity in all its shapes and forms discovered this corner of the galaxy. I curled up on a comfy seat, conveniently placed to face the view.

The scientist sat himself down with a big sigh, "Is it like that on your world?"

"You mean a bunch of windbags going at it hammer and tongs?" A short buzzing from the Com/ T followed by a pzzt.

He tapped the back of my hand laughing, "Yes!"

"Then absolutely, it is the same," I answered. The comet caught my eye as the suns were low on the horizon and I pointed. A few stars were spattered in the gathering dark.

"We call it the 'Dragon's Tail.'" He followed it with his finger. "In the past it was the bringer of good fortune for a superstitious people. Now it is a scientific phenomenon that we would like to spend time studying."

"Two of my friends are up there doing just that," I said.

"Are they now?" He said, with such longing I turned to look at him. His face was full of the desire a little boy might feel with his nose pressed up against the window of a sweet shop. "We are in our own solar system with shuttles and probes, but we don't have the expertise yet to chase the Dragon's Tail."

"I will ask Rani if you can come up to the Starfire. Na and Neff.P. would be delighted to show you what they have collected."

He nodded and carefully wiped a tear with the edge of his coat. I didn't see because it would have been an awkward moment for both of us. "Science seems to be universal," he said after a silence, "We all long for answers."

"We had a few tricky moments in the Middle Ages when religion did something unfortunate for several hundred years, then we got Einstein."

"Einstein?" He looked puzzled.

"E = mc2." I drew it in the dust at my feet. "Energy equals the object's mass times the speed of light squared."

"Ah," he said, "'char geta tewh,' it means, 'the secret kept by stars.'"

"Einstein was a great man with lots of hair!"

"I am sure he was," he said with all seriousness. "'We all walk in his shadow.'" Silence followed while we watched the stars as they spread across the sky and the comet as it disappeared over the horizon.

"Why are you not inside making a noise with the rest?"

"I'm a scientist. My life consists of long lines of mathematical formula interspersed with 'something odd happens here.' I don't need a parade I need a solution for the 'something odd.'"

"Exploration doesn't open as many doors as you would think," I said. He harrumphed, a universal sound that needed no help from the Com/T. I leaned back against the seat and looked directly up, no stars were recognisable. The Pleiades, the North Star, Ursa Major. It was a strange feeling to be seeing no shapes in the dark that you knew. There were still shapes though and someone had made up names and a history of ideas around them.

"Einstein said he wanted to 'travel on the crest of a wave of light.' That's what space travel is like." I hunched my knees up and tucked my arms around them. It was getting cold but I was not going back into the rooms, where I could see the lights on and a frustrated group of officials fighting a rearguard action for some presentation. I could sense Rani doing a good job of not punching a pompous idiot. I didn't feel it would be a good idea for me to join them because I would probably cause trouble.

"I can't wait," Civil:Moi interrupted my thoughts.

"What?" I was confused for a moment.

"For space travel." A companionable silence followed, which was strange because I was on a planet several light years from home, sitting next to a small green man who didn't speak my language.

A strangled cry was followed by Rani throwing herself into the seat and groaning with frustration.

"It's going well then?" I asked.

"Agh," she answered.

"That's good. I think it's important to be positive." Civil:Moi looked on with something like incredulity as Rani pretended to strangle me.

"You left me with the whole thing!"

"Yes," I said laughing, "I'm feeling really guilty about it."

"You are such a liar!" She rubbed her forehead and I pointed up to the bright sky full of stars and three moons, two close in and one much further out. A cold breeze moved the flowers and rustled the trees, making patterns on the ground in the moonlight.

"I offered Civil:Moi a lift up to the ship for a look at the information Ǹa has collected from the comet. Do you think the captain will mind?"

The scientist was trying to look as if it didn't matter to him one way or another, but his every nerve ending was stuck out like a porcupine quill and Rani understood that. "I think that would be okay." He was so pleased that I thought he was close to flinging himself at her. He contented himself with tapping the back of her hand and then brought it to his face gently.

It was a long time before the cold drove us back into the rooms with the still bickering officials. Asa/Et was a quiet figure, resolute and unmovable. I had got the impression that the arguing was just for the sake of face rather than in any hope of change. The charismatic grand commander was wisely somewhere else and Civil:Moi went off to collect his travelling things. I knew they wanted us to stay for a meal and I knew we should have stayed, but I longed for my own bed and some comfort food and I realised my aches and pains were making a return. Rani performed a lesson in graciousness and I hung on her coat-tails and we were out into the dark evening heading towards the SSV with an excited and chattering Civil:Moi. A small troop of guards escorted us to the door and snapped smartly around as we went in.

The lights came on automatically and the consoles lit up, humming a computer greeting. We did the checks together. Rani was tired, but she knew my body hurt and it was probably clear that of the two of us she would be the better pilot. I called the Starfire and got Jenny Smith, still sitting there. "How many hours have you got to do Jenny?"

A startled silence followed. "Bea, you have to give me a clue you know, I don't have your abilities, it's about another four hundred and sixty, are you on your way back?"

"Yes, Rani's done the equivalent of world peace in a teacup and I watched a sunset."

"We'll keep the light on." I gasped; there was no possibility she could have known that Ted had promised the same all those months ago but the sentence sent me spinning back with a moment of terrible longing pinching at my heart.

"Thank you for that, Jenny." I clicked off then remembered our visitor. "Oh Jenny, we have a scientist coming on a visit."

"I will inform the doctor to meet you at the docking bay." Rani had finished the checks and set the small ship for take-off. I sat down next to her and put the seat belt across my lap leaving the shoulder straps undone. Civil:Moi watched me and then did his own straps up by touching the key on the side of the seat.

He was nervous and excited in such large doses that it was making my ears ring. I tried to remember what my first time in the SSV had felt like and found it difficult, so much had happened. The atmosphere was bumpy and it let us go with a reluctant sigh, then the planet was below us.

Rani and I set the computer between us and she got up and stretched, then went back to the inner compartment and began brewing a cup of tea. I reached out a hand to Civil:Moi and pulled him to his feet. The window showed his world in all its glory, patterns of land and sea, the night side slipping into day as we moved further away. He was speechless and just stared.

We arrived back at the ship in one of those 'before we had left' moments. It was like heading west on earth, you could keep eating breakfast if you kept travelling. Most of the day was still to be had on the Starfire and I had already done evening and sunset on the planet.

It was difficult to know what meal was required, just that a meal of some sort was necessary.

The SSV slid gracefully to a dignified halt in the appropriate place in the docking bay, mainly because I wasn't flying it. Gatt.R. looked on with approval as no supply boxes needed to be retrieved from our path or anyone else's.

Civil:Moi had drifted into a complete and introspective silence, sitting by the window and watching the ship get larger and wider at a terrifying rate. He was leaning back in his seat when were came to a halt willing the craft not to crash.

Pui hopped on board as I opened the door. She sprayed each of us in the face in turn.

"Civil:Moi would you do me a favour?" I asked carefully. Rani stopped and turned around from the doorway.

"Of course," he answered. His gentle eyes were empty of any kind of suspicion.

"Would you mind if Pui did a body scan on you?" This was news to Pui, but she said nothing, not even a glance at me to see what I was up to. He nodded and shrugged. "I'll come with you," I said.

He loved the inside of the ship. The views from the windows and the rooms full of interesting people. The medical bay on level one was empty and it took no more than a few minutes for the scan to spin down from the ceiling and swirl around Civil:Moi. Some coloured lights, a few pings from the computer and it was done. "I'll take you to meet Na-Es-Yan and Neff.P." I grabbed Civil:Moi and said to Pui over my shoulder, "I'll be back in a moment."

The two Starfire scientists met the Admiran scientist with the nods and handshakes of brothers in a cause. It was instant identification and a spark of mutual fire and they were off into other worlds. I said I would be back later, but no one heard me. The collective heads were together over the information on the computer and several holograms of the comet.

The door slid closed behind me and Rani stepped up to walk with me back to the medical bay. She had stayed in the docking bay when I went off with Pui and Civil:Moi. Her face was impassive. "Are you okay with this?" I stopped and asked her.

She made a tiny shrug. "I don't know." We stood there for a minute. "I am a telepath too, Bea. What affects you affects me."

"Okay then," I said.

Pui looked up as we came in. She held up a small holo/computer and the tiny spinning image of the Admiran scientist was surrounded by information that appeared in visual form as well as the conventional writing on the computer screen. "What am I looking for?"

"I don't know." I came across and looked over her shoulder, after a moment Rani came too and stood the other side of Pui. They exchanged a glance the one that said this could be trouble. "Is there anything really different to us?"

Pui looked at me. "You're joking? You mean apart from the fact that they have two arms and two legs."

"Maybe we're going about this the wrong way," Rani said carefully. "Is there anything that would make them like us?" She pointed at herself and then at me and said in a quiet voice as if someone might hear, "I mean us." I was going to have to teach her about causing trouble.

Pui clicked the hand held computer and a hologram spun out and hovered around like a bad smell. "This is something; can you see the reticular formation?" I nodded and Rani screwed up her eyes. Pui continued as if we knew what she was talking about. "It's the part of the brain that deals with recognition and it regulates awareness and attention. You both have lots of activity in this area when you initiate your abilities and in the Admirans it's quite well developed." We tried to look as if we had a clue. "This is really interesting." Pui tapped keys and the computer seemed to spit out lots of little spinning balls. "Well now."

"Are these atoms?" I asked. Pui nodded and Rani was going to get serious wrinkles if she carried on squinting. "What's that?" I pointed to a stick-like object that was also spinning. It held a glowing light at its heart that was disconcerting. Looking at someone who was a living breathing being at the subatomic level seemed somehow impolite. More key tapping was followed by a sharp intake of breath.

"It's a photon." We were incredulous.

"You mean like Gurber?" I said.

"How do you know about Gurber?" Rani asked.

"He told me."

"We have only ever speculated about the composition of the explorers up to now. She pulled at her lip with thoughtful fingers." Pui looked on, a willing participant in a dangerous game. "I wonder why he told you," she added quietly.

I shrugged. I struggled to understand what everyone else just knew, like an endless first day at school: what was even more complicated was trying to comprehend what was not known. The doors slid open and Zeke walked in and all three of us leapt guiltily in the air like a group of drunken Morris dancers. "What's going on?"

"Umm," I said when I had finished having a heart attack.

"How is it possible to sneak up on a couple of telepaths?" He looked stunned.

"It's a lot easier than you'd think," Rani said, doing a good impression of someone who was up to no good. Pui of course had recovered quickly and hidden behind an oriental scowl of epic proportions. She had turned off the hand held computer and was holding it behind her back like a little girl with the sweeties she wasn't supposed to have before lunch.

"I persuaded Pui to scan Civil:Moi."

Zeke just nodded. He always seemed to have worked out what I was up to before I was up to it. "I can see why you would do that. Sam must have come here for a reason. The Admirans are a good place to start."

"Are you going to tell the captain?" I asked carefully. The hand held computer was out again and on again and we were all looking. He shrugged.

"I mean won't she have to tell the BNPs?" Everyone stopped and looked at me. "Bureaucratic nincompoops," I explained. They all nodded again.

"I think she's stuck her head so far out into uncharted territory over you, a few more cover up jobs won't be a problem," Zeke said. This was news to me and I tucked it away for later. We contemplated the photon, which was performing its function as part of the basic structure of the Admiran.

"Is *that* a photon?" Zeke asked.

"How do you not know what Gurber's race are made of?" I said, "I mean don't you scan people when you meet them?"

Pui raised her eyebrows, "What do you think; we say 'hi' and then zap them with a bolt of blue light. What for, why would we?"

"They do it all the time on Star Trek," I muttered.

"The explorers are electromagnetic life forms," Zeke said quietly. "Well, that answers some questions." He looked at Rani. "How did we come by that piece of information?" Rani nodded at me.

"You've never even tried to find out what they were?"

"They don't register on anything unless they feel like it," Zeke answered. We all did some mental shuffling around for a few moments.

"So what are we saying?" Rani speculated, "That the Admirans have a connection to Gurber's race?"

"But what does that have to do with us?" I struggled with all the pieces. "We don't have light particles at the subatomic level, do we?"

Pui shook her head.

"What happens at the science station on Deimos?" Pui looked puzzled. "Sam made two scientists disappear," I explained.

"Mainly quantum mechanics," Zeke answered. He leaned against the work surface and crossed his arms.

"So," I summarised, "We have a dead Gurber, who we now know are made of light particles." I tapped my fingers. "We have two missing scientists who are experts in black holes and we have the Admirans who have a photon or two swimming around at the subatomic level." I looked around for agreement.

"And we have you," Zeke added, which made my stomach do nine floors down without the aid of the lift shafts. There was nothing quite like realising that you were a small piece in a big puzzle, to make you feel vulnerable.

"To your knowledge," I looked at all of them, "Is it even possible to do anything with all of this. I mean what are we talking about here, time travel for anyone who can pay and an endless supply of telepaths?" Both Rani and Pui were pale. Zeke wasn't pale but he had a rather grim expression.

I had no idea, living on the Starfire with a crew of experienced space travellers and scientists, what the real world thought about either of those things, but from the expressions on the faces of the three people in front of me, it was not positive. Nothing about that surprised me. Most people didn't like big sweeping changes or little sweeping ones either.

"One thing I don't understand," I asked. Zeke looked up from his brooding, "I'm really not sure what I'm talking about but I didn't think that a photon had any mass?"

"Right," Pui answered.

"So how does he, Gurber, have a solid form without mass?" It was Pui's turn to look surprised. "We did have particle physics in my time," I said. Their collective shrug was sweetly insulting.

"Do you actually know what happened with the Gurber who was killed?" Rani and Zeke obviously knew.

"He self-terminated," Zeke said. This was news to Pui, who was horrified.

"So," I sighed, "There's a chance that Sam doesn't have what he needs." My back ached and my eyes were dry and scratchy and my brain was numb. "Trifle anyone?"

Zeke smiled, saying, "That sounds good."

"Okay. Pui, just one more thing those vials I gave you?" She nodded. "I think we'd better destroy them."

"Are you sure?" She asked calmly, going to a cabinet that was tucked behind her desk. She tapped in a sequence of numbers and the door sprang open.

I thought it might have been difficult for her. But it wasn't actually an embryo, just a collection of eggs and sperm in separate vials. She came over to me and I was conscious of Zeke watching with quiet interest. If he wondered why I hadn't told him, his face didn't give it away. "I could put them in permanent stasis for you?"

"Could you guarantee that some idiot wouldn't try and do the same thing, for the same reason?" She raised her eyebrows and then shook her head and sighed. I felt as if these people might be in danger if it got out that the vials were here, not that I thought they were worth anything.

Pui went over to a wall disposal unit and put the vials in. You could see the microbes doing their job through the clear plas-glass door. All that was left after a few seconds was a small amount of dust. I felt relieved.

Zeke, Rani and I left, leaving Pui to some work she had to do. I noticed she put the small scanner into her safe and locked it.

We walked in silence, watching the windows for the changing patterns of the Admiran solar system. At the doors of the upper restaurant I asked, "What's going to happen to Torriff's body?"

"His people are joining us in the next day or so to pick it up."

"I would like to be there." They both stopped, causing a bottleneck in the entrance to the restaurant. There were audible grumbles as people had to walk around us.

"I'm not sure," Rani started to say, but stopped when she realised my feelings, which were radiating from me like a supernova. Zeke put his arm around me and gave me a hug.

"Let's eat cake and pudding," he said. A man who understood the spiritual significance of cake would have been the perfect relationship except for the four hundred years or so time difference.

The place was buzzing. I could see Sig and Doz at a table by the window and we made our way over to join them. Mac grabbed me as I passed him. "It would be a good idea if we practised some more EVA drills Bea, I've cleared it with the captain."

"Why do you need to do more EVA?" Zeke asked too loudly, I looked at him in that couples way when the partner made an embarrassing comment about the neighbours. He got it. "Ah," he said.

Mark Limbu was talking to Tom Hatherley and Tim Asguard; there was a lot of hand waving and a whiff of basketball as we passed them. Asguard winked at me as Tom described a really vicious shot and he knocked the drink out of Mark's hand spilling liquid all over the two of them. They carried on arguing as if there wasn't coffee dripping down the front of Tom's uniform and he dabbed at the stain with an absent-minded cloth, which looked as if, in another life, it might have been a hankie.

I threw myself into one of the empty chairs while Zeke went off to fulfil his duty as a hunter-gatherer and forage for food. Rani had disappeared into the mass of people, talking to Ko-Yo-Na.

"Hi there Bea, how did it go today, ruined any planetary negotiations, caused any diplomatic incidents?" Sig asked in a sympathetic voice. I poked two fingers up at him. "I don't get that," he said looking puzzled.

"Bugger off," I said helpfully.

"Okay, that one I do know," he said.

It had occurred to me that I was home and these people were my friends and I really didn't want to be anywhere else and I was happy, the very thought made me nervous.

A slight uneasy feeling made me rub the back of my neck and I saw Sig's face trying not to twist. "Jad," Sig said and I turned in my seat. Jad Lassik was standing behind me with Calla. She looked battered but better and I felt a stab of guilt at not having been to the medical bay to visit her.

"Move Doz," I said. He leapt to his feet and I indicated for Calla to sit. She hesitated for a moment, some things were hard to let go of and a past filled with being the person no one saw must have been impossible to shake. To give Doz credit, if he felt anything about giving up his seat to a transgenetic ex-slave he gave no indication, helping her to sit down like the decent man he was.

"How are you?" I asked. She looked astonished, as if the thought that anyone should care how she felt was a new experience for her.

"I am very well," she spoke as if the words were from a dictionary up to now unopened, then smiled. "Very well, thank you."

"We're leaving," Lassik announced.

"What," I said, "Where, why?" I looked from one to the other and light dawned, here were two people who didn't belong anywhere.

"Are you sure?" I asked her quietly. I wondered if she didn't know what else to do and this seemed to be the only way. I understood, but I didn't feel easy about it. "You could stay here." She shook her head. The transgenetic issue must have been bigger than I had really understood.

"Okay." I stood up and gave Lassik a hug, which stunned him and just about everyone within spitting distance. Doz and Sig remained impassive, with the feelings of 'not appropriate' wafting around. But then what was the point of being different if you couldn't stir up the status quo every now and then. For a second the hug was returned and then they were leaving. I kissed Calla on the cheek and hugged her too. "Thank you for saving my life, I owe both of you."

I watched the retreating backs of the misfits and a part of me felt as if I should be going too. No one else seemed to notice or care very much and it made sense that they would each be a person the other could relate to. I wondered if he had talked much to his 'sister' and where she was. It was not likely that Captain Witherspoon would be joining us for an evening of relaxation. The 'it's tough at the top' hadn't lost any of its ability to spell the word alone in the twenty-fifth century.

Zeke arrived with a full, untouched bowl of chocolate trifle and two spoons. We sat down and I watched him carefully draw a line across the cream on the top, neatly dividing the pudding into two. He was just about to take a spoonful when Rani asked him a question on the whereabouts of Desi:Tig the Admiran grand commander. He turned for no more than a minute to answer and I smoothed out his line and drew one of my own, then tucked in from my side. He turned back and frowned as his spoon hovered over the bowl. "Oh my, it just has to be love," Doz said.

"Yes," said Zeke, "I think it must be."

Both marines were shocked by the public demonstration of affection. I was stunned myself. Rani joined us and Doz got another chair, by tipping a crewmember onto the floor and dragging it over to our table. "Doz!" Rani shouted, exasperated.

"Its okay, Rani." The young marine picked himself up and smiled, not looking the least bit bothered, he perched on the side of his friend's seat and carried on the conversation. Sig shrugged and he and Doz began a detailed explanation of the same basketball game Mark and Tom had been talking about, only this time it was the other side who were the 'stupid zudlocs.' They shovelled food in as they spoke, making it difficult to understand what they were saying, but they punctuated their remarks by waving forks laden with food which was literally hazardous if you were sitting anywhere within spitting distance.

"Where do you think Lassik and Calla are going?" I asked. They both knew something, but they both made a 'don't really know' face.

"I hope she's going to be okay," I said quietly. Rani patted my hand. I finished my 'side' of the trifle and began on Zeke's. For a military person he was a slow eater. I had had an older brother and you learned to eat fast or you learned to go without. The 'had' an older brother brought me up to a sense of the grinding loss I had put in a dark place for three in the morning to find. It was amazing how quickly you could start using the past tense when your heart hurt enough. My eyes welled with tears and I brushed them away finally admitted defeat with the pudding.

"Garobh! Bea!" Sig handed over a money disc to a grinning Doz. "That was supposed to be a safe bet." I looked at Zeke and he gave me an innocent grin.

I smacked his fingers with the spoon.

Na-Es-Yan tapped me on the shoulder and pointed to the other side of the room. "Civil:Moi is leaving," she said, "He wanted to say goodbye?"

"Of course," I hopped out of my chair only to have it appropriated by the marine who had lost his. He grinned. We made our way through the noise and hardly still bodies. Civil:Moi was standing by the door just watching, like a man trying to remember for later what he never wanted to forget.

"Did you have a good time?" I asked rather unnecessarily. 'A good time' was seeping from every pore. He tapped the back of my hand and then for a second held it to his face in a gesture of appreciation. "That would be yes then!"

I looked back at the crowded room and opted for escorting Civil:Moi and Na to the upper docking bay, scarcely a long walk as it was the same level and around the corner. We went through the doors to the docking bay and I stood at the top of the steps while the two of them made their way to an SSV. I saw as Neff.P. stuck his head out of the door to the craft and he looked up and smiled. The journey to the planet would give them more time to discuss everything. Civil:Moi turned just before he got into the SSV and raised a hand. Something about the gesture made me sad for a moment, my eyes welled with tears again and I stood there ridiculously waving, as if I was standing on the dock when the ship sailed away forever.

Gatt.R. came through the doors behind me and gave me a hug as he passed, he smelt of warmth and friendship and just a touch of cinnamon. Then he started yelling about kit not being moved fast enough which made me and a half a dozen techs jump. The SSV slid competently out of the bay doors.

I walked slowly down the corridor, thought for a minute about going back into the upper restaurant then went to a lift shaft, hopping in and going down two floors. There was something of the evening about the ship, a change in shift and pace. My door opened and Ollie did a little dance, which was nothing about being pleased to see me and all about food. I poured a crunchy meal into his bowl, tapped a key to clear his tray and put a cup under the hot water spout for a drink. I found bread and cheese and the sweet fruit pickle that Tariq made especially for me and ate some real food that had hardly anything to do with chocolate at all. I was the other side of the ship to Admira and I could see the distant and strange interaction of the two suns. I tapped the computer keys and fetched my sandwich and drink and sat in front of the holo/screen looking at the solar system inside my rooms and outside at the same time. Some things could only be heard in the silence.

Ollie joined me on the sofa and snagged a bit of cheese, chewing it carefully to get maximum spread all over the cushions. Half way through the serious munching the door chimed and Zeke came in. He sat down next to me and stole the rest of the cheese and pickle sandwich. He bumped me with a shoulder. "Are you okay?"

I nodded. "Will I ever understand what's happening here?"

He put the last mouthful of sandwich in and chewed carefully, then pulled me into a hug. We watched the spinning solar system, the hologram moved from planet to planet and finished with a swirl around the suns. "So, you're going to do some additional EVA practice tomorrow?"

"Yes, Mac felt I could do with a bit more." He sniggered. I leaned back to look at his face. "You're not buying it?" He looked back with an 'I wasn't born last week' expression. Ollie squeezed between us and settled down to wash, the rasping tongue on fur being the only noise for a while, that and the thoughts of the people on the ship.

I woke to the sound of the door chime. "Bea! Are you up?" Mac's voice came through the Com/T. I hopped out of bed, grabbing the pink dressing gown and a cup from the table as I went to the door. It was very early.

"Mac," I said as the door opened, "You need to get a life, this doesn't qualify as morning."

He stuck his head inside the door. "What makes you the expert?"

"I'm an authority on everything."

"Can you make a start in an hour?" His beautiful shiny face reminded me of a photograph I had once seen of a Native American warrior taken at the turn of the twentieth century, who must have been wondering what fate awaited his people now. I wished for a second I could tell the twentieth century man that his people were doing just fine. I filled the cup with hot water and added a slice of lemon. "Bea?"

"Yes, I'll be in the upper docking bay in an hour, go away." The door closed on a certain amount of exasperation and I went into the bathroom, the unkind mirror looked back at me. What happened at night that hair looked that way first thing in the morning? I tapped the shower on, nothing but water was going to do any good.

Half an hour and some shampoo and clothes later, I wandered into the corridor. Rani was heading in my direction. Early morning yawns and hellos and the lift shaft had taken us to the first level before I asked her where she was going. "With you, Mark Limbu has this new space-runner he wants to show me. Apparently it's fast."

"Like shit off a shiny shovel," I added helpfully. The Com/T buzzed in the quiet.

She looked puzzled. "That didn't go through the translator, I got something disgusting."

We went through the bay doors and down the steps. The ship was now very much awake. Gatt.R. and several crew members were crowded around a neat little space-runner. The usual clunky looking motorbike with a bubble on top was replaced by something smooth and sleek. I came up behind Mac and gave him a good shove for hurrying me when he wasn't ready. He hardly moved.

"Good grief, are you nailed to the floor?" I checked around his feet.

"Are you even from Earth?" He poked me in the face. I bit the waving finger.

"Give it *up* you two!" Rani scolded like an overworked parent. I had the sensation that you found brothers in all shapes and sizes, you didn't have to be born with one.

I pulled at Mac again and he came reluctantly. Just as we reached the door to the kit room Tom Hatherley caught up with us; he had something that looked like a pancake roll with a variety of aromatic meat and vegetable shapes spilling out of each end. Mac grabbed at it and successfully manoeuvred at least half of it into his mouth. "Hey!" Tom rescued his breakfast and offered me a bite of what was left.

"Tempting but no thanks, it looks as if it might be from a completely unknown food group."

He shrugged and pushed the remainder into his mouth, chewing like a man possessed. This didn't stop him from giving a complete rundown on his date with Jenny Smith the previous evening. He caught my slightly green nauseous expression. "You want me to shut up?"

"Yes please." We began suiting up. "I bet Jenny doesn't know you eat with your mouth open."

"Zudlocs no!" He looked a bit panicky. "You're not going to tell her are you?"

I looked back at him. "Power is a heady thing. I'm going to try not to let it destroy me." The waste disposal system in the suit suddenly engaged at that moment making all forms of communication on my part impossible. "Hell's bells and bloody blue blazes!" I said eventually.

"You see, I have no idea what that means," Mac said, "But I know what it means." He pressed buttons to engage his own suit. I waited to see if his eyes watered. They didn't.

"That's a good swearing sentence, I've got to learn that one," Tom said.

We checked each other out and I tapped Tom on his helmet to say he was clear. He in turn checked Mac, who then tapped me for all clear. "Bridge," Tom spoke into his suit com, "Three for additional EVA practice."

There was an unladylike snort, "If that's what you're calling it." The captain obviously wasn't buying the story either. I wondered if this could also be classified in the 'sticking her neck out for me' category. "Go ahead Tom."

We moved into the airlock and Mac did more checks before removing the circulating air. It hissed, leaving in a sinister way and then left us quiet. The door opened onto the ship's surface and a well of stars. The planet was above us. When you were in space it was not possible to say for sure what was stationary and what was moving. Na would have said motion was relative and there was a lot about time, distance and mass I should have had an opinion on.

I walked out after Mac and we stood for a moment looking up, or down, depending how the semicircular canals in your ears were doing. My feet snagged comfortingly on the ship's surface, like a good dollop of scientific chewing gum thanks to the gecko boots.

We did some drills for the sake of the few techs that were actually outside for a purpose and anyone else who might have been watching, as the ship's holo/cameras were scattered around everywhere. I went out on the line and swam around, only using my suit's power pack when I wanted to come back to the ship. "Hell's bells Bea!" Mac was a quick study with swearing. "If you mess up as a telepath you can always take on as a tech." Tom was nodding his approval which was not easy in a helmet.

"Yes," said Mac, "Any Mohawk back there in your family?" I was just about to say that no one had ever paid me a nicer compliment when the Com/T buzzed and Jenny's sweet voice advised us of a ship approaching and a partial docking. We planted our feet and I watched curiously as a large spiral shape moved close to the Starfire. The 'bump' was more of a whisper. "Great," Mac grumbled, "It's Torriff's lot."

Tom was doing some 'notice me' behaviour to the nearest camera, which had a red light on it. It consisted of pretending he didn't see that the camera was active. He bustled around getting us efficiently back to the airlock, he was so irritating that I almost gave in and told Jenny about his eating habits.

I took a last lingering look at the stars of out there. "Do you think that if we all close our eyes at the same time the universe will disappear?"

"Only if you don't live in this dimension of reality," Mac answered helpfully. Tom was too busy being 'responsible' to answer.

The ship that had docked so carefully was huge, like a big corkscrew, with the lighted windows dotted around the curve of each spiral. We removed the suits and put our indoor clothes back on.

"Thank you. I really enjoyed that."

"Are you sure about the lack of Mohawk?" Mac said, laughing.

"If there is, it's here." I tapped my heart and Mac smiled the little brother smile that shattered the place I was talking about into very small pieces.

We arrived in the docking bay at the same time as a small delegation of Vanerians. There were four, all in the familiar worn leather uniform. It made my eyes sting to see them. The captain was greeting the visitors with her usual diplomacy and Zeke had taken one of the soldiers to one side and was talking quietly, they seemed to know each other. There was nothing in particular, except an easy familiarity. Not so the rest of the crew. I think frosty would have been a kind description of the feelings I could sense. If the Vanerians noticed they gave nothing away. I walked over to Zeke and he put an arm around me in a gesture that made me feel part of something I hadn't actually sorted out in my head.

The Vanerian acknowledged me in a dignified and polite manner. Bowing his head, he held out a hand. I took it, warm and dry and sincere, it was all I could do not to sob for my old friend. "This is Bea," Zeke said, "Bea, this is Kartneff."

I kept hold of the hand and asked him, "You knew Torriff well?"

"We were brothers of the same family."

"Then," I said as if it could possibly make a difference, "I am sorry for your loss."

As the coffin was brought from the back of the storage units in the docking bay, I slipped up the stairs into a lift shaft and along to my room to fetch something. Running all the way back like a child afraid of the school bell, I was out of breath when I came down the stairs again into the bay. A small number of the crew had lined up on either side of the little group of Vanerians and were quiet and respectful.

I went to stand next to Kartneff and Zeke and the captain came over to join us bringing a tall, imposing Vanerian with her. He bowed over my hand. Kartneff spoke in a respectful whisper, "May I introduce Captain Gedhart." He stood the same height as Zeke and I had to tip my head back to get a good look at him. His uniform was nearly black in colour, denoting his rank. The rules of the game were printed large on his ridged face and his eyes were wheels of gold and green. Like Torriff's but without the light. He and Zeke nodded at each other and there was no trace of mutual respect.

Captain Witherspoon was making a face that neither of the two men could see. It clearly stated that I was to say nothing about the circumstances of Torriff's death.

"I want you to know, Captain Gedhart that Torriff did everything in his power to keep me from the renegade Roshii Samura." The man was too much of a politician not to notice the wording. But Kartneff's eyes filled with tears. Like Torriff, he had the qualities of an ageing professor. A gentle soul lost in the world of the warriors. I held out the disc.

"What is this?" He fingered it, looking puzzled.

"It's a piece of music, Kartneff, by Lennon and McCartney. Could you put it in the burial chamber for me? Torriff really liked this song and I want to be part of the ritual of death." He cleared his throat and I blinked some tears and everyone else examined the walls of the bay as if they suddenly had important news written on them.

"Then," he said clearly, "I will speak for you at the ceremony. May I ask what the 'song' is?"

"'The long and winding road,'" the words were nearly lost in the silence of all places.

The coffin hovered on air like the stretchers. Four Vanerians stood one at each corner, a hand resting lightly and they walked to the small tunnel that had been attached between the ships. It wavered as they began to walk along it. Captain Gedhart followed after a small nod between him and our captain. Kartneff waited. He shook my hand and then Zeke's. Eventually I gave him a hug and walked with him to the tunnel. The crew behind us began to disperse and I could sense the captain straining against the thought that I would say 'something.' She needn't have worried, nothing more was said between us, what could we have possibly said that would have made things right. He turned and walked away and I stood for a while to see if he would look back, but he didn't.

"Do you ever actually do as you're told?" The captain enquired, not unkindly. I thought about it carefully for a moment and she sighed and shook her head. Zeke came over to her and held his hand out so only the three of us were able to see, a small oval of crystal.

"What is that?" She asked. Even I knew it was a holo/disc, but I understood what she was actually saying. Zeke covered the disc with his fingers and they both sighed. "What now," she whispered.

The Vanerian ship pulled out from her dock and curved away into the dark. I saw the small lights that were rooms and laboratories and stores, the things we did, they did too, but it wouldn't matter to the people on either ship. They were all still looking for the differences.

"Okay?" Zeke asked. The disc had disappeared into his jacket. I wondered if I would find out what the 'what now' was.

"He was the scholar who should have spent his days discussing moth-eaten poetry with other neglected masterpieces." We walked up the steps of the bay to the first level. The captain was talking to Gatt.R. and she looked over her shoulder at Zeke, then turned back to the problems of the stores. "Instead," I continued, "He was sent on a quest no one could hope to achieve."

"Are we all supposed to be knights of the future to you?" Zeke asked.

I turned and gave him a hug, taking in the smell of strength and lemon soap. He hugged me back and we stood there blocking foot traffic into the docking bay and causing several people to have to pretend that they were walking around something that had always been there. "It must be several hours since you consumed something with chocolate in it, how about some food?" He spoke into the top of my head and I sighed, keeping the rest of the tears back. Later in the early hours would be soon enough to find them again.

The corridor was empty, people were doing something important somewhere else, but the upper restaurant had the late morning people. Rani waved us over to a pot of coffee and several large cakes with lots of swirled icing. She poured. "How did it go?" I reached for one of the cakes and ate the icing first with a finger. "That well," she said quietly. She didn't say why she hadn't been there and I didn't ask. It wasn't easy to understand the depth of betrayal she felt. Where did you stand, what did you say? So I said nothing.

"I suppose you and Gedhart swapped scowls?" She asked Zeke, he shrugged and drank coffee as if it was nothing. We were drowning in unexpressed feelings.

"Yes," I said. "There was some serious glowering going on. I take it you and the good captain had some history."

"He tortured and killed several people I was working with," Zeke answered, drinking more coffee and taking a cake from the plate on the table. "They wouldn't give me up."

I felt my hands tremble and I held on tightly to the mug as if the reality of a few years ago in someone else's life could creep into my bones like a damp day. I knew that most of what I experienced came to me second hand similar to music slightly out of tune.

"Are we going back down to the planet today?" I pushed the question out in an attempt to find something firm to stand on.

"The Admirans are holding their ceremony today and the diplomats are coming up to the ship this evening. We'll be meeting the Star Quest at the Ross 154 space station." Rani finished her weak herbal tea and clattered the cup and saucer down onto the table.

It was the silence that made the noise seem odd and out of place. I watched in fascination as the things on the table seemed to do a little dance, like a film where the crockery all burst into song when the people have left, except that we were here and the cups were still dancing. "Zeke," I pointed and he followed my finger, his brooding expression changed from the thoughts of old enemies to something that looked like fear. It was more frightening than a dark house at midnight on Halloween. He slammed out of his chair and ran towards the door, Rani grabbed my hand and we ran too.

I had no idea why I was running, but if running was required I was happy to oblige because all it needed was some really loud creepy discordant music. The noise of the ship's alarm sounding was deafening.

I tried not to feel the fear that washed around me like a tidal wave, but the faces of people going to their stations in the faint hope that this was a drill, made it difficult not to remember all the other running I had done in corridors lately.

Zeke was far ahead of us and talking into his Com/T. I couldn't hear what he was saying. The lights had gone to the emergency floor level again, though I felt that when you were scared it would have been good to see something other than your feet.

"What?" I asked Rani as we reached the doors of the bridge a second after they had closed behind Zeke.

The captain arrived at an impressive dead run. "Rani," she said, as she scooted past us to the main com. Zeke was already standing there with his hand on Yas Molina's shoulder, talking quietly.

I stood to one side trying to catch my breath. Rani closed her eyes and did a quick mind search. "Nothing," she said. In other words what was happening wasn't caused by someone hiding behind a convenient moon directing a death ray at us. I wondered, in my frazzled stupidity, if there was even a possibility of death rays lying in wait behind moons.

The bridge crew worked in almost complete quiet, just the noise of feverish activity. The ship moved out of the orbit of the planet and the shaking grating noise of a small tin can being pulled in two different directions stopped as we moved further away from whatever it was.

Jenny Smith spoke to the captain, pointing out something on a holo/screen. Yas Molina was flying. He looked at Captain Witherspoon for confirmation and she in turn looked at Zeke, he shrugged. It was a three syllable shrug, worthy of a French waiter. Yas shook his head slowly, the 'I hope you know what you're doing' clear in his expression. He spun the ship around in a handbrake turn that a speedway driver would have been proud of and which had us all hanging onto something.

"Rani what's happening?" I whispered.

"It's a gravitational radiation wave," she whispered back.

"A gravity wave," I shouted, making everyone jump. Rani looked slightly impressed, which made me feel slightly insulted. "I've been spending a lot of time with Na and Neff.P.," I offered in explanation. Though I was always stunned by how ignorant they expected me to be, including Rani who could see the inner workings. Would I have been the same with someone from the fifteenth century? Copernicus was studying the moon then but prejudice existed wherever people did. I tried to work out the next question, "How close are we to whatever caused it, I mean black holes, pulsars?"

Jenny answered me, "Close enough."

"So what happens now?" I asked no one.

"We ride it out," Jenny said.

A ship-wide announcement told everyone what was happening and gave out the twenty-fifth century version of hang on to something. "Do you think the planet will be okay?" Which was a stupid question as it was in the path of the space-quake just as we were. "Have you ever seen one of these before, Rani?" She turned to look at me. Her lips were white and her eyes looked like the colour had disappeared, washed into the fear of her dark pupils. "Can't Gurber help us?" I asked, frustrated and desperate.

"I don't think even an explorer can help with the compression and extension of the fabric of space/time," the captain said, the fear in her own voice stopped me in mid-thought and I wasn't able to quantify anything after that. Rani squeezed my hand and we waited.

The Admirans had been warned of the impending disaster and told to 'batten down the hatches.' Four hundred years after my time and we were still in the business of nautical solutions for quantum problems.

We hid behind a large gas giant, hoping our regenerating protection field that was explorer technology and the planets own natural radiation would deflect some of the wave, which felt a bit like hiding under a blanket behind a big rock to avoid a tsunami.

We waited. Zeke came over to me and put his arms around me and then I knew for certain he thought we were going to die.

It hit.

I was being pulled apart and squashed and pulled apart again. The room was distorted like a piece of chewing gum. I remembered the pain, but no time passed, then nothing for ages and more of the roller-coaster ride, there were dark moments when I crawled along the floor to a bleeding Rani. I touched her hand, it took an aeon.

Nothing about the flashing lights made any sense. People shouted. I wanted to go back to the quiet dark but someone was shaking me.

"What?" I yelled in a whisper.

"She's back, we've got her." I wondered where I'd been.

"Go away," I shouted as someone tried to move me. It wasn't even a murmur and no one did. A thought filtered through and I struggled against the lights and the restraining hands and the pain. "Ollie?" When the love of your life was fat, orange and furry it was amazing how strong you could be and I had left him alone. I screamed his name again, this time it came out as a really effective noise. I still couldn't see very well but a familiar voice spoke slowly.

"We got him too, Bea, he's alive, go back to sleep."

"You promise me, Sig?" I tried to reach for a hand I couldn't see.

"Absolutely I promise."

I was able to feel around with my mind before the sedative took effect. There were lots of people, but I couldn't find Rani or the gentle buzz that was my cat. The second I went under I realised I couldn't find Zeke either.

The sounds seemed to come back first, then I tried to open my eyes, everything swam for a while making throwing up a real option.

"How are you feeling?" Pui came over to me and put her hand my forehead in a way that good doctors seemed to have a qualification in. I was in the medical bay again. I raised my head and put it back down. There were people in beds and screens that I couldn't see through.

"Is everyone okay?" It was a stupid question that I knew the answer to.

"We lost seventeen of the crew Bea." She looked exhausted. "I won't lie to you Rani is not doing very well."

"What *happened* to us?" I felt the tears, but didn't bother to wipe them away. Pui reached out and brushed her fingers over my face.

"Well, there's a lot of science about time and space that I really don't want to think about right now. But when it all stops sometimes it puts things back together incorrectly."

The thought that Rani might not be quite 'back together' had me nearly out of the bed before I collapsed. A face I didn't recognise helped me to my feet and then back onto the bed. Pui, when I was able to focus, was scowling. "Don't do that again," she said. I thought, not for a while anyway, as the room spun in a dignified way.

"Who was that?" The medic went back to the desk and began checking vital signs by holo/computer.

"He's from the Star Quest; we were supposed to meet them at Ross 154. They rescued us. We were dead in the water."

I looked carefully at the screens that shielded the beds from the other occupants. I wondered which one Rani was behind. "Zeke," I asked carefully, waiting for the glass to shatter.

"He's on the bridge." She sounded as if she disapproved, which was interesting, because if it meant an argument between Pui and Zeke, my money would have been on Pui.

I waited until her back was turned and did some mental exploration. Rani was almost without thought. It was as if her mind had given into the pressure of pain and the tiredness that went with being alone. In my mind she looked fragile and transparent and something that surprised me, old. It made me hollow to see her as she saw herself. **"I'm not sure I can do this Bea."**

The quiet words were barely there. I was suddenly furious. **"Don't you dare leave me here on my own,"** I screamed at her. **"You brought me to this place,"** I raised my voice another octave, **"You get back!"** I battered her with my words.

Her face expressed shock and some anger and then a kind of resignation. The in-between was peaceful and hard to leave. I knew because I had tried to reach someone before and came back alone. **"You shouldn't be here,"** she said.

"I'm staying until you're strong enough to come with me." I reached out my hand and after a moment's hesitation, she took it.

I heard the monitor what felt like a second later and I opened my eyes. Both Pui and the unknown medical tech were heading behind the last screen to my left. Pui's voice was quiet but distinct, "You had us worried, Rani."

Captain Witherspoon came from behind the same screen, probably to give them more room to work. She sagged against the wall as if the relief was just one thing too many to deal with. I called her over. She pulled herself together, not realising that my screen had been turned off and I could see out.

"Bea," she said cheerfully, "How are you feeling?" I held my arms out to her and after a moment of shock she came over to the bed and let me cuddle her while her shoulders shook in silent grief. She was a mass of bruising and one of her arms had been badly broken, it had a slim brace from elbow to wrist. Her eyes were bloodshot with pain and damage and the sort of sadness that lived in your soul. She leaned back and took some wipes from the bed locker. "Thank you." We sat in silence with no uncomfortable spaces while they worked with Rani.

"Give me a hand please." I dragged myself out of the bed, which had curled around me and had been half way through a healing programme, because it bleeped with indignation. I leaned on the captain and we staggered over to Rani.

Behind the screen she was a mass of equipment and monitors. Her pale face was bruised like the captain's. My own face must have looked like that too. There wasn't an unbroken bone in her body. I went for the nearest chair and sank down. Pui looked as if she might argue for a moment, but she gave in without a fight and held up her hand. "Five minutes."

The door to the medical bay opened and Zeke came in. I tried to stand but failed and he squatted in front of me. His nose had been broken and both eyes were bruised. I could tell he was in pain. I rested my head on his shoulder and we did some completely non-verbal communication about things that were too close to call. I wondered just how close it had been. I wiped my eyes, "Have you seen my cat?" I asked hopefully.

"He's asleep on my bed. He had a broken jaw and some internal bleeding." At the expression on my face Zeke stopped abruptly. "Hey he's okay." My eyes filled with tears.

A small voice said, "Have I missed anything?"

"Rani," we all spoke at once, bringing Pui back to our side of the screen. She waved us all out, but not before I touched the cold fingers that moved carefully to reach for mine.

Zeke helped me onto the bed. I felt like a snail getting back into the safety of my shell and sighed with relief. "Does my face look like yours?"

"As if I've gone three rounds with the floor?"

"Yes."

"Then yes it does," he said helpfully. I pulled at the covers which felt like they were made of cashmere and reminded me of a child's comforter.

"Did the Admirans make it through?"

Zeke sighed. One of those big, 'I'm not sure how much more pain I can deal with' sigh. "They are being given all the help we can spare right now. We weren't the only ship caught in the wave and several Star League planets are in severe distress. Our resources are stretched to the limit."

"I think they hold the key to something important," I said dramatically.

"The key," he said, with scepticism.

"Well maybe not *the* key, maybe just *a* key." His sceptical expression was tinged with humour and he had the sort of black eyes only seen on careful pugilists. "Look," I whispered loudly, "You have to admit the photon was something."

He looked at me with incredulity and then laughed.

"Aren't you curious about Gurber's race about all the possible connections?"

"Well no, not really. Gurber has been around for as long as I can remember and before, it's not as if we've just discovered each other." He added after careful thought, "I think they are entitled to their secrets and they like their privacy."

"Yes, similar to Bill Gates liking computers! I wonder if they can glow in the dark." I said too loudly.

"Who glows in the dark?" The captain asked. I jumped guiltily. She looked from Zeke to me. I tried for innocence, but must have failed miserably. "Please tell me that this isn't something I'm going to get hauled up to answer for." I tried for puzzled innocence. "I'm going to bed," she said laughing. Zeke was being enigmatic which seemed to work better. She came over and gave me a hug.

"Get some sleep. That goes for you too, Zeke." He nodded.

I fell asleep with Zeke in the chair next to the bed. I made him promise that he would bring Ollie as soon as he could. When I woke it was to the sound of deep purring and Ollie's whiskers tickling my ear.

He was curled up in a tight ball and his fur was rough and hot. He had gone to sleep on my pillow with a paw pushed on my face. I was doing my best not to cry, but he was in some pain and I could feel it. They only person on board not wearing a blocking chip now was my cat. "Pui," I tried to make it a loud whisper. She was by the bed before I opened my mouth to call again. "Can you give him something, he hurts."

"I dare not Bea," she said gently. "He has to deal with the healing part himself. Everything else is okay." She made some reassuring noises.

The 'person' being discussed uncurled and gave a pitiful 'meow' pushing at my face with both his paws much as a kitten would do with the mother cat. I in turn looked helplessly at Pui. She dropped her chin on her chest and gave a pitiful sigh herself. "Let me try something." She disappeared behind the screen, which had been turned off both ways and came back a second later with some tiny needles, each with a different coloured tag on the end. I recognised them.

"Acupuncture needles." She put several around Ollie's neck and in the top of his shoulders. He didn't move except to give her an indulgent look. He washed a paw contentedly and in a few minutes fell asleep again in a much more relaxed position. I felt myself drift towards the clouds which had something to do with the medication in the small clear jelly on my arm that Pui had activated. "How's Rani?"

"She's fine; her bones are healing well, remedial exercise the day after tomorrow."

I thought it was going to be a bit of a shock for someone who had only ever lifted a cup of herbal tea as part of a regular routine. I forced my eyes open and fought the sedative. "Rani's piggiwig?"

"He got away without a scratch. His skeletal structure is rather like a sponge, very elastic." Her eyes were deeply shadowed and I wondered how long it had been since she slept.

"Are you okay?" I whispered, just before the cobwebs filled my head with old stories and quiet dreams. She nodded, the 'Ricky Ticky Tavy' of all time, 'all things to all people' and more.

After careful negotiation, worthy of a peace deal, I was able to go back to my rooms. I felt that I had got off lightly, only three days in the medical bay which was something of a record for me. The sensation of 'complete traitor' wafted into my head put there by Rani, who hadn't made it out.

My cat had taken to spending time with Zeke and was not there to welcome me 'home.' I stripped off and put the steamer on full and then filled the bath. My bones were aching and sometimes only lying in near-boiling water with lots of bubbles would do the trick.

I made coffee and found some cake that must have been put in my cupboard by Tariq. You were not supposed to be glad that the people you loved were the ones that made it through, because it meant the people that other people loved, didn't. I put my head down on my arms and rested on the table and indulged in the tears that it was okay to cry when you felt guilty about not having died. Then I put on clothes and makeup and went out to see if I could do something, anything, to help. The corridor showed windows with distant stars, I had forgotten we were on the move headed to Ross 154, leaving the Star Quest with the awful task of helping the Admirans salvage what was left after the space-quake. I had cowardly declined a trip to the planet before we left. The holo/screen had showed a consistent devastation and the sort of images associated with a long and bitter war. There was so much I could never put aside in the hope of peaceful sleep, I wondered if I had used up my capacity to grieve, like the number of heartbeats in a lifetime.

Sig came down the corridor as I was about to get into the lift shaft.

"Pui let you go then?" He smiled.

"I had to promise my first born son, but yes." He looked puzzled, even after all this time the Com/T was the last person to get the joke. "I was wondering if anyone needed my help." We travelled up to the first level.

"Well I'm going for coffee and then I'm back down to the engine room. If you felt up to it maybe you could have a 'look,'" he wiggled his fingers, "At the ship's systems, everything is slightly not quite right."

"I know how that feels." Coffee sounded good. Sig had the telltale look of someone who had been squeezed and squashed, bloodshot eyes, bruises and the sort of haunted expression that was about great pain and helplessness.

"How is Rani?" Tariq asked. I gave him a hug and he looked surprised.

"She's much better, thanks Tariq." Everyone had the shell shocked air of those who had made it, thinking about those who hadn't.

"How long will it take us to get to Ross 154?" I asked Sig.

He looked puzzled. "We're not going to Ross 154 space station, Bea. We're headed back to Earth." My cup dropped out of my hand and bounced onto the floor spilling coffee all over the place. I heard him shout after me as I sprinted towards the door.

I ran to the other end of the ship, out of breath, past the door to Gurber's rooms, past the laboratories, all familiar places that had felt like home. I didn't realise I was crying. Zeke came cannoning out of the bridge door just as I reached it. Sig had forewarned him. He grabbed me as I was in full flight and pulled me to him, trying desperately to comfort the comfortless. "When were you going to tell me?" I shouted. He held me away from him, shaking me gently and wiping the tears I didn't know about.

"You *knew* this was going to happen!" He looked as if the last thing he could cope with was a reality check for those of us who did denial in industrial strength.

"I just thought," I tried again, my voice no more than a whisper, "I just thought I would be allowed to stay." He did that thing when people didn't have an answer. He hugged me so tightly I could hardly breathe, in the hope that I could hear all the feelings he couldn't say. I just couldn't believe I was going back to the beginning of the book.

The captain came out of the bridge doors and swept both of us across to the conference room. She looked grey with old pain and something that looked like a new shock. As if the secret was really going to be too much to bear. We all took a moment to gather the emotions that had flown to the surface, each of us trying to deal with a different set of new circumstances. "Bea I..." That was as far as she got. Whatever the secret was, it shocked her to the core and she'd just survived a space-quake. The mechanics of bureaucracy were incomprehensible to most of us and usually dealt with acres of inaction followed by a nightmare of patronising red tape.

The fact that they were insisting on 'something being done' filled me with fear. "It's to do with the timeline Bea and..." she tailed off again.

"I see," I said helpfully, "You can change my reality, but there's a law about changing your reality?" Zeke nodded. The captain was still dealing rather badly with her inner demons. "That's reality discrimination," I added. We sat in silence all trying to get a grip on the facts as we knew them.

"How come *Sam* gets to stay?" The injustice of it made my voice sound squeaky. Nothing much had changed, I felt like I did as a child when he got away with a prank and I was left looking guilty for the both of us. The captain shrugged. I really believed she actually didn't know the answer to that question, whereas I could tell she had a good idea about my intergalactic hiccup.

I sighed and got up, the anger had dissipated leaving just the sense of loss and loneliness and I was back in the world where I came from without leaving the room. There was much to think about. From the expressions on Zeke's face and Harriet Witherspoon's, they would be doing some thinking too and some of the thoughts would sit like an ugly toad squatting in the dark places of the mind. In my case it would include a relationship to a race of photon blobbies, **"no offence intended,"** I thought carefully. The Gurber equivalent of **"none taken,"** wafted back to me, which was also interesting as it meant he was doing some high level 'listening.' I'd never noticed before, but for someone who no one else ever seemed to remember was there for most of the time, it must have been a good way of keeping up with important information.

This 'whatever it was,' had both of them looking as if they had swallowed some bitter poison; sometimes the 'path' for good people took them through the back yards of those who really didn't care about anyone else but themselves.

"You're not going to say that this is the best thing for me are you?" Zeke was not listening, like many people he had selective hearing. The captain tried hard not to give away her feelings, but a poker player she was not.

The Com/T buzzed and a plaintive voice said, "If you don't come and rescue me now Bea, I am never going to lie to Pui about you exercising again." As this was a real threat and the fact that I had been lying to Pui for weeks about the running machine in the gym, I got to my feet.

"I'm on my way Rani." I pointed at the door and shrugging my shoulders went toward it. I wondered if she too had been 'listening.'

"Bea," Harriet Witherspoon was at a loss for words.

"Yes me too." I think her utter despair was worse than the fear.

I walked rather than ran to the upper medical bay and stood for a moment in front of the doors, took a deep breath and tapped the key to open. I came nose to nose with Rani who was just the other side and looking grumpy. I tried not to smile as it made a change for me to be rescuing her from Pui. "Ah, Bea," said Pui. Rani and I both cringed. "Have you got time for a check up?" I opened my mouth trying to think of some reason why I needed to be somewhere else, but everyone knew it wasn't actually a question. Pui pointed to a spare bed and I sighed, going over and lying down while the automatic instruments beeped their results. Rani sidled towards the door again, 'every man for himself' overtook all loyalty when it meant getting out of the medical bay.

"Rani, I suggest you wait for Bea," Pui said, using the 'eyes in the back of the head' tactic commonly employed by all parents. "You're unsteady on your feet and I want you to go straight back to your rooms and lie down."

Over Pui's shoulder Rani was mouthing 'how does she do that?'

I mouthed back 'I don't know.'

"Right, I want both of you to get some rest. Is that clear?" I got up off the bed as she tutted at my readings. More sidling took place and

Rani tapped the door key. For a change Rani leaned on me. We were out of there like convicts going over the wall of a maximum security facility.

The trip to Rani's rooms was uneventful except for the fact that both of us were green in the face when we got there. Collapsing onto the sofa, not a word was said for several minutes. I got up and made something with the hot water and one of the aromatic teas Rani kept on her kitchen shelves. I gave her the hot drink and she cradled the cup in her slightly shaking hands. The bones had healed but the trauma was deep in the body and hard to overcome.

"I'm going to go down to engineering and see if I can help with the," I waved my hands around in the air, signalling a vortex. She nodded, sipping tea carefully, her eyes closed, her body slumped in a most un-Rani-like way.

"When will we get to Ross 154, do you know?" I was stunned and my being so made her open her eyes wide. "What is it?" She sat up.

"We're not going to 154 Rani we're headed back to Earth."

"*What!*" She shouted.

"I'm going home," I added, trying for brave, but failing when the tear slid down my face and I didn't wipe it away.

She tapped her Com/T. "Harriet?"

"I'm on my way Rani," was the immediate answer.

"I'll go," I said, heading for the door. "I've already had this conversation once and I didn't like it the first time."

I made it out of the rooms just as the captain turned the corner and I hid around the curve as Rani's door slid open. As the doors closed behind her I heard Rani say, "What is going on?"

I would have liked to have known the answer myself, but no one was going to tell me.

Engineering was busy and there was rather a strained atmosphere. Ko-Yo-Na was pleased to see me on several levels and there was a bone cracking hug that took all the air out of my lungs and desperation like a solid wall. "Please tell me you are here to help?"

"I'm here to help," I said helpfully. I got another hug that I was unable to avoid without causing serious offence.

"Bea!" Doz leaned over the upper level and he was joined by Sig and Sofred. "Please say you're here to help?" I pointed upwards to a harassed Ko and she nodded. The upper deck was crowded with engineering crew all looking as if things were not going well.

"Where would you like me to start?"

"Can you see why this won't catch?" Doz asked. I had no idea what that meant. He was pointing at an open console. "It's the bio-energy feed to the microbe waste system." I was none the wiser for the explanation but I nodded.

I 'looked,' reaching into the empty cold bits that were what made up the mechanics. A small unit seemed to be leaking blue fluid in a tiny cloud, which attached itself to anything and seemed to make it disappear in a very short time. Even I knew this was not good.

"Okay," I said opening my eyes to see expectant faces, "The thing that looks like a big lady, which is attached to the saucepan with large handles, is not quite attached to the thing that looks like a bathroom tap." Everyone was quiet. All faces waited for the Com/T to get over itself.

Doz spoke, "Right, well, it's a start."

"It's good to feel useful," I said.

I did some more 'looking' and we all got the hang of my interpretation of the inner workings, except for the Com/T which was reduced to plaintive beeping. "It does look like a big lady," Sofred said thoughtfully as he did some dangerous twiddling with a laser cutter.

"Are you okay Bea?" Sig asked. He gave me a hug. People knew something was wrong, just not what. "You know, it's just the journey Bea; don't worry so much about the destination, we all end up in the same place eventually."

I looked at him. "What does that mean?"

"Good question," Doz added, crawling out from under the console.

Sig searched around for an answer. "I have absolutely no idea. It was something I heard Pui say. Does it help?" He asked hopefully.

What was a comfort was the generous spirit in the face looking at me. We all needed to feel that someone understood and was on our side no matter what, and both these people would and had done everything to prove that, so the loneliness lifted in the wash of friendship.

"Anyway, stop being a whinge and give us a hand with this one," Sig said indicating that anything meaningful was over.

Sofred sighed with real tiredness, "I don't understand it," he said, "I've reattached the big lady to the bathroom tap and fixed the saucepan with the large handles, so why doesn't it work?"

After a short silence, which involved several crew members not smiling with great difficulty, Doz said, "Let me have a go, 'Soffers' I'm better with big ladies than you are."

I did my best with the next problem, a tricky little situation that involved a 'doorbell' being back to front, thus preventing power to the storage bins on the lower docking bay.

The day passed and I hardly noticed the time because strangely enough I was having fun. Hunger drove me out of engineering and up to the level eight restaurant, the rest of the 'fix it' team had decided to have food sent in, Sofred was even greyer than usual, I gave him a hug which he returned. Pui had said several of the other Katinads had died in the space-quake because their fragile systems were harder to put back together again, though I knew she had nearly broken herself in two trying.

We were all still suffering from physical injury, but the worst of it was the empty spaces where friends used to be. I called Rani on the Com/T, "Do you want me to bring you some soup and bread?"

"Please. And some of that 'gloop' you eat."

"Could you be a little more 'gloop' specific?"

"Anything with chocolate." This was bad, that the guru, who called her body a temple to the lettuce leaf was after one of the poisons of the universe, was very bad. The 'what is going on' conversation clearly hadn't gone too well.

The trip to the lift shaft was perilous due to the loaded tray. I felt that soup and tea wasn't going to be of any use to either of us. So I had picked a pasta dish and a large pudding, which fulfilled the 'gloop' criteria. Thick coffee and cream completed the felony.

My arms ached by the time I got to Rani's door, which slid open without me knocking.

She was lying on the sofa draped with lots of things in bright colours. I put the tray down between us and we each picked up a fork. With her head still bent, not looking at me she said, "Bea, I am so sorry." I nodded and we ate pasta before either of us could start crying.

I went back to my rooms for a shower and the evening things that happened on board ships. My cat had been fed and Zeke was sitting with his feet up on my coffee table in the dark. "Why didn't you come and have supper with us?"

"I thought you'd be angry with me."

I was stunned. "Why would you think that?"

"Because I can't protect you."

"Zeke, since I got here you've done nothing but protect me; it's like having a guardian angel with aftershave and a great body!"

He looked surprised for a moment then laughed. I sat down next to him and he took my hand, "I just thought we'd have more time," he said.

"You're joking about the time thing."

He hugged me, crushing my bones, in the desperation of someone who couldn't find a way out. Like one of those nightmares where you got through one door only to find another room and the claustrophobic thoughts that seep into the edges of your mind, when all you wanted was fields and trees. For the first time the ship felt too small. "How long do we have?" I asked.

"Six or seven days." So short a distance, yet half way across the solar neighbourhood. "Two star-jumps and then the time-jump," he tried to say something, "I..."

"Its okay, Zeke, anyone who has no regrets is a fool." We sat for some time, holding hands like teenagers who had been forbidden to go out together. "Let's go and get drunk," I suggested.

We went to the coffee bar on level four and started on some beer. It came in a bottle with the galactic equivalent of a worm in the bottom of the clear glass-like container. I up ended the last of the liquid and narrowly missed swallowing the creature. It had several legs, I focused carefully. "This looks suspiciously like a cockroach?"

"Not technically." Zeke slapped his bottle down on the bar and waved the crewman over.

Sab Wheelan smiled, bringing two more beers. "Is this going to be an all night job?"

"It's unlikely, Bea gets drunk on fumes. Another half an hour and I'll have to carry her home."

I thumped him on the arm. "Ouch," I said, "That hurt." I stood up, shaking my bruised fingers. "I'm not even a little bit drunk yet." I swayed and Zeke helped me sit down again. "Okay maybe a little. Give me another cockroach Sab." He handed me the beer, a big grin on his face.

A voice behind me said, "Can I have one of those?" The captain pulled out a stool. "Is this all right with you?"

"Sure," I shrugged.

She sighed and we sat in silence like the three wise monkeys, only we had seen and heard the evil.

"You know," I said, examining my trainers, which had suddenly become fascinating, "I love high heeled shoes, but they do make you want to commit a crime of passion after four minutes." Both Zeke and Sab nodded after serious consideration. The captain hadn't had enough beer so she just looked puzzled. "As for the thong, it's just steel wire heavily disguised with a few frills." Sab sprayed beer over the counter. Zeke choked.

The first star-jump was a disaster. All the things that had only just made it through the space-quake gave up under the additional strain. All over the ship loud sirens were sounding off and people were scurrying around like ants in hot water. I stood with my hands pressed over my ears in a fruitless attempt to make staying sane possible. "Do you still have a hangover, Bea?" Sig asked, with no sympathy whatsoever. He grinned as he shot past me in the level one corridor.

I tapped my Com/T. "Zeke."

"Yes Bea." His voice sounded busy.

"Do you want me to go to the bridge, or head back down to engineering?" At least it sounded as if I might possibly know what I was doing.

"See if you can help Ko and Sofred, Rani's up here."

I made a face and turned to go back down to the lift shaft. A floating image appeared inside my head of Rani poking her tongue out at me something I wished I could do. I stepped into the shaft without checking and fell; a scream was snatched out of me by a net the thickness of a spider's web, stopping my descent. It lowered me to the next level doorway, which turned out to be level six. I would have screamed again when I realised, how far I'd fallen but no air remained in my lungs and I scrambled out of the net getting tangled in it trying to avoid the large gap between the doorway and the corridor.

"You should know better than stepping into a lift shaft without checking!" Asguard looked stern. I tried not to stagger.

"I'm fine; really, there's no need to fuss."

"If you're going to engineering, you'll have to use the maintenance shafts." I must have been able to express horror because he sighed and said, "Come on, I'll go with you."

"You know, it's nothing personal, but I'd rather hoped not to be using any of these shafts ever again." I grimaced as he opened the door and the emergency lights came on inside. The noise of the sirens was actually louder as we climbed down one level and then cut off abruptly as if someone had had enough.

"I can't say this is my favourite place to be either Bea," I heard Asguard say quietly. We stopped to catch our breath on the next level. I patted him on the back, as speech was difficult.

"What will you do after the Starfire returns to Earth?" I asked him. His face was in shadow and that didn't count the ones he carried with him.

"I was thinking about getting that bar on the outer colonies anyway."

"Well," I said, after a pause which included me biting back the tears, "I will be your first customer."

"It's a dream really, let's face it Bea, neither of us is free to do what we want, are we?"

I didn't think anyone had actually said it in so many words before, but as we climbed down to the ninth level and the engineering section I realised that he was right. I wasn't free to do as I liked and while I stayed, I never would be.

I was met at the door to engineering by Sofred. "You look a bit flustered Bea, are you okay?"

"I just fell down the lift shaft. Then I had to climb down the rest of the way through the maintenance shafts, so yes I am a bit flustered, but thank you for asking."

He looked cross. "Really Bea, you should know better than to get into a lift shaft without checking."

"Sofred, you shouldn't overwhelm me with sympathy. It makes me all mushy and I can't concentrate." He huffed and walked away to a console, but his back was doing something that looked as if he was suppressing laughter. Sarcasm, amazingly enough, didn't just exist in one small corner of the universe.

I did my best to help with the problems blossoming around me like spring flowers, but frustration got the better of me once or twice and I found myself jumping up and down shouting, 'the doorbell on the left I said, not the balloon on the right!' Ko tried really hard not to be astounded at my lack of knowledge but her non-existent eyebrows seemed to be permanently welded to her wild punk hairline.

"What's this?" I asked. A console with very few flashing lights covered something that felt to my mind like a discordant bundle of anomalous bio-mechanics. It had a light at its centre that flickered.

"It's a quantum teleportation device." Ko answered, "We've had the technology from the Gerber's for a while but it's not something we use very often, it's dangerous."

I felt like saying 'aha!' But I made an effort not to.

"It's not something I would ever use at all," Sofred interjected wryly. "This one was taken from a renegade ship. Did you have anything like it in your time?" He asked curiously.

"I think I remember there was tentative experimentation about sending the information in a photon from one place to another." They both looked surprised. I shrugged. "I'm not sure about the details."

Ko tapped a few keys and put a welding tool on the pad over the console. It shimmered and then disappeared, reappearing on a pad near the engine. "Oh," I shrieked, "Its magic!"

"You don't really believe that do you?" Ko asked anxiously.

I tapped her Com/T. "Hello, is there a sense of humour in there?" She gave me a friendly punch, which would probably need arnica later and Sofred laughed out loud. It was a universal constant, laughter, like atoms, stardust and dentists who always asked you a question after they'd put the drill into your mouth.

I felt dusty and tired and the thought of food and coffee sent me out on an expedition to see if the lift shafts had come back on line and the restaurants were doing anything. Having had a free skydive before breakfast I was more careful to look before stepping in through the doorway. A green light flashed and the whooshing sound meant that things were good. I hoped the food was in the same state of repair.

Rani had beaten me to it in the upper restaurant and was tucking in to her usual fare of herbal tea and a plate of vegetables. I grabbed a bowl of pasta and something that looked like a cheese sauce to go with it. The coffee mug was the size of a soup bowl and I sniffed it before gulping. All the frustrations seemed to be wafted away in the steam swirling from the cup. I sat down. Rani had something to tell me, but she was waiting until I had eaten, which was making it difficult to eat.

"What now?" I said eventually, banging down the fork.

"We have to go to Restra before we go to Earth."

"Why, I thought the Star League had given up on them?"

She did a sort of eyebrow shrug that I had tried out for myself in front of the mirror, without success. "It seems they've been rather quiet of late. We need to check up on them." She added, "No contact, just a look."

"Do you think the space-quake damaged the planet?" My appetite had suddenly disappeared.

"No," she said carefully, "It happened before that." We did an exchange of a mental flip flop and I dropped my head onto my hands.

"Sam?" I said. She did the eyebrow shrug again. "When do we get there?"

"We'll be there in a few hours."

I began eating the rest of my meal. Tariq came over bringing a beautifully decorated cake, carefully dodging the hands of several crewmen who were eager to help with the task of dismantling it. He showed it to me proudly and I dutifully paid homage to his abilities, which were considerable. He cut a large slice and I scooped a spoon through the rich icing.

"Wait!" Rani said as Tariq turned to go. "I think I'll have some."

A look of astonishment swept across his face for a moment but it was gone by the time he turned towards her. Another slice of cake appeared on a plate on the table and she ate the first mouthful. "This is your fault." She pointed at me.

"Cake is vital as part of an important learning experience," I said. We scraped the plates and got up to go.

"I'm so worried about the fact that seems to make perfect sense to me," she muttered.

We walked onto the bridge an hour later; the people on the way were still bustling about, trying to fix the unfixable. I saw Mac Ibarra and another crewman working on a holo/computer, they were both hunched in silent frustration. Nothing short of a full scale overhaul was going to make the ship shipshape.

The bridge had the usual slightly dramatic dim lighting and tense concentration. Jenny waved from the pilot's seat and Yas smiled at me, looking up from his holo/console in-between tapping and adjusting. Zeke, the captain and Mark Limbu were huddled in a corner.

The central windows showed the star of the Restran system in the distance and the curve of the nearest planet. I could hear a steady bleeping pattern, which was the Restrans version of Morse code. I could feel Rani reaching out. I knew it was a necessity, but sometimes it made me feel like a milk cow. Zeke looked over to us and then the little group broke up and they walked across to see what Rani had found. She opened her eyes and shook her head, a bleak expression on her face. I must have looked puzzled. "There's nothing," she said, "Absolutely nothing."

"Maybe the cake is affecting your abilities," I said flippantly. Jenny smiled.

The crew were puzzled, not worried. Rani was worried, not puzzled. I felt the smile slide off my face like a child's wobbly ice cream on a hot day. Gradually the concentration became stunned incredulity. Holo/screens were showing the Restran planet. Yas pointed silently. The main windows showed we were still too far out, but the hologram in the centre of the bridge had a close up. It looked like a chewed tennis ball. There was a deathly hush, quiet enough to hear the individual breathing of every person in the room. My own breath seemed to be banging in my ears. "What did this?" I whispered.

"A very powerful sonic weapon," Yas answered after a moment of silence, when he realised no one else was going to. "They were bombarded from space. It takes time to cause so much damage and more than one ship."

Zeke put his arm around me. "We can't save everybody, Bea."

"We didn't save anyone," I said, not able to take my eyes off the hologram. I thought of the woman who had put the note into my hand, 'don't forget us,' she'd said. "They must have waited and waited and no one came," I gasped.

"They made a deal with a family," the captain said, her mouth turned down with the sick feeling that came when you were just too late.

"They made a deal with Sam, and not all of them Harriet," I said. "Some of them wanted to make one with us." I knew I was stating the obvious but my mouth was talking and my brain was frozen solid. "What do you mean 'more than one ship?'" I swung around to face Yas. The information had filtered through. Yas looked at Zeke for help.

"He means that Sam must have had access to more than Roshii Samura's ship." Zeke answered me.

"More renegades?" I asked. He shrugged and I got that 'middle of nowhere' feeling. It crept into my bones and inched up my spine until the tips of my fingers felt afraid. Selfishly I wondered what was going to happen to me. Usually people didn't get to see the future until it happened. I couldn't see my own past, as if I'd had a blackout that lasted for years. Everyone else had experienced the time except me.

Rani steered me towards the door, her warmth and kindness the usual comfort blanket around my spirit. I felt guilty that I was made to feel it wasn't my fault. "It isn't," she said.

"Then why does it feel like it is?" We made our way past the frustrated people still trying to fix things. All standing and looking out of the windows at the planet. There were lots of mixed feelings, but mostly there was pity, a sense of lost possibilities which was really what life cut short meant.

I tried to rest in my rooms but the ship buzzed and I couldn't concentrate. Ollie gave up trying to sit on my lap and went out to find more peaceful people to pester. Of course I found myself outside Gurber's door. A small crack of bright light became a blinding supernova as the door opened, a hot, white star exploding, something to measure the expansion of the universe and time travel for the eye.

I walked through the mass of dust and matter. The computer pinged and a hologram superimposed itself over the spinning clouds with the result of protons and electrons combining to form neutrons. The matter and energy seemed to disappear inside itself and you could see ripples of nothing. I realised I was watching a black hole form, the details were clear to me and I wondered if Na and Neff.P. had any idea of Gurber's enhancements to the computer.

I gave him a hug, he felt warm and squishy. The rumble of not quite laughter filled my head.

We didn't talk; I couldn't say I missed the deeply informed statements that usually left me with a profound sense of the smallness in my abilities to reason. Instead he showed me the distant Andromeda galaxy, 2.2 billion light years from Earth; it was a spiral of 200 billion suns. If the words were there they would have said 'experience and learning are all we have, it makes us what we are; the light from Andromeda began its journey at the same time as humans began living on Earth. If the past was a puzzle, then so should the future be.'

My cat came in and settled on my lap as I curled on the floor. He first had touched his nose to Gurber, who seemed to glow a little at the contact. It was a good way to spend an evening and half the night. Like a college room full of students and booze and noise, except with none of those things.

I went back to my rooms with my sleepy cat on my shoulder. Some of the crew were still working on the damaged ship, their frustration had a quiet tired edge to it, but everyone said 'good night' and everyone meant it. I took a book off the shelf in my rooms and swept my hand over the covers of the remainder. There was magic in a book and it was a good place to spend time. I flicked the pages and the smell of old words wafted back to me, stronger than a spoken spell. Middle of the night feelings were always more complicated. Ollie and I nested in the blankets on the sofa and I had a mug of milky coffee and cake and Jane Austen and somewhere between the shadows and the books I hoped I would find the answers.

The second star-jump was nearly as bad as the first. All the alarms went off again and lots of people lost their temper, including Jenny Smith, who I didn't realise knew those words. "Jenny," I said, "You've been spending too much time with Tom Hatherley!" She blushed and it was a beautiful pale pink that went to the roots of her hair. It was difficult not to tease someone who could do that and still look as if she could fly a starship through a space-quake.

I was standing on the bridge next to the pilot's seat, so Jenny's impressive range of expletives were easy to hear. The ship did a wicked shimmy worthy of a dance floor hostess and settled eventually. The captain was talking into her Com/T and to Mark Limbu at the same time. Zeke got hold of my arm. "Are you okay?" He asked.

"Yes, I though that went well," I shouted above the alarms. He tutted at my inappropriate humour, but he smiled as well. Rani was already in engineering trying to do her best with bits of metal and bio-mechanics.

I tried to help with the holograph repair, but it was out of my league and much more complicated than the flash crash of the lower decks. Couzins came through the bridge doors and did his medic routine with one of the crew who had taken a liking to the floor at some speed and caught his head on the edge of a console. I decided to wait before suggesting seat belts on the bridge. No one was really interested in my brand of sarcasm even when the ship wasn't falling apart.

"Are we nearly there yet?" I whined in the tradition of every six year old that had ever gone on a journey. I didn't expect comprehension, never mind an answer but Jenny smiled.

"Shut up and stop kicking the back of my seat!" She snapped back.

"Jenny, you have my respect," I said solemnly.

"That child was me," she said by way of an explanation and began tapping keys in the vain hope of making something work. A fizz bang left her hopping back from the console and sucking singed fingers. More salty language followed.

"I vote we go somewhere and get drunk," I said helpfully.

"I'll think I'll join you," I heard the captain mutter.

The star-jump had brought us within two days of Earth. Not in my time, but one step away from whatever happened next. There was a never a point when I didn't believe in 'something out there,' even when I was encouraged to stop looking, the universe had its rules and it wasn't done with me.

I tried 'looking' at the main pilot's console. The outside was still smoking slightly and Jenny was carefully trying to get a response from the flashing lights without getting singed again. It seemed to have something in a space behind the keypad that shouldn't be there. I drew a curly shape in the air which looked a bit like an ace of clubs.

"Really," Yas Molina said, "It sounds as if the projection system has moved." We went over it again, me with my hands waving around to help with the description, him with a double frown of concentration.

"No, that definitely shouldn't be there," he added sadly.

A small fire started in the holo/systems at the back of the bridge. Zeke was swearing as he pulled a red tube from the wall and began spraying a gel on the unit surface. The man who had been working at the station held his hands out and Zeke sprayed them with the multi-purpose gel. Couzins checked him over, adding more protective layers to the burns which were obviously painful.

Everyone looked tired in the emergency lighting, an unflattering yellow cast over every face emphasising lines and shadows under the eyes, we were limping home with our tails between our legs, like an old dog caught fighting a bigger, meaner foe for the pleasure of losing. They seemed to be walking through syrup. I pushed up my sleeves in an effort to appear more businesslike in helping. The bangle that was part of my every day and therefore never noticed any more was glowing in the half light. I looked carefully at it. Maybe it was my imagination. I had assumed that Gurber had removed whatever he had put on it after the possibility of Sam was gone.

"What?" Zeke asked sharply, ever aware of my vulnerability, even with all the noise and smoke and all the way across the other side of the bridge, he was grumpy and smudged faced as he came over to me.

"It's nothing." He gave me a look, the one that said 'get on with it.' "My bangle, I think it was glowing, but that's not possible is it?" He grabbed my wrist and we both looked at the shiny silver/gold sheen.

"I must have been mistaken," I shrugged. Zeke seemed to drift away from me into the warrior zone of speculation which made me feel as if I was at the edge of a battlefield with the only person who could get me to the safety of the other side.

"Hmm," he said. I looked for a moment at his face and then put my arms around his neck and gave him a kiss. He seemed astonished and then that combination of pleased and embarrassed that went straight to the heart of everyone who had ever had a heart. He strode over to the captain and spoke quietly to her and Mark Limbu.

"Is there a queue I can join?" Yas asked dryly.

"I can't believe there isn't someone somewhere sending you a kiss, Yas."

"Not even if I look really mournful?" I thumped him and he pretended to be knocked back by the blow. "Oof!" He said. The whispering over in the corner was distracting me from tormenting Yas and Jenny Smith was prepared to take over and tease him about some girl on Ross 154 space station, so I walked over to join Zeke.

I held up my arm, to show them that the bangle was not doing anything. "It could have been the jump," I said, shrugging. They stopped talking to each other and all looked at me. "You've got to be joking?"

The captain said to Mark, "Do a scan. See if you can find anything that shouldn't be there. Anything at all," she added.

Zeke got hold of my hand. "Let's get some food. It must be all of two hours since you last ate. Do you want something sent up?" He asked Captain Witherspoon.

"Yes, thanks. It doesn't look as if I'll be going anywhere but this chair for the foreseeable future." We left, taking Jenny Smith to the medical bay for her burnt fingers.

"It's going to happen soon, isn't it?" I asked Zeke when we were alone in the corridor. He hugged me, but he didn't say 'what are you talking about?' It was like walking into dark places and everyone else was just watching you go, as if the things that had tied us together were slowly becoming untied and the memories were dusty. I reached for his hand and it was strong and warm and he kissed my fingers, but the fear was out there still.

Sleep was something of a gift and there were no presents for me that night. I made a hot drink from some of the tea Rani had given me the type that smelt like old socks but tasted okay.

Zeke was curled up with my cat in the nest of the bed and they both made gentle muttering noises in unison. I watched them for a while and then slipped into their dreams, quiet movement through thoughts. Dream watching was uncomplicated, it required no effort. The blocking chip didn't protect dreams, because it was not about active thinking. It was a place I would never usually go, because no one should walk into your dreams uninvited and understanding them is like organising sand.

Ollie was all speed and blurred sense, like a picture painted by a child, bright splashes of shape and sound. Zeke's dreams were dark, linked with loss and sorrow and the puzzle that was living with lies. He also had a strange preoccupation with trying to find his boots. I put an imaginary pair by his bed for him and his restless noises stopped.

Into the corridors I pushed my thoughts through into rooms. People usually slept at the same time and in the same way. I listened, trying to remember experiences, storing up memories, feeling the familiar minds for the day when I would be alone again. Na-Es-Yan stretched out, with her hand reaching open palmed for more stars, Neff.P. still watching over her, even in his sleep. Pui was restless and half awake, worrying about someone else and with some weird thoughts about DNA. Ko-Yo-Na, organised, self-contained, composed even as she slept, her rooms were full of technical things, the type of toys clever people liked to have around them. Gatt.R. and Yas Molina, strong, positive, like book ends from different places in the wild sky. I tried not to feel too much but the pain of loving people was like walking on broken glass. I remembered a time when I thought I would never care about anyone again, but you didn't get to choose. Mac and Tom, sleeping sprawled on the sofa after working themselves to a standstill. I leaned in to touch them, a wisp of thought, haunting the spaces between breathing. Exhaustion etched on each face and dirty hands. Mac had fallen asleep with one boot still on. I could see their jumbled dreams. Tom's were a mix of broken holo/computers and a smiling Jenny. Mark Limbu was shut away even in sleep, just a dark brown wave I couldn't get past.

I was aware of her of course. "**How long have you been there?**" I asked Rani. My own rooms were somewhere on the periphery of my vision. But I could feel her watching me her own dream watching was so much softer than mine.

"I didn't think you should be doing this alone." More of a whisper than real thought.

The possibility of Sam being around had not really made much of an impression on me. I just didn't think it was likely. We drifted back to my rooms and I felt the familiar swirl of air that linked in with the breathing of your own body. Rani's thoughts were gold and green and wispy, a few moments later she came to join them and me and we sat drinking more of her ghastly tea. If I could have seen the sun coming up I think it would have been a good night.

Zeke came into the main rooms from the bedroom. He had a purring Ollie tucked under his chin. He reached out a hand and squeezed mine and he and Rani exchanged a glance that said nothing. "It's today isn't it?" I asked as I watched a tear slide slowly down Rani's face. Nothing prepared you for eternity.

"Ah!" I dropped a box as Mac came up behind me and grabbed me around the waist where I was ticklish, something my brother used to do before he had turned into a madman. I smacked him and he laughed.

"I dreamed about you last night." He lifted up the box and put it back on the coffee table. I added more books and he examined one that had fallen on the floor. "My grandfather had some of these. He said he 'needed to feel the words in his hands.'"

"Your grandfather was a wise man." I was nearly packed. All the clothes I had acquired on the ship were going back to the recycler. As were most of the things I had brought with me that hadn't survived the trip around the solar neighbourhood. Rani had commandeered a pair of my HKM jeans though quite what she was going to do with them I didn't know. Ollie was doing the rounds and sulking. He made a point of ignoring me as I fed him. I knew how he felt. Being 'sent home' was bad enough but I kept sensing an underlying wave of tension not my own, it felt like a low level hum, the kind that you got with slightly faulty air conditioning and it froze my nerve endings until my head ached with words not said.

It was amazing how quickly you could pack, even when you were trying really hard not to. Mac helped by getting in the way. I sat down with coffee and cake and sometime after I had made a second cup and Mac had told me about his love life, which involved Tova Gordon and too much information about low gravity assignations Doz and Sig wandered in and helped themselves.

Then Tom Hatherley came in with Jenny. "Who's flying the ship?" I asked, clutching my forehead in my best panic-stricken impression. She made a face at me and Tom made her coffee, dancing attendance on her as if she couldn't manage the water or cups.

What they didn't say and the feelings not spoken I really appreciated. My hands shook a little but no one could see I was scared. It felt not so much as if I was leaving, but being left behind.

Going back made me nervous on so many levels, the fact that I actually now knew what happened to your atoms in a time-jump was just one aspect of it.

"Don't you have a problem with the time-jump?"

"Oh yes," Mac said. "Have I gone white with fear? I don't like anyone to see me with my lips quivering." I blew a raspberry at him right up close, something I used to do to my brother before the crazy happened. "Okay that's good I'm feeling much better now." He made a big thing about wiping his face. I had forgotten how young they were, when you were young everything was possible and nothing mattered that much.

The door slid open and Zeke walked in. I stood up abruptly and spilt my coffee. The conversation ended like a knife had cut through the words, but no blood fell, just the coffee spill dripping off the edge of the table.

The room emptied and Zeke came to stand next to me as the noisy siren warned about the jump. He took my hand and held on tight and the room tipped and we seemed to be miles away from each other.

My head exploded into coloured lights and I thought I heard

someone shout a really rude word. The stars settled back outside the windows where they belonged and I clutched my eyes which hurt. "That was as bad as the first one!" Zeke held onto me and tried desperately to stop his feelings from spinning us both out of reality. I went over to the window. We were behind Earth's moon and back in my time.

We walked around each other while the boxes that contained my life so far were taken to the upper docking bay. Ollie was put in his travel basket and did a cat double take at the indignity of being asked to get into the small space.

Zeke began a sentence again and then didn't say anything except, "I'm sorry that we had such a rough time, all the incidents I mean."

"It could have been worse," I said cheerfully. He gave me a Zeke look, one of those which included 'I don't understand you on any level.' "Well there could have been shooting," I explained.

"As I recall there was." He tried again for the words he really wanted to say and came up with nothing.

"Zeke, apart from the obvious, the 'age difference' I mean." I pointed out the window at the moon in my time. "Relationships seldom work when one of you is hiding a big part of yourself."

"I thought that was what you were supposed to do." A small smile masked the dryness of the words. He folded me in a hug that felt as if it would have to do for a lifetime. I wondered whose that would be, mine or his.

"Your previous relationship lasted how long?" I said to his shirt. He kissed the top of my head and then we walked out into the corridor and up to the first level docking bay.

The door slid quietly open on the hum of waiting people and the possibility of emotional leave-taking, everyone was crammed into the bay. The rush of goodwill swept up to meet me and I wanted to say something clever and thought provoking, but my teeth were clenched on a tidal wave of tears and I just hugged the waiting friends and hoped they would understand. Gatt.R. took his translator off and spoke in his own language. It sounded like Native American, warm and lyrical. The words reverberated around as if the walls were leaning in and listening. He touched my arm and then held his over his chest and bowed his head. I reached out and touched the hand folded like a fist and he radiated the warmth and gentleness of a spring day.

The SSV was full of my boxes and Rani sat in the co-pilot seat. Captain Witherspoon stood outside by the door as I got in, followed by Zeke. Her face was clouded with unsuppressed emotion, there were feelings there too complex to read, but I could see something that surprised me and that was anger. Somehow it made me more afraid than anything else I had come up against.

We swung in a dignified loop towards the bay doors and I could see faces looking up and hands reached to wave and my heart felt as if it was being ripped in two. If you really wanted to crush someone, give them hope and then take it away. "What did Gatt.R. say?"

"It's a Des.Ran. chant, it means 'travel safely loved person.'" Rani was not looking at me, examining her hands as if they had the answers. Zeke tapped the console keys with studied concentration.

Gamblers looked for physical 'tells' to give away emotional feelings and therefore the possibility of the cards. Telepaths looked for the same thing but it was more as if you could see the cards first then the emotions. Three people on the Starfire knew what was going on and all of them were dealing with it badly. As goodbyes went it was awful, but the rest of the crew had just thought they were dealing with the day-to-day decisions of the bureaucracy.

I sighed, looking out of the windows at Earth closing in fast and the blue-green swirling promise of home. I rubbed the bangle on my arm. Both Sig and Doz had tried to remove it by using a range of cutting implements. In the end the captain just shrugged and said, "It stays." Pui flatly refused to put the medical condition I had arrived with into my system. They really had been told to put me back as they'd found me. How stupid could some people be, experience couldn't be unlearned.

We were all connected by something. Even the 'little green men' made sense, in fact maybe them more than most. It wasn't as if mankind had gone out and terra-formed other planets leaving a little of themselves in each place along the way. It was more as if a panspermia of 'us' had started in different parts of the galaxy at the same time.

The middle of the night was curved around my side of the planet. Skimming to my little corner of England, we set down on the hill behind the house. The doors to the SSV slid open and I could smell rain on the wind. Quietly, out of the trees a shadow moved towards us. Ted hugged me and reached in for the boxes Zeke handed out. It was done in a moment, all that passed between them were the boxes. Ted began taking my sad collection of books and shoes down the hill and I stood on the slightly damp grass looking up at the faces in the dark doorway.

Rani reached out a hand and took mine and we did something without speaking that wouldn't make much sense unless you understood the colour of friendship. Then she turned and disappeared into the SSV. "I don't want to leave you here," Zeke said.

"I didn't get the impression anyone was offering us a choice," I whispered back. A sudden rustling in the distant trees had both of us jumping apart in a most undignified way. The fact that he was an armed warrior and I was a telepath added to the sense of the ridiculous. A startled deer spun around and went back under cover.

"You know we could try to find a more isolated and windblown spot. If it was really cold and raining that would be good, too." He sounded spooked and angry.

"You're being sarcastic?" I asked helpfully, reaching for Ollie's travelling case and putting it down on the ground. Ollie was unnaturally silent.

Zeke hugged me and we stood there in the shadows of old feelings until Ted arrived back to pick up some more boxes and when I looked back at the SSV, the closing door made me realise what alone really meant.

I followed Ted down the path, a small slip of moon reflected back from waving grass. A sigh escaped me as I heard the almost silent engine noise change and I turned slightly to see the craft lift off. Nothing but numb disbelief filtered through, but Ted put down what he was carrying and took my hand in both of his. We stood there in the empty spaces of my mind. I noticed the light in the window of the cottage Ted had promised to keep on for me and I picked up Ollie's basket again.

We walked on towards the house in silence apart from the wind stirring the leaves and the trees creaking like the deck of an old ship with its sails billowing.

Ted helped me put the boxes on the upper landing and I opened Ollie's travelling basket. The cat stalked over to the bedroom and leapt onto my bed, his tail swishing and I wished, not for the first time, that I had a tail to do some swishing of my own.

"Would you like a cup of tea?" Ted asked.

The kitchen felt like an alien place and home at the same time which was not a good sensation. I looked hopelessly at the kettle and Ted sighed, taking over as I slumped at the table. He produced home-made chocolate cake from out of a cupboard, milk and mugs, and eventually the kettle boiled. My chin was resting on my hands and my hands were flat on the table. "Do you know someone called Tariq Azel?" Ted snorted, so I assumed that was yes.

I reached out automatically like a little child looking for old comfort and found nothing.

"Where's Edie?" I sat up, spilling tea. The house next door was void of her gentle spirit and seemed to be mocking me with its large empty corners. Ted pulled out a chair. He filled his cup with milk and then tea from the pot and stirred in four spoonfuls of sugar before he answered.

"She's gone, Bea."

I tried not to sob, "What is this, some sort of test in loneliness?" We were quiet for a moment. "Sorry," I added, then wiped the point-less tears and grabbed for a slice of cake.

"It's okay. I'm pretty angry myself right now." He picked up his tea and added one more thoughtful spoon of sugar and tried for some-thing, but ended up silent. "Just understand it's not the end."

"I don't know if that's supposed to make me feel better." The cake was really good and several cups of tea made with water that hadn't been around a spaceship and its occupants half a dozen times tasted wonderful. "Are you going to leave me too?" I asked carefully, not making eye contact.

Ted looked down at his hands and spoke deliberately, "I will be here while you need me." Even I knew that wasn't really the right answer.

Ollie and I were swathed in downie and sitting by the open window. He did his burrowing routine when he realised that we would not be returning to the bed any time soon. I looked hopefully for falling stars and any sign that someone would change their mind. I had been lonely all my life, but I waited until the night stretched out and grey fingers crept across the grass and I was stiff and chilled with the cold.

I pulled on more layers of clothing and left my sleeping cat in the folds of the bedding and went out into the early garden. Ted had done a good job. The flowerbeds were rich with shoots and nearly-open daffodils. The trees were that sudden green of early spring and an ice blue sky was blooming behind the sunrise. I sat on the doorstep and drank coffee, sipping the rich taste like a lifeboat in a storm. Sometimes it was the little things that kept you afloat.

Ted came up the garden path a few hours later. I had fed my cat showered and unpacked and listened to the radio. It felt like déjà vu, but without Edie. "Ted, how long have I been gone. In this time, I mean?"

"A week."

Those people really didn't care whose time they messed with.

S ometimes life was about hiding out where your fears couldn't find you and sometimes it was changing things until life fitted a little better.

The house didn't feel as if it was home any more with Edie gone. I was constantly listening in the dark for echoes and looking for lost things. Ted was silent on the questions and desperate on the pleading, so I stopped. Days of waiting were replaced by the sudden need to look in estate agent windows. I was full of self-pity and painful second hand history and then asked Ted to help before my restlessness drove me crazy. Living in an old house was like sleeping next to a lion, there was always something on your mind. What I needed was new bricks.

Ted surprised me by not trying to dissuade me from house hunting. He introduced me to a middle aged man who was planning to move in with his partner. This was not the type of person who had spent a huge amount of time thinking about closets and we got on really well. He was bright and vibrant with an acid wit and a really good eye for a bargain. After some careful negotiation over a large coffee cake and some serious levels of alcohol, we agreed to swap and they would then buy the other half of the house. Ted unsurprisingly seemed to have complete power of attorney over Edie's property and it gave me several sleepless nights to think that she wouldn't need it any more. I sent silent thoughts out to the stars that she was out there somewhere, safe.

The last night in the cottage I spent roaming the hills where the SSV had landed, worrying that no one would be able to find me and I would be lost to them forever. Then I cursed and cried because it seemed they had forgotten me anyway.

Ted arrived in the morning and looked exasperated at my exhausted pale face. Once more the grumbling Ollie was put in his travelling basket and the small van we had hired was filled in less than a morning with books and shoes. Ted drove the van and I followed in my much-abused Mini Cooper, crashing the gears occasionally when I forgot that there wasn't a computer on board. Ollie yowled in the seat beside me and I cried all the way to the nearby village in the next valley, up a small hill and wiped my tears as we came to a stop.

The small village sat in contented and tidy silence in the Exe valley. The hill behind had a few scattered modern houses, built much too fast and in all the wrong places. But the view down the valley was the thing of dreams; forty miles of fields with the river winding its way through the different greens and soft trees and sheep on the far hills in the distance.

I stood on the balcony and drank coffee and the view in great gulps. It was like letting go of a drowning man, a part of me was over-come with guilt and the rest just felt relief that something really impossible was over.

Ted joined me and I put my arm around him and we hugged for a while and I said thank you in silence and he smiled. "Rani said you were a really strong telepath, she was right."

I didn't ask him just when he'd had that conversation with her. Ollie was crunching loudly. He missed Tariq, who, I suspected, had cooked him something special every day. The dried food out of a bag no longer received the same level of interest.

The house was spacious, two bedrooms and a bathroom upstairs and a kitchen and living room down. It was ultra modern, open plan and most of the large windows brought light and the view of the valley in. The two men had added top of the range cooking equipment and a sense of fun and laughter that danced in the beams of sunlight on the light wood floors. There was barely a hint of things past. They had left a bunch of flowers and a bottle of champagne on the kitchen counter. We scattered my meagre collection of furniture around the house and it had taken me twenty minutes to put my shoes away in the fitted cupboards and two to open the bottle because it was important to prioritise.

I wandered around in my dressing gown, emptying my book boxes and stacking them against the wall where I intended some shelves to go. I pulled the last book out and discovered it was the copy of Sense and Sensibility that Torriff had given me. I sat on the floor and tucked the folds of my nightwear around me. In a beautiful hand he had written a note in the front cover. It wasn't readable, some language far away, faded, as if it had been written a long time ago instead of not yet. I put it aside to see if Ted could read it for me. He was an ageing hippie so by definition it was bound to include a few obscure languages.

The evening light did little to move the rich shadows from the valley. I breathed deeply, listening carefully to the sounds of the night. Ollie wound his tail around me hoping for a cuddle. I picked him up and sniffed warm fur. My thoughts wandered and I found myself wishing that one of my not yet born friends would just come by for a cup of coffee and a chat. It was amazing how many shades loneliness came in. At the back of my mind was a stray thought, something I couldn't quite get a grip on. It whispered in and out and then finally came to rest; my brother.

It was easier to get a signal to a fuel carrier in Proxima Centauri, I knew because Doz 'phoned' his mother every week in 2428, than it was to find a phone number for a mobile-less someone in Scotland that you only had a partial address for in this century.

I pulled a small bag from the cupboard and began throwing things into it. Ollie looked on with that expression on his face which could only be described as 'you have got to be kidding.' His orange whiskers twitched and his gold eyes flickered. "Look," I said, whining like a little kid, "If I can stop Sam from going to the future and turning into Mr Crazy than I think I should give it a try." The irony of discussing time travel with my cat was not lost on me. "Well," I said, "Are you coming?"

The packed bag sat by the front door and I did all the usual checking you needed to do for a journey. Credit card, phone, clean knickers, family size bag of Bassett's Dolly Mixtures, cat. I locked the doors and crept to my car as if someone was watching me. Ted had gone back to his cottage in the village over the hill and as far as I knew no one was the least bit interested in my whereabouts. I tried not to tie myself in knots about the fact that I might be doing the something that I was supposed to be doing.

Driving to Scotland from Somerset was mostly straight lines with a few squiggles in the middle around Birmingham. I spent a lot of the journey vacillating between guilt for not telling Ted where I was going and that wonderful 'let out of school early' feeling.

Music blared along empty night roads and I stopped for coffee and a loo at transport cafes full of illegal cigarette smoke and heart-stopping fried food and other tired people who seemed like me to be going nowhere at middle of the night o'clock. Ollie had slept most of the way on the passenger seat curled up on a travel blanket, his ears flicking at the loud music and his opinion on the journey evident in every irritated 'huff' if I tried to stroke him.

Truck drivers were a remarkably cheerful lot, even at two in the morning and the transport cafe was full of them. They were curious but not rude about my appearance in their midst and I drank several cups of coffee and ate a fried egg sandwich, which was one of those middle of the night snacks you couldn't possibly manage at any other time. I got back in the car and gave Ollie my peace gift, a packet of crisps which he ate noisily. Making a nest of the blanket he went back to sleep, crisp crumbs stuck to his whiskers.

The false dawn saw me somewhere near the Scottish border and I stopped the car in a quiet lay-by before I drove into a hedge trying to avoid the weird hallucinations that kept springing up in front of my tired eyes. I stretched out, locked the doors and pulled the blanket with Ollie over to my side of the car. It was cold and we burrowed together and I slept.

I dreamed of the Starfire and Zeke, they were looking for me and I kept shouting and he just couldn't see me and eventually they went away and I woke up in a blind panic clutching at Ollie, who was not a clutching sort of cat. He objected very strongly by scratching me in an effort to get away.

We stopped at a petrol station and I filled up the car, stocked up on sweets and coffee and asked to use their loo. I did as much washing as I could in the small sink and slopped on moisturiser and mascara. My hair would have frightened a yeti at the best of times and I wet it, running my fingers through it. The young man running the till looked at me curiously; we were somewhere near Fort William and it was bleak and hilly wherever you looked.

I went back to the car and let Ollie out to do his business. He sniffed around for a while and then hopped off behind some cover for a bit of privacy. It was cold and it didn't take him long, he sniffed the air, gave me a look that would have frozen water and hopped back onto the front seat.

I knew that Sam lived near a place called Kingussie, pronounced King-oosie, which was near Aviemore. In the absence of any satellite connection I pulled out my road map and did some driving with my index finger on a small B road.

Eventually after several hours of weary travel and spectacular views, I stopped by a river and got out of the car to stretch. Ollie hopped out too and wandered around sniffing at the strange smells. For a cat he was more like a dog, though I would never have told him that. I could see for miles, the air was crisp and clear and the Cairngorms were snow capped in the background. I could see why Sam would like it here, something about the place made you think of lost legions and a wild past, as if warriors would ride through the trees on some noble Celtic cause.

The sun was doing its best but a chill wind sent me back to the car for my Gore-Tex jacket. Ollie had had enough and was sitting on the top of the car watching me. He rubbed his head up against my face and said, 'prroww' which was about as forgiving as it was going to get. I tickled his chin and we studied the map together.

I went around in circles for another three hours until I gave up and asked at a small cottage that looked friendly with its spire of smoke curling up until it met the bitter wind. A puzzled woman answered the door. "I'm looking for my brother, Sam Markam, I know he lives around here somewhere."

"Oh aye," her face was slightly suspicious. She had been baking and the delicious smell of new bread seemed to cloud around her. Her hands were covered in flour.

"It was supposed to be a surprise, but I'm not doing very well," I finished lamely.

She looked at me carefully. "Yes, you're his sister all right. You have his way about you." I stepped back mentally as well as physically and remembered that people around these parts were often fey. She tilted her head to one side.

"We look out for each other as there's not many of us live here. This is the way of it." Her voice was soft with that hardly there highland accent. I nodded and smiled again, pulling my jacket around me and zipping it up.

I waved a hand back down the road, "Umm?"

"Oh right." She came out of the house and pointed. "Back down the road, turn left at the three pines, no more than a track, then all the way to the end, you'll see it, a small bothy." I nodded my thanks and looked at the lowering sky. As I got back into the car she came over.

"Sam said he was going away for a while soon and not to worry about not seeing him. If he's not there you come back now, it's not a time to be out here alone."

My face must have betrayed the panic I felt, because she stood on the doorstep and watched me go.

The evening seemed to have arrived without a moment of an afternoon, as if the mountains were in too much of a hurry to bother with the end of the day. The sun was setting behind the trees and there were long shadows in all sorts of places, like my heart.

As I turned by the three pines, I put my headlights on and bumped along the road, trying not to worry about the occasional crunch from under the car as the wheels spun on the stones.

Something made me look up. My panic caught at the back of my throat and I shouted through gritted teeth, "Oh no!" A small craft was slipping down quietly through the trees. If you didn't know what you were looking at you probably wouldn't have noticed. I stopped the car and shut the door on a grumbling Ollie.

The foliage was thick almost to the back of the bothy. A small garden with spring flowers made me stop for a second, the thought of Sam digging holes and planting was about as surprised as one person could be about another. I moved forward slowly as the quiet voices carried on the tide of evening.

Everything went silent. I crept around the side of the building, my back was up against the cold wall and I peered out toward the front, a large bush hid me from them. I felt silly hiding behind a few leaves. Three men were loading the SSV with boxes and one of them was Zeke. I leaned back and slid down on my heels with my fists pushed against my closed eyes. Not in a million years would I have thought of this. Part of me was angry and most of me hurt, but I couldn't seem to find the strength to go with the pain. I heard a voice whisper a quiet word, "What?"

I flattened myself against the wall. I could sense the searching of a telepath, but this was not the Sam of the future, the Mr Crazy with the power of madness, it was easy to deflect and hide from him. Still, I could feel his puzzlement. I took a breath and pulled myself upright.

The SSV doors had slid shut and the engines were changing to the barely there noise that meant they were ready for take off. I moved quickly out into the open and banged on the side of the craft. I could sense shock and then the SSV lifted, it turned and there were the faces in the front windows, their mouths open in speech and something that looked as if a plan had gone wrong. Sam was shrugging his shoulders, 'No he didn't know who I was.'

Zeke's look was strained and angry and then something else, he didn't know me, but he would remember me. He looked again, all in a few moments of panic and surprise and anger. The jumble of my emotions coalesced into a desperate longing and I watched as the craft sped away. Just wanting to touch someone was like breathing.

I dropped to my knees in exhaustion and put my head in my hands, but my eyes were dry. Eventually I went to fetch my car and my cat and I opened the door of the house and turned on a light and pulled myself to a chair and then I found some tears left.

Cold and curled up into a ball I realised there was someone at the door. For a minute I couldn't remember where I was and it was dim except for one small light on a table, Sam's house. For a mad moment I thought they might have come back, but only in that place between sleeping and waking where hope lived. I opened the door to find the woman from down the road and a man standing close behind her with a lantern, they looked tense.

"Sam's gone?" She asked. I nodded, too tired to speak, then I moved out of the way so they could come in.

"We were worried," the man said his voice as soft as his wife's.

"My name's Duncan by the way and this is Stella." We shook hands, which seemed a little strange, but not, at the same time.

"We brought you some milk and some of Stellie's home-made bread."

"Oh my goodness me is that a tiger?" Stella swooped down on Ollie and swept him up into a cuddle, something that would have earned a mere mortal a great deal of disdain. The smell of home-made bread had gone a long way to making Ollie a good friend and he purred.

They turned on some more lights and Duncan put the bread and milk in the kitchen end of the bothy. I sat back down in the chair and after a moment's hesitation Stella began making tea and cutting bread. Ollie wrapped his furry body around her ankles and she leaned down and gave him a slice she had buttered. He took it under the other chair in the living room end and chomped noisily.

I sighed, bone weary from too much driving and the emotional baggage that came from being too late.

The bothy was basically one long room, kitchen and table at one end, chairs and books at the other. Sam had built a second level above the kitchen and the bedroom and the bathroom were up a small spiral staircase into the roof. I could see a laptop by the bed and thought I might have a look later.

"Why did you say 'it's not a time to be out here alone?'" I asked Stella. She put the bread knife down and brought tea over to me and Duncan, who had plonked himself into the other chair. She and he exchanged a look that had apprehension as its main ingredient.

"We've had strangers around here for a few weeks, nothing really you could put your finger on, but they just didn't feel correct." She brought bread and butter and cheese and some of the best honey I had ever tasted and we sat on the floor and had a carpet picnic. Ollie swooped in for the occasional kill and retreated just as quickly with it back under the chair.

"What will you do now?" Duncan asked me.

I shrugged. "Go home I guess." I felt defeated and alone.

"Not tonight!" Stella looked horrified.

"No, I'll go in the morning." I grabbed my cat before he finished up the butter and made himself sick. Stella began clearing away the debris. Duncan stayed where he was looking thoughtful. I wondered what they would say to each other later about the brother and sister who had missed each other because they didn't speak.

"You could come and stay with us for the night, so you wouldn't be alone up here."

I was stunned, their kindness was overwhelming and I stumbled over words, "Thank you, I will be fine I'll come by in the morning before I go."

"Well, if you're sure." They both looked worried.

"Honestly, I'll be fine."

They fussed around a bit more. Duncan checked the generator

which was something that would never have occurred to me, so that I wouldn't be plunged into darkness. Stella put the food on a tray and covered it with a damp cloth. Eventually they left and I breathed a sigh of selfish relief. I brought my bag in from the car and Ollie demanded to be let out for a prowl. He disappeared into the dark, an orange blob on the back of my eye.

The bathroom was basic but there was plenty of hot water, thanks to Duncan and I filled the bath and stepped in, steam swirled up and out of the open window. My whole body ached with the sense of being alone, that feeling where you thought no one would ever touch you again.

I padded around the house in my pyjamas, opened cupboards and looked at books. Ollie tapped on the kitchen window with a paw and I let him in. Then I checked the door. It had seemed pointless to lock it, because the only 'stranger' that was left was me, but I did it anyway.

We sat in a chair for a while. I stroked Ollie's glossy fur and thought about how much I missed Zeke, the loss was like bereavement and it made my heart feel like a stone. I closed my eyes and I could almost smell the deep warmth of him, but I just couldn't quite see his face. The feeling of walking along the edge of time was very real.

The computer by the bed was as silent as the moon drifting through the clouds. Sam had put in a password that defeated me. I had tried all the usual things, our mother's maiden name, the local pub he used to get thrown out of regularly, plus the names of a few mountains I knew he had climbed. I could feel him laughing at me all over the house. I curled up in the cold bed with Ollie who had made a nest between the pillows and was purring like a train. The bedside table had a little, almost hidden drawer, which was incongruously facing towards me rather than the room. I reached out and pulled it open. By the light of the lamp I could see a letter and a small framed picture.

'Bea. If you're reading this, it's because something has happened to me and you're going through my stuff. I think I'm doing the right thing, though I don't entirely trust the people who I have gone with. Nothing sinister, I'm not joining a *cult and I'm not going to do anything crazy. Be on your guard. I need you to be safe. Sam.'*

The picture was one we had taken before our mother had died. She had a scarf wrapped around her head and her eyes, so like Sam's, were dark pools of suppressed pain. She was laughing though and so was Sam, I was looking at both of them, they had seemed to me at the time so in tune with each other. His arm was wrapped around her protectively and he held my hand. I thought the memories that came rushing in would break me in two. I leaned on the bed to fight the waves as if my pain was a thing I could control.

Three computer passwords were printed at the bottom of the letter.

In the early dawn I drank coffee sitting on the doorstep with a blanket wrapped around me. I watched the trees change from guardians of the night to growing things going about the business of photosynthesis.

I used the bathroom and then went around tidying and bleaching and turning off switches. Nothing in the house was of any great value but I locked it up, taking Sam's laptop and the photo with me. As I went down the road the house disappeared around a curve and a part of me thought that it was as lost in time as Sam.

It was still very early, but the smoke from the chimney stack was a welcome question mark over the house. I stopped and before I tapped on the door it swung open. "I was just about to send Duncan up with some more supplies." Stella smiled. "You might not be eating much, but your cat would surely starve!"

She made me strong sweet tea and more of her bread, this time with home-made jam. It felt like a slice of sunshine spreading across your tongue. Some people had abilities that are not so clear and Stella's was to put her love into her food. "Would you take the key for Sam's house, Stella?"

"Of course, I will check up there and let you know if anything needs doing, you don't think Sam will be back." It wasn't a question and I shook my head, she gave a small nod as if it confirmed what she herself had thought.

I went on my way with a lifetime's supply of honey, jam and bread, and a bunch of early flowers, which she had wrapped in damp cotton wool and paper. I hugged her and she hugged me back, as if trying to give me some of her peace and contentment which was a lost cause.

Ollie sat in the back window of the car; he looked like one of those plastic dogs and frightened the passing cars when he did something cat-like and real. I just drove, for hours. I didn't feel tired, except in my spirit and you couldn't cure that with sleep.

I stopped three times on the way home, but I couldn't eat anything, just drank some coffee that tasted how I imagined very old engine fuel would. It made my eyes judder and I think I must have done irreparable damage to my kidneys, but it did the trick. It took all day and most of the evening and then I was home.

As an exercise in futility it was very successful. Ted was making supper and had a large brandy and no questions in his hand as I opened the door. He picked Ollie up who couldn't wait to 'tell' on me and whose loud complaining was only subdued by a huge plate of fresh fish.

I fell into the sofa in the kitchen which Ted must have moved and curled up in a heap. The first brandy didn't touch the sides the second seemed to have had an effect on my eyelids and the third I didn't finish.

Waking up in the early morning I couldn't remember where I was, for a moment I thought I was back on the Starfire and my heart squeezed as I came to a little more and I realised the noise I could hear was not the air filtration system but my coffee machine. I pushed back the blanket and stood up swaying like an old bag lady without her shopping cart.

There was that thought going around in my mind about putting the future behind me and if I didn't I would end up as crazy as my brother.

Ted stuck his head around the kitchen door. "How are you doing? Okay, forget I said that, I can see for myself."

I avoided the small talk and went for a large glass of water and a small coffee. "I saw him." I sat back down after I finished the water and sipped the coffee.

"Sam?" Ted came over and helped himself to a cup, adding loads of milk and enough sugar to make a dentist whimper. He looked earthy. A light trail of soil led from him out of the kitchen door and his boots seemed to be depositing neat little wavy lines of dirt on the tiles.

"I mean Zeke," I said. Ted sat down next to me. "He looked younger and he didn't know me." I pulled the framed photograph out of my bag. "When we first met, he said he'd seen a picture of me and it stayed with him. I think it was this one." Ted took it from me and looked at it carefully.

"He must have seen it in the bothy before Sam hid it in the bedside drawer. I wonder how long it took him to work it out. That I was Sam's sister, I mean." I took the picture back from Ted. "Oh wait," I said sarcastically, "Of course you would know the answer to that." Ted looked really uncomfortable and I felt mean. "I feel like the character in the play who's the only one who doesn't know that it's the end of the second act." We finished our coffee in silence.

"Come and look at your garden." He took my hand and the feeling about missing my brother seemed to ease a little. We checked out the tiny front garden, which had been mainly grass and a few bushes and was now transformed into a haven of ornamental trees and flower beds. I hadn't noticed in the dark and in my haze of exhaustion. The back garden was on three levels and had been rather plain with one border and lots of gravel. It now looked Italian, with lots of places to sit and running water and a little bit of magic.

"Do you have an army of munchkins who work at night?" We sat and looked at the view and I eventually went in for a shower and we drank more milky sweet coffee and I read an actual newspaper for the first time in a million light years. The sky was blue and you could see forever. Ted went home to do his own garden, leaving me supper and a sense of something over that couldn't be sorted and was best left. Ollie chased butterflies and I tipped my head back and looked up until my mind swirled with the size of the sky.

If I'd thought about it for too long it would have been put back in the attic. I was going through flight logs and jump logs, sorting out photographs and sifting through the past. Nothing prepared you for growing up and you were even less prepared for growing older. I didn't have much in the way of belongings, but what I did have made me feel restless for the things I hadn't done. I thought about retaking some exams and doing a little flying. The plane I had bought had been sold a long time ago when I realised what the true meaning of the word 'syndrome' meant. Chronic illness and altitude didn't go together. It would have been interesting to try and log the hours I had spent in the SSV. I took my rig downstairs and pulled the canopy out of the container.

A parachute was a personal thing, I knew men who would have rescued their kit before they went back into a burning building to get their children. I stretched out the lines and examined the material, holding some tight to my mouth and blowing, not a real test for porosity, just something I'd seen a rigger do years ago. Being anally retentive had had its advantages. The 'firelite,' a small neat canopy was clean and had been stored out of the sunlight. The design had long been overtaken by the minute swoopy 'squares' that were banging their owners into the ground with alarming regularity. I didn't pop the reserve because the days when people packed their own reserves were long gone.

I stretched my arms above my head, leaned back, closed my eyes and fell mentally backwards through memories. The ability to do something wasn't always a good reason for doing it, but the canopy rustled in the breeze from the slid open patio windows and the sound whispered inside my head and it felt as if some doors didn't need to stay closed.

Ted called from the front door, "Hey Bea,"

"I'm in the living room Ted." He came in and flung himself into one of the chairs I had bought. The sofa had stayed in the kitchen, which was where we usually ended up sitting anyway. The chairs had come from a second hand shop, they were comfy and worn, one had been leather in a past life and a long time ago the other had had a paisley pattern. It was hot and Ted looked exhausted. I had never asked what he did to get so tired, mainly because the idea left my head as soon as it entered, which was very irritating and while it was allowed to exist as a thought I knew he wouldn't answer anyway.

"What are you doing?"

"Checking my kit, I have no idea if it's still jumpable but I think I'll make a phone call."

Ted tried to look impassive but I could feel the anxiety radiating from him. "You're thinking of selling it?" He asked hopefully.

"No Ted," I said quietly, "I'm thinking of jumping it." Something slid around the room like cloud shadow, greasy and cold. "Tell me that was my imagination?" We both looked about us like the pair of extras in an old film whose names you had never bothered to learn. I shook my head, Ted seemed to be puzzled, which was a bit creepy too. I had thought the only person who wouldn't know what was going on was me.

I untangled the lines on the canopy and began laying it out, the familiar moves settled in as I straightened and smoothed. Ted watched impassively. When I had closed the last container flap with a pull-up cord and patted down the edges he said, "That looked like a dance."

"If it's done properly, it feels like one," I smiled. It did, you had to know exactly where each part went and sometimes late at the end of a really good day's jumping, with the possibility of a beer, you remembered that you'd packed but not how, like a tango with a really good looking partner, it was only when the music stopped you knew what your feet had been up to.

We sat in the evening light talking and eating and avoided all conversation that meant I would have asked questions that he tried not to lie about. "So where will you go?" He picked up plates and took them over to the sink.

"Dunkeswell, or maybe Netheravon." He nodded as if both of those places were familiar to him. It wouldn't have surprised me if he had done some skydiving himself he looked the type who would be happy to live on the edge of a drop-zone, packing reserves for beer money.

"I'll have to get my canopy checked and the reserve repacked. You can't just walk onto a drop-zone these days and put your name up on the board. I imagine there will be some reserve drills to go through and quite a lot of humiliation to be taken with good humour." He nodded again. "You just let me know if there's anything that's not going according to plan."

"Bea, it's not like that!"

"Okay, what *is* it like Ted?" He sat down and covered his face with his hands. It made my mouth dry and my head spin and I felt the line of control that kept me from losing it was starting to thin at the edges. I sat down next to him. "Tell me."

"I can't Bea," he said quietly. "We both have to go through this."

I nodded. His mind was like a steel trap, but leaking out at the periphery, like smoke around a door holding the fire in, was fear.

I came up to the barrier and stopped the car. "Parachute centre," I said to the soldier. He invited me to step out of the vehicle while he examined it. There was a lot of looking underneath with mirrors on sticks and general rifling through my spare underwear.

"Sign in over there ma'am." He pointed to the guardroom. I moved the car and took my driver's licence into the office. A sergeant with lots of good teeth pushed the book over to me and I filled the line in, stopping only briefly to look out the door and check my number plate. This was accompanied by him with much eye rolling and clicking of teeth and tongue. I smiled my best smile and got some serious grins back.

Nothing much had changed in the few years since I had given up jumping. I parked and grabbed my kit, slinging it over one shoulder.

The journey up to Netheravon in Wiltshire from my home had started early. A peach-like sky filled the windscreen and I emptied the verge on both sides of the road of wildlife with Boston's 'more than a feeling,' which was serious skydiving music and should always be played loudly whilst accompanied by off-key singing. Driving over

Salisbury Plain felt like 'groundhog day,' some of it was going home and some was going back, a stupid combination of feelings.

The buildings were exactly the same configuration of practice area, indoor packing, offices, canteen and bar. The rigging room was an embarrassing walk through unknown curious faces and surprised familiar ones. "Hey Bea, been taking fashion tips from Miss Piggy?"

"Yes, that girl is hot!" I shouted. The laughter followed me.

Skydiving was a clan, an extended family, not always kind, a dangerous belonging to a closed group. They watched and waited to see how long you were going to last; when you were on the inside, they looked after their own, endless personalities and monumental egos. They also had the best parties. You'd have had to be crazy not to understand that it was dangerous and it could become all consuming and obsessive. But it was fun, lots of fun, sometimes though you had to give it up before it gave you up.

The grumpy rigger looked over my kit. All riggers were grumpy because they stayed inside fixing things while other people were having a wild time outside in the sunshine trashing things they had just fixed. They were non-discriminatory grumpy, they hated students and sky-gods equally, but they really, deeply, despised those returning jumpers with incredibly old kit.

"Shall I get you some coffee?" I smiled my best smile again because it had worked with the squaddies.

"Mm," he grunted. I took that as a yes and went to find the canteen. I sprung for a coffee and a bacon butty because if you were going to bribe someone food was a good place to start.

The canteen was full of nearly awake people all propping up coffee cups with the monumental hangovers of the evening before. I tiptoed carefully through old memories and quite a lot of halitosis. When I got back to the rigging room he had pulled the reserve out and was checking it sadly like an old man thinking of all the things he could have done in life that didn't insult his integrity the way that this did. He grumbled again, but it had a more amenable tone as the smell of the bacon wafted in, mingling with old sweat and that unmistakable aroma of parachutes.

The man of the 'Miss Piggy' crack came in and gave me a hug. "It's good to see you, what have you been up to?"

The question was right up there with 'tell me about yourself,' as having the most disaster potential of any enquiry in the English language. Anything to do with your life should have been something to get past as soon as possible. I paused before replying as if the Com/T was still working and I was waiting for some help from the computer, I found I was still listening for the click.

"Who does this pile of junk belong to?" He asked the rigger, I thumped him hard on the arm.

"Right, vintage stuff, I can see the attraction." He rubbed his arm, mouthing 'ow' at me behind the rigger's back. I scowled at him. Mike Stillis, I remembered him from my pathetic early attempts at freefall, he had been a keen young officer then; training students at the weekend and himself as an instructor with a tandem rating.

He reminded me of Sig, chunky and blonde with the scars of bad decisions in far away places worse for the fact that most of the decisions had been someone else's stupidity, not his. He was in the Royal Marine off duty uniform of jeans, T-shirt and trainers. He looked older and there were the squint lines of laughter and hot dry countries around his eyes. I knew from a drunken evening how he felt about most things, it had been a long evening and I respected him as one of the best skydivers I had ever met. He opened his mouth and I thumped him again. "Whose side are you on?" I hissed at him.

"Yours, mainly because you're standing next to me and you hit harder than he does," he whispered back. He rubbed his arm again which was rubbish as punching him was like coming into contact with a brick wall.

"Shall I pack the reserve mate?" Mike asked the rigger. The grunt of a reply must have meant something positive because he moved over to the table next to the rigger and began pulling the canopy straight and setting it out for a repack. Knowing my place, I went for more coffee and food.

I spent the rest of the morning talking to Mike 'the marine' and getting the 'wets' in when required. Apart from a small bit of stitching on the parachute container and the verbal abuse, it had been a relatively painless experience. "Do you want to come and do some reserve drills Bea?" Mike pointed towards the door. It wasn't actually a question. I swung in the harness practising cutaways until he had had enough and my arms were like jelly.

We went and sat outside and watched the board fill up with names and the crowd of people moving like the tides, dirt-diving, jumping and packing. I got nods of recognition from some and a complete sense of indifference from most, things moved on and the centre of any group changed.

"Are you happy to get out and just do your own thing for a couple of jumps?" Again this was not really a question.

We were sitting at a table by the main building. I nodded. Mike went over to put my name up on the board and two young men walked over. I recognised the faces, but the names remained in that place where crossword answers went to die. "Bea! How is it going, I hear you're jumping crap kit?" I leaned forward and banged my head gently on the table.

"What is she doing?" He asked his friend.

"She seems to be banging her head on the table," his friend replied with exaggerated helpfulness.

"I can see that, why?"

He considered carefully. "I think to express frustration."

"Ah." They sat down and helped themselves to Mike's coffee, something that was more stupid than brave. "What have you been up to, Bea?" There was that question again.

"It will be about twenty minutes. I've stuck you on with a high lift. Get out about eight and just enjoy the view." Mike sat down. He stared at his coffee cup and then looked at the face of the young man holding it.

"I was just looking after it for you."

The aeroplane was still 'burning and turning' as we climbed in; there were usually two lifts of eight jumpers and one of nine before each refuel; I squeezed in next to an excited eight-way team, they were young and full of last nights good ideas dreamed up by an unrealistic dirt-dive in the bar. I watched my altimeter climb and listened to the plan for their jump, they had as much chance of pulling it off as Wile E. Coyote had of beating that running chicken.

The Islander pilot called 'running in' and I scooted back and opened the door. A rush of air hit me and the powerful turbine engines throttled back. I used to pride myself on a decent ability to spot my own exits but I mouthed a grateful 'thank you' to the girl who offered to look over my shoulder for a second opinion. I shouted one correction to the pilot and looked at her. She gave me the thumbs up. "Cut!" She yelled at the pilot and I dived out of the door.

The feeling of throwing yourself out of an aeroplane door fulfilled all the little primeval needs that were written on your DNA. I read once that even monkeys would watch something that frightened them over and over again, screeching in excitement until their fur stood up all over. We all got something from experiencing fear.

I turned to see the 'plane moving away from me and saw the hands wave out the door and smiled into the up rush of air and felt my lungs fill with the sense of being out there that for me was flying. But you were not you were falling and from eight thousand feet it was only about forty seconds of freefall and I couldn't defy the laws of physics any more than a brick, or Wile E. Coyote, so I tracked a little just for the fun of it and then pulled, the solid wall of slowing down catching me under an arc of canopy.

It was always good to be under a perfect sky, but really any sky would have done. I could hear people talking on the ground and I did my best to do a clean flare. It was a pity I did it too high, 'stoofing in,' in front of the telemeters so that I ended up in an undignified heap. I hoisted up the canopy and tried to slide by the little knot of grinning instructors.

"What was that?" Mike asked.

"I think this parachute is having a bad day." I smiled my most winning smile.

It had exactly no effect on Mike. "I know how it feels."

I said grumpily, "Do you want me to sit on the naughty step for the rest of the afternoon?" He shook his head sadly.

I finished the day doing a neat little four-way with Mike and the two guys who had tormented me earlier. Lots of effort on their part had made it a really nice dive, yes they had built the formations around me, but I was there and in my mind I felt that it was a plus in the great tally in the blue that I hadn't disgraced myself, by being 'out to lunch.'

I sat looking up at the cloudless sky, the grass was still warm from the sun and my head was propped up on my rig. The beer lamp had been lit and the bar was full of light and skydivers reliving old moves. I let the barrier down that kept me from the thoughts of those around me. It was like a tidal wave and I blocked it out in an instant. It was not good to feel other people's feelings when you had your own, but I'd done it because I could.

Mike came over with the two young men who had made the last dive of the day with us, and a beer for me. We sat and watched the sun go down until we could barely see each other. The light from the bar was a beacon of noise streaking the ground with laughter, spinning out beyond the dark jagged edge of the building to the plains.

They talked about the things that had happened to them in Iraq and made jokes out of serious situations like soldiers had done for ever. There was a path for those who fought for us shaped like a pattern in time. Somewhere in the past there were Roman soldiers sitting in the wilds of England, with one syllable nicknames, who had a really awful sense of humour, I knew this because I had met their future.

The drive home was a dark tunnel of music. The crepuscular creatures were my only company and I was content to be alone, no voices, anywhere.

I jumped through an early summer and picked up old habits and old conversations and took some exams for my pilot's licence. I even contacted my old editor, who was not even slightly pleased to hear from me. Things had 'moved on' to the internet and no one was interested in 'my sort of work.' I sent him something I had written on the fifteenth century in Florence. I wrote it as if I were watching the 'bonfire of the vanities' actually take place and I was one of the young men who'd collected the books and art for Savonarola and stacked them in the main square for burning on Shrove Tuesday.

He called it self-indulgent and over-worded, but he published it and he paid me. It had had several letters of complaint by the following week, which he grumbled to me about, but like most editors all that had ever really worried him was indifference.

Ted came around less and less, until one week it was not at all. I panicked; I mean really panicked, great gulping loss of air and red mists of a panic. I phoned and he arrived in a flurry of dusty wheels and we sat for the rest of the afternoon, talking about Rani and Zeke and the space-quake and the Starfire, until I was sure I hadn't forgotten a detail and therefore they couldn't have forgotten me.

I was sitting in the canteen at the parachute centre watching a group of skydiver's dirt-dive an eight-way. They shouted at each other in lieu of encouragement. It was seriously complicated. "Do you ever get the sense that they're reinventing the wheel?" Mike said, looking on with a critical eye. He shook his head and turned around to face me.

"I never even found the wheel, what do I know?" I was grumpy with something that might have been a hangover, if I could only have remembered what I had been drinking.

Sleeping in the car and the showers at the centre had added a certain something to the grumpy mountain. I had left a text message on Ted's phone asking him to feed Ollie, so guilt might have been a big part of the equation.

Mike watched bemused while I cut off the top of a chocolate muffin, it had a thick layer of icing and I performed the procedure like a surgeon with a cause. I ate the bits loaded with icing. Mike pinched the discarded layer of cake. "I don't think I've ever seen anyone do that before." He finished his coffee and got up for a refill, taking my cup with him.

"I have," said a quiet voice behind my right shoulder, just what was needed to go with a hangover, a cold shower and a guilty conscience, an ex-husband. I turned around.

"Max," I said politely, "How nice to see you." The coffee arrived and I gulped the steaming hot liquid a little too fast. Mike patted me on the back, a wicked unhelpful grin on his face. In the absence of any skydiving people loved a good show.

The blonde who stood next to Max seemed to my watery eyes to have more than a passing resemblance to Dolly Parton. I blinked, wondering if maybe I was still a little drunk. This was the sort of person who never missed an opportunity to wear a thong and stilettos. I might even have been gaping. The thong without a doubt was this century's version of the hair-shirt and the pain of high heels had probably resulted in unidentified crime sprees. It felt as if unfinished business was out to get me. I sighed.

She spoke, "I have to say I'm a little disappointed!" She managed to get three more syllables into the last word than the Oxford English dictionary had designated. And the voice was 'deep south' no more than frog hopping distance from the Tennessee boarder. "I," she pronounced it as 'ah,' "Was led to believe you had horns and a tail." I looked at Max who had a suitably horrified expression on his face.

The voice continued, "Not Dumbo here," she pointed at Max's big ears, "The ugly sisters!"

Mike was grinning, he couldn't believe his luck; the floor show was turning into a spectacular. In fact selling tickets was becoming a possibility. I was having a warm fuzzy glow of my own.

Whole flocks of chickens were coming 'home to roost' before my very eyes. That this four foot ten inch babe had got the better of Max and the measure of his family, was something that made my heart glad on all sorts of levels because my own tactic of lying down and letting them walk all over me had not, of course, been an unqualified success. I smiled, all of me smiled.

"Honey," she said, "We have to talk." I thought for a moment that the SAS and Navy Seals would benefit from a conversation with her. I knew whole star systems that would.

"How did you two meet?" I managed to squeeze out between grins.

"He was on board the boat I was working on. My, he was sick. The guy was so bad even his ego was projectile vomiting!" Max was squirming, literally. Mike's laughter added to the layers of discomfort and I felt a door slam so loudly in my head I had to look around.

"Lola Marie, give me a break!" Even the name was a gift. I felt my hangover melt under the spotlight of Lola Marie's platinum hair. All marriage guidance counsellors should have had this woman's number.

Anyone who has had a failed marriage knew that it was about being alone in a not quite socially acceptable way. There was always the 'someone left, everyone got hurt' feeling and people could be judgemental and unkind, they took sides, death could be easier to deal with. At a parachute centre you were just this week's entertainment. They employed an 'if you don't like it, marry out' rule.

Lola Marie carried on talking and it didn't take me long to work out that underneath the 'look' was the 'brain.' She turned out to be a lawyer; a lawyer who skydived and sailed.

"How did that go?" She asked the bickering eight-way as they came in for coffee.

"It went better in the bar," one of the team answered.

"Well your exit was the problem honey." It was very hard to give advice to anyone wearing a parachute, so I could hear the general sucking of teeth coming from all four corners of the room.

"Really," was the sarcastic reply.

"Sure." Lola Marie got up and walked over to them. In what seemed to have something to do with particle physics she had lined them up in their exit and then moved and shoved the team into a different configuration, talking the moves through. Mike was giving the whole thing the nod.

"Could work," he said grudgingly which was skydiver language for 'I think she's got it.'

"I bet you've never lost a case," I said as she sat down, leaving the eight-way with a bad case of 'did that just happen?'

"Well, not unless it was supposed to be that way." She patted me on the arm, an old fashioned gesture more in keeping with a maiden aunt. I wondered about her age and pushed a little at the corners of her thoughts for other clues. Something pushed back and I looked around. A small darkness like witch's fingers crept across the room.

"My!" Lola Marie said, "Someone just walked over my grave." She shuddered. My head felt like cotton wool, but then, I rationalised, the hangover was still more 'hang' than 'over.' "Honey, is there any chance that some time soon you'll be able to jump out of that 'plane?" She pointed to the Islander as it moved off to the fuel pump.

I caught a shift in the light that seemed to sigh inside my head and I looked at her carefully.

"One more icing-laden muffin should do it," I answered. Over her shoulder I thought I saw Ted walking past the canteen window. I stood up to get a better look and then covered my foolishness with a trip to the hatch. The smell of frying bacon sounded like rain on the roof for a moment. It was as if my senses were giving me the wrong signals for everything.

"We're going to get our kit?" Max spoke from the door. I nodded, cake and coffee in my hands. Mike reached for my cup, tipping half of it into his. "I'd bonk her," he informed me.

"How do the girls stay on their feet when you're around?" I asked wonderingly. He gave it his serious consideration and shrugged.

"Come on, let's see if your ex can fly stable yet." He pulled me to my feet.

The 'kit' belonging to the southern belle was of course bright neon pink. She pulled on a day-glow jumpsuit and we dirt-dived something that made my eyes spin, the possibility of me being in the right place after the first three moves was seriously in question.

"Any chance you could make that a six-way?" Cookie asked from the safety of several thousand more jumps than I had. Lola Marie looked them up and down like someone had ordered take away without showing her the menu.

Mike did the introductions. "Jeff Cook and Les Jackson, both really mediocre, but it could make it more interesting; Cookie, Jacks, this is the stupid prick who divorced Bea and his current Doris, Lola Marie, who is far more woman than he deserves." They shook hands and we got down to dirt-diving a head-whimpering dance that made me sure I wasn't going to be there after the exit.

Our names went up on the board and we did a gear check. I sat in the sun, my eyes were half closed behind dark glasses. The wind whispered across the plains, ruffling short blades of grass. A haze was beginning to settle on the distant fields. I thought I heard a rumble of thunder, but the sky was still clear.

Lola Marie plonked herself down next to me, cancel that, the woman had never plonked in her life. "Don't worry it's one of those dives that isn't as bad as it looks. Anyway Max said you were good, you just don't know it yet." I think my eyebrows must have disappeared into the fuzz I called my hair because she laughed, like an emptying drain; it was a good laugh, one that made other people look around and smile.

We sat in companionable silence waiting for our turn. I thought about my cat and what I would have to do to make up for my non-appearance the previous night; a serious amount of grovelling was not going to be enough. I turned and examined her profile, at her small sharp features and the sweep of smooth hair. "You're a walking paradox aren't you, Lola Marie?"

She laughed, "I know men who wouldn't be sure what walking meant, never mind paradox. We all hide behind what we are to other people honey it's about how people see you."

"Did a really smart lawyer teach you that?" I smiled.

"No, my really smart mama did."

Mike did the sign for twenty minutes from the manifest room. I nodded and smiled again. "Daft twit," I sighed.

"It's funny but I just can't imagine anyone telling you what to do." She pushed back her hair, a move that caused serious strain on the top half of her jump suit and I think several people forgot where they were for a moment.

"Yes well, some people don't have a strong sense of their own mortality."

"So *why,*" she paused dramatically, "Did you let Max and his family bully you?"

It was a good question and one I had asked myself for several centuries. I shrugged. "I think I felt sorry for them." She looked astounded, which was not easy when you were that beautiful. "Then there's Martin Luther King."

"'It's not the words of our enemies we remember, but the silence of our friends,'" she quoted. It was my turn to look astonished. She patted at her considerable chest which again caused some minor injuries due to coffee scalding and walking into walls and said, "Lawyer, remember?"

We sat in the sun in silence. "This life," she said quietly, "It grabs you back and closes around you, no real questions asked. It's dangerous and exciting and all the things that we're supposed to grow out of."

"Is that why you do it?" I was surprised.

"No honey, I just like making patterns in the sky!" She pulled me to my feet and we geared up, tucking and tightening. The group gradually drifted together and did a last minute dirt-dive as the 'plane slid in to land.

We climbed on board in roughly our exit positions. Two people were getting out before us and were going to get their own pass; they nodded and squashed themselves into the back of the 'plane. I didn't know either of them and was too busy trying to remember what came after the exit to examine them much or to speak. They looked like central casting's idea of servicemen. Mike nodded at both of them which in the Royal Marines passed for detailed conversation.

I closed my eyes and tried to catch the stray wisps of fresh air that came around the edge of the 'plane door. The journey up to altitude, never usually a fragrant experience, was enhanced by the after effects of the home-made curry some sadist had decided to cook the previous evening once the beer supplies had been severely affected.

Lola Marie had her head resting on Max's knee; he was sat behind her and she seemed to fit comfortably in the space he had made and he had his arms around her. I felt a pain somewhere in my stomach, it could have been the coffee and cake, but it seemed more as if old memories were trying to get into the right place in my mind. Max saw me looking and he smiled and the guilt and sadness seemed to lift a little. I smiled back.

The pilot called 'running in' and I shuffled back out of the way to let the two men have a good shot at the door, because it was irritating to trip over someone's feet when you were trying to ace an exit. The one nearest me asked for a second opinion on the spot, which was odd because I hadn't jumped that day. The door was open so we didn't speak, he just pointed at his eyes, then me, then down at the ground. I shrugged looking at Mike who was by far the best choice. Mike had his head back and was snoring; I decided not to wake him because you should never come between a marine and his sleep. We scrunched in the doorway. I turned my head around for a moment trying to orientate myself, there were trees and no buildings, we were miles away from the drop-zone, I looked at the man next to me; his eyes were pale green and shone behind his goggles like the edge of an empty lake. I was suddenly aware that I didn't like him, it was not unusual to meet people you didn't like on a drop-zone, it had happened to me all the time, it was just that I usually didn't get on a plane with them. He shrugged. I was going to shout to the pilot that he was miles out; when it occurred to me they might have asked for a long spot for some sort of tracking exercise or high opening, in the case of the high opening they shouldn't have been getting out before us. People bumping into each other in freefall or under canopy without prior arrangement were usually frowned upon in the skydiving fraternity as it often ended in body bags.

I shouted at him, "Did you ask for a long run in?" He nodded and pointed down. I looked. Contrary to popular belief there were lots of trees on Salisbury Plain: we seemed to be passing high over a wooded area. I turned to see Lola Marie's puzzled face, then her eyes opened slightly wide and I felt the second of the two-way half stand behind me. The plane didn't throttle back as I was grabbed and spun out of the door. There was a scream somewhere, not mine, in the moment we left the doorway. I was hooked between the two of them. I knew this wasn't a bad joke that would get the two of them grounded for the rest of the day for ruining a dive. From thirteen thousand feet I punched and kicked as we spun around, no one was flying this knot of pain and fear to keep it stable. I pushed at their minds for any clue, wasting precious seconds against what must have been blocking chips, something no one had for several hundred years.

I sunk my teeth into a hand nearest my face and drew salty blood into my mouth and across my goggles. The rush of air and noise and the cold mingled with a pushing and shoving of no contest. I cried; I knew I did and fought with all my heart. Some long hidden atavistic pattern of behaviour manifested itself in the sort of strength that you only saw when mothers rescued their children from burning cars and I punched and bit blindly, pointlessly, not connecting with much, as my arms were pinned in an awkward and ghastly embrace like being drowned by a dead lover.

From altitude it was about sixty seconds of freefall. A safe pulling height was about three thousand feet, I couldn't see my altimeter, but the internal proximity warning device that kept blind people from bumping into the furniture was going off inside my head.

What I couldn't understand was my AOD not firing.

Suddenly there was nothing, the two men let go and I felt light and disorientated. Spinning over to get stable, I saw them as they tracked off. I looked down and saw that there were trees and eighteen hundred feet on the altimeter. I dumped my main and waited for the pull of the opening canopy, nothing. I looked up, nothing, one thousand feet. I pulled the yellow reserve handle, a stiff two handed and one foot pull, again nothing.

Who of us had never ranted at a god, never argued and never pleaded, cried, screamed and begged. Fear tasted of metal because your mouth was full of adrenaline.

I hit the trees, a lightening rod of jagged sound.

Life... the winter sky a perfect eggshell blue, watching sleeping puppies breathe, running in the early morning through a peach dawn, the unexpected phone call of old friends, rain on the wind, a cat's yawn, shared laughter, the sound of the sea any day of the year, the curve of each smile, the first step on a mountain, the goodbye kiss, the light from distant stars, a last breath.

Somewhere, backwards and forwards in time, the gulls were in from the sea again. Wheeling and diving on the winds beyond the storm.

ꗇ 4 ꗄ

This was more than the dark dreamless sleep that felt like death. Time was broken in some places. Faces were like chewing gum. I waited, nothing, consciousness, surprise, pain, whispering; a voice, full of sadness, soft deep words reading something.

It wasn't a bed. I was encased in jelly, breathing through the liquid, hearing my breath in my head, like holding a shell to your ear. I moved my hand, looked at my fingers but couldn't remember what they were, or why I was. Acres of time passed by in the closing and opening of my eyes. Thoughts, gentle peaceful memories were planted like seeds in the warm earth. Sleep. Little pieces put together, the puzzle of me. Then awareness, I moved my head, which was a big mistake, I was spinning, spinning. Still, gasping for breath. Sleep. Light, feelings that seemed to link together, thoughts that had reason. The world came to a stop and I could see the people.

"Hi." I said. Someone sighed with relief. Not me. "You know you could have just told me." I tried to laugh, but I cried instead, about dying.

It didn't excuse what had happened when you heard the other side. It just made the solution more complicated. The faces were familiar and I came upon great chunks of my life in moments and lost the little words for days. "So why did I go through this?" I asked again for what must have been the millionth time. I couldn't remember the question until I had asked it and then its shape sounded familiar in my mouth.

"We had to go through it." I remembered the answer and then the person.

"Pui." She smiled at me and came over and put her arms around me and I leaned on her shoulder, with bits of my body still wrapped in the jelly stuff and I breathed in her strength and remembered who I was, but mostly why.

The moments linked together until whole days were like a string of pearls, each one perfectly connected. I still had bad days, when Pui sedated me and I was grateful for the dark and the quiet and the space without fear and the faces that made no sense, their words a panic of jumbled sound.

"How did it happen?" I asked one day. Pui looked carefully at me and checked the readings on the bio-bed. Then she called Rani. I knew she had done this before, it was just I had difficulty retaining the memory of it. Rani hugged me.

So, you're asking questions?"

"Will I remember the answers if you tell me?" I shuffled in the bed, as much as the jelly packs would allow. She closed her eyes and began a gentle thought that swirled around me like mist on the moors, little fingers of assessment, pressing against something that felt like a raw bruise, only deep inside my mind. I cringed and she stopped.

"We'll go at this slowly." She smiled, holding my hand. I nodded.

"We rescued you at the moment you hit the ground." I opened my mouth, but she carried on, "We used the quantum teleportation device that was 'taken' from a renegade ship like the one you were on. It's dangerous and we still don't know how they store the pattern for reintegration.

I absorbed this information. "Where was I?" It was a difficult question.

"You didn't *die* Bea, you were never dead."

Pui came over because something about the tone of our voices made her check readings and watch my face. I wondered as I looked back at her and I rested my head which had begun to ache with this pathetic amount of personal history.

"How many times have we had this conversation?" Rani glanced at Pui and she gave her permission for whatever.

"This is the fourth time." They both looked like a couple of kids waiting for exam results, hopeful but wary. It was a shock and it showed. Something heaved itself up from my consciousness.

"Ollie," I shouted. Pui rushed over waving Rani away. Little keys were tapped and small bleeps were heard and the bits of my head that felt as if they were exploding went back together like a rewind of the bullet hitting the watermelon.

"He's here!" Rani shouted back.

I stopped reaching for something I couldn't find. A small furry orange ball uncurled on a bed of blankets and stretched out paws, whiskers flattened back against the pink tongue and fierce teeth in a big yawn. "I'm okay." I tried to reassure Pui who looked as if she was about to pull the plug on any conversation for the next ten years.

"So, my brother tried to kill me." It wasn't a question. The death of a Gurber, the kidnapping of scientists, all things pointed to him trying to get the key for time travel. A small worm of thought passed between the two women and I caught it, as if the bit of my brain that could quantify a look had finally come back on line again. "You don't know if it was him?"

I remembered my conversation the next day and the next and the thoughts seemed to push past the blanks without me having to think about thinking.

Gradually I realised Pui was rationing the visits and I went from gratitude to boredom to irritation to complaining. One day I asked her after much careful thought. "Didn't they wonder where the body had gone?" Pui came over to the bed and smoothed the crumpled jelly that was still wrapped around my legs and midriff.

"No," she said quietly, watching my reaction.

I tried to think of all the possibilities of 'no body' causing 'no reaction' and couldn't come up with anything but the reality filtered through eventually. "The DNA you took when we first met, could that have anything to do with it?"

Pui sighed and I could see her working up to an explanation, I wondered how many times we'd had this conversation. "No one would have known the difference."

"Right," I said. The thought made me feel queasy and I tried not to think too much about 'another' me, because that way lay a really restless night.

"So let me see if I've got it all so far." I sat up for effect. "You snatched me back from my century a second before someone succeeded in murdering me, we don't know who, but there's a short list." I tapped my fingers. "You put a body in my place and you bring me back here with my brains scrambled and just about everything broken, so far so good?" I looked at her. She nodded.

"But *why*," I asked. She looked puzzled. "I mean it's an awful lot of effort for one telepath?"

"You're supposed to be here," she explained simply. I nodded as if I understood and then it turned into a head shake because I really didn't. Her exasperation was sincere, "Bea, it's not where you're from, it's where you belong."

"How did you heal my head and I don't mean the technical treatment," I added hastily as she began to give me details. She sat on the bed which was never a good sign.

"Rani held your memories and we kept her in stasis until your brain was healed enough to take them back." She looked pale and tired and I wondered again if this was the first time we had got this far or if this was déjà vu for her. She licked dry lips. "It's not something I've ever tried before." There was a long silence while we both waited for what she had to say next. "I'm not sure how successful it's going to be."

"Where's Zeke?" I asked in a very small voice because a loud one might have brought me to the notice of the galaxy. The karmic pudding having been stirred beyond all culinary cosmic safety levels.

She smiled. "He was here for a while in the beginning. He sat and read you all your favourite books. Night after night, he just kept reading."

Her words, loaded with emotional content were delivered without any. I remembered the whispered stories like a film with subtitles. The sounds still didn't make sense, but I knew what they meant now.

"When you began to stay conscious for longer periods he seemed to cause you distress." I must have looked stunned.

"You kept saying something about him 'not knowing who you were and that he left without you.'" It was odd how the barely there mind could play tricks on you. My trip up to Scotland to see my brother must have been the one thing that I had remembered without help.

"Have I asked to see him before?" She nodded. "How did it go?"

"Not well."

"Poor Zeke, can we try again now?" She pretended to deliberate, but I thought she was curious to find out how far we had come 'this time.'

He looked terrible and sad and hopeless. I watched him as he stood in the doorway. I held out a hand and he walked over and took it and we sat in silence because it was important not to create something so powerful between you, that explanations and apologies became useless. Eventually I asked, "Are Sig and Doz behaving?"

"No." He smiled and sighed like the shadows at the edges of his heart were something he would just have to put up with.

"Zeke, I will learn to live in my head again, it's not as if there weren't any dark corners there before." We sat in the quiet for a while, watching Pui with little slides and a holo/ microscope that projected beautiful deadly patterns of dying tissues. She hummed and talked to herself and it was restful and interesting at the same time. I knew what time of the 'day' it was by her routine and this was the evening.

"Can I have a cuddle?" I asked politely. Zeke looked stunned for a moment. He sighed and stood up, stretching his body with his hands above his head. I shuffled over to one side of the bio-bed and he lay down, his legs nearly off the end, his body curving a space for me that felt as if it had been waiting and Pui looked up and smiled. The bed must have been giving confused readings, because it beeped uncomfortably for a while until she came over and turned it off.

I rested my head on Zeke's chest and fell asleep.

———

I staggered down the corridor, limping and swearing. Sig stopped and sighed, "Did you fall off the running machine again?"

"That thing hates me," I answered and swore by way of an explanation. He put my arm over his shoulder, which made me swear even louder and helped me to the lift shaft and up to the medical bay. We did our three-legged race in through the doors.

Pui turned around. "Did you fall off the running machine *again?*"

"Ah!" I shouted.

I sat where she indicated and watched the little dance that the two of them did to avoid showing how much they cared for each other.

I tried to breathe without using my ribs which was not actually possible, my mouth was open like a fish and I had the red spots before my eyes that usually meant I had broken something.

"You've cracked several ribs." Pui looked at me accusingly. "Which bit about 'try not to get yourself into any trouble' did you not comprehend?" I hung my head which usually worked with Pui. "I'm not buying it!" She looked grumpy.

Some bone knitting treatment and an ear stinging lecture later and I was walking slowly back to my rooms. The walls of the ship were zinging around due to some really good analgesia. I staggered over to the sofa by the windows and sank down. The rooms were now filled with my possessions. Even the old chairs and my own bed had been brought up to the ship. Books were stacked against the walls as I hadn't yet bribed the ship's carpenter to make me some more shelves. It was odd how easily my possessions had fitted into the rooms, as if I had always been collecting and decorating the same space in my mind.

I sat up and pulled the computer over to me, shuffling the books on the coffee table and trying to get myself in a position that didn't feel like spikes were being driven into my side. I tapped the holo/keys and accessed the Earth records, scrolling back. I fished around finding dead ends and lots of things that didn't make much sense. What I didn't find was a blank screen. The block was off, which meant no going back.

Eventually the computer gave up trying to confuse me and I found what I was looking for. The records were surprising detailed considering the length of time that had passed, though it was mostly old newspaper reports. There was a picture of the funeral, my funeral. The death was classed as an open verdict. Both the lines to my main canopy and the reserve had been cut. I looked at the faces of people long gone, who felt in my heart like a moment ago. Old secrets again, carried deep within, like a promise never forgotten. It said that the case was being pursued by an American lawyer who wouldn't put up with the English legal system's 'ass attitude.' Lola Marie. I could just hear her saying it. I scrolled around until I found the details about Edie. Her death had been described as 'after a long illness.' I turned off the computer, maybe later I would try and find out more and maybe not. It felt as if I were reading the faded pages of some long ago lover's letters, smudged with tears.

The doors slid open and Zeke and my cat came in at the same time.

"Did you fall off the running machine again?" I sighed, looking for some sympathy. "You have got to take it easy, Bea." He looked cross.

"I've already had that lecture from Pui." Then I was sorry because he hadn't got past the panic stage and always behind the normal was the unease. It was going to take time and the effort that goes into normal. "Would you make me a cup of coffee?" I asked hopefully. He put the cups out and turned on the hot water. "Zeke." He looked over, his expression half enquiry and half exasperation, I looked at my hands. "What happens now?"

"Well," he said, walking over with the full cups and something that looked suspiciously like cake which had magically appeared from nowhere, "More of the same, you getting into trouble and Sig and Doz whinging about getting you out of it."

"Where will you be?" I asked quietly.

He smiled and said, in that quiet voice, "I'll be here."

We sat without talking for a while. "I'm sorry." He spoke so softly that I wasn't sure I had actually heard it, more a stray thought passing between us that had accidentally got snagged on a moment. "I know this is really difficult for you and I know how hard you try to make it seem okay." He pulled me into him and I avoided squeaking by a narrow margin.

"I thought we were going to be like 'The Ghost and Mrs Muir'" I said, "and that I would only see you again when I died. I just didn't realise that dying was going to be so soon." The Com/T was buzzing and we were quiet for a minute.

"You're going to have to explain The Ghost and Mrs Muir?" I laughed and leaned back to look at his face.

"It's a story. I think I have the book somewhere. She's a widow and she buys a house near the sea and he's the ghost of an old sea captain that haunts the house. They write a book together and then he goes away and she thinks she's dreamed him and she has to wait until she grows old and dies before she sees him again." I found that the tears were there before I could stop them. "I'm sorry, but when I saw you in Scotland at my brother's house that's how it felt." He kissed me on the forehead. "There's still so much I don't understand," I added.

The door swept open again and Rani came in. "We're going to pay a visit to your green friends."

"Great," I said, not moving.

She began to make herself a drink and the door chimed. Doz wandered in. "Hi Boss," he said to Zeke, who waved with the hand not on my back. "Will you make me a coffee Rani?" He sat down in one of the tatty chairs and grabbed a book from the stack next to it. "Bea, did you fall off the running machine again?"

ACKNOWLEDGMENTS

Without Robin Phillips of Author Help this book would have stayed in the shadows.

I had been 'advised' by an agent to write it in 'chick lit' style as science fiction wouldn't sell. Robin helped me turn it back into the book it was supposed to be. (AuthorHelp.uk)

The cover is the wonderful work of Henry Hyde. (HenryHyde.co.uk)

Kat Morgan for her kindness and all the help with my website, Twitter and Instagram. (Kat@seasideweb.co.uk)

I am grateful to Captain Bill Canning for all the navel information on the ship.

Eric Cottrell for finding the single point engine for me and for being a sci-fi friend.

Pete Guest and Mike Wills, who is out there already, for the Royal Marine and parachuting advice.

Gill Baderman and Sara Pearcy for listening to my incessant worrying and always being there.

Patricia Gilpin who knows where all the secrets are.

This book was originally written between 2001 and 2003. It was published for the first time by Stephen and Irene Clark of Paradox Publishing in 2006.

Printed in Poland
by Amazon Fulfillment
Poland Sp. z o.o., Wrocław

65415656R00294